OverLondon

George Penney & Tony Johnson

SWASHBUCKLER PRESS

CONTENTS

To the memory of Sir Terry Pratchett, whose wonderful books brought us together.

FOREWARD

Hail Dear Reader!

We welcome you heartily to the first OverLondon novel.

In the following pages you will find an assortment of swashbuckling pirates-turned-privateers, rogue artificers, exploding priests, kleptomaniac ferret girls and many more characters bubbling around in the rich soup that forms OverLondon, the best worst city on the globe!

As your eyes dance over the pages, you may notice that the words are written with English spelling. If you're American, that will mean you'll see an "s" where you're used to seeing a "z", a "u" in words like "colour", and an extra "l" in words like "travelling".

The reason for the spelling is our mortal fear of the Vengeful Queen Anne Boleyn, who was known for making her displeasure terminally clear when people went against her wishes. In 1554, she dictated that all books about OverLondon must use English spelling. Since she was holding a red-hot poker at the time while dressed as a massive chicken, no one—including our humble selves—were inclined to disagree with her.

There may also be one or two words you might not recognise because they are quintessentially English, or just plain made up, but never fear! Just go to our website, www.overlondon.net where you will find a magnificent glossary that we've made just for you.

Make it reign!

George Penney & Tony Johnson

CHAPTER 1

A GLARING ABSENCE OF GIN, COIN AND SHIP

CLOUDS DRIFT BETWEEN THE mould-dank edifices that line OverLondon's Theatreland, which tilt over the streets like gossiping aunts. The moist air wilts the plumes on the floppy hats of the promenading dandies showing off their finery, chills the street urchins eavesdropping for news to sell to the hourly Cry and delights in loosening the Femur's Animal Glue sticking old playbills to crumbling plaster walls.

Mist sharpens the voices of the touts flogging overpriced tickets to drunken tourists, now destined to see a show about dancing cats that they'd otherwise avoid like gonorrhoea. Halfway along Drury Lane, where the unique aroma of Mister Jim's Mysterious Pies assaults the air, the mist curls around the sign for The Armory with its iconic painting of a snarling badger gnawing on a mime's leg.

Inside, we find Captain Alex Reign, former Dread Pirate Purple Reign, who was, until a day ago, the most wanted individual in all of England. She is sitting slouched under a notice stating: *NOE Sonnets, NOE Limericks, NOE Rhyminge Couplets And NOE Soliloquies. Or Face THEE WRATHE Ofe GREGOR*.

On the table before the captain sits an unfurled letter of marque signed by the OverLondon Academic Council, pardoning her piratical actions and naming her as the city's only official privateer. Albeit a ship-less one.

A LEX REIGN TIPPED HER flying helmet back before raising her third pint of gin to her lips, draining its contents and huffing a sigh of frustration at her inability to get drunk. Outside, Drury Lane's crier took up the Cry, bellowing with a theatricality that fit the location.

Hear ye! Hear ye! The Dread Pirate Purple Reign has been pardoned by the Academic Council and has been granted the title of privateer for services to the city in thwarting the scurrilous OverParisian cowards. Stop. Cardinal Chudleigh denounces all the snivelling worms who aren't fasting during New Lent and laments the recent drop in sales of hair shirts. Stop. Another lemming Hare Krishna has fallen off The Edge. In response, the Woodkin Council demand nets under each gangplank surrounding the city and more education about homo lemmus. Stop. Ye've heard! Ye've heard! This bulletin was brought to you by Axiom wig powder. The powder with power. Get powdered with Axiom today!

Alex didn't find the news about the lemming Hare Krishna amusing, unlike many of the pub's other inhabitants. No one knew why the various woodland creatures on the globe started to mix their genetics with humans late in the 16th century, but there were many theories about how it happened, most of them unflattering. She didn't appreciate hearing them rehashed by this room of glorified stage moppers, nor did she appreciate the reminder of her current predicament.

She glared at a nearby table of guffawing actors, making note of their tatty clothing and too-shiny weaponry, no doubt stolen from the prop cupboard of some dire off-Lane production. Curs.

She slammed her tankard down and caught the eye of a passing barmaid before pointing decisively at the glaring absence of gin.

"I don't think it's working, Captain." At Alex's side, Sid Potts employed his usual capacity to state the obvious. His years of being the Purple Reign's bo'sun had left him with a face resembling the lovechild of a potato that had made love to another, homelier potato. His ever-present brown bowler hat only added to the impression.

"No, Sid, it's not, but there's merit in trying. It's either try to get drunk or storm the docks and take back the Purple Reign, and I don't think that's such a good idea. Do you?" Still glaring at the actors, Alex slumped down the wall until her chin rested on her chest. They were so *oblivious*. Didn't they understand they were doomed to unhappiness, should some stuffed frilly shirts from a stupid university decide to take away their most prized possession—their very livelihood?

Sid shrugged before downing his pint of Long John's Extremely Uncomfortable. The movement strained the brass buttons on his waistcoat, which was the same faded brown as his hat. Sid liked brown. "Look on the bright side—they were nice to give us that pardon once you convinced them you were really a privateer only *pretending* to be a pirate to fool the OverParisians." He poked the letter of marque with his forefinger. "Especially when they caught us with the booty we'd snaffled from that OverManchester merchantman."

This had involved some fast talking on Alex's part. But since no one from the south of England ever visited the north, except to sneer or to be overcharged for gingerbread while holidaying in the Lake District, she'd been able to convince the authorities that her looted cargo of woolly vests, flat caps and strong tea was a Frenchman's ploy to *pretend* to be English.

"Were they?" Alex checked her empty tankard, just in case a gin fairy had left a little something extra in the bottom. "I'm not so sure."

"Yes, Captain. Professor Bottomley was gracious, letting you argue your defence like that. If you hadn't been so convincing, our bits would currently be nailed on the Wharf Gate and I, for one, don't think my insides would look good on the outside. Gates aren't meant for kidneys and whatnot. Especially not mine. I have sensitive insides." Sid stifled a burp with his fist.

"While I appreciate your efforts to depress me to the point where my metabolism slows and I can achieve inebriation, I'm going to have to kindly ask you to shut up," Alex said, enunciating her words carefully.

A shadow fell over the table and they looked up at Gregor, The Armoury's proprietor and one of the few *homo meles* in OverLondon. The badger man's huge face was contorted into a cantankerous scowl, the black stripes over his eyes stark against the white skin of his cheeks and neck. The black tip of his broad white nose was turned up in disgust.

"I believe this is yours." From behind his back he brought an arm bulging with muscles, thrusting it towards Alex. Her cabin boy, Flora, hung limply from his fist, which was wrapped around the scruff of her shirt.

Flora was wearing the benign smile that only *homo furo* could manage. The ferret girl's floppy red velvet cap with its bedraggled chicken feather was askew, and the mousy hair sticking out from beneath it was a picture of chaos. Her pointy, fawn-coloured face, with its brown mask around the eyes, was fixed in a dreamy smile even as her torso—much longer than the average human's—swayed like a rubber pendulum. Her shirt had ridden up to reveal a brass navel ring above her red breeches and mended black stockings. She was wearing the same heavy hobnail ship boots as Alex and Sid—although, if anyone looked closer, they'd see that the soles of Flora's boots had been augmented with an extra layer of soft rubber. All the better for sneaking.

"Hello, Captain," Flora said dreamily. "I think Gregor's upset."

"Daft ferret. Where'd you find her?" Alex asked Gregor.

"With one hand in my coin chest and the other in my pockets." Gregor gave Flora a shake and something tinkled to the floor.

A silver spoon glinted in the sawdust. They all studied it.

"That's not one of mine," Gregor said. "She must've got that off someone else. Who'd you get it off, girl?" He gave Flora another shake, dislodging five threepenny bits.

Alex ran a hand over her eyes. "How much did you take?"

"Nothing much. Just some shiny things from here and there. And a few more shiny things from inside and under, and a few more from out and up," Flora replied in a singsong voice, her small black eyes alight with happiness. "I'll return them all once I've looked at them. I promise."

"You'll return them now." The vibration of Gregor's growl liberated another coin and what looked like a brass ring. "And give me back my buttons."

It was only then that Alex noticed that the big man's shirt was undone to his waist, exposing a penny-sized longevity trinket, closely resembling a clockwork ladybug, attached to his chest. The complex opalescent patina on its cog-shaped carapace betrayed its worth and explained Gregor's exceptional health and indeterminate age.

"You took his *buttons*?" Alex asked Flora. "When?"

"While we were looking at the spoon," Gregor said.

Alex rolled her eyes. "Vengeful Lady's spittle, Flora—what are the rules?"

Flora radiated innocence. "Don't take shiny things from Gregor?"

"Don't take shiny things from Gregor," Alex repeated. "Now give them back."

Flora reached into one of her many pockets and produced five pewter buttons. Her legs were still dangling in the air, but she'd now crossed her ankles. Alex suspected this was to stop yet more objects falling out from wherever she'd hidden them.

Gregor snatched up the buttons, then dropped Flora onto the sawdust before collecting the coins, ring and spoon. "If she does it again, I'll bite her head off." He stomped back to the bar, snarling at anyone who got in his way.

Alex held out her black-gloved left hand. "Now he's gone, hand the rest over."

Flora jumped up from the floor, her body swaying from side to side as she straightened her shirt and then reached into her pockets. Another spoon and four more coins clinked into Alex's palm.

"And the rest."

There were a few more clinks.

"And the rest."

Flora pouted. "Can't I keep one shiny thing?"

"Is it yours?"

"It *could* be mine."

"But is it?"

"It is now."

"Give it here."

Reluctantly, Flora held out another ring, set with a green stone. Given the high density of impoverished actors in the vicinity, the stone would inevitably be glass. Flora then dived under the table and slunk to the seat on Alex's right. With the extra height afforded by her torso, she was a few inches taller than Alex when sitting down.

Now that Gregor had gone, Sid finally found his voice again. He'd been shy of speaking in Gregor's company ever since he'd once drunkenly announced that badgers spread disease, and Gregor had threatened to terminally ensure he never caught anything again. "That badger is going to eat you one day," he said. "Stupid ferret. And if he doesn't, you're going to end up wanted by the beadles. Do you want to end up on one of these?" He gestured to the wanted posters plastered on the wall behind them. "I know I don't. I like my neck attached to the rest of me. It's the right size, my neck. Not long, or stretched, or nailed to something. Like the Wharf Gate—"

"Alright, Sid," Alex cut in. "You'll kindly remember that I'm on one of those posters." She nodded to the large notice that Gregor had tacked behind the bar some years ago in an uncharacteristic display of good humour. It featured the woodcut of a painting Alex had regretted sitting for ever since its inception.

The portrait was a minor work of Giuseppe Blowhardi, the notorious Over-Florentine artist who'd once insisted Alex kidnap him for ransom. He'd then spent a month lounging on the Purple Reign's deck, demanding Alex fly him somewhere with better light.

In true Blowhardi style, Giuseppe had decided against depicting Alex as a passingly handsome woman of medium height and stature, instead opting for a questionable interpretation of Botticelli's Venus in a flying helmet and goggles, with a chest that would cause even the stoutest woman severe back problems. At least the scar slashing across her left cheek was accurate, but the rest? The woman in the painting was otherwise naked except for her hands because, Alex suspected, Giuseppe didn't know how to paint them. Instead of the usual black leather glove on her left hand, he'd inexplicably given her crimson gloves with gold rings worn over the top.

The woodcut artist who had replicated the painting for the wanted poster hadn't bothered with colour, but they'd enhanced Alex's chest to the point where the woman depicted would never have to worry about drowning.

Sid glanced at the poster and then back at Alex. "Well, Captain, it's not as if it really looks like you, so there was never any fear of them capturing you, was there? And you always said that it was a good advertisement for your services, although I never quite knew what that meant."

"True." Alex spent a pleasant moment thinking of all the services she'd performed over the years for the multitude of ladies and gentlemen who'd expressed a desire to be plundered by a notorious pirate.

"I mean, no one would know it's you because there's a lack in the..." He cupped his hands in front of his chest. "Height department."

"Thanks, Sid."

"And you said it yourself—that poster meant you were able to walk around OverLondon without fearing capture for years. Because you wear clothes, and you don't have the same sized—"

"Yes, yes." Alex contemplated banging her head on the table when Sid opened his mouth to speak again. "No, Sid, really, if you say one more thing, I'll tell Gregor that you said the thing about badgers again. Understand me?"

"Yes, Captain, but—"

"The *important* thing is working out what to do for coin now that we've lost the Purple Reign. *Privateer*," she sneered. "Who ever heard of a privateer without a ship?"

"We'll get it back, Captain. All we have to do is pay off that big tax bill the Academic Council said you owed since you never declared any of your privateering income."

A pounding started behind Alex's eyes. When she'd come up with the privateer argument to save their skins, she hadn't anticipated accountants getting involved.

The barmaid brought over another tankard of gin, and Alex used one of the coins Flora had stolen to pay for it.

"If you need money, you could let me keep my shiny things," Flora said hopefully.

Alex considered this. While she was a lying, stealing, dreadful pirate, The Armoury was the closest thing she had to a home in OverLondon. She knew every fetid street, alleyway and dead end in this overpopulated floating cesspit like she knew her own mind. This city was *hers*, and after losing the Purple Reign she couldn't afford to lose it too. It would be like having a limb amputated. "Or I could just turn you upside down, shake out the rest of whatever you've got hidden in your pockets and turn you over to Gregor. I'm sure he'd reward me for my troubles."

Sid spoke over Flora's alarmed squeak. "That wouldn't work, Captain. She'd just steal them back off you. It'd be like that thing the academic blighters found out about last year... What's that thing called when a snake eats its own tail?"

"Regret?" Flora asked.

"No, no. The thing where it's happening continuously, like. Only heard it the other day. Wrote it down..." He rifled in his pockets and pulled out a scrap of paper covered in his heavy-handed scrawl. "Ouroboros!" he exclaimed.

"Bless you," Flora said.

Sid ignored her. "What I mean, Captain, is that we'd have more luck rounding up one of the coves on these wanted posters and turning them in than shaking out Flora's pockets." He guffawed. "Wouldn't that be a laugh? First time anyone was turned in by someone who wasn't a relative, or some blighter sick of their mate drinking all their gin. But then you'd have to work out who to turn 'em in to. Some of these posters are for the same blighter from four or five different parish beadles. Look at these!" He waved at a set of woodcuts of varying quality, all of which requested the capture of Lemmy Coghead, a squat man with stringy black hair and a huge mole on his cheek, who specialised in everything from making an unreasonable ruckus to flower snaffling in locations as diverse as Westminster, Soho and Whitechapel. "Wanted by the Bad Habits, the Ushers *and* the Lepers. I can tell you who I'd want to be handed in to and who I wouldn't. All the Ushers would do is make him an extra in a bleedin' play until he died of boredom, the Bad Habits would give him an arse caning—unless he messed with a cat—but the Lepers would tear him limb from limb. Cog cursed devils. I don't like 'em. I don't like 'em at all. The things they do to people. It's worse than the Wharf Gate. It just isn't right. I don't—"

"We get the idea, Sid." The Whitechapel rookery's notorious beadles, the Lepers were a feature of the city Alex wasn't too fond of discussing. She'd take Mother Superior, the head beadle of OverLondon's official ecclesiastical body, the Church of Vengeful Acquisition any day.

Mother Superior was considered mild-mannered compared to many of OverLondon's other religious and civic leaders, with the exception of her love of cats, which was all-encompassing to the point that she got a little Leper-like when she suspected anyone of mistreating a cat. This meant OverLondon's feline population was the most coddled on the globe. Alex liked cats, so she approved.

Alex studied the posters, her eyes alighting on the number on the bottom of the nearest one. Two pounds. That was a lot of coin. Funny how she'd never noticed that before—probably because *her* poster hadn't offered a financial reward. Instead, it had offered the slimy double-crossing bottom feeder who turned her in a certificate of life-long immunity from prosecution by the Over-London Academic Council. *Bastards.*

To erase the sting of recent memory, Alex took a slug from her new pint, but it was no use. Anyone who'd accumulated as many trinkets on their body as she had was doomed to an extraordinarily long life of healthy sobriety.

"Why *doesn't* anyone go looking for these idiots?" she said. "If they're stupid enough to stay still long enough for someone to draw their picture, they must be stupid enough to catch, and I say that from experience." She downed the rest of the gin for the hell of it. At the very least, it was safer to drink than the water in this city.

"Because people can easily get money other ways?" Flora said brightly. Alex noticed that the pile of coins on the table had disappeared and that Flora was back to her normal cheerful self.

"It's obvious." Sid rubbed his stomach in a self-important fashion. "No beadle is going to cross the parish boundaries, are they? Could you imagine the Lepers crossing Utopia Street from the rookery to the artificer district? The Hammer Men'd be on them in a minute." He snorted. "It'd be all-out war again. That's what the treaties were all about, wasn't it? No more war between the parishes as long as no beadle crosses into another beadle's turf. In fact, I'd hazard to say that due to being listed as privateers for the entire city, we're the only people in this city *not* attached to a parish in any way!"

Alex tapped her chin. "That's a surprisingly complex answer for a man with a brain as unique as yours, Sid."

Sid's chest swelled with pride. "I have my moments."

"And he overheard Gregor talking about what your letter of marque meant yesterday," Flora said. "It was with that Bad Habit who came in to ask him to hang up a poster. I saw Sid's mouth moving as he memorised it all. He even wrote some of it down on that piece of paper he's holding, and he didn't return my pencil."

"Lying ferret! I can come up with ideas on my own."

"If someone gives you a running start, a step ladder and an explanatory pop-up book. And give me back my pencil!"

"Now would be the time to be quiet. I'm thinking." Alex was rewarded by a momentary blessed—though slightly resentful—silence.

She did some arithmetic. There were at least fifteen posters on this wall and although they were old, there was never a shortage of wanted coves in this town. If she could find enough current ones, she'd have enough to pay off her tax debt and get the Purple Reign back. And the next time, she wouldn't be caught.

"Sid," Alex said as the idea started to take hold.

"Aye, Captain?"

"You've always been a dab hand at finding our crew before embarkation." It was a sacred tradition for the Purple Reign's crew to get bladdered the night before setting sail and to wedge themselves somewhere they swore they'd never be found, only for Sid to inevitably wake them up with a bucket of water the next morning. Finding crew members was one of the many abilities that made Sid one of the best bo'suns in aeronautical history. That, and being reliable, trustworthy and in possession of a stubborn streak which meant that it was impossible to dislodge an idea once he'd grown attached to it.

Sid's chest swelled with pride, straining the buttons on his vest. "There's no rock too small for me to look under. No hole too deep. No mountain too high—"

"No bawdy house too bawdy, no dive too divey," Flora added.

"—be it rain, sleet, hail or typhoon, I always find my man, woman or woodkin."

"Along with their pies, their gin and their spare change," Flora said.

"Along with their— What are you talking about, Flora?" Sid said indignantly. "I never took anyone's spare change."

Alex ignored them. "And Flora—take that damn spoon out of your pocket and put it back—you can find anything that's got a shine to it."

"If it's shiny, it's mine." Flora's dreamy smile contained a lot of sharp little white teeth.

"And I've got brains," Alex stated. "An abundance of magnificent brains." She steepled her fingers beneath her chin as she considered the letter of marque with renewed interest. Maybe the Academic Council hadn't screwed her down as hard as they'd thought.

"I don't like brains," Flora said. "They're not shiny."

"But you do like money." Alex stood up abruptly, tugging her flying helmet firmly down on her head.

"Where are you going?" Sid asked, looking alarmed. "Captain, you know what happens when you get ideas. That expression on your face says you're going to drop us right in it."

Alex's gold incisor tooth glinted in the lamplight and the scar that slashed down the left side of her face momentarily caused a nearby table of actors to wonder openly if she *was* the real Purple Reign, despite her lack of "height".

She retrieved a cigar from her doublet, lit it and blew a smoke ring into the air. "I'm going to drop us in money, Sid, that's what I'm going to do. When I get ideas, things *happen*. So why don't you mind our table while I go ask Gregor what he's doing with the room upstairs now that he's kicked the stomp ballet school out?"

CHAPTER 2

A VERY ENGLISH CRIME

L ET'S NOW TURN OUR attention to Bloomsbury, where artisans and tradespeople are streaming from the great publishing houses at the end of the working day. Huddling from the night's chill, they dodge food vendors and penny dreadful hacks who've set up their writer's blocks on street corners, scrawling out copies of the latest tawdry tale for anyone looking for a quick thrill.

Some have eyes that are red rimmed with the strain of illustration. Some wear smocks covered in ink and the Femur's Animal Glue used to bind the books destined for the specialist shops and librarians of the city and the universities beyond.

Here and there the Editors, Bloomsbury's beadles, patrol the streets, ever ready to write up infraction notices with their regulation red pencils.

In the centre of Chaucer Street sits St. Smeaton's Cathedral, with its remarkably lifelike statue of Queen Anne the Vengeful tearing up Henry VIII's order for her execution. The church is home to the Blessed Press, the only remaining printing press in England. It's a notable stop for any tourist who believes the thirty glowing fictional reviews in the pamphlet titled *Whye You Snivellinge Cretins Aren't Goinge to Appreciate thee Magnificence of What You're Aboute to See,* by Cardinal Chudleigh of the Church of Vengeful Acquisition.

The press had been a reconciliation gift from OverVatican City, an effort to end the Three Hundred Year War. The conflict started when the Vatican had expressed its displeasure over Queen Anne declaring herself a deity before founding the Church of Vengeful Acquisition and diverting money from their coffers to hers. Consequently, OverVatican City and OverLondon played a city-sized version of bumper carts for the next 300 years. Surprisingly, few people were hurt, on account of cities being bad at sneaking up on each other.

The Blessed Press has so far printed two million Books of Vengeance. Only a small fraction of them have been distributed to the faithful. The rest were foisted onto every boarding house and bawdy house the Church could convince to take them, except for the ones that asked for the pages to be softer and the books to have a hook on the cover so they'd be easier to hang on the privy door.

The cost for non-believers to view the press is tuppence. However, all members of the church's congregation are able to see it in action for free, as long as they pay the farthing congregation registration fee. As a result, St. Smeaton's is the envy of every clergyman in the city, having the largest on-the-books congregation and yet the lowest attendance in OverLondon.

The interior of the church is notable for the pews made from the printing presses the Vengeful Queen ordered destroyed after ascending to the throne. In many places, the wood still bears the scorch marks from those glorious times.

Behind the altar, you'll notice the three iconic stained glass windows. The first depicts Queen Anne the Vengeful sealing the famous Icelandic floatstone pact with King Christian III of Denmark. It incorporates an excellent tableau of the first discovery of floatstone when a volcano erupted, flew into the air, and flipped upside down.

The second window shows Queen Anne the Vengeful announcing her ascendency to godhood while famously holding a dagger to Pope Paul IV's neck, and the third shows Queen Anne the Vengeful supervising the elevation of OverLondon. The latter window includes a particularly pretty sequence showing the city's inaugural voyage around the Thames Valley with the help of its two hundred piloting airships, each of their balloons emblazoned with the flaming hen of Anne.

There are a lot of theories as to why Queen Anne thought levitating OverLondon was a good idea, but no one asks a natural disaster its business plan. Either way, the Vengeful Queen was a doer, and the things that she did stayed done. And once the globe had one floating city that routinely hovered over its enemies before emptying its sewers, it wasn't long before there were more.

While the church windows could keep us occupied for an age, it's the room to the right of the nave that concerns us. It's protected by a reinforced bronze door that owes its exceptional shine to the vigorous licking given it by pilgrims, in the belief that it cures dullness.

Today, the door is ajar. Slipping through the crack, we can plainly see what the fuss is all about. The Blessed Press is a majestic machine, made of intricately carved walnut, six feet long by nine feet high, with a shallow basin to hold the trays of type on its bed and a giant slab of polished pink marble that can be lowered to press the paper to it. The printing blanket that goes over the back of the paper is so holy that anyone prone to religious spasms must take medication before viewing it.

On a normal day, this divine machine is operated by Father Inigo, but he has taken ill. Today, there are five priests grouped around it, radiating the air of schoolboys looking at naughty woodcuts. The impression is enhanced by the vellum pamphlet one priest is holding, which is far more inflammatory than any naughty illustration, no matter how many wobbly bits it might have.

While four of the priests seem excited about what they're about to do, one of them has the kind of facial lines that only an Olympian stress-addict can achieve. We'll call him Father Worrier. The others we'll call Father Confident, Father Cheerful, Father Pious, and lastly, Novice Smug, for reasons that will soon be obvious.

"**A**RE YOU SURE THIS is okay? I mean, if Mother Superior finds out what we're doing, our entrails will be spread all over Westminster Abbey. This is *New Lent*." Father Worrier swallowed convulsively.

Father Cheerful, a large, jovial priest, waved a hand dismissively. His black cassock was tight around his midriff and he closely resembled any one of the deities in charge of fine wine and good times. He was the one holding the woodcut pamphlet and, without checking, anyone would know his hands were sweating. "Don't worry about her," he said. "We're pressing paper, not cats. The worst we'd get is a bottom paddling, which we all know you'd enjoy." His body shook as he laughed at the look of outrage on Father Worrier's face. "Father. It was merely a joke. I understand your concern, but as I told you, the paper is blessed, and the words were written by a nun. How wrong can it be?"

"But it's not right! The words... They're not holy words!" Father Worrier's hands wrung together like two mating octopi.

"Father, Father. Any words written by a member of the church are holy." This was said by Father Pious, a tall man with a hatchet face and hunched shoulders. "Like our father here says, Sister Lascivious is a nun. And you have heard how Cardinal Chudleigh and Mother Superior want us to modernise and celebrate our female members. This is merely an extension of that desire. In fact, I see it as our *duty* to spread these teachings." He all but bowed despite the titters of the other men in the room.

Father Worrier was not to be dissuaded. "But what if you're wrong? What if there's unholy retribution? Remember Father Spatula? Remember the smell of his shoes? Now that we're here, about to *do* this, I'm not sure—"

"Oh, *Father*. Not this again. We all know that Father Spatula died of untreated athlete's foot that was so bad that his feet tried to run away from him," Novice Smug said. He was a young, sweaty priest wearing a novice's grey robes, and he radiated the air of someone who'd looked up little girls' dresses when he was in short pants.

"Father, would it help if I showed you?" This came from Father Confident, who was currently adjusting a lever on the press. He was a commanding man with a sonorous voice. "I'll take the punishment should any lightning bolts come from the sky or flames from the ground." Father Confident waved his hand expansively and the gold ring on his index finger caught the light. "This is merely a printing press. There were once many of them about, used for whatever people wished in the times before our Vengeful Queen decreed they were an abomination and a threat to her ascendency. The evidence is in the wood of the pews just outside this door. The press prints the holy Word and we are holy men, thus, every word we feed it is holy. At this moment, I could arrange these letters any way I like, and the words would be consecrated by my hand. And as I've already told you, I spent time aiding Father Inigo before I took on my own flock at St. George's, and even he, great man that he is, prints the odd non-religious item, usually to make sure the press is working correctly to receive the divine Word."

"But..." Father Worrier said, "I don't know about this and the... other thing. I'm not sure I'm comfortable collecting it in plain daylight."

Father Cheerful's cheerful façade dropped. "Father, no one said we'd *collect* it ourselves. He said he'll deliver it to me in the evening after he's finished with his shift. I'll arrange distribution of your shares by teatime tomorrow."

"Show him, Father." Novice Smug tugged at Father Confident's cassock. "Print something."

"Give me the pamphlet." Father Confident held out his hand.

Father Cheerful held the pamphlet to his chest, his smile dimming. "No, *not* the pamphlet. Not for something so trivial. Do something else, like you just said Father Inigo does."

"Okay," Father Confident said. "What's the time?"

The nearby priests checked their pocket watches, Father Pious tapping and winding his and mumbling about forgetting to have done so that morning.

"Nearly ten," Father Cheerful said.

"Then the Cry should be— Ah. Open the window, Father."

Even as Father Worrier walked to the window, Crier Frank, stationed at the front of St. Smeaton's, began his hourly update, the words echoing around the small room.

Hear ye! Hear ye! A survey by Miss Ignatia Crump's Agency for the Correction of Wanton Stupidity has revealed that the city's ignoramus count has increased by twenty percent over the past ten years. Miss Crump recommends mandatory distribution of library books and preventative neutering for repeat offenders. Stop. The Academic Council will be debating a parliamentary bill concerning the trade of OverParisian prisoners of war tomorrow at midday. Clockbows at thirty paces, no handicaps. Odds are two-to-one on the Latin department due to the width and density of their Armour of Supporting Documents. Stop. Ye've heard! Ye've heard! Want to try dying without the tiresome bit? We put the fun in funeral! Call on Kanker and Son's Living Funeral Parlour in Leaky Street today. Book your fun-eral today!

Father Confident's fingers danced over the trays of type as he arranged the letters one by one in rapid fire. "Width *and* density... That will do, Father. You can close the window now. Here we go." He inked the type quickly and placed a fresh sheet of paper over the top before draping the printing cloth over it and turning a handle. The block came down with a muffled thud.

He raised the block, retrieved the paper and handed it to Father Worrier, who held it like it was something that had been dropped in a midden.

"There you go." Father Cheerful slapped Father Worrier cheerfully on the back. "I think you'll find that there are *no* flames. No lightning bolts. In fact, I do believe our Father here could print the Cry every day and hand copies out in the street for a ha'penny each with no issue."

"Of course." Father Pious patted the printing press. "Through us, the words are blessed."

Father Confident clapped his hands together. "Now that we've got that out of the way, are there any other objections?" He looked around with the air of a physical education teacher itching to dole out push ups. "Good. Once I clear this type, we'll get down to business."

Father Worrier crumpled the paper in his hands. "But to do this during New Lent—"

"Harmless, Father. New Lent only applies to the common man. We priests don't need New Lent to understand deprivation of self and the gift of wealth to Our Lady. We've been deprived our whole *lives* and have already given so much." An incongruous scowl of impatience marred Father Cheerful's jovial features.

"I didn't get to have a bath this morning because there was no more hot water in the boiler," Novice Smug said. "That's deprivation."

"You never wash anyway. I can smell you from here," Father Pious muttered.

"That's not my fault. I would have, if I could have."

"And pigs tap dance on pinheads."

"Fathers," Father Confident cut in. "No need to schism. I think we can all agree that what we are doing is nothing more than a little harmless fun, in an age where we have so little to enjoy. And may I remind you that for us to truly understand the depth of temptation that our flocks face daily, we must from time to time sample those temptations, so that we can be truly empathetic." He puffed up as he saw that his words had found their target. "Now, time is running out and, bar our young novice here, we all have sermons to write and nightly prayers to recite."

Novice Smug smirked. "I've already said my prayers. Twice."

"Vengeful Lady roast your entrails, you didn't!" Father Pious growled. "You've never said your prayers twice in all your years."

"Read the first passage!" Father Confident commanded, rolling his eyes at Father Pious's vehemence. There's always one in every group who is that little bit *too* devout.

Father Cheerful opened the pamphlet. The room fell silent and there was a noticeable charge, the kind that usually fills a room before an attractive lady steps onto a stage and starts removing her clothing. He cleared his throat. "For anyone who wishes to delve into the sensual delights as can be found in the moist depths—"

There was an audible groan from Father Worrier.

"—one must realise that a *hardness* of character is required."

"Oh yes. Very hard."

"Father." Father Confident swiped at his forehead with the back of his hand. "Hmm?"

"The paper. Get me some paper. And keep reading."

Some hours later, the four priests and Novice Smug scurried from the church, each clutching at the newly printed pamphlet hidden under their cassocks and novice's robe.

In their haste to leave, they didn't notice the urchin crouched near the brass door. But then again, her livelihood depended on not being seen.

She waited until the last of the priests had merged into the still-crowded street before she set off. She had valuable information. The Clockmaker would want to hear it, and maybe others too. In this town, information was money, and she'd be making a few stops before she got to Whitechapel.

CHAPTER 3

A Rogue Artificer Investigates a Most Unusual Scene

"ELIAS ADAZE DOOLEY—MAY OUR Vengeful Lady forgive you! Stop playing with it, foolish boy. This is the house of Our Vengeful Lady. Not a place for you to be fiddling with your *thing*." Elias Dooley's mother probably thought her words were a hissed whisper, but since she was more accustomed to communicating over the din of a hundred coglooms in the factory she supervised, they echoed around St. George's Cathedral at least three times.

In the pew across the aisle, Mabel Archer, Euphemia Dooley's next-door neighbour and arch-nemesis, snorted in disdain. Elias's mother snorted in return and they were soon huffing and puffing like disapproving steam engines.

With a swift movement that came from seventeen years of practice, Elias avoided an elbow aimed at his ribs and maintained his focus on Phillips, his test-subject trinket. He cradled the small cog-shaped crustacean in his left hand, while in his right he held a fully articulated clockwork toy soldier's arm. Making this piece of equipment had cost him his latest artificer apprenticeship two days ago, but he was particularly proud of the workmanship when it came to the minute hooks and levers poking out from the shoulder joint.

As he ran the arm over Phillips, the flat surface of the creature's opalescent back rose—somewhat resembling a beetle lifting its wing cases—to reveal the complex biomechanisms packed underneath like a toolbox for all eventualities. Elias touched the small hooks he'd built into the arm's end to Phillip's crimson petal-like cogs, hoops and levers. There was a faint whirring sound before the wing cases closed and Phillips's carapace was smooth again, with the exception of the miniature prosthetic arm sticking up from it like an odd-shaped barnacle, which made a lot of sense when one considered where trinkets originated from.

They had been discovered in the English Channel feeding on omnicite seaweed, coincidentally around the same time that woodkin began to appear in the world. It wasn't entirely understood how they extended people's lives and filtered one's system of most transmissible diseases, toxins and poisons (including the recreational kind), but they were good-natured little creatures that rarely made a fuss while happily acting as a spare liver and kidneys. Their additional ability to connect prosthetics to the human body had proven to be a welcome later discovery, and there was a good chance Elias was on the cusp of making that discovery even more remarkable.

He allowed himself a small, satisfied smile.

Now all he had to do was get Phillips to power the arm without being attached to a human body. He prodded the trinket with his finger, but all Phillips did was extend his twelve tiny ultramarine blue legs, making a high-pitched cooing noise that meant he was enjoying the contact. The arm didn't move.

This was most unsatisfactory.

"*Elias.*"

"What?"

"Father Bartholomew will be here soon! Show some *respect.*"

Although Elias had travelled from his lodgings in the rookery to walk his mother to church, it was only now that he noticed she was wearing her best hat with the extravagant wax pineapple on top. That meant her cold war with Mabel Archer was heating up again. A haberdashery arms race was confirmed by Mabel's hat, which was adorned with four bunches of grapes and, inexplicably, a slice of honeydew melon.

Realising that a show of solidarity was probably in order, Elias made a mental note to compliment his mother on the pineapple after the service. With luck, it would soften the news that he was no longer pursuing an apprenticeship with the Guild of Artificers and that he'd established his own business in a questionable part of the city. However, that could wait, because he had a more immediate concern.

Elias flipped Phillips over to examine his underside. The little trinket's legs waved in the air and his orange suction mouths extended, seeking out Elias in a habitually friendly manner. Elias had long hypothesised that Phillips was the most eccentric trinket he'd ever encountered, but he'd yet to do the experiments to prove it, mainly because he suspected that Phillips was so eccentric that the trinket would act normal while any experiment was underway, specifically to thwart his efforts.

Elias frowned at the dangling arm. Maybe a few drops of blood would help to simulate the human connection. The only problem was that he hadn't brought anything with which to pierce his skin, and he wouldn't be returning to his new workshop for another two hours.

The extravagant pineapple loomed in Elias's peripheral vision, giving him an idea. "Can I borrow a hat pin?" he asked.

The pineapple quivered ominously. "Why would you need a *hat pin*? Useless boy who can't keep a job more than a month, may our Vengeful Lady bless your soul."

"So I can prick myself to draw blood."

This time the maternal elbow connected, and he yelped just as the verger started hammering at the pipe organ. Elias didn't recognise the song, but people frequently commented that the verger didn't recognise the songs either.

He stood up along with everyone else as Father Bartholomew marched to the pulpit with the confident air of a general leading his troops into battle. His altar boys scampered after him, their wildly swinging thuribles barraging the air with the overpowering scent of frankincense.

The priest was a large, commanding man, with an aristocratic, high forehead and a broad nose with nostrils that flared whenever he recited fiery passages of scripture. It was a handsome face, and the women in his congregation frequently speculated that he was an illegitimate son of some OverBenin royal. They never quite answered Elias's questions about why someone with such an illustrious ancestry would be guiding a congregation of weavers in a city almost three thousand miles from his home country on the African continent.

Under the International Treaty of Royal Exchange, Elias had no doubt that an OverBenin royal had, at some stage, been in residency at Westminster Palace. In order for the Royal Exchange to work, each participating monarchy had to maintain a thirteen-strong plump of royals. Given the recent failures of global royal breeding programs due to congenital stupidity, it was inconceivable that any monarchy would knowingly allow an illegitimate spare to go astray. Especially one that could walk and breathe at the same time. In recent centuries, it had become common knowledge that the globe's royals had become experts in producing heirs with chins like the wrong ends of icebergs, overbites that made them look like walking mushrooms, and less intelligence than a senile pigeon.

All evidence pointed to Father Bartholomew having descended from the same West African merchant class as Elias's mother's family, his ancestors presumably having emigrated on special request of the Vengeful Queen in the decades after the city's elevation. The idea had been to reinvigorate England's stale economy with ideas, talent and heads that were still attached to bodies.

Whatever the truth of the priest's ancestry, Elias suspected the adoration he received was largely a result of some kind of underlying female mating urge. Elias had once tried explaining this to his mother, but she'd hit him on the head with a cooking pot.

At the priest's curt gesture for everyone to take their seats, Elias checked to confirm his mother was focused on Father Bartholomew's flaring nostrils.

Once the priest started talking it was impossible to stop him until he was ready, which meant Elias had at least four hours of uninterrupted time to focus. This was precisely why he accompanied his mother to New Mass every week. It took care of a mandatory family obligation and provided him with time for quiet contemplation, even though he questioned the underlying tenants of the religion in which he'd been raised.

Queen Anne the Vengeful had admirably prioritised the separation of religion and intellect in forming the Church of Vengeance and the OverLondon Academic Council, but that didn't mean she hadn't been deranged. All the priests in the Church of Vengeful Acquisition did was repeat a long-dead—and by all reports, rather psychotic—queen's adaptation of someone else's holy book. The result, as far as Elias could see, was three thousand pages of demands that people fill the church's coffers in one fashion or another, and no one questioned it. They didn't *think*.

Whereas Elias was currently working on the solution to a problem of great magnitude that would affect the future of the whole of humanity. If he could get a trinket to power a prosthetic limb without being attached to a human or woodkin body, he'd be able to create automatons. If he could create automatons, he'd be able to release the working classes from the tyranny of labour, and his mother could leave her supervisory job at the textile factory and do whatever she wanted. This would probably involve her tyrannizing him more than she already did, but he was willing to take the hit for the greater good. Yes, the chances of Elias succeeding were slim, but he was a scientist and experimentation was vital, despite what the Artificers' Code said.

As Father Bartholomew's sonorous voice filled the church, Elias studied Phillips with a frown. He didn't have blood, but he had omnicite dust, a residue from the seaweed pods found in deep waters around the globe, which compositionally resembled an extraordinarily energy-dense coal. Maybe if the trinket associated the arm with a reward, it would power it. He fished around in the pockets of his waistcoat and located the pod of omnicite that he'd used to feed the mild-mannered longevity trinket attached to his chest that morning. He shaved off a small amount with his thumbnail—enough to heat a small room for an hour—and held it out.

Sniffing food, Phillips rose to attention, his blue eyestalks extending and waving in the air. Phillips sucked up the dust and shivered with happiness and Elias's cautious anticipation turned to elation when the tiny arm twitched. Maybe the unpleasant disagreement with Master Proops had been worth it. Maybe all the failed apprenticeships, all the times Elias had been called abnormal and stupid had been unjustified. Maybe—

He was distantly aware of the drone of Father Bartholomew's voice ceasing abruptly and then… something else. The noise wasn't quite what he would later associate with an explosion. It was more of a loud, wet splat.

He became conscious of a lot of moisture coating his person and the sound of screaming. He wiped a hand over his face and examined it. Red.

He looked around. In fact, there seemed to be a large amount of red, and a general theme of chunks.

He felt a faint tug on the skin on the back of his hand and looked down. While his attention had been distracted, Phillips had latched on. The anaesthetic in the creature's saliva made the attachment painless, but that didn't stem Elias's annoyance. The little clockwork arm waved at him, which only served to irritate him further. The damned trinket was definitely abnormal.

He'd have to deal with that later. Right now, he had a crisis to attend to.

His mother had fainted and the extravagant pineapple was nowhere to be seen. He checked her pulse, loosened her collar and made sure she didn't have any obvious injury before evaluating the wider situation.

The church was full of screaming people tripping over pews and bumping into each other, which was not constructive activity. The verger had left his post at the organ and was running in circles around the pulpit, wailing and trying to rescue his sheet music. One of the altar boys, now entirely coated in red, was standing in the aisle and picking his nose. The lad was no doubt in shock, perhaps concussed by the thurible at his feet, which had a considerable dent in its side. The other altar boy was tapping his ear, making strange "mawp mawp" noises.

No one was trying to help Father Bartholomew, who was distributed evenly around the front of the church, while a pair of smoking shoes lay where his feet should have been.

Elias's nose twitched at the disturbing mixture of barbeque and incense filling the air.

He knew that he should be demonstrating some kind of shock at this moment, but he'd lived in a boarding house in the Whitechapel rookery ever since his first apprenticeship. After four years of seeing what the Lepers did to those who didn't follow the Rules of the Rookery, he'd grown somewhat immune to seeing a person's insides. And for all the mess, this particular death had been strangely non-violent.

Elias strode down the aisle, gently moving the nose-picking altar boy out of the way and dislodging Mabel Archer's sudden grip on his arm. He didn't have time for other people's hysteria. This was a time for science.

He reached the general perimeter of Father Bartholomew's remains and circled it slowly, frowning.

This was not correct. Priests were not meant to explode, at least in any level of Elias's understanding of how New Mass should work. This did *not* fit.

Elias studied the spatter covering the pulpit, then noted the way the priest's arms were on separate sides of the church and how his head was lodged amongst the organ's pipes. With luck, that would mean the verger wouldn't be performing another of his infamous recitals any time soon.

"What happened, bruv?"

Elias looked down at an urchin's upturned, grease-smeared face, which contained all the world-weariness of a five-hundred-year-old.

"A man has exploded," Elias said.

The urchin raised a dog-end to her mouth and blew a smoke ring towards the church's domed ceiling. "Who?"

"Father Bartholomew."

"Why?"

"I'm not sure."

"Do you have a quote for the Cry?"

"No. This is most irregular."

"Most irregular," the urchin repeated, lowering the cigarette. "What's your name?"

"Elias Dooley."

"Thanks, bruv. Nice one." She sauntered off, skirting around a woman who was screaming for the Sewing Circle, the textile district's beadles. This was despite the obvious fact that Church of Vengeful Acquisition matters—including exploding priests—were the domain of the Bad Habits, and that it would take them at least an hour to reach Stepney from Westminster.

Elias turned back to Father Bartholomew. Why would a priest explode?

He immediately ruled out any ecclesiastical reason. He'd read the church's *Bumper Book of Sins for Filthy Perverts*, which had been less instructive than he'd hoped, being mainly about thinking impure thoughts. He doubted that Father Bartholomew had had many of those. Besides, Elias didn't consider the term 'pure' as a suitable measurement for units of thinking—ostensibly, any thought was *purely* the possession of the person thinking it—so as he squatted down to examine the priest's remains, he decided he was searching for some other cause.

There were the usual insides of a person, albeit more jumbled than normal, and the bizarrely smoking shoes. There was also a confetti of paper fragments that had presumably come from the holy book Father Bartholomew had been holding.

Elias retrieved a screwdriver from his utility belt and sorted amongst the bits in front of him until he came across a scrap of fabric that didn't fit.

Having spent his early childhood as an errand boy at his mother's workplace, Elias knew satin when he saw it, even when it was soaked in blood. During New Lent, followers of the Vengeful Queen's faith weren't allowed to wear anything more sumptuous than coarse cotton weave. In fact, Father Bartholomew had given a sermon on the sins of extravagant textiles only last week.

A fragment of paper also struck him as odd, mainly because of the blood-flecked word *moist* printed on it.

Deciding that both items deserved further investigation, he produced a sheet of wax paper from his pocket and was wrapping up the fabric and paper when he spotted movement near his boot.

A longevity trinket was hobbling around on injured legs, its eyestalks waving about in alarm. Half of its carapace was buckled, revealing the minute red workings underneath.

Elias knew he shouldn't take it, but he was unable to leave the creature in such a state of distress, so he painstakingly scooped it up, carefully enveloping it in his handkerchief to avoid harming it any further. Feeling the vibration of Phillips's coo of greeting rather than hearing it, he placed the injured trinket and the other things he'd collected into a pocket.

As Elias stood to better study the scene, the Cry momentarily overcame the hysteric din inside the church.

Hear ye! Hear ye! This is an exclusive emergency bulletin. Stop. Father Bartholomew of St. George's Cathedral has exploded during New Mass. Bystander Elias Dooley was quoted as saying, 'This is most irregular.' We will update as developments continue. Stop. Ye've heard! Ye've heard! This bulletin was brought to you by Gobbles Milk Pellets. Satisfies the ravenous child like nothing else. Now in cow flavour!

Knowing time was limited, Elias took out his notebook and jotted down his observations. He then measured the blast radius, dodging the hysterical verger in the process. Deciding that he'd gathered as much information as possible, he strode back to his mother.

She was still unconscious, so he awkwardly hefted her into his arms and left the church, stepping over the unfortunate wax pineapple which was now in almost as many chunks as the late Father Bartholomew.

CHAPTER 4

THE REIGN AGENCY OPENS FOR BUSINESS

A LEX IGNORED THE FLOW of Drury Lane's morning traffic around her and inspected the sign Sid was screwing to the wall between the two second-floor windows of The Armoury. It read, *The Reign Agency: Home of the Dreade Pirate Purple Reign. An OverLondon Privat Ear.*

She rolled her eyes, raising her voice. "Sid, have you read the sign?"

Sid wobbled on the ladder as he looked over his shoulder. "Aye, Captain. It says exactly what you told me to paint."

"Yes, but the last words. Privat ear, Sid? Privat *ear*?"

"Is there a problem, Cap'n?"

Alex spent a couple of seconds contemplating the average OverLondoner's reading ability. "No, no. It'll do." She turned her attention to the skull and crossbones painted next to the words. That had been her idea. With luck, it would bring in the punters. People in this city liked pictures much more than words.

Behind Alex, a couple of actors dressed as a pantomime horse were attempting to busk by banging the horse's head on the bottom of a wooden bucket. To her right she could hear the squeaky wheels of the cart belonging to Sweet Pete, Drury Lane's resident ice cream pusherman. In a true testament to the average OverLondoner's compulsion to eat ice cream, he was doing a brisk trade despite the number of skin-chilling clouds drifting through the streets.

That distinctive squeak had been a local fixture since Alex's childhood. The only thing that had changed was the size of Pete's ice cream scoop. It was a brass prosthetic attached to his left arm in lieu of a hand, and he used it to flail at the urchins surrounding him. In much the same way that sabre-toothed tigers had developed bigger teeth to combat their prey's increased speed, dexterity and thickness of hide, Sweet Pete and the local urchins were engaged in an evolutionary arms race. This had resulted in the urchins evolving bullet heads and bodies that were only able to survive on a diet of sugar—the mere sight of a vegetable sent them into anaphylactic shock—while Pete's scoop had been upgraded incrementally until it had become a weapon worthy of being hung on the walls of any great castle.

"Can I come down now, Captain?" Sid asked. "You know I don't like heights."

"Sid, you've spent the past forty years living on an airship. Where's your faith in your pig and chicken tattoos?" Alex asked, referring to the way airmen had followed the tradition of sailors in centuries gone by in tattooing a pig and a chicken on their feet to ward off drowning, using the rationale that in shipwrecks, the crates of pigs and chickens were always seen bobbing on the water. For airmen, the logic was slightly different, but still held. The reasoning went that any airman who fell from an airship would develop the flapping powers of a chicken, or alternatively become a delicious roast dinner for some unsuspecting farmer below. Either way, people figured that it was a happy ending for someone.

"They only help in the air," Sid said. "I don't like heights on land. There's so much more air between me and the land when I'm on a ship. I don't think either the pig or the chicken would be much help at this height."

Alex had to grant this logic its due.

As Sid climbed down and yelled at a nearby beggar trying to steal his toolbox, Alex placed her hands on her hips and gauged the reaction from the street. The busking actors had noticed the sign and the horse's backside was wondering out loud where the great Dread Pirate Purple Reign was. That was a start, at least.

"Where's Flora got to with those wanted posters?" Alex muttered to herself.

"I'm here." Flora bobbed up next to her. She had three ice cream cones clutched in one hand and a wad of posters crumpled in the other. "I brought you something sweet. Because I'm sweet."

Alex took the cone with a scoop of strawberry ice cream on top. Then she looked at Sweet Pete's cart. A couple of seconds ago, Flora hadn't been anywhere in sight. "Who'd you snaffle these from?"

"No one." Flora darted her tongue out to lick at the scoop of vanilla ice cream. Her floppy hat had a speckled chicken feather stuck in it today.

"No one?"

"Maybe someone."

"Who is someone?"

"No one important. Sid! I got you something." Flora skipped over to Sid and thrust an ice cream cone at him. He took it automatically while continuing a philosophical argument over the ownership of his toolbox.

Alex was about to ask Flora's opinion of the sign when Sweet Pete scurried up behind her, his cart squeaking, his scoop waving. "Here! She didn't pay for those."

He was a small man with an unfortunate boil on his forehead that he tended like a pet, and a permanent air of dissatisfaction with his lot in life—no small feat for someone rumoured to be over two hundred years old, with a longevity trinket struggling to keep him looking a permanent, unhealthy forty. His physical resemblance to an over-sucked lemon was contradicted by his costume. Like every other member of the Sugar Gang, Sweet Pete wore the red-and-white-striped sequined suit that their boss, Big Ivan had made compulsory.

Big Ivan liked a bit more sparkle than the average megalomaniac, but no one was going to comment on it in a public space where it could get back to him. People who got on the wrong side of Big Ivan tended to find themselves terminally lacking in the things required for living. And then there was the rumour about the thing he did with the carrot...

Alex glared sternly at Flora before taking another lick of her ice cream. "Do you have evidence?" she asked Pete.

"She asks if I have any evidence?" Pete wailed in a high-pitched voice made for complaining. "I'm missing the three cones that I made up for those blokes over there, aren't I?" He waved his scoop towards three dandies who were talking heatedly amongst themselves.

"Hey! You!" one of them called out with an accent that oozed money. He was dressed in the regalia of a Maye Fayre fop and sported a bejewelled prosthetic nose, no doubt thinking it would make him look like he'd suffered some kind of gallant duelling injury. Alex thought it made him look like a tit. "That sign your man just nailed up. It says Dread Pirate Purple Reign."

"Yes," Alex said.

"Are *you* the Dread Pirate Purple Reign?" His accomplices chortled at the question.

Alex gave him a long, hard stare. "I prefer to be called the Dread *Privateer* Purple Reign nowadays, thank you."

"You can't be her!"

"Why not?"

"Well, for one thing, I've seen the picture and you're not the right..." He made cupping gestures in front of his chest with his hands and looked pointedly at Alex's doublet. "Height."

"And?"

"I'll credit you for the costume. That clockbow is a convincing prop." He gestured to the weapon holstered at Alex's hip. "The flying helmet is spot on, too. And Tarquin and Vulker want to know who did the scar."

Behind him, his friends tittered. Their prominent Adam's apples were poor substitutes for the chins they wished they'd been born with.

"A low-flying shark," Alex said calmly. "Now if you'll excuse me, I'm busy." She tilted her head towards Sweet Pete, who'd just smacked away one urchin's searching hands, while two more tried to jab stolen cones into his tub of vanilla.

"But you haven't answered my question!"

"I think it's time for you to run along now," Alex said coolly.

"Who are you to tell me what to do? Do you know who I am?"

There was only so much a pirate could put up with, and such a tired cliché had to be met by the response it deserved. Moments later, the man was a huddled ball on the muck-strewn cobblestones at Alex's feet, with an ice cream cone functioning as a serviceable gag.

"I'm someone who's much taller now." She straightened her doublet before turning back to Sweet Pete.

"How much do we owe you, Pete?"

"It's not that. It's the *principle*! If it were anyone else but you, I'd report her, I would." Sweet Pete waved his scoop at Flora, barely missing a passing actor dressed as a fair maiden who scowled and stomped off. "And she'd end up with horrible things happening to her. It's not right. I'm an honest man, earning an honest wage, putting up with harassment every day—" As he said this, he smacked yet another urchin on the head with a clanging sound. "And what thanks do I get?"

"A four hundred percent markup on the product and the protection of one of the scariest bastards around?" Alex smiled ingratiatingly. "How about I pay you double for the cones?"

"Triple. It's emotional trauma."

"Okay, triple. Pay the man, Flora," Alex commanded.

Flora started to protest, until Alex glared at her.

"Alright." She riffled through her pockets before dropping the coins into Sweet Pete's hand.

"Bleedin' cursed. You're all the same," he muttered, before pushing his cart away fast enough to avoid Alex's reprisal.

"He shouldn't have said that," Flora said.

"No." Alex put a hand on Flora's shoulder, picturing how Pete would look with his scoop inserted somewhere sensible.

"We could tell Big Ivan."

"We could." Alex scratched her cheek. "I've always been curious about what he does with the carrot."

"Yeah." Flora sighed. "But then we wouldn't have any ice cream. It's okay, really. I got my money back." She opened her hand to reveal the coins Alex had just seen her drop into Sweet Pete's hand.

Alex patted her head. "Good girl. You got the posters?"

"Yes. Lots and lots of them. All of them new, like you asked."

"Good. Come into my office." Alex gestured to the door of The Armoury with a smile. As Flora skipped ahead of her, Alex turned to catch Sid's attention, but since he was currently buying his toolbox back from the beggar who'd stolen it, she left him to it. Behind her, the Cry approached, a ripple of sound from Westminster to the City's edge.

Hear ye! Hear ye! OverLondon will be piloted twenty miles-off course tomorrow to avoid an incoming hailstorm. Air Controller Hendricks was quoted as saying that it'll all be over by teatime if we don't ram OverBristol. Stop. An envoy from the University of OverMunich will be arriving as a guest of the Academic Council tomorrow. Anyone making fun of lederhosen during the next forty-eight hours will answer to Porter Gluggins. Stop. The Dread Pirate Purple Reign has opened the Reign Agency above The Armoury in Drury Lane to find wanted citizens for a fee. In response, a Drury Lane local, Sweet Pete, was quoted as saying, 'What is the world coming to?' Stop. Ye've heard! Ye've heard! This bulletin was brought to you by the Reign Agency. Trust a pirate, because honest blighters don't exist.

Flora hooted. "That's us! In the Cry *and* in one of the advertisements you paid for."

"Yes." Alex rubbed her hands together, feeling the same excitement she usually experienced when her ship got the drop on a gold-laden merchantman. "That's us. The bait's been set. All we need to do is wait for our quarry to have a nibble!"

CHAPTER 5

A SHOP DIVIDED

T HE CRY WAS SUBSIDING as Elias placed his paintbrush into the tin of gold paint by his feet and studied the words he'd painted, one letter per diamond windowpane of the shop before him. *Ingenious Mechanisms*. He allowed himself a brief moment of satisfaction.

Earlier that morning, he'd visited the Cry's office in Westminster and had paid five shillings for an advertisement to be read every day for five days, starting from tomorrow. Selecting the right wording for the advertisement had been difficult, especially given the distraction of the steady flow of urchins, beggars and members of the general public looking to sell information at the Cry's intake desk.

However, he'd got lucky when Mister Vernon Gripes, the Master of Information, had offered to help. Sensing Elias's dilemma in not wanting to alert the artificers that he was setting up his own workshop outside their district, Mister Gripes had suggested that Elias limit his advertisement to offering the repair of small mechanical items. Elias had seen the intelligence in this, as the artificers wouldn't bother themselves with someone doing what they considered 'busywork'.

The professionalism of the man had impressed Elias considerably, as had his polite praise of Elias's utility belt. On the spot, Elias had decided that he would attempt to grow a pencil moustache similar to Mister Gripes's, as it projected an air of intellectual competence while also conveying pleasant approachability. He felt that a moustache would demark the change from the boy who'd apprenticed at numerous workshops in the artificer district, to the business-owning man he was now.

In simply crossing Utopia Street from Shadwell's artificer district and opening Ingenious Mechanisms on the Whitechapel rookery's side, Elias was now free to both earn a living and continue his experiments without risk of being fired from yet another apprenticeship. He'd no longer have to concern himself with his mother's questions about keeping gainful employment. Also, he'd never again be asked to terminate a trinket just because it wasn't behaving in a conventional fashion.

Although, Phillips had been trying his patience for the past twenty minutes by attempting to snatch the paintbrush from his hand. He rolled his eyes at the way the arm on Phillips's back was flailing around. He should have removed the creature by now, but the additional hand might be useful one day, once Elias and Phillips had reached some kind of interspecies agreement that would inevitably involve additional omnicite treats.

All around him, the citizens of the Whitechapel rookery hurried by, deliberately not paying attention. In their experience, businesses on this side of the street came and went.

If Elias were on the other side of Utopia Street, in the neat world of the artificer district, people would've stopped and asked questions, free in the knowledge that their rights were protected by the Hammer Men who patrolled the streets in their brown leather aprons, their traditional nail-studded wooden mallets slung over their shoulders. On the Whitechapel side, asking questions made you a 'known associate', and you didn't want to be one of those when the Lepers came knocking—that's if they bothered to knock. Usually, they just smashed a window or came through the roof.

As Elias picked up his paint pot and brush, preparing to enter the building, two Lepers turned the corner from More Lane and started purposefully towards him as if summoned. Their heavily modified crimson uniforms and stovepipe hats stood out against the dinginess of the street, and their unwashed stench spread through the air. One of them had three mechanical legs of brass, bronze and rusted iron that ended in sharp points, which stabbed the cobblestones with every step, while her right hand possessed the Lepers' distinctive rusted-blade fingers. The other appeared to have his original legs, but each of his arms had been cobbled from multiple limbs and a patchwork of scrap metal, modified to be extra-long and multi-jointed. The tips of his finger blades scraped against the cobblestones with the sound of a knife on a whetstone. He must have been a handsome man until The Clockmaker got hold of him. Now he had one dummy rusted metal eye and a disjointed jaw that was more mandible than mouth.

Centuries ago, people had feared and degraded London's lepers under the misapprehension that their disease was contagious. Then The Clockmaker had come along and had taught them how to lean into that fear. His argument had been: "Let's give them something to be *really* scared of." After trinkets were discovered, curing leprosy and almost every other ailment known to man, the original lepers had largely retired to top-floor rookery tenements. This meant that nowadays The Clockmaker required all enterprising applicants to take off their longevity trinkets and hack off a significant limb, trusting him to revive them and recreate them as monster clockwork creatures who would police his parish with maximum sadism. The job attracted a specific type of individual, generally the sort who tortured small animals for recreational sport.

"What's this, then?" the female Leper asked, clinking her knife-fingers together. Her mouth had been modified as an extra-wide gash in her face, her teeth metallic, her breath fetid. "It looks like we've got a shop for the thinker. To think his little thoughts." She nudged the long-armed Leper next to her and he made a rasping sound like a saw cutting through bone. Elias wondered how many people in the rookery's dank alleys had heard that noise just before they died.

"Yes." He took great care to keep his expression polite.

"They kick you out over there?" She jerked her head at the other side of the street where a pair of Hammer Men were watching on with an air of vigilance.

Elias shook his head. "I left voluntarily. I'm starting a business."

"Sharin' with the funny little bookman? Rumour 'as it that the two of you hate each other's guts."

"Yes."

She laughed. It was a sound even more chilling than her companion's guttural rasping, as if some toxic liquid was bubbling up from her insides. Then her smile vanished. "Heard on the Cry you were there when that priest went pop yesterday. Did *you* do it?" A rusty-blade finger poked the underside of Elias's jaw, not quite breaking his skin. He'd heard once that they rubbed the metal in vinegar to make it corrode quicker.

"No," he murmured, barely moving his lips.

"Because if you did, I'd slash you now. You're lucky there were witnesses, or you'd be a pretty souvenir for me to take to The Clockmaker. He likes Mother Superior. He'd be sure to send your corpse to her with your guts tied in a bow." She stared into Elias's eyes and he could see the banked insanity there, could feel her impulse to fillet him like a fish.

Sweat ran down Elias's back and his longevity trinket twitched at his unease. Phillips emitted a low-frequency hiss from the back of his hand.

The blade pressed at his skin for another tense second, until she withdrew her hand with a guttural chuckle. "We'll watch your business with interest." With that, the Lepers walked away, parting the mass of people on the street like two nightmare creatures at a children's party.

Elias reassured himself they weren't coming back before hurrying inside his shop. He rested his back against the door, allowing the air trapped in his lungs to escape.

"Mind the line!" The shout came from behind a pile of books to Elias's left. He jerked in surprise, almost spilling the paint in the pot.

He looked down and realised that one of his shoes had indeed crossed the newly dried red line that stretched down the middle of the space, separating the Happy Times Bookstore from his own business. He moved his toe a little more into the book-logged section.

"I see what you're doing!"

"Don't you have better things to do?" Elias finally spotted the one-book hole in a carefully constructed wall of books, pamphlets, and tomes. Two eyes were glaring through it.

"Why don't you get on with setting up your disturbing little shop and leave *my* business alone. I never would've rented the space to you if you hadn't looked so *pitiful* when that prosthetic place gave you the boot."

"Nice book dam."

"It's *not* a dam!"

"Forgive me if I'm wrong, but a dam is a wall. Made of sticks, mud and branches generally, but from what I understand, *homo castor* can dam in any environment. Didn't you once dam all the books in the library at your college at OverOxford? Wasn't that why they asked you to leave before your exams?"

"I am *not* woodkin! I was *adopted* by woodkin! I do *not* dam and I am *not* a beaver!" There was the sound of something—most likely a book—thumping on the floor. "Besides, at least *I'm* not the one who was fired from... how many apprenticeships?"

"Seven," Elias said. It was common knowledge.

"Oh? Seven? *Seven*. Ha! Go fondle your bugs. Hurry up and fail."

The tension in Elias's shoulders eased. He'd known Vikram since the day he'd taken a room at Mrs Nevins's Boarding House for Respectable Young Gentlemen four years earlier. It turned out that Mrs Nevins had unwittingly conflated Vikram being a book seller with respectability. If Mrs Nevins knew what was really contained in the books piled on Vikram's side of the shop, she'd call an exorcist and excommunicate him from her premises.

There were woodcuts in some of the books in Vikram's shop that showed people in positions that Elias knew were anatomically impossible. This was because he'd taken one of the books to the Southwark butter district and had asked a milkmaid there her professional opinion.

The butter district was the part of Southwark where affection was arranged on a by-the-minute rate—sometimes even by the second. Rumour had it that the name came from the old tradition of milkmaids devising new and interesting ways to make additional income. As far as Elias knew, this was only partially true. He'd recently learned that the name had been coined by milkmaid, Bess "The Gripper" Smacker, who'd diversified her business after her advertisement for cows to be 'Milked in Five Minutes. Satisfaction Guaranteed,' began to attract an unexpected—and very un-bovine-like clientele. Seeing there was money to be made, she'd declared that cows were awful tippers and had changed her core business strategy.

Sometimes Elias indulged himself in remembering how much the milkmaid he'd showed Vikram's book to had laughed. On days like this he wished he could have bottled the sound to bring out and release whenever Vikram did something particularly vexing.

During their first meeting, Vikram had called Elias an 'unwashed mass' and they'd been archenemies ever since. According to Vikram, he'd offered to lease Elias half of his shop space so he could watch him fail up close.

Elias had accepted partly because the rent was cheap, but mostly because no respectable member of the Artificer's Guild was going to admit they'd ever visited Vikram's shop.

He inched his foot over the line until a satisfying amount of resentment simmered in the air, then turned to his side of the room.

He'd yet to organize his crates of cogs, nuts, bolts and tools, as his first priority had been setting up his trinket aquariums on a series of shelves above his desk. It filled him with warmth to see them bubbling away with his specially designed cogpumps airing the water. The little creatures—all of them rejects that would have been terminated by his previous employers—were clinging to lengths of omnicite weed that he'd brought at the Covent Garden fish market. The weed had to be purchased fresh once a week, but Elias had worked out the creatures still found it comforting. In the wild, they lived on the omnicite pods that grew on the weed, but they were satisfied with the sprinkle of shaved omnicite Elias gave them once a month.

The injured trinket he had found after Father Bartholomew's explosion was now housed in one of the smaller aquariums, above a brazier which heated the water to blood temperature. Four of its legs had been carefully splinted with slivers of wood fastened with silk thread so as not to cause further injury. Its carapace was still crinkled, but Elias was confident that, with time and care, the creature would recover. Surprisingly, its suction mouths hadn't been injured, which was a puzzle. Either it had disconnected from Father Bartholomew's body shortly before the priest had exploded, or it was a very lucky beast indeed.

Elias tapped the tank, then wiggled his fingers as the injured trinket poked out its eyes, studying him quizzically. He placed the paint pot on the second-hand desk he'd purchased with a significant fraction of his modest savings. His enlargoscope was already set up in its centre, ready for him to examine the paper and fabric fragments he'd collected after Father Bartholomew's explosion, but that would have to wait. Being church business, it was more a matter of curiosity than urgency. Mother Superior and her Bad Habits would soon have an answer, no doubt, albeit an incorrect, non-scientific one.

Right now, Elias had a workspace to organize.

Soon, customers, and hopefully money, would start coming in, and he'd never again be berated for having a head too full of brains.

CHAPTER 6

AN URCHIN WAKES

T HE URCHIN GIRL NAMED Grub woke up and sneezed before yelping at the pain shooting from the back of her head. She gingerly ran her fingers over her scalp, examining the egg-sized lump there. She'd been coshed, and whoever'd done it had been an amateur. It was widely known she was one of The Clockmaker's urchins, which meant he'd have their guts for pulley wire when he found out.

Swiping her nose on the back of her hand, she took stock of her surroundings.

She was in a cold, dusty dark room, but someone had covered her with a blanket that smelled of goats, and had given her a pillow. She'd never had a pillow before. She sat up and squeezed it to her chest, waiting for her eyes to adjust to the light, but they didn't, because there wasn't any.

She shivered and felt around until she worked out that she was lying on a pile of hay.

The dust tickled her nose and she sneezed again before standing up, carefully navigating the room, the pillow still clutched to her chest. It was a small space, and the walls were damp stone. The floor was made of dirt, and uneven. A cellar.

She found a door and fumbled at the handle before pulling the hairpin she used as a lockpick from her tangled mop of hair. She tried to find a keyhole, but there wasn't one. An old door, maybe barred on the other side, or something leaning against it.

Hugging the pillow tighter, she considered her situation.

It was too dark to have an idea of the time of day, but from the size of the lump on her head she supposed she'd slept for a while.

Someone had inexpertly hit her on the head and snaffled her, but they'd made sure she was warm and they'd given her a pillow, which meant they hadn't wanted to kill her.

She returned to the makeshift bed and huddled under the rug.

Someone would notice she was missing soon, if they hadn't already. The Clockmaker would send someone after her. All she had to do was wait. Her shivering was only due to the cold and because she was getting hungry. She wasn't scared. She wasn't scared at all.

CHAPTER 7

THE REIGN AGENCY'S FIRST CLIENT

A LEX STRODE THROUGH THE Armoury and wove around tables, heading for the stairs leading to her new office.

Gregor was shirtless as he swept up yesterday's sawdust, and she made an effort to leer, but only out of professional courtesy. Alex had a reputation to maintain, and leching was a mandatory quality in a pirate—not that she'd gotten a lot of that in over the past couple of years. She'd largely spent them evading the OverLondon Fleet, the OverParisian Fleet, the OverMadrid Fleet... Oh, and there was that time they'd offended the OverAlexandrian Fleet. She shuddered at the memory. Never offend Egyptians, especially not when they are trialling prototype poison-tipped ballistas from OverTimbuktu. To this day, she couldn't mention the Songhai Empire without Sid turning a virulent shade of purple and ranting about Alex almost getting him killed by weapons created by the world's most proficient producers of floatstone and armaments. In her defence, the Purple Reign had been on holiday, but having a giant skull and crossbones on one's ship had been known to offend.

Alex reached the top of the stairs to find Flora nibbling on her nails and idly swinging back and forward in one of the three hammocks that hung in the corner of the room that was now the Reign Agency's headquarters.

The tarnished copper teapot on the hob simmered politely. It featured a skull and crossbones on the side and was one of the few items Alex had been able to rescue from the Purple Reign before its confiscation.

Earlier that morning, Sid had constructed a shelf above the stove, which held some basic foodstuffs and Sid's modest collection of penny dreadful paperbacks. They all had lurid woodcut covers of scantily dressed women and titles like *Thee*

Darke Alley, *Afraide of Heights*, *The Bavarian Ducke* and Sid's favourite due to a questionable bathtub scene, *Mentalley Desturbed*.

The crumpled wanted posters Flora had collected were scattered on the cracked marble-top desk that Alex and Sid had raided from the prop cupboard of a nearby theatre. They'd also snaffled a tattered green velvet armchair, a small table and chairs and three mismatched but impressive-looking fake treasure chests covered in paste gemstones. They had clearly been made by someone who'd never met a pirate, because if they had, they'd know that pirates didn't bury their loot, they spent it. The chests now contained Alex's, Sid's and Flora's belongings. Alex liked to think the furniture added a refined touch, inasmuch as their addition was better than the room being empty.

The bathroom accessible through a small arched doorway was decorated in an eye-watering pink dancing pig motif, care of Horatia Causation's Stomp Ballet School for the Rhythmically Disadvantaged, which had previously occupied the space.

Over the years, Horatia Causation had become something of an OverLondon legend, if legends were something that caused people to shudder slightly. Horatia was an eternal optimist who firmly believed that anyone could achieve their dream if they weaponised positive thinking and perseverance, and it was frequently said that the term 'blast radius' could be applied to her business model. As a result, her enterprises frequently proved *too* successful and were inevitably shut down by neighbours wielding blunt instruments. In addition to her wildly successful stomp ballet school that had been shut down by Gregor, who'd wielded a mallet with maximum prejudice, there had been her school for megaphone orchestra and her *avant-garde* institute for yodelling poodles.

The other relics of the school's occupation were the various warped mirrors nailed to the wall, and the faint waft of desperation and aggressive liniment. But the bathroom was fully plumbed and had a wardrobe that they were using to store sacks of potatoes and onions, so Alex wasn't complaining.

Giving Flora a side-eye, Alex lounged behind the desk, put her booted feet up on its surface and smoothed out the wanted posters. She lowered her specially made opti-goggles from their perch on her helmet, looking around out of habit to make sure no one other than Flora was going to see her wearing them.

"Let's take a look. Ah, there are some promising ones here. This one's for a pound, this one's for two pounds…"

She inspected the one-pound poster. It was for a cove named Dirty Robert who'd been accused of petty theft at Canary Wharf. "'Wanted with his hed sandpapered with a sharkes aresole or ded'," she read. "Given our low stock of shark's posteriors, I think we'll give him a miss. The Neptune Guards are definitely an odd bunch. Where'd you find this, Flora?"

"The conveniences in Hyde Park."

"Oh." Alex pursed her lips. "I think that one may have been a code for something we'd better not address in your company. What's this next one?" She shifted her attention to the two-pound poster. The rough woodcut depicted a woman who looked like she'd spent a lifetime working as the business end of a battering ram. "'Wanted extremely dead with her entrails scooped out and her eyeballs on toothpicks by Mother Superior for illegal theft of a kitten in Westminster.' Now this is a possibility—a kitten thief doesn't present much of a challenge." Alex read the small print at the bottom of the page. "No, I rescind that. She's also wanted for murdering fifteen gin brewers using a piece of chalk and a handkerchief."

She re-examined the picture for any sign the woman was woodkin. "Flora, do you know any species that could murder people with a piece of chalk? Gregor's the only badger I know of, and you're not exactly lethal…"

"Wolverine."

Alex's eyebrows rose. "There are woodkin wolverine?"

"I don't think so, but if there was, they could."

"True. Okay, well, for one thing, I don't want to deal with someone who may or may not be a psychotic death creature, and for another, I'm not so sure I want to deliver anyone who has offended a cat to Mother Superior."

"Too messy." Flora waved a hand idly, watching how the dusty light from the window streamed through her fingers. "She doesn't like people who hurt cats and neither do I."

"Quite." Alex looked at the next poster. It was written in a rusty red colour and the only illustration was a stick figure. "'Wanted ded by Lepers. Don't kare how'... No, I don't think we'll be associated with the Lepers." She supressed an involuntary shudder. Anyone who ventured into Whitechapel's fetid alleyways would've seen the Lepers' work nailed up above doorways or smeared across walls.

She riffled through the other notices. "'Wanted shirt ruffled or shoe scuffed by the Butlers of Maye Fayre.' 'Wanted bollock stifled or man titty motorboated'—that'll be the butter district. Yes, it's the Milk Maids. Not exactly something I really fancy doing. Especially for five shillings. Where did you find this one? No, don't tell me—"

"The Hyde Park—"

"Conveniences." Alex sighed. "Wasn't there anything better than these?"

"Yes. Maybe. I'm not sure. I got distracted."

"Of course you did."

"I started thinking about all the things I could have, that could be mine, if only people would let me have them."

"I always said you made a perfect pirate."

"Thank you." Flora smiled dreamily.

"Captain! Captain! We have a visitor! Captain!" Sid's words echoed up the stairs, as did the sound of his puffing and the thud of his boots.

Alex swung her boots off the desk and sprung to her feet. "We do?"

"We do." Sid appeared in the doorway, his bowler hat clutched in his hands, beads of sweat running down his cheeks. "And she's a lady of quality!"

"Is she now?" Alex hastily removed her goggles, then gestured for Flora to get out of the hammock.

Alex had just tucked in her shirt and straightened her doublet when a woman walked through the door.

Her face and body were immediately pleasing to the eye. Wisps of mousy hair escaped from an oversized white bonnet and she wore the kind of blousy blue velvet gown that was all the rage with OverLondon's well-dressed and brainless set.

However, despite the velvet, Alex noticed subtle signs that spoke of a humbler life—the steel buttons, the cambric trim, the scuffed black boots. A highly paid servant, maybe, but not gentry.

"Welcome!" Alex exclaimed, tipping her flying helmet and coming around the desk to bow. "I'm Captain Reign. I'm delighted to be at your service."

The woman came to an abrupt halt, the shock showing on her face. "*You're* the Dread Pirate Purple Reign?"

"The Dread *Privateer* Purple Reign, at your service."

"Privateer. Yes. But... well... but you're... No offence, but you're not as..." The woman made a fluttering gesture at her chest. "*Tall* as your picture suggests."

Alex's smile didn't falter. "That's what I've been told. I really should have shot the artist when I had a chance. May I ask your name?"

The woman blushed prettily. "Oh. Manners. What must you think of me? I'm Miss Sadie Simms."

"Lovely to make your acquaintance, Miss Simms. Can I offer you a seat?" Alex gestured grandly to the armchair.

"Oh. Yes." Miss Simms hurried to it, sitting with a stiff-backed, rigid posture that was unaccountably regarded as ladylike by the less enlightened. Alex had no doubt that she would have been quite alarmed to learn that real ladies slouched something fierce. In Alex's experience, real ladies saw posture as something that servants took care of.

"Can Mister Potts get you a refreshment?" Alex gave Sid a wide-eyed look. He was standing by the door, still clutching his hat as if he didn't know what to do with it. It was only then that Alex remembered that Sid had never been good with women who preferred bustles over breeches.

Miss Simms blinked. "Refreshment? Oh yes. I would like a tea. Or maybe a coffee. Or maybe a glass of water. What do you have?"

"What do we have, Sid?" Alex asked smoothly.

"Everything. I mean— I'll just—"

"Make it so," Alex commanded as she leant against the desk. "And what can I help you with, Miss Simms?"

"Knickers," Miss Simms blurted, then put her hand to her mouth. "What must you think of me? I should be clearer. It concerns a pair of knickers, and it's a matter of some urgency and delicacy."

"Knickers usually are quite delicate," Alex said.

"And can sometimes be quite urgent," Flora interjected.

Miss Simms twisted to look at Flora before turning back to Alex. "Yes, well, be that as it may, this concerns a particular *pair* of knickers. Red satin ones."

"I'm not sure I follow," Alex said.

"It's the priest, the one that exploded. He was wearing them."

"Priest?"

"The one from yesterday that was 'most irregular,'" Flora added.

"Ah. *That* priest." In Alex's wide and varied experience, an exploding priest was a long way down on the list of the oddest things she'd encountered. "Yes, I heard about it on the Cry. But isn't this something for the Bad Habits to take care of?"

Miss Simms grimaced. "That's the problem. I don't want them to take care of it. Or to be more precise, I want *you* to take care of it before they do."

Alex pictured herself with a shovel and a bucket full of priest. "It's been a day, Miss Simms. I'm sure they haven't left him in the church overnight."

"On the contrary, they have. I can only assume it's because they want to thoroughly investigate what killed him. Which means no one's, ah... They haven't examined the, ah..."

"Remains?"

"Yes," Miss Simms said gratefully. "And when they do, there's a chance they'll discover that Father Bartholomew was wearing red satin knickers."

Alex prided herself on her blank expression. "I see. And you have some connection to these red satin knickers?"

Miss Simms nodded. "I made them." She looked around furtively, as if expecting Mother Superior to jump out of one of the walls with her caning stick in hand. "Is this entirely confidential?"

Until now, Alex hadn't given a thought to confidentiality, but when she answered, it was with a reassuring smile that would make any self-respecting life-insurance salesman proud. "Yes. Assuredly."

"Well, it's like this. A lot of the clergy come to me and I make *things* for them." Miss Simms waved to her midsection in a self-conscious gesture. "It's a considerable part of my income."

"I see."

"And I've heard from a source who was at St. George's that a man dressed in black inspected the remains just after the, ah..."

"Incident?" Alex supplied.

"Yes, that. I can only assume he's with the Church. At the moment, they may still assume that the satin comes from another source, but on further investigation of Father Bartholomew's... If *she* finds out that priests are wearing salacious underwear during New Lent, it will be disastrous! You know what the Church of Vengeful Acquisition is like at this time of year. I'd be made an example of!"

"And you'd lose a large amount of money due to priests fearing the wrath of the Almighty, or failing that, Mother Superior's walloping stick." Alex sucked in her cheeks. "I'm beginning to see the light."

"Yes. That's why I need you to discover what, or *who*, killed Father Bartholomew, and to spread it around before the Church investigates, so they won't bother looking too closely. I'm willing to pay you three pounds."

"Three pounds," Alex repeated slowly, willing Flora not to make a noise. As it was, the ridiculous ferret was doing a silent sideways dance behind Miss Simms's back, her hands thrown up in the air, her mouth curved into a wide, pointy-toothed grin.

Miss Simms bit her lip. "Isn't that enough? I can pay you more. Will four pounds be suitable?"

Alex spent a couple of seconds trying not to swallow her tongue as Flora began pirouetting. "I'm sure that will be sufficient."

Miss Simms's perfect posture momentarily relaxed. "That's such a relief. You know, it's not just the Church I'm worried about. If it got around Southwark that I was working with the clergy... You know what it's like with the parishes. The wars are over but that doesn't mean the bad feeling isn't still there. It's not easy. And with the Church being associated with Westminster, it's complicated."

"You make clothing for the butter district?" Alex asked.

"I do," Miss Simms said primly. "It's an honourable job and my butter district clients always pay on time, as do the gentleman priests."

Alex digested this information. "And they're all wearing red knickers, the priests?"

"Oh no. Some of them like pink. Some like white. A few like black, so, you know, it doesn't seem so sinful. But Father Bartholomew likes—*liked*—a bit of flash." Miss Simms sniffed and swiped a tear from the corner of her eye.

Alex put together everything she'd heard on the Cry. "He certainly liked to make a splash—no, that's bad taste. Yes, I think we can take care of this for you, Miss Simms," she said, just as Sid burst through the door holding a tray that seemed to contain every beverage available in Drury Lane. "Ah, here's refreshment."

"Thank you." Miss Simms smiled gratefully as Sid stood before her, exuding awkwardness. She selected a cup of what looked like tea, but was probably gin, given the badger on the side of the mug. Maybe she wasn't so proper after all.

"Just out of curiosity, where did you hear of our services?" Alex asked.

"On the Cry. I was in the area making a delivery and I came right over, the minute I heard."

Alex looked at Sid. "See, Sid, it pays to advertise."

Sid—who'd been pretending he was a statue—flushed. "I'm not saying it doesn't, Captain. I just don't trust those blighters yelling in the street, waking everyone up every hour. Anyone who needs to yell for a living just isn't right."

"You used to yell for a living. On the ship," Flora chimed in.

"Yes, well, that was honourable yelling. I was yelling at actual people, not just the air."

"I'm sure," Miss Simms said, looking somewhat bemused. She turned back to Alex. "When do you think you can solve my little problem?"

"Oh, I can't imagine it'll take too long," Alex said with utmost confidence. "This is the *precise* thing we excel at."

CHAPTER 8

HOW WOULD A PIRATE DO IT?

"RIGHT, CREW. AS YOU know, we have our first job. It's not exactly a job we know how to do, but it's a job nonetheless!" Alex paced the room as Sid and Flora stood to variations of attention, which involved Sid's chest momentarily sticking out further than his stomach and Flora twirling a strand of hair around one finger while gazing up at the ceiling.

In the time it had taken Sid to show Miss Simms out, Alex had considered the situation and had concluded that—as inadvisable as it was—three heads would be better than one when it came to devising a plan.

The sound of Gregor making it clear to some unfortunate soul that he was not a morning person echoed up the stairs. Maybe Alex should have consulted him instead. His first impulse was to bite something, but Alex had to concede that was frequently the correct solution.

"Right," she said again. "We need to find an idiot stupid enough to blow up a priest belonging to the Church of Vengeful Acquisition."

"Do we know who the idiot is?" Flora asked.

"No," Alex said decisively. "No idea in the slightest."

"Excuse me, Captain."

"Yes, Sid. You can relax, by the way."

This led to a slumping of Sid's shoulders and a restretching of his waistcoat. "Captain, if we don't know who did it, how do we find them?"

Alex turned on the ball of her foot. "And now we reach the crux of our dilemma. To find them, we must work out who they are. Which is a somewhat sticky issue."

"The Cry said it was more chunky than sticky," Flora chimed in.

"Your contribution is valued as always," Alex said. "There has to be a way to attack this problem, although I'm damned if I can think of how to start."

"If you don't mind me saying, this was a lot easier when we were pirates. There wasn't any of this *thinking* when we were pirates," Sid said.

"Aha!" Alex exclaimed. "Excellent observation. We *are* pirates—ex-pirates." She held up a finger to silence Sid. "And while we've never blown up a priest, it is not inconceivable that we wouldn't have, if the opportunity arose. Using that logic, we should think of our quarry as some kind of priest-exploding pirate." This line of thought felt good. Her tone became more confident. "All we have to do is ask how a pirate would blow up a priest, and work backwards from there. Yes, Sid, you don't need to hold up your hand. I keep telling you that you never need to hold up your hand."

"A cogcannon, Captain. They'd use a cogcannon. Someone could've wheeled a dirty big cogcannon into the church and fired it when no one was looking. That would do it."

"Yes... it would definitely do it. Although I'm relatively sure someone would've spotted a cannon being pushed into the church before the event. Good suggestion, though," Alex added as Sid deflated, only to rally at her praise.

"Could it have been a tummy ache?" Flora asked. "Maybe he ate something bad. When I eat something bad it feels like I'm going to explode. Like last night, after eating that pie with the extra mustard and mango sauce with the onions and the sardines on the side."

"She's right, Captain! A gut ache would do it. Certainly one caused by the sort of food this silly ferret eats." Sid rounded on Flora, waving an admonishing finger. "I told you that pie from Mister Jim's was a bad idea. You could've exploded!"

"I'll grant you that Flora's diet could do with some reform, but I don't think that's the solution to our problem." Alex held up a finger. "Hold it! Why don't we pretend this priest is a pirate? Who would be the first cove to blow up a pirate?"

"Oh, oh, I know this one!'

"Yes, Flora?"

"Mister Lemons."

Alex slapped her hand over her face at the sound of her former first mate's name. "What have I told you about mentioning that name in my presence?"

"You told us that if we ever said Mister Lemons's name in your presence again you'd nail our boots to the floor."

"Yes. That's *precisely* what I said I'd do."

"But he would be the first one to try and blow you up. He was the one who turned you in."

"He was, Captain," Sid said quickly. "Not that I'd mention his name in your presence in all my years. I've sworn never to mention Mister Lemons's traitorous name ever again as long as I live."

"Thanks, Sid."

"But she's right, Captain, he would be the one who'd do it."

Flora's eyes brightened. "Does this mean that Mister Lemons did it?"

"No, Flora. It doesn't mean that Mister Lemons did it." Alex wondered momentarily at the wisdom of keeping these two on, after her pardon. However, Sid had taken on the role of blustery uncle from the day Alex had signed on to her first ship so long ago, taking her under his wing and teaching her everything he knew, until she worked out how to unlearn it all and teach herself properly. And Alex had known Flora since she'd been a tiny ferret woodkin that Alex had rescued from a rookery gutter after being left for dead by thugs. Like it or not, they'd been family ever since. In fact, they were currently giving Alex the kind of feeling that family did right before the beadles were called in to intervene during what the Cry frequently called a 'domestic disturbance'.

"Mister Lemons couldn't have done it because the bastard was last seen on the deck of a vessel headed for OverVenice, with his pants down, directing his backside at us in what in common parlance is referred to as a 'full moon'."

"Could it have been the Vengeful Queen?" Sid asked. "The priest was wearing lascivious underpants. I don't approve of that kind of frippery. A man is meant to let his vulnerable parts air. It's more natural that way. If you coop them up, they'll get ideas, and then where would we all be?"

"We'd have anthropomorphic private parts?" Alex shook her head. "If it was the Vengeful Queen, there'd be a lot more exploding priests, and nuns for that matter. No, but I'm beginning to think you might be onto something."

"I know I am. A man should never wear constrictive underwear. Especially not these hulking great codpieces that've come back into fashion. They're the devil. Especially the iron ones. Who wants his nethers to look like an elephant's trunk, anyway?"

"I'm sure there's many who would agree with you there."

"Like I said, my privates will never have strange ideas. Mine are free, unfettered—you could even say liberated."

"I think that's all we require on that topic, Mister Potts," Alex said sternly. "What I meant is that if Mister Lemons would be the first person to blame if *I* exploded, then who would Father Bartholomew's Mister Lemons be? Who is the person closest to a priest?"

"The verger?" Sid asked. "Last night's Cry quoted him. He said 'Agh', and then he said it again."

"The verger!" It was as if a ray of light had shone from the heavens to illuminate Alex's existence. "No one would suspect him, which makes him the perfect suspect."

"*We* suspected him," Flora said.

"Yes, but it's like the books, Flora," Sid said self-importantly, nodding to his shelf of penny dreadfuls. "We're heroes, and the heroes in books are always highly suspectful."

"I thought we were pirates."

"Absolutely!" Alex said. "As I've told you many a time, pirating is an inclusive profession. You can be anything you want to be, as long as you are also a pirate." She rubbed her hands together. "Yes, crew, this verger shall be our first port of call. I'm sure he's our man. I don't know how he did it, but I'm *sure* he did it. He is Father Bartholomew's Mister Lemons. Crew!" She raised a finger in the air. "I will go find this verger, capture him and claim our reward by the end of the day. Sid, you stay here in case we get another visitor."

"Yes, Captain! I will, Captain!"

"You don't need to salute. Flora, you're coming with me." Alex marched to the hooks by the door, grabbed her black satin cape and swirled it onto her shoulders with a flair that came from hours of practice in front of a mirror. "Let's make it reign!"

CHAPTER 9

ELIAS EXAMINES THE EVIDENCE

E LIAS CAREFULLY PLACED THE small fragment of paper from Father Bartholomew's explosion in the viewing area of his enlargoscope.

This was his reward for creating order. He was going to conduct his first bit of deductive science in his new shop, which now featured an arrangement of shelves containing the various oddments of his trade, hooks for his tools and his desk set out precisely how he liked it.

Anticipation was a very real thing.

He was just hunching over the scope when someone banged on the door.

"Vikram," he said, "that'll be for you."

"Me? Never!" Vikram paused in disinfecting the cover of a used book. "My customers are perverts, you ignorant cretin! They don't knock, they skulk through the back door from a fetid alley as befits them. I even make it extra fetid so they feel at home."

The bang came again but Elias doggedly ignored it. If he gave in now, Vikram would make his life hell in perpetuity. It would be like that time Elias had allowed Vikram to use his more convenient bathroom slot at Mrs Nevins's boarding house. Vikram had claimed it ever since, leaving his toenail clippings in morbid piles on top of the soap, like little *memento mori*.

Phillips poked at Elias's hand but Elias ignored that as well. What he was doing was important. As an artificer, it would be remiss of him not to give the matter at least a cursory investigation.

He focused on the scrap of paper, jotting down the words just visible through the dried blood. "Luscious, moist... insert," he murmured. He rotated the han-

dle on the side of the scope, and a new lens clicked into place. "And 'plump'."
He straightened and examined the words he'd written.

This was strange.

Thanks to his mother's insistence on a pre-bedtime ritual of contemplating endless damnation, Elias had read the Book of Vengeance numerous times. He was positive that these words weren't in any of its three thousand densely print-ed pages, including the Book of Anne, which even religious scholars admitted was little more than a hysterical rant about bees.

After an unfortunate incident with a honey sandwich during her yearly 'Viewing of the Peasants', the Vengeful Queen had declared war on all of Eng-land's bees. The ensuing conflict had immediately been coined the '*Other* War of the Roses' and had consisted of Anne rampaging through Westminster Palace's flower gardens while brandishing a broadsword and screaming incoherently at anything that buzzed. The Vengeful Queen had been declared victorious at eight o'clock that evening after her powerful screeching triggered a sunset, thus forcing her foes back to their hives. An overnight siege had then been forestalled by the palace's beekeepers offering the queen honey as war reparations, which many believed was the origin of the phrase "Victory never tasted so sweet." Although, that felt a bit too tidy to Elias and he had a suspicion some creative writing had been involved when recording the story for generations to come.

He turned his attention back to the words.

"Moist." He scratched his head.

"Are you reading my literature?" Vikram demanded. "I told you that you weren't allowed on my side of the shop!"

"I wouldn't be seen dead touching one of your so-called books. I doubt trin-kets can filter that level of depravity from the bloodstream." Elias re-examined the fragment, now ignoring the words and focusing on the print. Each letter 'e' featured a tiny spur that he knew all too well.

Everyone knew the Blessed Press was used exclusively to print Books of Vengeance, so that left Elias with two questions. Why had the item been printed on the press when it was against the law for anything other than the Book of

Vengeance to be printed in OverLondon? And why had Father Bartholomew
had it on him when he'd exploded?

The banging sound was getting more insistent.

Irritated, Elias twisted around and scowled at Vikram. "I've yet to advertise.
Ergo, they're here for you. Aren't you going to see who's so stupid they can't
open an unlocked door?"

"No." Vikram glared over his round wire-rimmed spectacles, then licked his
finger and turned the page of the book he was reading. He was narrow faced
with a contrived, wind-blown hairstyle that was all the rage with OverLondon's
bluestocking and intellectual crowd. A hank of hair was hanging over one eye.
As always, he was wearing at least two noxious yellow and brown woollen scarves
and an awful green cardigan. His gloves had the fingers cut out, and the tattered
threads of yellow wool caused a small part of Elias's brain to twitch.

"You could be turning away a customer," Elias said.

"Yes." Vikram turned another page. "But if they're too stupid to open the
door, they're too stupid to open a book."

Elias peered out of the leaded windows that faced into the street, but Over-
London had encountered some thick cloud cover and all he saw was white.
"The agreement we wrote this morning stipulates that you answer the door on
Mondays."

Vikram turned yet another page, sniffing in a way that drew attention to his
sharp, pointed nose. "Every *second* Monday."

"It's the second Monday of the month."

"It's a leap month."

"They don't exist."

"It's a leap week."

"That's irrelevant. And, *again*, they don't exist."

"Prove it."

"To do that, I have to get up and walk to the calendar by the door, which
means that I may as well open it."

"What a *wonderful* idea. Why don't you do that?" Vikram fluttered his
fingers. "Go on. Trot trot."

Elias stomped to the door and wrenched it open.

A young man was hunched over on the step, puffing furiously, his fist raised mid-knock. Elias blinked when he recognised his mother's errand boy from the textile factory.

"Jeffrey. Come in. What are you doing here? The door was unlocked."

"Hello, Mister Elias, sir," the boy said between puffs. "Walked in something iffy, sir. Didn't want to bring it inside."

"That's considerate of you. Thank you." Elias's nose twitched at the smell of something that was definitely 'iffy'. "May I ask why you're here?"

Jeffrey swiped the back of his hand over his brow. "It's your mum. She says you've got to come straight away. She paid me a ha'penny."

That was a considerable sum for a message. "Was she standing up, breathing and speaking clearly?"

Jeffrey swallowed and clutched his chest. "Aye."

"She asked you to run here?"

"She said it was urgent and she said you'd pay me another tuppence if I got here before eleven. She said something about the exploded priest. About some big church git visiting St. George's to decide if it's a miracle."

A miracle? This was deadly serious. "Was she holding a large handbag?"

"Size of a bleedin' continent."

"How loud was she speaking when she gave you the message?"

"Nearly blasted my ears off."

Elias checked his pocket watch. It was ten fifty-eight. He pulled out his coin pouch. He didn't have a lot of money, but at the same time, the boy had obviously been through an ordeal. "For your troubles."

Jeffrey gave him a gap-toothed smile as coins were dropped into his palm. "Thank you, sir. Thank you. You're a toff. Thank you."

He ran off and Elias swiftly closed the door and walked up to the painted line. "I have to go see my mother."

Vikram looked over his spectacles. "And?"

"Please don't touch or move any of my things. That includes my enlargo-scope. No trying to make any parts of your revolting person bigger than they need to be."

Vikram looked down at his book again, turning the page. "What filthy predilections you give me."

"Realistic. You could also clean up. Your business reflects on me too." Elias gestured to the great piles of dusty books on every single surface of Vikram's side of the room.

"You think someone from this part of town cares about dust?" Vikram waved at the windows. "No one comes to Whitechapel to put on airs. They come to arrange putting someone away terminally. Or to find a substitute for putting their something into someone's something else."

"Be that as it may, your side of the shop could still do with a dusting. And the privy's growing new life forms."

"What *is* dust? After the first five years, it's merely more of the same."

"I'll bring you coffee."

That got Vikram's attention. "From Ruddick's—none of that muck you get from Bumbridge's. And a bun. I haven't eaten breakfast."

"If I have time." Elias shrugged on his coat before retrieving the black arti-ficer's flat cap he'd had made after deciding that he'd never wear apprentice's green ever again. He swiped his protective goggles from his desk as well—one never knew with his mother.

"What do you have, other than time?" Vikram asked sardonically.

"I'm more worried that I'm running *out* of time." Elias fitted the goggles over his flat cap. "If there's even a suggestion that Father Bartholomew's death will be declared a miracle, the congregation at my mother's church will be desperate to collect any relics they can."

Vikram snorted. "Nix the coffee. Bring me back a finger bone instead. Relics earn big money."

"That's what concerns me," Elias said under his breath as he exited into the soupy fog outside.

CHAPTER 10

A HOLY PROCLAMATION

ALEX IGNORED THE WAY Gregor was banging the head of a soliloquizing playwright on the bar and marched out into the fog-swamped street to hail a passing hack. It had a black awning featuring the words *Black Hack* painted in red. The drabness of the carriage matched the decrepitude of the driver, who was wearing an unfortunate smock and a conical hat that had once been black. A badge for the Anti-Longevity League was pinned to his chest, which meant he was vehemently opposed to wearing a trinket, like a certain vocal minority in the city who were opposed to anything 'unnatural' interfering with their systems, except for parasites and plagues which were perfectly natural, as they had the capacity to permanently cleanse the body of all toxins and impurities by means of making sure that body was buried in a nice sunny patch of grass, somewhere in nature.

Or, alternatively, he had another reason. Given the stench of stale booze, Alex had her answer. Some people preferred the right to pickle themselves into short-lived oblivion. Sometimes she envied them the ability to drink to forgetfulness, and their lives of mere decades rather than centuries. And sometimes, like today, smelling this cove, she didn't.

"Welcome to my Black Hack. Kids today don't know what's good for 'em," he intoned, giving Alex a grimace that revealed he was competing with his goats for least teeth and most stained beard. He spat a wad of tobacco in a perfect trajectory between one of his goat's ears. The goat didn't budge.

The man was a prime example of the ideal employee championed by Smelton 'Would-You-Credit-It' Boob, who had founded the Black Hacks in the early 17th century. Boob had been an astute businessman who reasoned that since customers expected hack drivers to be cynical misanthropes, it would be a shame to disappoint them. As a result, every Black Hack driver was expected to say one of the three hundred company-sanctioned cynical, world-weary catchphrases whenever they picked up a fare. Everyone in OverLondon knew them by heart.

"How much to St. George's, near The Edge?" Alex asked, referring to the great fifty-foot wall that surrounded the floating city.

The driver scowled. "That's near Brixton Hill, right? Gotta cross London Bridge to get there, don't I?"

"No. Not across the OverThames Reservoir. It's this side." Alex braced herself for the ordeal to come. All Black Hack drivers were reputed to be trained in 'the Wisdom', a mental map of OverLondon that enabled them to strategically get lost, gaining them the maximum fare with the minimal effort. Alex had long suspected that this rumour had been started by the drivers themselves to cover up the fact they couldn't navigate themselves out of a privy pipe if someone pulled the flush chain twice.

The driver scowled. "I know, I know. I was just testin' you. The Edge. Yeah. The Edge. St. George's is in the nobby part of town, Chelsea way, right?"

"Wrong part of The Edge. Stepney. Past the Tower of OverLondon, towards the docks." Alex pointed in the correct direction.

The driver was already shaking his head. "Sketchy drive to get there. I've got to go past the rookery. There's the psychological hardship of seeing the Lepers. Then there's the wear and tear on my goats. They don't like going along the reservoir. Damp gets in their lungs and deflates their bellows. It's not good for 'em. It's not good for me either."

Alex looked him up and down. "That's evident."

"It's traumatic, seein' water."

"How much?"

"A half shilling."

"I'll give you a half groat," Alex said, just as Flora wandered up behind her.

The driver looked Flora up and down. "Is she cursed? I can't be having cursed in my vehicle. They stink."

Alex rolled her head from side to side like a boxer before a fight on hearing the slur. "Do they?" she asked silkily.

"And they scare my goats. I can't be having some ferret or weasel puttin' 'em off their feed." He gestured to his uninterested animals. One of them was in the process of fertilizing the cobblestones.

"Is that so?" Alex cracked her knuckles.

"Captain, I don't need to ride in some stinky hack." Flora tugged at Alex's sleeve. "So you don't need to do what you're about to do. It won't change anything."

"But I do, and it will change things eventually, even if I have to do it to every idiot in this city." Alex gave the driver a too-shiny smile. "Have you ever heard of the Dread Pirate Purple Reign?"

The driver shoved another wad of tobacco into his cheek. "Of course I have. Everyone has."

"Well, what do you think the Dread Pirate Purple Reign would do to you if you insulted one of her crew?"

His face screwed up. This was advanced thinking. "Well—"

"Picture the worst thing you could possibly imagine."

"Why?"

"Because the Dread Pirate Purple Reign is currently holding a clockbow to your head and telling you to." Alex unholstered the weapon from her belt and flipped the safety catch, causing a bunch of tightly wound helical springs to transfer their energy to the firing armature with an oily whirring noise. To the trained ear, those noises made by cogs, gears, springsteel and leather meant several hundred pounds of force was now just sitting around, waiting for some excitement to happen.

She watched the driver's eyes drop to the words *Make it Reign* embossed on the clockbow's obsidian finish, and then focus on the barbed bolt pointed directly between his eyes.

"Here, you can't do that! Those things are illegal in Theatreland!"

Alex's eyes widened. "Are they?" She looked sideways at Flora. "Did *you* know these are illegal here?" She asked, knowing full well what the man said was true.

After a spate of actors meeting untimely endings care of unsatisfied theatregoers, it had been decided people could submit their negative reviews with rotten fruit and vegetables as per long-standing tradition.

Flora shook her head. "I don't know nothin'."

Alex cocked a brow at the driver. "You never did answer my question."

"What question?"

"The one about the worst thing the Dread Pirate Purple Reign could do to you."

The man was cross-eyed looking at the bolt. "That would be a start."

Alex *tsk*ed. "You can do better than that."

"I guess there's the thing with the pinecone and the bale of straw." He shuddered. "That'd be an 'orrible way to go."

"Oh? Then that's exactly what I'll do to you if you don't give us a lift to St. George's. But it'll be even worse. I'll even throw in a—" She paused for effect. "Yew branch."

"Not a yew branch!" The driver momentarily forgot the immediate peril he was in and accidentally cracked his reins. His goats moved an inch before he had the sense to halt them.

"Yes. So are you going to apologize to my crew and give us a ride to St. George's? Or am I going to have to show you how I got my reputation?"

"Alright, alright, I'm sorry. Get in, get in."

Alex looked at Flora. "Is that a good enough apology?"

Flora shook her head. "Nope."

Alex looked down the sight of the bow. "Try again."

The driver swallowed loudly. "I'm *very* sorry and won't do it again?"

"Flora? Good enough?"

"For now."

"I'll take that as a conditional yes." Alex stared the driver dead in the eyes as she gestured for Flora to climb into the carriage. She then re-engaged the safety catch on her clockbow so that the tension would be transferred back to the storage mechanism. She gave the tensioner a few top-up winds before holstering it and climbing into the carriage herself. "It's so *nice* when people are polite."

The driver shook the reigns and the carriage jerked into motion. He looked over his shoulder at Alex. "Here, if you're the Purple Reign, you don't look as—"

"Tall as my picture? For that you're getting a ha'penny and no more. If you're lucky, it won't be administered somewhere uncomfortable."

They were well on their way to the textile district when Flora leant in to Alex and whispered, "If you do the thing with the pinecone, can I do the thing with the yew branch?"

"Most definitely," Alex said. "I'll even give you two yew branches. And four bales of hay."

The driver's back straightened and he yelled to hurry his goats even faster, swerving them around the other carts, sedan chairs and pedestrians, scattering stray dogs, cats and chickens along the way.

Traffic slowed as they approached Stepney and the stench of the Whitechapel rookery was overwhelmed by the even stronger waft of the tanneries and woad plants further on, and the nearer, humid smell of textile mills. Alex told the driver to stop and let Flora pay the fare, knowing full well that she'd picked the man's pocket only minutes before.

The hack did a U-turn and clattered away, leaving them standing before a tableau of what would charitably be described as OverLondon's finest rabble, who were given a more mystical air than they deserved thanks to the low cloud cover. The fact that they were being attended by hot potato and chestnut merchants indicated that they'd been there for some time. The textile district's beadles, the Sewing Circle, were also heavily represented. Dressed in tunics constructed from fabric oddments, and patched, mismatching hose, they were moving amongst the crowd with purposeful gaits, their wooden clubs with knitting needles sticking out of them swinging at their sides.

A Sugar Gang pusherman was also navigating his cart amongst the crowd, his sequined suit flashing in the weak sunlight. Noting his scoop was normal sized, Alex glanced judgementally at a nearby grubby child. The kid's lack of enterprise was an insult to OverLondon's fine institution of moulding its urchins into the best scrambling, thieving, cajoling survivors on the globe.

Just as she was about to ask someone where St. George's Cathedral was, the unmistakeable sound of the approaching Cry rolled over them.

Hear ye! Hear ye! A fracas has commenced at St. George's Cathedral. Stop. Cardinal O'Connery from the Bad Habits Special Branch is on the scene. Stop. The Lepers have apprehended a thief. His insides will be spread over the cobblestones of Munge Street and viewing will commence at three this afternoon. Stop. This year's Great Royal Exchange will commence next Tuesday. Queen Charlotte Tudor is a hot favourite to be exchanged with Emperor Zhu of OverBeijing. An unnamed palace source was quoted as saying, 'Damned if we'll keep Charlotte another year. She's a dribbler.' Stop. Ye've heard! Ye've heard! This bulletin was brought to you by Newsome's Pear Drops. Beware the stare of the pear.

Standing on tiptoes, Alex could just see the spire of St. George's. The only reason OverLondoners mobbed like this was for free street theatre, but the only execution mentioned in the Cry was happening in the rookery. Here in the textile district the entertainment was just a visiting cardinal. Why would anyone get excited to see a cardinal? OverLondon was full of cardinals, imams, rabbis, priests, gurus, shamans and soapbox evangelists, but people rarely gathered to gawp at them. Albeit, priests weren't in the habit of exploding that often.

"I hope we get Emperor Zhu," Flora said, oblivious to Alex's train of thought. "Queen Charlotte lost me two groats that last polo match. According to his Top Toff card, Emperor Zhu's good at polo and knows how to play chess without erupting into boils."

"I'll never understand your thing with royals," Alex said as she began elbowing her way through the crowd. Flora had been collecting Top Toffs cards for years now. Each card featured a picture of an aristocrat, followed by their statistical likelihood of breathing without their servants reminding them to, and any special skills they possessed, e.g. walking without concussing themselves.

"They wear shiny things and sometimes, when I bet on them, I get shiny things," Flora said.

"And here I was thinking it was something complex, like the exchange of royals each year guaranteeing global diplomacy and the fair exchange of goods that can be pirated by discerning individuals like ourselves."

"That too," Flora said. "I liked it when we took that ship with the OverCuzco prince. He was wearing lots of shiny things. You must have liked him too, because he spent a lot of time in your cabin."

"That I did." Alex sighed at the memory. She and Prince Kronk still exchanged letters whenever they could be bothered. Well, not letters exactly, more like explicit diagrams with arrows and explanatory labels. For some reason he liked calling her his 'little squirrel'.

It took a studious application of elbows, but finally they reached the front of the crowd to find that St. George's doors were open. A 'fracas' was definitely underway inside and had spilled out onto the church steps. The main theme seemed to be 'well-dressed church lady brandishing body parts'. There was no sign of a cardinal, or a verger for that matter.

Alex blinked. She knew the Church of Vengeful Acquisition had some odd ideas, but she was relatively sure smacking someone around the head with a dismembered arm was not common practice. A nun came into view, blocking a church lady's exit while wielding a regulation cane. Like all Bad Habits, she was big, scary and dressed in a black habit with a flame-red wimple. Two members of the Sewing Circle stood guard at the front of the onlooking crowd, sharing a cigarette and smirking.

Alex frowned. "Flora, I think the verger is already occupied."

"If he looks like a lady in a flowery dress holding a dead person's arm, then he definitely is," Flora said pensively.

"We may have to come up with another plan—"

"If it isn't the bastard pirate scoundrel who scuppered my ship! Pox be on you, you mangy cur, and buy my daffodils or I'll set Daphne onto you!"

Alex spun around, a grin already stretching her mouth ear-to-ear. "Slasher Harry?!"

Behind her, the crowd was being cleared by a huge man with a fiery mane of dreadlocks, a bushy russet beard and an eyepatch. His good eye was pale blue, and his mouth was curved in a grin that contained a bank's worth of gold. Curiously, he had a tray of flowers hung around his neck and was wearing a pastel pink apron with a small, vibrating, hairless dog wearing a matching eyepatch nestled in the top pocket. It looked as though the mutt had stored all the rage in the world in its tiny body.

"And Daphne!" Flora cried as the dog snarled.

"The one and the same." Slasher Harry used his articulated hook hand to catch a bystander by the collar and yell in his face, "Buy my daffodils, you cur! Buy them before I shove them down your throat and Daphne widdles on them."

Alex and Flora waited until Harry's unfortunate victim had coughed up some coin and Harry had wrapped a posy of daffodils in pink tissue paper.

"Harry, what the hell are you doing here?" Alex asked incredulously. The last time she'd seen Slasher Harry, he'd had a clockbow in one hand, a cutlass strapped to his hook, and had been swinging from the rigging of his airship by his teeth, while Daphne committed unspeakable acts of carnage on the deck below. He'd also been stark naked, his three mechanical peglegs whirring in the air like a deranged starfish.

"Selling bleedin' posies to the undeserving. What does it look like?" Harry retorted. "I sold the Elegant Buttercup, pensioned my crew and am pursuing a lifelong goal to share my love of bleedin' beauty with the world." He jiggled his tray of flowers. "What are *you* doing here? I should let Daphne tear you into tiny little bits for what you did to the Buttercup the last time we met."

"She wouldn't do that. She loves us." Flora wiggled her fingers at the dog, whose snarls became even louder. "See?"

"I'll grant you that. She's always had a soft spot for her favourite ferret." Harry rewarded Flora with a benevolent smile, then patted Daphne on the head with his ham-hock-sized hand, ramming her down into the apron pocket, which vibrated like a rage-filled tuning fork.

"We're here to talk to the verger in that church, Harry."

"The verger?" Harry's bushy brows rose. "What do you want with a verger?"

"We're trying to find out who exploded the priest," Flora said. "For money."

"Oh?" Harry stroked his beard. "You're going to have trouble there. The Bad Habits are already on the case." As he said this, another nun appeared in the doorway and smacked a church lady over the head with a rubber thurible.

Alex nodded. "I can see that. Do you have any idea what's going on?"

"Relics! These birds turned up to see about the smashed priest and then launched into a feeding frenzy when they learned that some cardinal could declare it a miracle. There hasn't been one of those for years. I'd be in there myself if it weren't for Daphne's sensitive constitution." Harry patted his growling pocket.

"A miracle?" Alex asked, still not understanding why a woman who looked like she belonged in a church choir would be attempting to wrest a dismembered arm from a nun's grasp. "I'm not following you."

"Are you touched, woman?" Harry looked incredulously at her. "If this is declared a miracle, then the priest'll be declared a saint. If the priest is a saint, his parts will be worth a bleedin' fortune. A fortune! And if you didn't already know, the Church of Vengeful Acquisition loves wringing the maximum amount of money from the world, and they'll be hoarding relics to drive the price up. Watching them at work brings a tear of pride in his city to this old pirate's eye."

"A fortune, you say?" Alex looked at the church with renewed interest. "How many Bad Habits are in there exactly?"

"Oh, five or six."

"Interesting. Church ladies?"

"Seven or eight. Terrifying women. One of them bought a daffodil from me and she had a look in her eye that made me almost widdle my breeches. Daphne was scared stiff."

"Is that so? Harry, if you were to enter that church, how would you do it?"

"Do I have my clockbow and cutlass?"

"No, you have brains and stealth."

"Down that alley, through the nave."

"And if you wanted to collect some religious relics and a verger in the process, the best exit from this vicinity would be?"

"Prod Alley. First right, then second left. If you're carrying someone heavy, I'd suggest you use the barrow you'll find halfway down Rube Lane. It's mine and you'd owe me half a crown rent."

Alex coughed. "Half a crown? Are you trying to beggar me?"

"The last time we met, you scuppered my ship. I half expect you to scupper my bloody barrow too."

"You can't scupper a barrow, Harry."

"You can never be too cautious."

"No, you can't." Alex was about to venture forth valiantly but paused. She didn't have half a crown and waiting for Flora to acquire one from this crowd of beggars and ne'er-do-wells would take far too long. Maybe it would be smarter to reconnoitre the situation, especially since Harry had good reason to double-cross her. Scuppering another pirate's ship—no matter how justifiable the grounds—wasn't something to be forgotten in a hurry.

"Flora, how do you feel about doing a reconnaissance mission?" Alex asked.

Flora's eyes brightened. "Can I take any shiny thing I see?"

"Listen to the ferret! What pirate doesn't take what they see? Good on you, girl!" Harry bellowed before collaring another unfortunate with his hook. "Want flowers? Of course you bloody do. Buy them or die!"

While Harry was selecting some purple tissue paper for his posy, Alex briefed Flora. "Take as much as you want, as long as no one notices. But your primary job is to locate the verger and pocket any body parts you can. Got it?"

Flora nodded. "Find the verger and get chunky parts."

"I wouldn't word it like that, but yes. Go through the nave. That's the side bit down that alley."

Flora disappeared into the crowd just as a serious-looking young man approached the church purposefully, pushing up the sleeves of a black overcoat. He was tall and lanky and in possession of a dark brown, smooth complexion that screamed youth on a face that radiated earnestness. Oddly, he was wearing an artificer's flat cap, but instead of the traditional blue or apprentice green, it was black.

The fighting nuns and women in the church's doorway were too distracted in thurible-to-severed-arm combat to notice him as he strode inside. He emerged moments later with a sturdy woman slung over his shoulder. She was wearing a floral dress and was flailing at his back with a massive, full-to-bursting red handbag. The crowd parted to let him through, laughter following in his wake.

Not long after, a priest emerged from the doorway with the sedate gait that marked all high-ups in the Church of Vengeful Acquisition. If his bearing and austere black cassock hadn't immediately marked him as the cardinal mentioned in the Cry, the sudden silence in the crowd would have.

"Here we go. This is the big cheese," Harry murmured as a number of women in floral dresses, carrying bulging handbags, scurried from the church. They were followed by a battalion of Bad Habits who lined up either side of the cardinal on the top step.

There was no sign of a verger, or Flora.

One of the nuns handed the cardinal a speaking cone, and his voice rang out in the nasal drone of someone who probably sniffed pencils for fun.

"After my examination of Father Bartholomew's remains, which was somewhat hindered by a few of our faithful congregation—" He glowered at the departing church ladies. "It is clear to me that Father Bartholomew was so full of the holy Word that he combusted with rapture and is now dining, as befits his station, on an upper-middle-class diet in the Halls of Vengeance. Let this miracle sent by Our Vengeful Lady be an example to us all."

The nuns around him looked pointedly at the crowd and slow clapped with the air of schoolmistresses who'd be handing out detentions in the very near future. Soon there was a smattering of applause, a couple of cheers and a snarl from Daphne.

The cardinal held a hand up for silence and then continued, "I'd also like to say, that if anyone—*anyone*—has taken parts of Father Bartholomew from the church today, I will go very hard on you. You have five minutes amnesty."

The words were met with silence.

"Four minutes."

There was a shuffle in the crowd.

"Three minutes. Please deposit your ill-gotten gains in Sister Lilly's holy receptacle."

A nun with an impressive moustache stepped forward. She was holding a hessian sack with the word *POTATOES* painted on the side. The church ladies who'd just exited the building returned in a hurry and a series of squishy-looking handbags were emptied into the sack, accompanied by sad squelching noises.

"Yes. Good. Two minutes. I know you're out there. There's at least one more of you." The cardinal eyeballed the crowd.

There was a tense silence.

"One minute and then it's disembowelment time."

The woman who'd been carried from the church marched forward. Glaring at the young man in the black artificer's flat cap, she emptied her handbag into the sack and stormed off.

"Excellent." The cardinal rewarded the crowd with a benevolent smile. "I knew you'd see the light. St. George's is officially the site of a miracle. Anyone who wishes to come through these doors will be charged two shillings per non-believer, or one shilling for members. Give your payment to Sister Tribulation. Be blessed and bring us your wealth." He made the sign of the pound and walked back inside.

The nuns glared at the crowd. One of them, presumably Sister Tribulation, cracked her knuckles threateningly. She had a lot of knuckles and it went on for a while.

"He'll be declared a saint before the year's out," Slasher Harry chortled as the nuns disappeared back into the church.

Alex looked at him sideways. She'd never taken Harry for an ecclesiastical expert. "You think so?"

"I know so. You heard the cardinal. The man exploded for his faith. How holy can you get?"

Alex winced as her four pounds evaporated before her eyes. If a miracle had killed the priest, then the church wouldn't be looking too closely at his remains past sectioning them up into saleable relics. That meant a priest's knickers weren't going to be on the church's agenda, which meant that Miss Sadie Simms no longer had a problem, which meant that Alex didn't have a job.

"Harry, I've been scuppered by the divine."

Harry burst into booming laughter. "Serves you right."

Flora popped up next to Alex. "I'm back. What did I miss?"

"Your captain's been thwarted by a cardinal," Harry said.

"Oh. I didn't find the verger. He's been taken away."

"Where?" Alex asked, scrambling for a way to save the situation.

"Somewhere. Maybe here, maybe there." Flora jammed her hands into her pockets and did a side-to-side wiggle.

"Very helpful." Alex ran her hand over her face. "Did you pick anything up, at least?"

"A finger!"

"Oh?" Alex brightened. A future saint's finger would be future gold. "Where have you put it?"

Flora shrugged. "I gave it to a nun when she asked me for it."

"That was helpful of you."

"Her name was Sister Barry. I told her that I'm a girl even though I'm a cabin boy and she said she's a boy even though she's a nun. I like her."

"Right now, I'm not finding that comforting," Alex said.

"I also found this!" Flora held out a gold signet ring, dropping it into Alex's palm.

Alex held it up. It was yellow gold, heavy and had a Gothic 'S' set into it in red stones that shone like rubies. "Where did you get this?"

"Off the finger. It was hidden under a piece of glove."

Alex was about to bite the gold to test its give, but then she remembered where it had been. No matter. Suddenly, the day was improving. They'd lost four pounds, but if this ring was genuine gold, she'd be able to pawn it to put a dent in her tax bill.

"Excellent work, Flora!"

"Can I have it back?"

"No. You can have this penny instead."

Ignoring Flora's pout, Alex turned to Harry, who'd just finished wrapping up yet another posy for a well-threatened member of the public. "It's been nice seeing you, Harry. Drop by The Armoury in Drury Lane one day and I'll buy you a pint."

"When hell freezes over, you mangy cur!"

Alex bowed to Harry, swirled her cape around her and headed through the crowd. She may have just experienced a defeat, but she'd soon be sailing the skies again, and this time, there'd be no Mister Lemons and she'd not get caught.

CHAPTER 11

A NEFARIOUS MEETING IN MAYE FAYRE

N OW TO ANOTHER PART of OverLondon, where the streets are wider and cleaner, the buildings are imposing and ostentatious and the residents are bestowed with more ear acreage than brain acreage.

Maye Fayre. Home of OverLondon's overfed and inbred.

Lucius Rumpus, lecturer for Brain Science at Magdalen College, OverOxford, once conducted a survey of the parish, which revealed that the rats at Canary Wharf demonstrated greater intellectual acumen than the average OverLondon aristocrat. This was deemed satisfactory. Ever since Queen Anne had ruled that the gentry couldn't participate in politics or the military unless they could tie their own shoelaces unaided, their lack of neural capacity hadn't been a concern to the city's population. In fact, OverLondon's aristocrats are frequently likened to a breed of particularly stupid peacock. They're nice to look at from a distance, and sometimes to throw things at when they squawk too loudly.

A skin-prickling drizzle has driven most of the parish's residents indoors or has left them huddled in plush carriages as their liveried goats trot through the streets.

One such carriage trots down Raleigh Street, past Krabb's, the city's most exclusive private members' club, owned by the notorious Krabb brothers.

It is rumoured that Benny and Bobby Krabb grew up on the harrowing streets of Whitechapel, eking out a grim existence before they struck it big by blackmailing an aristocrat over his sock-darning fetish, resulting in enough money to open Krabb's Private Members' Club. However, it was also rumoured that they were Swedish myrmecologists who'd come to OverLondon in search of the perfect type of jam to weaponize picnic ants. After merely managing to attract OverLondon's aristocrats with their jam roly-poly, they gave up and started a private members' club instead. OverLondoners tend to pick whichever story suits their mood on the day.

Krabb's is an imposing stone structure of the Gothic persuasion, complete with gargoyles wearing bowler hats and enough faux crenulations to give people a little too much information about the architect's sanity.

It's said that anyone who has to ask the cost of a yearly membership at Krabb's isn't suitable to join. This is true, mainly because buying things without questioning the price is a sure indicator of the determined inbreeding for which the OverLondon aristocracy is renowned.

A man who appears to be one such aristocrat is framed by a third-floor window.

His name is Count Guillermo Mendacium, and in the three years since his arrival in OverLondon, he's gained a reputation as the enigmatic dinner guest that every society stalwart hopes to secure.

He cuts a remarkable figure. His snow-white wig is a towering torrent of ringlets that flow around his shoulders. His jacket and breeches are scarlet brocade, and are cut in a way that endows him with what he hasn't got in the shoulder department and subtracts from what he does have in the stomach. Following the current men's fashion trend in this part of town, his skin and all of his facial hair has been whitened with Venetian ceruse. His eyebrows are painted slashes across his forehead and there is a small crescent-shaped beauty mark to the right of his thin, rouged lips.

Most remarkable, however, is his prosthetic right hand, which is decorated in intricate brass filigree with mother-of-pearl inlay. The brass and pearl sleevette covering the trinket attachment at his wrist is an example of what an artificer can do when given an unlimited budget.

At this moment, the hand is clenched into a fist in response to news that the Count has just received from the two men standing awkwardly behind him.

Both men radiate the air of employees picked for their height and shoulder width rather than their intellectual prowess. One of them is trying to surreptitiously wipe something he's just picked out of his nose onto an antique chair.

COUNT MENDACIUM WAITED JUST long enough to taste the discomfort in the room, before speaking in a measured Bohemian accent. "Gentlemen, you had one job, which was to make a problem with a priest go away quickly, discreetly and efficiently. I'd devised a plan. It was, in fact, a brilliant plan. But what happened? Instead of carrying it out to the letter, you two somehow managed to blow the man up in front of his *entire* congregation! Do you have *any* idea what could have happened if those imbeciles hadn't declared it a miracle?"

The man who'd imparted the bad news swiped the sweat from his brow. "Yes, boss, but we did it all like you said. Everything."

The Count turned with snake-like swiftness, his eyes narrowed. "*Everything*? Because there's a priest being shovelled up at St. George's, which indicates something wasn't done correctly, and since you were the one doing that thing, the *common*—" he sneered the word "—denominator is *you*." He retrieved a perfumed lace handkerchief from his frockcoat, raising it to his nose to calm himself.

"Honestly, boss. We did it like you told us. Step by step."

He studied their large, sweating faces. "Well, something has gone wrong, because there is priest in the St. George's chandelier. I would like to know how it happened *a day*—one *entire* day—after it was meant to happen, and why it didn't happen in the man's home, with minimal fuss and even less of an explosion."

The second man shrugged. "Don't know, boss."

"Not good enough." The words were said in a murmur. He wouldn't strain his vocal cords for these two imbeciles.

He calmed himself. He hadn't reached his position in society by letting emotion rule his judgement. He was a man of refinement, of observation, of *intelligence*. "Take me through everything you did. Step by step. Don't leave anything out."

He listened intently as they stuttered through their story, looking for any tell-tale signs of a lie or an omission, but there were none. He couldn't fault their actions. It seemed that they had done everything he'd asked, but somehow the priest had exploded spectacularly in a place and at a time that should have been impossible. He needed to think through the variables again. And the possibilities.

"Are you *sure* you're telling me everything?" he asked finally.

He was met with two nods.

"Fine. Have you dealt with the girl?"

"We put her in the cellar like you said, boss."

"The cellar. Good. Good." He tucked his handkerchief away with a flourish. "I want you to take care of her. Hear me?"

"Yes, boss. We gave her a pillow an' Keef got her a blanket, so she'll be nice and warm. Keef an' me was gonna get her one of Mister Jim's pies on the way home—"

The Count stared at them for a long moment, unable to comprehend the sheer *stupidity* of these cretins. "No. Not take *care* of her. I mean I want you to kill her! Dispose of her. Do it today, and bury the body in the cellar so no one sees you with it. It *has* to be in the cellar. Do you understand me?"

The men looked at each other before Keef spoke. "Are you sure that's okay, boss? I mean, you never told us we'd have to scrag a kiddie. Roddy and me—we don't hurt kiddies. And if The Clockmaker found out we scragged one of his urchins, our guts'd be all over Utopia Street before the end of the day."

The Count glowered at them. "Of course it's okay! The Clockmaker? What does *he* have to do with this? He's got so many brats running around the city, he wouldn't notice one missing, and even if he did, how could he possibly know who took her and where she is now?"

"But boss, the Lepers, they've got ways—"

"No arguments! Kill her and bury her in the cellar, or I'll be forced to reveal the information I possess about last year's little *faux pas* to Big Ivan. Almost stealing a sugar shipment? How much was it again? Ten kilos of premium brown? I hear that's a fortune on the street, and Big Ivan still has a handsome bounty on your heads. If I turned you in, what punishment do you think he'd give you? Remind me."

The men looked at each other again, their resigned misery evident. "He'd give us the carrot, boss." Keef swallowed loudly. "But we didn't know that cart was Big Ivan's. We thought it was—"

"Ah yes," the Count said silkily, interrupting him. "He'd give you the carrot. Do you want the carrot?"

"No, boss," Roddy answered.

"I imagine not." The Count fluttered his fingers. "Now go do your job before I send a message to Big Ivan anyway. You're tiring me."

He turned back to the window and looked out at the rain until he heard the sound of the door shutting.

Why was everyone in this city so *stupid*?

Why couldn't they see how it worked, like he did? This city was merely a system of petty hierarchies and rules that were barely held together by greed and money. No one looked beyond their own selfish desires. No one *thought*. No one realised that it was just a game to be played, if one understood the fundamental rule: There were no rules as long as you didn't get caught.

CHAPTER 12

FATHER POLK IS WORRIED

T HE TEN O'CLOCK EVENING Cry had just echoed along Utopia Street when Father Polk skulked from shadow to shadow on the artificer district side, furtively checking over his shoulder to make sure no one had seen him. As always at this hour, the arched doorway of St. Weston's Cathedral was occupied by a loudly snoring complement of a better sort of beggars and stray dogs. On the other side of Utopia Street, omnicite lamplight limned a patrolling Leper wearing a tattered red uniform and stovepipe hat. His footfalls clanked along the cobblestones, his cogwork leg prosthetics no doubt containing all manner of dreadful mechanisms.

Father Polk instinctively froze until the Leper disappeared into Whitechapel's depths before he tiptoed down the alley that separated St. Weston's from Gorbal's Beautiful and Brutal Weapons. He reached the door of the rectory and cursed quietly when he saw that the windows were dark, except for a faint glow from a basement window at the rear of the building.

He picked up a pebble and threw it at the glass. It bounced off. He repeated the action and this time he heard the sound of footsteps. He hurried back to the doorway to see that Father O'Malley's rotund shape now filled the entrance.

The plump priest was holding an omnicite lamp. The way it uplit his generous face, casting ominous shadows around his eyes gave Father Polk a deep chill.

"I need to talk to you." Father Polk clutched his wealth beads in his hand, causing them to clatter together softly. "It's urgent."

"Father Polk? Come in, come in! Let me take your coat," Father O'Malley said cheerfully as he ushered Father Polk inside. He then stuck his head outside and looked either way before closing the door, taking care to bolt it. "And may I ask why you're here at this late hour?"

"You know why I'm here," Father Polk hissed, sending spittle flying. He wiped his mouth with the sleeve of his cassock. "It's about *him*. I've tried to see the others, but neither were in. I'd almost believe they're hiding from me. Isn't anyone going to talk about it?"

Father O'Malley patted him on the shoulder. "Calm yourself, Father. Of course we're going to talk about it. Everyone's talking about it. It's impossible for a priest to experience the Word in such a divine way *without* people talking about it. Come, let's discuss this somewhere warmer." He led the way down a short hallway, then descended stairs leading to a modest stone-walled kitchen. A cast-iron baking oven in one corner radiated heat, and the plate, wine goblet and earthenware jug set out on the table made it apparent that the priest had been indulging in a late-night snack. "Take a seat and let me offer you something to drink. Tea? Wine?"

Father Polk took a seat and made the sign of the pound. "It's New Lent!"

"Is it? I had no idea." Father O'Malley picked up the jug and filled the goblet, sniffing the wine and then taking a sip.

"Don't you think we should be—that we should... He exploded!"

"Yes, he did. It was a miracle," Father O'Malley said calmly. "Or are you saying that Father Bartholomew wasn't blessed by Our Vengeful Lady, as Cardinal O'Connery proclaimed?"

"Yes. No. I don't know! All I know is that we've done something sacrilegious! Something wrong!"

"Have we? Because I seem to remember we've been through this." An hourglass on the table flowed the last of its sand into its base bulb, and Father O'Malley bustled to the oven and opened its door. The aroma of baking wafted through the room. "I've just made the most delicious scones. I'd be delighted to share one with you. In case you're concerned about Mrs Smith discovering my little midnight activity, I've given her the evening off to see her sister." Wrapping a cloth around his hand, he pulled a tray from the oven and brought it to the table. Upon it were twelve perfect, golden scones. They steamed. "I have to indulge myself at least one evening a week. The things Mrs Smith does to fish should be labelled a criminal offence. I despise fish and frequently wonder why the Vengeful Queen had to keep the fish during New Lent. Or why she kept Lent at all, for that matter. Granted, it's an excellent means to increase the church's coffers, but I don't understand why fish had to come into it."

"Some traditions are too strong to break." Father Polk reached for the jug of wine, but then froze when he noticed the sinful printed thing they'd made on the table beside it. He flipped it over so he wouldn't have to see what they'd done. He couldn't believe Father O'Malley would have left it just *sitting* here!

He grimaced in revulsion. At least he kept his copy hidden in the privy and only looked at it in small doses.

"Have a little *something*." Father O'Malley waved a hand at the scones.

The only thing Father Polk had eaten since Father Bartholomew's explosion had been his housekeeper's fish-based elixir for indigestion. He looked at the scones and the acid in his stomach burned. "I don't know. I don't know if I can! The temptation is unconscionable. We've already done so much wrong. What if it wasn't a miracle? What if it was punishment for what we did, and what we've done, and what we're doing?" He threw his hands in the air. "What if she has the same punishment in store for us?"

Father O'Malley flicked a scone onto a plate. He sucked his fingers with a smacking sound, drawing attention to the signet ring on his index finger, the same signet ring that Father Polk had hidden at the bottom of his clothing chest. How could Father O'Malley be so blatant? The rings had been made only to wear at society meetings, but some of the priests disregarded that rule, vainly wearing them either on their fingers under gloves or on chains around their necks. Father Bartholomew had led the way, with far too much confidence that he'd never be caught—although there'd been no reports that suggested he had been wearing his ring during the awful incident.

Father O'Malley grinned at Father Polk. "Delicious. I've doubled the sugar for that extra shock of sweetness, and the butter is divine. You really must try it." He waddled over to the icebox and returned with a giant apothecary jar. "We can't have Mrs Smith discovering my little indulgence. She thinks this is a haemorrhoid unguent." He sat down, unscrewed the lid and scooped out a generous dollop of butter, spreading it on one half of the scone before taking a bite.

"I don't think you're taking my concerns seriously." Father Polk shifted uncomfortably in response to the sound of chewing.

"Father, please don't mistake me. I'm taking it *very* seriously." Father O'Malley popped the rest of the scone into his mouth, chewing and swallowing with relish.

"What we've done is wrong! What we're *doing* is wrong!" Father Polk gestured at the pamphlet on the table. "What if it happens to *us*? What if I wake up tomorrow, sit on the privy and explode?"

"Father, Father..." Father O'Malley wiped his fingers delicately on his cassock. "Need I remind you that our dearly departed friend met his demise whilst reciting New Mass to his congregation. It wasn't while he was in the privy. It wasn't while we were together printing our little pamphlets." The priest gestured to the *thing* on the table. "Which would've been the perfect time for divine retribution. This is a completely unrelated incident. He was a holy man and our Vengeful Lady honoured him—"

"By splatting him everywhere!"

"In a euphoric moment of ecstatic rapture!"

Silence fell while Father O'Malley found a second goblet for Father Polk and filled it to the brim with wine. "Drink."

Father Polk's shoulders slumped. "Alright."

Father O'Malley lost his ever-present smile and his tone became serious. "If it were divine punishment, we would've all exploded by now. And we haven't. So it's not."

Father Polk chugged the entire contents of the goblet, warmth filling his empty belly. "You may be right."

Father O'Malley's smile returned. "I know I'm right." He slid the plate of scones towards Father Polk. "You really must try one. They're delicious. And why don't we toast the late Father Bartholomew? May he soon become a saint." He refilled Father Polk's goblet.

Father Polk's tension eased. It might have been the wine, it might have been Father O'Malley's reassurances, but he didn't feel so worried any more. "May he soon become a saint."

They sipped their wine.

Father O'Malley looked at him sideways. "Did you get yourself a relic?"

Father Polk stifled a burp. "I have some fingernail clippings he once left on the washstand in my rectory. He was a devil for leaving them everywhere." He didn't really. The clippings were his own, but he'd already decided that there'd be no way for anyone to tell the difference.

"I have a couple of whiskers he left on a razor he borrowed from me a few years ago. I have two razors, so I never got around to using it again. I was hoping to go to St. George's to retrieve something more substantial, but that idiot verger told the congregation about the imminent miracle announcement and sent them into a frenzy." Father O'Malley rolled his eyes. "He deserves everything Mother Superior is giving him right now. May they paddle his backside in perpetuity."

"Amen." Father Polk shuddered. "If I could operate my parish without a congregation, it would be a perfect world. They're all so *needy*. I hear they were stuffing their handbags!"

"What do you expect? I had a small trunk ready and waiting. Unfortunately, the Bad Habits were on guard at St. George's all last night."

"But handbags? They didn't even bring shovels! They used their hands! The sacrilege!"

Father O'Malley took another swig of his wine. "Take heart, Father—should you ever miraculously explode, I will assuredly scoop up your remains with a shovel."

Tears sprung to Father Polk's eyes. He wasn't a drinker and he'd barely slept or eaten these past days for worry. "That is an incredibly sweet thing to say. You're a true friend. I assure you that I will do the same for you."

Father O'Malley's body shook with laughter. "Sell me for a fortune!"

Father Polk nodded solemnly. "I'll sell you for a fortune *after* I've used a shovel. You will *never* be placed in a handbag. I promise."

"I'll drink to that!"

CHAPTER 13

RODDY AND KEEF TAKE CARE OF GRUB

RODDY AND KEEF, PART-TIME thieves and odd-job men, stood huddled around the stove situated in the middle of the abandoned stables they called home. Around them lay the detritus of the now defunct Beazel's Whitechapel Livery Company.

The Beazel Sisters had adopted a self-service business model where customers could pick up single-passenger goat carriages at special stations all around Whitechapel, then return them to any other station. Whitechapel's residents had quickly taken to the system, although they didn't quite understand the 'return the goat when you're finished' bit. The sisters went bust when the rule about thieving in the rookery was suspended on account of The Clockmaker deciding that unattended goats being left all over the place counted as litter. No one knew where they'd gone and Roddy and Keef hadn't asked too many questions. It never paid to ask questions in the rookery.

Goat harnesses lined the walls and a stale-hay mustiness haunted the air.

Despite the building's decrepitude, there were touches that showed someone had tried to make it nicer. A milk bottle on a table contained a bunch of daffodils that Roddy had bought from a shouting ex-pirate in Stepney. Beside the flowers were two delicate china teacups, two teaspoons, two bowls and two forks. While the china was chipped and one of the forks was missing a tine, the neatness of their arrangement suggested a certain care and sentimentality.

"I guess... I guess we're not gonna give her this pie, then." Roddy looked glumly at the brown paper bag in his hands.

After leaving Maye Fayre, they'd stopped at a pub on the way home, drinking their pints in silence, unable to look into each other's eyes.

"No." Keef shook his head. "You shouldn't have got it, Roddy. You knew you wasn't gonna be able to give it to her."

Roddy's shrug triggered a woozy sway. He only had one small trinket and it hadn't got rid of the alcohol in his system yet. "Yeah, but she's so scrawny. It's not right, Keef. When he got us to go collect her after he knocked her on the head, I fought... I fought we was just gonna be hidin' her or somefink. Not this. Here's you an' me planning on one day gettin' out of trouble an' maybe going somewhere different. Maybe adoptin' a kid or two an' startin' a family. Maybe getting a farm an' lookin' after some goats. You like goats. None of that involved *scraggin'* a kiddie. Especially not a little one like that."

Keef put a meaty hand on Roddy's shoulder, his mouth downturned. "Yeah, but fink of what'll happen if we don't. His Lordship'll tell Big Ivan about us an' we'll be dead sooner'n you can blink."

"You never should've admitted to His Lordship that the sugar thing was us! When he came and tol' us he knew about it, you should've lied. If you'd lied we'd never have got stuck workin' for him, havin' him look at us like we're muck. Him wiv his fancy airs an' his fancy clothes an' his hoity-toity voice," Roddy added, in a high-pitched approximation of the Count's accent. It would normally have made Keef laugh, but not tonight.

"He said he had witnesses. You were there. You heard 'im."

"Yeah, but how? Have you ever wondered how a toff like him'd know the goings on of people like us? How'd he know we took that cart?"

Keef had wondered the same thing. He wasn't a smart man, but he understood facts and he knew when the facts weren't in his favour. "Did you ever think that he's got more brains than the average aristo?"

"Yeah. I did think that. He's got buckles on his shoes, so he doesn't have to worry about tyin' laces or nothin', but he's still smart."

"Too smart, I'm thinkin'. He knew all the important stuff. He knew we were drunk. He knew we took the cart, an' where we left it when we realised it were one of Big Ivan's. An' if someone like him knew, then others did too. He kept 'em quiet, otherwise someone would've grassed on us to Big Ivan by now. He's kept us alive, Roddy."

"Yeah, but at what price? To do his dirty work whenever he flutters his fingers." Roddy waggled his own sausage-sized fingers in the air. "To kill a kiddie? A kiddie who works for The Clockmaker? Even if I didn't wan' to kill her, I'd still fink it's suicide. If The Clockmaker found out, we'd be Leper bait. Mark my words."

"He said we 'ave to do it, so we 'ave to do it," Keef said.

Roddy slumped down onto one of the crates they'd been using for chairs. "You can do it. I can't. Tiny little tyke, she is. It's not right."

"No, it's not. But it's got to be done. It's her or us. That's just how it is. This world ain't fair an' we've gotta survive, Roddy. We've gotta do what we have to until we work out how to get outta this mess. That's just how it is," Keef repeated, running his palms over his chest like he was trying to wipe away the horrible thing they had been asked to do. "I'll just... I'll do it. How hard can it be to break a neck that small?" He picked up a lamp from a shelf, marched to the cellar door, removed the bar locking it and wrenched it open.

Sick to his stomach, Roddy watched the flickering light that illuminated the darkness beyond the door, and he listened for the sounds of a crack or a crunch to indicate Keef had done the job.

It didn't come.

Instead, Keef emerged a few seconds later. He closed the door with pained care.

"Did you do it?" Roddy asked, his voice a croak.

Keef swallowed and swiped suspiciously damp eyes. "I couldn't. She was asleep, wiv that bump on her head. It didn't seem polite. So I pulled her blanket up and made sure she weren't cold." He set the lamp down and slumped on the other crate at the table.

Roddy nodded. "Yeah. You can't scrag someone who isn't feelin' well. Poor mite. Size of a stone, that bump was."

Keef looked at the floor. They were silent for a long moment before he spoke again. "Roddy?"

"Yeah, Keef?"

"You know how he said... how he told us to take care of her?"

"Yeah. He said that."

Keef's words came out in short bursts, as if his brain were straining with the effort. "What if we didn't hear the other bit? What if we just heard *that* bit? And the bit about the cellar. If we took care of her in the cellar... that would be doin' what he said, right? Cos I have trouble wiv my ears sometimes. An' I remember you said you did too."

Roddy studied him for a painful few seconds, the words taking their time to line up properly. He nodded solemnly. "Yeah. Bad hearin'. Got to be gettin' old. I can barely hear anyfink any more. An' he's got that funny accent. Hard to understand him if my hearin's bad."

"Yeah... yeah." Keef looked at the paper bag containing the pie. "So if we was gonna take care of her, the right fing to do would be to give her some water an' that pie, wouldn't it? An' maybe we could give her some candles an' let her use the proper bathroom an' that. An' there's that woman who sells dollies from that stand near Bumbridge's Tea Shop. Little girls like dollies, don't they? There was this dolly of Big Liv, that sociology professor from the Academic Council. It came wiv her Armour of Supporting Documents, an' a Club of Equal Distribution wiv a nail in it and everyfink. She'd like that, wouldn't she? Somefink to play wiv?"

"Yeah. I fink so."

"And when His Lordship asks, we just tell him that we took care of her an' she's in the cellar. That way he won't say anyfink to Big Ivan. An' maybe we can mess up the cellar floor a bit to make it look like we buried her there, just in case he checks."

"Yeah. Keef?"

"Yeah, Roddy?"

"I fink it's time we worked out how to leave this city."

"I fink so too, Roddy, but it's just gotta be the right time. He seems to know what we do all the time. It's like he's always got someone watchin' us. We've gotta pick our time."

"Yeah." Roddy looked at the door leading to the cellar, his prominent brow creasing into a map of lines. "We've gotta pick our time."

CHAPTER 14

FENCE AND FENCIBILITY

THE EIGHT IN THE morning Cry had barely finished when Alex knocked on the door of Hamish Leek's Experience of a Lifetime, located at the intersection of Utopia Street and More Lane. A light rain was falling, washing a generous amount of muck into the gutters, including the remains of some unfortunate soul who'd had a terminal appointment with the Lepers. She checked her boots to make sure there wasn't any victim attached to them. She'd spent enough time on these streets to know not to question what happened and to whom. Generally, people who fell foul of the Lepers gained a fast and thorough cure for their stupidity.

It was amazing how many people had trouble following the Rules of the Rookery, which stipulated that all rookery residents must pay The Clockmaker's tax—the Rent—on time, must not steal from fellow rookery coves, must not murder fellow rookery coves, must not take The Clockmaker's name in vain and finally, must not whistle in the alleyways.

Rule breakers were frequently newcomers who didn't understand that despite its reputation for being the city's very own den of iniquity, Whitechapel was the most crime-free parish in OverLondon. The Lepers saw to that. The fact that the rookery exported its crime to the rest of the city was incidental.

Utopia Street was busy despite the early hour, and banging, clanging and tapping echoed from the workshops in the artificer district. On this side of the street, things were different.

It was said anything could be found in Whitechapel. One of those things were pawn shops that enabled enterprising thieves to sell goods acquired from other parts of the city. Of these, Hamish Leek's Experience of a Lifetime was the most established and notorious.

Alex banged on the door again. This time, it opened.

A waft of pungent incense escaped into the street, and then Alex was confronted with a spectre in purple velvet. There were velvet ruffles, ribbons, puffs and bows. Somewhere amongst it all was a dark-grey-skinned man with a pointy face and huge silver buck teeth. His hunched posture spoke more of him being *homo rattus* than elderly. Hamish had been an institution in Whitechapel since the signing of the Parish Agreement of 1635 had stopped the Beadle Wars. That was centuries ago, and no one knew exactly how long he'd been alive before then. All Alex knew was that he was a shifty bastard who'd somehow secured The Clockmaker's undying affection and protection without having any limbs chopped off.

"Well *hello*. Who could be so eager they'd arrive on opening?" Hamish asked, giving Alex a smile that managed to be both lascivious and business-like. "How can I help you?"

"Hamish. It's Alex Reign. Remember me?"

After a moment, the smile widened. "Alex Reign? Or should I say Dread Pirate Purple Reign? I haven't seen you since you tried to pick my pockets—when was it? Far too long ago to count! Look at *you*. Haven't you *grown*? Although, I notice, not in all the same places as your painting." He gave a bawdy laugh. "Not to worry, dear, I'm sure you'll get there one day."

"I'm sure I will." Alex rolled her eyes. "Are you going to let me in?"

"Depends on whether or not being seen in your company will be detrimental to my health," Hamish said coyly. He was wearing a floppy hat that partially obscured one beady black eye. A peacock feather stuck out rakishly, but since this was Hamish, it had a price tag attached to it.

"I need to sell something," Alex said briskly, looking around to make sure she wasn't attracting attention. Luckily, a Sugar Gang pusherman was currently being accosted by a Hammer Man on the other side of the street for illegally parking her ice cream cart. The cart was surrounded by urchins taking advantage of the situation. Oddly, one of them was munching on the bottom of the

Hammer Man's leather apron with the air of a vegetarian taking a walk on the wild side.

"A former pirate wants to sell me something. What could it be?" Hamish narrowed his eyes. "Is it from the rookery? Because you know the Rules."

"No. From the textile district. I got it yesterday."

"Well, that's different, then. It was *rather* interesting there yesterday, wasn't it?"

"You could say that."

"Is the thing you're looking to sell a... miraculous find?" He raised his eyebrows.

"Let's just say that I've been blessed."

"In that case, come in!"

Alex was ushered into a space that resembled a glittery bowerbird's nest. There was a reason she hadn't brought Flora with her this morning. There was only so much stimulation a ferret could take.

"Tea?" Hamish bustled over to a stove, which was partially obscured by sparkling ephemera. A brass kettle was on the boil.

"Yes please." Alex scanned the shop, exercising the caution she knew to use around this particular acquaintance. She paused when she spotted an empty stretch of wall covered in filigree wallpaper. This shop had never contained an empty stretch of wall in all the time Alex had known of it, no matter how small.

Hamish poured Alex a misshapen mug of tea and handed it to her. "Have a cuppa, darling. I promise you the water's fresh. Barely a tiddler in it before I boiled it."

Taking the mug, she walked closer to the bare patch of wall, immediately spotting two small holes. "What are these?"

Hamish waved a hand. "Don't mind that. It's a new enterprise I'm experimenting with."

"What?"

"It's a thing where people pay to watch me interact with customers."

"Why?"

Hamish made a sweeping gesture that encompassed his shop. "Living theatre! Pathos, darling. Observing the everyday *mundanity* of it all, making people feel more... *more*. It's a whole 'Will they or won't they walk out the door richer in money or richer in belongings?' thing. Or even better, will there be disappointment? Not that I supply much of that here." He batted stubby eyelashes. "And just in case you're tempted to inform the Ushers that I'm infringing on Theatreland turf, this is purely amateur interaction. No actors in sight."

Alex frowned. "People pay you to watch everyday business transactions?"

Hamish hunched his shoulders with glee. "Oh *yes*, darling. They love it! I've had a queue of people in there from daybreak, all waiting for their ten-minute interval at the snoop holes. I call it 'reality viewing'. A lot of shops are doing it. There's a nail salon in Scrutt Lane with a year-long waiting list to watch ladies of leisure get their feet filed. Then there's the cart maker over the road... What's it called again? Oh yes, Whore my Wagon. They do all those little unnecessary add-ons to people's goat carts. Then there's the opera house. People pay a *fortune* to watch the ballerinas audition. It's all the rage. It's a pity you didn't charge people to view your trial. You could've made a pretty penny."

Alex looked at the snoop holes again. If she focused, she could make out a set of eyeballs. "No witnesses to this meeting, Hamish."

"I'm not so sure about that, darling. It's an infringement on my profit margin."

"Do you want to see what I have or not?"

"Oh, alright, but I'll have you know that you're creating an undue sense of anticipation in my viewers that I'll now have to accommodate by creating some kind of scene later." Hamish tottered on towering purple heels to hang a painting of a duck flying a kite in front of the snoop holes. There was a muffled complaint from the other side of the wall.

"Suspense, darlings. Who knows *what* will happen next?" he yelled, then gestured for Alex to join him at his counter. "Now show me what you've got."

Alex handed him the signet ring that Flora had taken from the exploded priest's finger. She spoke in a low voice so as not to be heard by the paying voyeurs in the next room. "It's solid gold with rubies." In truth, she had no idea what the stones were, but she wasn't going to admit that to Hamish.

Hamish's face acquired a magnifying eyepiece. He studied the ring in detail, turned it over a few times and then held it up to the light. "Yes. Hmm. Ah."

"And?" Alex asked.

Hamish looked up sharply. "Where did you get it?"

Alex lowered her voice. "Off the exploded priest's finger."

"You *never*," Hamish whispered.

"What do you mean, I never?" Alex whispered back.

"It's New Lent. There is no way a priest would be wearing something like this during New Lent. The whole idea of New Lent is that priests are meant to go without, to set an example to the public. How else would the church convince its followers to give away forty percent of their year's earnings? I should know—half the stuff in here is from people who go to St. Weston's." He fluttered his fingers at the window, the gold lace on his gloves catching the light. Alex could just make out a cathedral through Hamish's clutter of sparkling wares. "Every year they hock themselves to the eyeballs so they can make their New Lent payments and gain accommodation in the Halls of Vengeance once they croak."

Alex had been prepared for some bargaining. "It was definitely on his finger, so he was definitely wearing it when he exploded."

"Wearing this?" Hamish held up the ring.

"Yes."

"On his finger, openly, during New Mass, during New Lent?"

Alex's cheek muscles ached from forcing a polite smile. "Yes. Under a glove, at least. Maybe it was exempt from the rules or something."

"*Never.*"

"How much, Hamish?"

Hamish sucked his teeth. "Well, as you can see, I've got a lot of stock right now, and the demand for gold rings with red stones *pretending* to be rubies isn't exactly high." In that moment, seeing the sparkle in Hamish's eyes, Alex knew without a doubt they were rubies. She was being out-pirated and didn't like it one bit.

"How much?"

"One pound and it's a good deal. You won't get any better. You won't get anything at all if Mother Superior hears you've been trying to pass off a ring like this as belonging to her miracle priest. She's on the warpath, looking for anyone who scarpered with relics yesterday. I heard she's handing out the full kidnapped-kitten treatment. Very messy." He shuddered. "I wouldn't want to be a part of it."

It took all of Alex's willpower to stop herself doing something that would leave Hamish's viewing public talking for years. "Are you threatening me?" she growled, not caring now if anyone heard.

"Oh no, of course not! Don't hurt me!" Hamish raised his voice to match hers, projecting it towards the snoop holes, before leaning forward and whispering. "*Delicious* drama, darling."

"I should strangle you right here and now," Alex hissed.

"Temper, temper!" Hamish directed his words to the painting on the wall. "I'm just an honest merchantman!"

"It's worth at least seven," Alex whispered. "And if he's declared a saint, it'll be worth even more, so don't mess me around."

"Yes, but it's only worth seven if I can find a buyer who isn't scared of Mother Superior," Hamish whispered back.

"Six pounds," Alex said. "Melt it down and take the stones."

"Nineteen shillings. That's my best price. You know I always start high and go down."

"Five pounds."

He sighed. "They never listen. Fifteen shillings."

"It was nice seeing you." Alex snatched the ring out of his hand. "I'll take my business elsewhere."

"No one's going to speak to you," Hamish said in hushed tones. "A Bad Habit was around to The Clockmaker with a special request only last night."

Alex stared at him. "You could've told me. You were never going to buy it, were you?"

"No, but it's content, darling. Content." Hamish jerked his head to the painting covering up the snoop holes. "Come back and finish that cuppa the next time you've got an actual thing to sell me."

Alex thunked the mug onto the counter, sloshing tea over the rim. "You've been absolutely no help."

Hamish's eyes sparkled with the reflection of a thousand shiny things. "If you could slam the door on your way out, I'd be most grateful. The drama, you see."

"Happy to oblige." Alex stormed from the shop, slamming the door as hard as she could, ignoring the furtive looks from passers-by.

She'd just jammed the ring into her pocket when her shoulder was grabbed from behind.

"A minute of your time." The words had all the timbre and feel of something extruded from a snake's insides.

Alex kept very still, her eyes straight ahead. An unwritten rule of the rookery was *never run*. They always chased you if you ran.

"I'm entitled to be here."

"Yes... and no," the Leper said. "There's a little matter of the Rent."

"I don't live here. I'm a privateer for the city, which means I don't have a parish. I have a letter of marque from the Academic Council that says as much," Alex said calmly, as a woman clutching a child to her chest scurried past. "The Parish Agreement says that only people operating businesses and living in Whitechapel have to pay the Rent."

"That's an interestin' conundrum. Isn't it?" Something sharp poked at the back of Alex's neck. It gave a whole new meaning to the phrase 'making your point'. "Because my master heard on the Cry that you're findin' people from wanted posters. *We* put up a lot of wanted posters."

"But that's working for your master's benefit," Alex said. "And the coves that I'd be looking for wouldn't hide out in Whitechapel if they're wanted by The Clockmaker, unless they're extremely stupid."

"True, but you'd be returnin' them to Whitechapel, expectin' money. Which means you've got business here. Which means you owe us the Rent, no matter what your little piece of paper says."

Alex could feel blood trickling down her back now. "How can I help you?"

"One of our employees is missin' and we want you to find her." The words bathed the side of Alex's face with the stench of a clogged privy. "Last seen in Bloomsbury. Near St. Smeaton's."

"Do you have a description of some kind? A drawing? A name?"

"She was small. Slept at the church most nights. Gave us information about the comings and goings. Named Grub."

"That's all?"

"We want to know who took her and we want her back. No one takes one of ours and gets away with it."

"Fine. Fine." Alex swallowed, being particularly careful not to do anything that would drive the blade in deeper. Longevity trinkets could do a lot, but they couldn't fix a severed spinal column at the neck. "And if I can't find her?"

"The Clockmaker will have a very special word with you. He's been wantin' to try out some new devices. Find the girl or die."

With that, the blade and the vice-grip on Alex's shoulder withdrew.

As Alex scrabbled in her pockets for a handkerchief to staunch the blood, she turned and caught sight of a four-legged horror in a red coat and stovepipe hat scuttling into More Lane, no doubt to tell his master that the message had been delivered.

She made eye contact with Hamish, who was staring out the window of his shop, his eyes round.

No one else made eye contact with her. In the rookery, helping bleeding people wasn't good for one's health.

When she was certain the wound was staunched and that her trinkets were doing their job, Alex hailed a passing hack.

The driver, a plump, jolly-looking woman, reined her goats to the curb. "Welcome to Black Hacks," she trilled. "What's this world coming to, I ask you?"

"How much to take me to The Armoury on Drury Lane?" Alex asked.

The driver looked Alex up and down, obviously making a calculation of Alex's wealth and then doubling her usual fare. "A shilling."

"You've got to be kidding me! I'll give you six farthings and no more."

The woman gave her a pained grimace. "But you see that'll mean driving my goats past water. It makes them unhappy, water."

"Their bellows will be fine. One of your colleagues tried that one on me yesterday."

"Oh. Then there's heavy cloud cover that way. Heavy cloud's harder to drive through," the woman said with a hopeful smile.

"Would you credit it?" Alex exclaimed through gritted teeth. "Let's cut to the chase. I'll play you thruppence if you can get me to my destination as quickly as possible with minimal conversation, which is two more than you're due. If you deliberately get lost, I'll start using your hat as target practice." She placed a hand on the hilt of her clockbow. It wasn't something she was proud of, but she'd just had her life threatened and was in a filthy mood.

"Right you are!"

As the driver urged her goats into action, Alex slouched in her seat, evaluating her situation. She now had to find a missing urchin or the Lepers would kill her gruesomely. She was in possession of an illicit ring that she couldn't sell without getting on Mother Superior's bad side. Her ship was impounded at the docks, and last night she'd received a note from Miss Sadie Simms stating that her services were no longer needed. She also needed to pay Gregor the first instalment of rent by the end of the week or he'd bite her head off, or worse, kick her out of her favourite pub.

It was obvious that she needed to start solving these problems in order of importance.

After a few more moments thought, she tapped the driver on the shoulder. "I've changed my mind. Take me to Hyde Park." Maybe Flora hadn't taken the better posters from the conveniences.

Afterwards, she'd drop by St. Smeaton's and go on an urchin hunt.

CHAPTER 15

THE EXTRAORDINARY POWERS OF PORRIDGE

E LIAS WAS WOKEN UP by Phillips smacking him between the eyes. He sat upright, saw the muted daylight seeping around the curtains and snatched his pocket watch from the bedside table.

He'd slept in.

Feeling out of sorts, he got out of bed and dashed to the washstand in the corner of the room to see that Phillips had migrated to his forehead overnight. The creature waved at him cheerfully.

"You're abnormal." He reached for the bottle of absinthe beside the basin, dampening a handkerchief and holding it over Phillips's cog-shaped form, momentarily flattening the arm. Phillips detached with a cooing sound, his eyestalks waving in a dreamy fashion thanks to the wormwood.

Rolling his eyes. Elias placed Phillips on the back of his hand, making sure the trinket was attached before examining his forehead.

He dabbed at the small ring of pinpoint lesions that Phillips's mouths had produced, then brushed his teeth. He was experimenting with a new tooth powder recipe and decided that it still needed some improvement, but at least it wasn't as bad as the sand-adulterated stuff sold by the apothecary, who'd no doubt partnered with local dentists to drum up business. He then hurried to the bathroom for his bath, got dressed and went downstairs, only to meet his landlady in the hallway.

Mrs Nevins was a single-minded woman, and at this hour of the morning her single-minded fixation was porridge. With her pale white cheeks, and cream-coloured dressing gown with faux pearl buttons, she even looked somewhat like porridge.

"Mister Dooley, will you be having porridge this morning? Mister Belvoir assured me that you would be *particularly* interested in my newest flavour. It's curry. You'd like that, wouldn't you?"

Damn Vikram. Elias had tried Mrs Nevins's porridge only once, on his first day at the boarding house. It had been her speciality, 'beef and kidney'. He still woke up some nights in a cold sweat remembering the aftermath. He forced a smile. "No thank you, Mrs Nevins. I'll take my breakfast at my new workshop."

Her eyes widened with the same expression of alarm she'd showed every morning for the four years Elias had boarded at her establishment. "But you must have porridge! Porridge is the perfect fuel for the citizens of our fine city. We OverLondoners have achieved greatness on full bellies of porridge, and just think of the things a growing lad like you could achieve if you started your day correctly." Her eyes lowered to Phillips, who was waving at her. "I've never seen one with an arm like that. And why's it attached to your hand?"

"It's an experiment, Mrs Nevins. I assure you it will not be an issue. Now if you'll excuse me, I must go." Elias donned his flat cap and fitted his goggles over the top.

"Can I pack something for you?" Her face lit up. "I don't even have to! Here. I packed it for Mister Lewis, but since he's not come down yet, you can have it." She hurried into the dining room and returned holding a hefty lunch pail.

Elias took it. "Is this porridge?"

"Oh yes."

"Curry flavour?"

"The other gentlemen have told me it's *delicious*."

"Thank you."

"It was *so* kind of Mister Belvoir to allow you to take half of his shop, wasn't it? Especially since woollens are *so* important this time of year for the dear little things." She smiled benevolently. As far as Mrs Nevins knew, Vikram owned a bookshop specialising in knitting patterns for cats.

"He's certainly one of a kind Mrs Nevins. Thank you. Good day." Elias backed away, maintaining eye contact so that Mrs Nevins wasn't tempted to find more porridge to give him.

The contrast between the neat, furniture-polish-and-porridge world of Mrs Nevins's Boarding House for Respectable Young Gentlemen and the dank street outside couldn't have been starker. Elias had once asked Mrs Nevins why she'd established her boarding house in such grim surroundings, and the answer had involved a fervent defence of the power of good hearty meals and a woman's touch in reforming the dark parts of the world. Although, Elias had a suspicion that by 'hearty meals' Mrs Nevins meant 'porridge'. Having a mother who frequently expressed evangelical zeal, Elias well knew the signs of someone who lived by a belief system. If Mrs Nevins ever wanted to expand her faith, Elias had no doubt she'd succeed in gaining ready converts. As long as they were ready for porridge.

This deep into the rookery, the buildings were so bowed towards each other that light didn't reach street level, but Elias knew every single cobblestone of this part of Whitechapel and hurried with his head down, ducking low-hanging washing lines and ignoring the miasma of smells until he reached Utopia Street.

His first impulse was to go directly to the shop and inflict the porridge pail on Vikram, but instead he crossed the street, heading for Bumbridge's Tea Shop for his breakfast. Since St. Weston's was on the way, he'd stop by and enquire about the odd fragments he'd found at the site of Father Bartholomew's explosion.

While yesterday's proclamation meant the Church wouldn't be investigating the matter further, Elias still had questions about the scrap of printed paper and the piece of red satin he'd found. He would potentially have even more questions after examining the lining of his mother's best handbag, but that would involve braving her fury over forcibly removing her from the church yesterday. He had no doubt that at this very moment she was trying to work out how to mummify the bag so that it could be determined a relic at a later date.

On this side of the street, the shop fronts were all freshly painted and maintained, the diamond-paned windows sparkling, the wares inside displayed with the goal of attracting the discerning customer. Even the Artificer's Foundling House, this parish's solution to the many orphans and poor children within the city, was tidy, with neat boxes of flowering plants in front of its ornate metal doors. Across the road, Whitechapel's urchins were under the protection of The

Clockmaker, who made sure they had accommodation and food should they need it. The fact that most urchins slept anywhere but the rookery pointed to how Spartan that offered accommodation and food was.

One would assume that given the ability of trinkets to extend people's lifespans, that there wouldn't be a lot of orphans in the city. However, in making this assumption, one wouldn't be taking into account OverLondon's rather lackadaisical approach to industrial safety.

Elias had worked in almost every major workshop in the artificer district, and he returned the waves and good-natured greetings of some of them and ignored the stares and mutters of others. The reputation he'd gained during some of his apprenticeships was unfortunate, but it didn't worry him as much now that he'd opened his shop.

Having reached St. Weston's, he spared a proud glance down the road towards Ingenious Mechanisms, before stepping inside the church's cavernous interior.

St. Weston's was famous for its three massive stained-glass windows depicting the Church's interpretation of the events leading to OverLondon's levitation. As he always did, Elias paused to appreciate them.

The first window depicted floatstone's discovery in Iceland after a great volcanic eruption. The second showed the Vengeful Queen's famous dream about floatstone's possibilities, in which she imagined she was a giant hen flapping through the sky, raining fire on unbelievers. Theologians were conflicted as to whether or not 'hen' could be interpreted as 'dragon', but in this case, the window showed a great white chicken with fire shooting from its beak. The fact that the chicken also somewhat resembled a dragon, an irate teapot, or an upside-down incontinent duck—depending on which angle it was viewed from—was a testament to how skilled OverLondon's glass artists were in hedging their bets.

The third window showed the great engineering feat of undermining the city and floating it after its rebuilding in the wake of the Great Fire of Anne, which had burned the original landlocked London to a cinder. The many smaller surrounding windows told the story of the various other volcanic nations discovering their own floatstone resources, the elevation of the other great cities of the globe and the resulting Floating Cities War of 1560. A final window to one side, appearing like an afterthought, showed the drawing up of the International Treaty of Royal Exchange.

While Elias doubted that the windows showed an accurate accounting of events, he thought the glasswork had been well done, and enjoyed the peacefulness of the church when no one else was here.

That wasn't the case today, though, as Father O'Malley was standing by the pulpit, talking to a small boy wearing too-large leather boots and a threadbare black smock that stamped him as a Black Hack employee.

CHAPTER 16

FATHER O'MALLEY DOESN'T FEEL CHEERFUL

FATHER O'MALLEY WAS HAVING an exceptional morning. Despite the sleepless night, care of Father Polk's visit, he was looking forward to greeting the members of his congregation as they arrived with the day's New Lenten offerings.

He had it on good authority from Hamish Leek that a sizable proportion of his congregation had visited Hamish's shop to sell their valuables. Father O'Malley expected those funds to soon plump St. Weston's coffers. Last year, his congregation had paid an average of fifty percent of their yearly income instead of forty, which had earned him a Sash of Rampaging Acquisition from Cardinal Chudleigh. He hoped to be as blessed again this year.

However, he first had to deal with the task at hand. He liked children as a rule, but the one standing before him had been known to tax his patience. Today was no exception.

He placed a hand on the boy's shoulder. "Michael, to answer your question, I assure you that your parents donated the required sum to gain themselves *more* than adequate accommodation in heaven. They are no doubt looking down on you from their reasonably priced tenement right now, proud of everything you've accomplished since they left us."

The child frowned. He had wiry black hair, a face older than his years and ears that could be used as soup ladles. "Is it a tenement in a nice street?"

Father O'Malley gave the question the solemnity it deserved. "Yes. I assure you it's a nice street. There are no bad streets in Vengeful Heaven."

"Do they have a nice big bed?"

"Yes."

"And a puppy?"

"If they wish to have a heavenly hound, they can." Father O'Malley chortled at his own turn of phrase.

"Would it be a puppy that died here and was then sent to heaven? Because if it is, it might belong to someone else. Does that mean when *they* get to heaven they'll ask for their puppy back?"

"I'm sure there are spare puppies in heaven."

"And what you said the other day... when you said heaven is endlessly big... How big is that?"

Father O'Malley rubbed his stomach. The conversation was triggering his indigestion. "Big enough to fit a multitude, my son."

That got a solemn nod. "Okay. But what about the other heavens? Because Mister Khmalo at the Artificer's Foundling House, he's a Blacksmith's Brother, and they've got an endlessly big heaven too. Is it the same one? Because if it is, they're selling reasonably priced tenements at half the price. Does that mean that I could maybe sell my parents' tenement through you, then buy them another one through the Blacksmith's Brothers?"

Father O'Malley looked down into the clear eyes of a child who would soon progress from a muckraker to either a lawyer or a real-estate merchant. "I'm afraid your parents made a non-refundable purchase."

Michael's face screwed up in concentration. "Yeah, okay. But. Okay. How about this? They've got a spare room. Can they take in a lodger? What if someone here wants to just have a room in a reasonably priced tenement in heaven, but not the whole thing? What if I prayed and told my parents to take in a lodger? Can I do that?"

"That is a big question, and I'm going to have to consult a higher power than myself to answer it." Father O'Malley patted Michael on the head. As he wiped his hand on his cassock, he noticed Elias Dooley standing nearby. "I'll make sure to let you know the answer the minute I have it."

Michael studied him with narrowed eyes. "Does that mean you're going to pray, or that you're going to talk to Mother Superior and Cardinal Chudleigh?"

"I'll let you know when I decide. You have to run along now, because I have to talk to this young man." Father O'Malley gave the child a gentle push in the direction of the door.

Michael stopped in front of Elias. "Hey mister, would you be interested in a comfortable room in a modest tenement in heaven?"

Elias studied him solemnly. "No. Would you be interested in this pail of curry-flavoured porridge?"

"Curry?"

"Yes."

There was a long moment of thoughtful silence. "Yes."

"Here you go." Elias handed over the pail and the boy's shoulder jerked as he took its weight. "My shop is Ingenious Mechanisms, not far down the street on the rookery side. Return the pail by the end of the day and there may be another one tomorrow. It probably won't be curry flavour."

"Thanks, mister!" The boy left the church, lugging the pail with an uneven gait.

"Hello my son, how can I help you?" Father O'Malley greeted Elias, noting his new black artificer uniform and wondering what the colour meant. The new clothes reminded him that the boy had grown up in the past four years, from being a short, chubby lad of thirteen to tall and rangy, with an honest face and enquiring brown eyes. Seeing Elias reminded him of the lad's former priest, the late Father Bartholomew, rest his soul. The thought caused a pang of loss to push past Father O'Malley's good cheer.

"I have some questions to ask, if you have the time. Also, my mother told me to send you her regards the next time I stopped by."

Father O'Malley supressed a shiver, but kept his smile firmly in place. "How *is* your dear mother? She has a truly formidable reputation as one of our most devoted followers."

"She's well, and I'm sure she'd be happy to hear that," Elias said solemnly. "I'm sorry for the loss of Father Bartholomew, by the way."

Father O'Malley waved a hand, ignoring the sharp pain in his chest produced by the mention of his late friend's name. "He is now at our Vengeful Lady's side, living in his luxury upper-middle-class mansion. It's not a loss, but our Vengeful Lady's gain. Let's move on to other matters. What questions do you have to ask me?"

"It's about something I found at the site of Father Bartholomew's explosion."

It was only then that Father O'Malley noticed the odd little trinket on the back of Elias's hand. He was about to comment on it when Elias produced a small square of wax paper, unfolding it and holding it out. "It's some printed paper, but I don't think it contains words from the Book of Vengeance."

Father O'Malley's back teeth locked together as he saw what was enclosed within. He cleared his throat, running his hands over his stomach to cover up a stab of fear. Why in the Vengeful Lady's name had Father Bartholomew taken the pamphlet to his sermon? Father O'Malley had his moments of arrogance, and, admittedly, he was wearing the society's signet ring on a chain around his neck at this very moment, but it was out of sight. He'd never carry the pamphlet in public!

"Was that your name I heard on the Cry the day it happened, son?" he asked, seeking to divert attention from his less-than-ideal reaction.

"It was."

"It must have been a terrible experience for you and your mother. Mixed with the rapture of witnessing a miracle, of course."

"It was confusing," Elias said earnestly.

"Yes. Yes, it must have been. You know, my vision isn't as good as it used to be. May I?" He reached for the fragment in Elias's hand.

"Yes. But I'd appreciate it if you didn't—"

"Oh my, how did that happen?" Father O'Malley feigned alarm as the piece of paper fell to the floor. "Here, let me... I seem to have— Yes, it's fallen into the crack there. I am so *terribly* sorry. Never fear, let's get something to fish it out," he said, grinding his shoe until he was satisfied the paper was now irretrievably lost between the carved flagstones that demarked the many crypts situated under the church. The name *Tabitha Noop* was just visible by his foot.

"If you step back, I can pry it out." Elias knelt on the floor, producing a screwdriver from the utility belt at his waist.

"Oh yes. Please do." Father O'Malley's stomach roiled and he slumped against a pew, blotting his brow with the back of his hand. "You'll have to excuse me, my son. I was up quite late last night and I'm a little under the weather—" The stabbing in his stomach intensified until he had trouble breathing. "That's strange. My— seems to be— Yes, it seems to be—" He felt his longevity trinket detach from his body and scuttle over his chest and along his arm. He tried to capture it under his cassock. Just when he thought he'd caught it, it darted free of his sleeve and dropped onto the back of Elias's neck.

Father O'Malley's last thought was that he'd paid too much for it.

CHAPTER 17

A STICKY SITUATION

A GREAT WET THUDDING sound filled St. Weston's, and something threw
Elias backwards. His head hit the flagstones and everything went dark.

He regained consciousness with Phillips pinching the back of his wrist. He
opened his eyes, then immediately had to scrunch them closed again to clear
away the stuff on his face with his fingers. His ears were ringing and his vision
was wavering. Something had obviously gone terribly wrong.

Stumbling to his feet, he focused on the spot where Father O'Malley had
stood moments before, only to see that the walls, ceiling and floor were coated
in priest, with the exception of a pair of smoking shoes.

He spotted his cap and goggles under a nearby pew and stumbled over to pick
them up, jamming his cap onto his head and ramming the goggles into his pocket. This reoriented him enough to try and piece together what had happened.
He'd been intent on retrieving the lost fragment of paper and then... this. As he
blearily examined the clear patch of flagstones where he'd lain moments before,
a runnel of blood trickled between the cracks and along a series of inset words,
until *Tabitha Noop, Rest In Vengeance* stood in crimson relief.

Elias tried to think logically through the pounding in his head. Another priest
had exploded, but this time Elias had been the only witness—

His eyes widened. *The only witness!*

He stumbled backwards as he recalled the Leper's words about gutting him.
He had to leave.

The front doors of the church were still open, and he spotted two Hammer
Men striding through the heavy cloud that enveloped the city. He could call

out to them, do the right thing. But would that be the right thing, in terms of keeping his insides inside him?

It didn't take a scientific mind to conclude that Mother Superior and Cardinal Chudleigh would see him as the common denominator of two priestly explosions. They wouldn't recant the miracle proclamation from St. George's, but they could make sure Elias was no longer around to rampantly detonate any more priests in the future.

This was not the time for scientific investigation of the type he'd been able to conduct after Father Bartholomew's explosion. This was the time for self-preservation.

It took some searching, but Elias located another doorway behind a tapestry near the confessional booth. The tapestry had once featured the Vengeful Queen at the hunt, chasing the members of the final Tudor parliament through a wooded glen, and now the tableau had been augmented with a lot of realistic blood. As he moved the fabric aside, Elias heard a faint tinkling sound. A gold ring shone on the floor.

He picked it up, frowning at the 'S' set in red stones.

On the vague chance it could provide a reason for the explosion, Elias tucked the ring into a pocket before opening the door and slipping into an alley.

He had timing on his side. The cloud cover was thick enough for him to be invisible. However, to be cautious, he hurried into the depths of the artificer district, weaving furtively through the narrow lanes, flattening himself against walls and ducking out of sight of any passers-by. When he felt he'd got far enough away from St. Weston's, he looped back to Utopia Street where a traffic accident on the artificer district side had distracted people. He spared a brief glance for the rolled goat lying on its back, its legs in the air. It was chewing cud with disinterest as Whitechapel onlookers rushed to loot the beer barrels that were rolling off a smashed cart. They wouldn't be worried about breaking The Rules because theft from the artificer district was perfectly fine as far as The Clockmaker was concerned.

Once Elias reached Whitechapel, he slowed his pace. While no one would question a bloody man walking in the rookery, the Lepers would be sure to give chase to a running one.

It seemed an age before he reached Ingenious Mechanisms. He looked back towards St. Weston's, and was about to enter the shop when a voice stopped him.

"Hey mister! I've brought your pail back."

Clutching his chest, Elias spun around. Michael, the boy from St. Weston's, was running towards him with the porridge pail in hand.

"Here. I ate my fill and then gave the rest to my favourite goat. I don't think it'll give her the bloats, because she once ate half of Mister Muthalaly's special curry sauce and only backfired once on a ride to Bond Street."

"Thank you." Elias took the pail. "Now if you don't mind, I really must get to work."

The boy shifted from one foot to the other. "Will there really be more tomorrow like you said? Only I have to share the goat food most days."

"I assure you there will be a pail for you tomorrow." Elias was entirely confident in Mrs Nevins's ability to manifest porridge. Right now, Mrs Nevins's porridge was a rock of stability in his otherwise shaky reality.

"Thanks, mister." Michael looked Elias up and down with a frown. "I know it's none of my business, but what did you do?"

"Do?" Elias asked, his body tensing.

"For the Lepers to do you over like that. Covered in blood, you are. You must be rich to have enough trinkets to survive all that." Michael's eyes dropped to Phillips. "How did you get one like that?"

"I made it." Elias was about to make his excuses again, when a thought occurred to him. "I'll make you one too, if you don't tell anyone you saw me at the church today."

"Why?"

Elias flailed for a reason. "Because?" This summed up his ability to communicate with small children.

Michael opened his mouth, no doubt to ask more questions, but then he paused and his eyes narrowed. "You'll definitely make me one like that, with an arm on it, if I don't say anything? For free? Because I don't have a trinket. No one in my family's ever been able to afford a permanent one. I have to settle for borrowing Mister Khmalo's spare one for an hour once a week."

"You have my word that I'll make you one with an arm on it, just like this one, *if* you don't tell anyone—and that means *anyone*—you saw me at the church today."

"When? When do I get it?"

Elias was about to offer up Phillips, then it occurred to him that it may be smarter to wait. "One month from now. I have to make the arm first and select the right trinket. It'll take some experimentation to find the right one. Some trinkets are best for longevity, some are good for prosthetic attachment."

Michael considered this. "Alright. Alright, but I still get a pail of porridge every day, right?"

"Most certainly. There will always be porridge. Porridge is inevitable. Come by tomorrow. If I'm not here, the other man in the shop will give it to you."

Michael's face screwed up. "What, the beaver man?"

"*Adopted* beaver man," Elias corrected him, though he had no idea why. "Do we have a deal?"

"Yeah, but you won't get in any more trouble with the Lepers between then and now, will you?"

"I'll do my utmost to avoid all trouble," Elias said.

"Yeah. Alright." The kid tipped his cap, which was prevented from covering his eyes by his oversized ears. "I'll be seeing you." With that, he ducked and wove across the street, leaving Elias free to enter the shop.

Inside, he shrugged out of his coat, bundling it up in shaking hands.

"You're late."

When Elias didn't answer, Vikram poked his head above his dam of books. He was wearing a mustard-yellow beanie that made him look like a noxious, literary inclined puff ball, possibly a critic. "What happened to you?"

"A priest exploded." Elias strode to the fetid privy at the back of the shop, hung his hat and coat on a hook and washed his face and hands, watching as the water in the basin turned pink. This was so much worse than Father Bartholomew's explosion, which had only necessitated some spot cleaning at his mother's lodgings after he'd taken her home. He realised that his new waistcoat was also covered in blood, so he took that off too, only then noticing the additional bump beneath his shirt.

An unfamiliar trinket was attached to him, beneath his right collarbone.

Prodding it, he frowned. It was a large creature, the diameter of a walnut, and extraordinarily expensive—far more expensive even than the one he'd rescued from Father Bartholomew's explosion.

He searched his mind and, in a jolt of clarity, recalled the sensation of something landing on the back of his neck before Father O'Malley had exploded. Had it been this trinket? If that was the case, it had known the explosion was about to happen. But how had it sensed it?

He looked around for some absinthe to remove the trinket, but gave up when he realised that any alcohol unfortunate enough to end up in this place had been drunk years ago.

He paused. Absinthe!

It could have caused the trinket to drop off Father O'Malley. But no, if it had been wormwood, the trinket would've been too inebriated to attach to Elias so soon.

Putting the matter aside for now, he decided the trinket wasn't going anywhere and that he was benefiting from it being attached to him. Instead, he proceeded to empty his pockets, rediscovering the gold ring he'd found at the church. That was another thing to deal with, but later, once he'd found a bucket to rinse his clothing in. He finally found one hiding behind the door beneath a pile of mouldy old penny dreadful paperbacks of the sort that always ended up in privies. Its wood was mildewed from misuse but it was still serviceable.

"Do we have soap?" he called over the sound of the running water.

"What is this strange thing you speak of?"

"This is not the time to be amusing." Elias caught his scowl in the cracked mirror and realised that he still had to wash the gunk from his hair. He removed the now full bucket from the sink and placed his head under the tap until the water ran clear. He then searched through the various boxes and cupboards Vikram had piled around the privy until he found what appeared to be a hard, cracked sliver of soap that had obviously tried its best to escape from the filth that otherwise pervaded the small room. He dropped it in the bucket and worked up an insipid froth before washing out as much blood as possible from his waistcoat and coat, then hung them on pegs on the back of the door. All he had to do now was give his damaged clothing to Mrs Nevins to send to her washerwoman. Being based in Whitechapel, she'd be accustomed to removing blood and not asking questions. The colour would help. When Elias had had the clothing tailored to his specifications, he'd decided that black would be a wise choice, and was now satisfied that he'd been correct.

He inspected his breeches and shirt. His coat and waistcoat had taken the brunt of Father O'Malley, so it was merely a matter of another few minutes of scrubbing at the hems and cuffs and wiping off his shoes to make them presentable.

Finally, he rinsed his goggles off and then inspected his flat cap. He'd designed the fabric himself to ward off almost every liquid imaginable, so it was the work of minutes to rinse it and wring it out before it was somewhat limp, but presentable. Ramming it onto his head, he shoved the items that had been in his waistcoat pockets—including the priest's ring—into the compartments in his utility belt and walked back into the shop.

"If anyone asks, I was here all day," he told Vikram.

"Where else would you be?" Vikram demanded. "It's not as if you have a glittering social life, unless you count taking mother dearest to church. Are you going to tell me what really happened?"

"I visited St. Weston's on the way here to talk to Father O'Malley, but he exploded while I was there," Elias said.

"Pull the other one, it's got little gold and silver bells on. No, just wait. I'll pull it myself. There's a book somewhere in this pile that'll tell me how to do it. If you give me an hour, I'll find it."

Elias ignored him. Now that he was telling someone, the words poured out. "There was no warning. One minute we were talking, and then he was spread all over the church."

"And I suppose no one else saw this miraculous event? Only you," Vikram scoffed. "I know a doctor who has special pills for this kind of delusion. If you're lucky he'll even proscribe oral ones."

"No, but there was someone there just before. A small child. I gave him a pail of Mrs Nevins's curry porridge. He just returned it to me." Elias realised he'd left the pail in the privy. With luck, it wouldn't grow mould before he went back in there. "I've asked him not to tell anyone he saw me in exchange for a pail of porridge a day and a trinket with a prosthetic on it." Elias held up his hand and Phillips waved obligingly.

Vikram appeared over the top of the book wall, studying Elias with the air of a chicken who'd just discovered where deep-fried drumsticks came from. "You're not joking, are you?"

"No," Elias said. "See this." He unbuttoned his shirt to expose the rogue trinket. "I think it was Father O'Malley's—it must've jumped off him before the explosion."

Vikram stared at it for several seconds. "You bastard!" He disappeared behind the books again. "You've made me a bloody known associate by telling me, haven't you?" Elias heard a shuffle and a thud, and realised that Vikram's beaver-by-adoption ancestry was inspiring a spate of panic damming. Vikram was making crenulations.

Unsure of what to say and aware that he himself was still not thinking rationally, Elias retreated to his desk.

Finally, Vikram spoke again, his voice muffled. "And I'm guessing this urchin works for the Cry?"

"He was wearing a Black Hack uniform, so I don't think so."

He flinched as the bell on the door rang and someone entered. One of Vikram's crenulations tumbled to the floor.

A skinny man with a bushy beard, wearing a tan overcoat, looked everywhere but at Elias's face. "Is this where I can get the books about the... special fruit?"

"This side," Vikram said. "Shelf at the back. We've got a surplus of bananas and cucumbers—before you ask, yes, they are a fruit—and you'll find the peaches at the bottom if you can drag your eyes off the melons."

The man warily looked at Elias. "Yeah, yeah. Right. I'll just—"

"No returns, buy two get one free, but if you ruin the pages before you buy, you pay full price and go on the list," Vikram said crisply.

Elias and Vikram waited in silence as the man spent an inordinate amount of time shuffling through the shelves, before finally approaching the counter holding six books, which were then duly wrapped in brown paper.

The minute the door closed behind the customer, Vikram's head popped up again. "You'd better pray they declare this one a miracle too, because if they don't, and that boy talks, your insides will be Mother Superior's plaything."

Elias touched the bump of the extra trinket under his shirt. Trinkets never left a person voluntarily. He just wished he could think clearly enough to decipher what had caused the explosion.

"Or I could determine what killed Father O'Malley," he said.

"How?"

"There has to be some kind of scientific explanation."

"You want to explain *science* to the church of eternal vengeance and carnage? Impossible! You'd be better teaching pigeons to clean statues and goats to fly!"

"Then what else do you suggest?"

"Find out *who* killed him instead. Come up with someone to point the finger at, *point* that finger and back away quickly. One priest splattering the walls? I'll buy that it could be a miracle. Two? It's definitely murder, especially if you were the only witness. You're the last person on the globe to inspire a miracle, other than causing entire rooms to be vacated out of extreme boredom."

Elias grimaced. "It could have just been an accident or an unfortunate series of events. I can't count that out."

"Never! It was murder. Why would priests accidentally explode themselves?" Vikram's nostrils flared. "Let me put it this way, if you don't find out who did it and manage to clear yourself, I'm kicking you onto the street and sending for Mother Superior myself before The Clockmaker decides to do her a favour. There's no way my entrails are getting spread all over yours. I don't swing that way. So get to work. Trot trot." He made a shooing gesture and then ducked out of sight again.

Elias glared at the pile of books Vikram was lurking behind, frustration rising within him. Then the Cry sounded in the street, and his entire body tensed as he waited to hear his name.

Hear ye! hear ye! Mistress Fenderpossum of the Artificer's Guild will be demonstrating the incompetence of the OverFlorentine ballistic cherub to civic leaders at the Artificer's Guild Hall today. We stand by to report injuries and fatalities. Stop. Big Ivan of the Sugar Gang announced an imminent sugar deal with an as-yet-unnamed city. When queried, he said, 'If you don't get out of my face, I'm gonna give you the carrot. Don't make me give you the carrot. Trust me, people don't like the carrot.' Stop. Ye've heard! Ye've heard! If you need to find someone, choose the Reign Agency by the sign of The Armoury in Drury Lane. Trust a pirate to catch a thief, murderer, goat worrier or annoying person. The Reign Agency. We'll snaffle your booty in no time.

Vikram snorted. "It sounds like no one's found the splatted priest yet, but the minute they do and that urchin talks, you're going to be worth as much as the stuff they skim off the OverThames every summer."

"The question is, how do I extract myself from this situation?" Elias said.

"You heard the Cry. Hire the bloody pirate! And don't come back until there's no risk of Mother Superior turning up with a rubber thurible. I like my head round and bursting with ingenuity, as opposed to merely bursting, thank you so very much."

Elias's head ached. Every part of him wanted to reject Vikram's idea, but it was the best option at the moment. *Damn.*

He cleared his throat. "Can I borrow your spare cardigan?" He looked at the repugnant woollen mass hanging on a hook by the door.

"Why?"

"Because there's priest all over my coat and I need to hire a pirate."

CHAPTER 18

THE HUNT FOR GRUB

A LEX STEPPED DOWN FROM a hack and tucked the wad of posters she'd just collected from the Hyde Park conveniences into her doublet. With luck, there'd be some cove worth enough to pay her rent, but right now she had an urchin to find.

Despite Bloomsbury's proximity to Drury Lane, it had been years since she'd been in this part of town, but the presence of Sweet Pete plying his trade added a sense of familiarity. His cart was surrounded by the usual clamour of urchins. Seeing them, Alex had an excellent idea. She wandered over to the cart.

Pete looked even more disenfranchised with the world than normal today, his skin grizzled in contrast to his sequined uniform and the boil on his forehead so large that Alex wondered if his trinket was up to snuff. The creatures lasted for centuries, as far as anyone knew, but since no one really knew how old Pete was, his could be geriatric.

Alex sized up the urchins surrounding the cart. "Greetings," she said, only to be the recipient of at least twenty belligerent glares. "I require some information and will be paying Sweet Pete here for a theft-free triple-scoop of the flavour of your choice if you can provide it."

There was a momentary stunned silence.

"You're going to what?" Pete asked, not even looking as he dinged an ice cream-seeking child around the ear, producing a bonging sound. "Are you trying to get done by the Editors for soliciting unlicenced fiction from these little fiends? Get out of it!"

"I grew up on these streets, Pete. I'll know if they're lying." Alex surveyed the kids. A couple of them were picking their noses, one of them looked like he needed the privy, while another appeared to no longer need the privy, if the puddle at his feet was any indication.

"What do you want to know?" asked a girl who came up to Alex's waist. Her expression was so calculating Alex was tempted to peer into her ear to see if her brain had been replaced by an abacus.

"I'm looking for someone named Grub." Alex scanned their faces, hoping to see a reaction. Even though half of these kids were no doubt employed by The Clockmaker, she didn't mention his name. Hearing The Clockmaker was looking for someone tended to clear the streets, because no one wanted to risk finding out they were the cove he was looking for. "Rumour has it that she sleeps in St. Smeaton's most nights."

Pete spat on the cobbles. "That'll be half of this lot here. Father Inigo is too soft on 'em. He lets 'em sleep on the pews when they should be at the rookery hostels. Pews are too good for 'em." His expression transformed into an approximation of a smile as he greeted a plump woman in a large white bonnet. "Hello, my good lady, and how may I take your order today? We have every flavour imaginable. Strawberry, vanilla, lemon and chocolate. Whatever your heart desires, provided it's strawberry, vanilla, lemon or chocolate." He managed to say this while flailing his scoop behind his back to create an urchin-free arc.

The woman looked distinctly embarrassed. "Oh, I don't want an ice cream. I want some... Do you have any... you know..."

Sweet Pete tapped his nose. "Say no more, madam. Say no more. How much do you need?"

She smiled in relief. "Half a cup. Mister Tums has run out."

"The brown or the white?"

"The white, if you please. This isn't a special enough occasion to warrant the expense of the brown. You're always *so* helpful! We're so lucky to have you." The woman gave a girlish chuckle.

Pete simpered. "I live to please."

One of the urchins made a vomiting face.

Taking advantage of Pete's distraction as he scooped and measured out white sugar from a small sack kept in the base of his cart, Alex tried again. "The question stands. Anyone here know Grub?"

"Are you just offerin' ice cream or are you givin' money too? Because we can get ice cream whenever we want, but money is harder," said a boy who seemed to be constructed primarily of grime and snot.

Alex pursed her lips. "If the information is good, it could be negotiable."

"Why'd you want to know?" This was from a girl whose face was smeared with what Alex could only hope was chocolate ice cream.

Alex shrugged. "I just want to find her. Anyone know her or know why she hasn't been seen around here lately?"

She waited. They stared at her. She waited some more. They stared some more.

She clasped her hands behind her back, whistling nonchalantly.

One of the children wandered off to pick up a stray ginger kitten. Alex might have thought the picture quaint if he hadn't then wiped his nose on its fur. The kitten didn't seem to mind.

She shrugged. "I'm going to speak to Father Inigo, then I'm going back to my office above The Armoury in Drury Lane. If anyone wants to pay me a visit..." She let her words hang in the air. Another child scratched his head, revealing that it was possible to have more dandruff than hair on a human scalp.

"You don't look like your picture," a boy said, giving her a look that was a hundred years old.

"No. Which is why you should never trust anyone holding a paintbrush." Alex bowed. She'd planted the seed, now all she had to do was see if it would grow. "I bid you farewell."

She walked towards St. Smeaton's without looking back. As she passed the statue of the Vengeful Queen, she nodded her respects, noting the way the pigeon droppings gave old Anne an even more psychotic air.

It had been an age since Alex had been here. She was pretty sure the shine on the door to the Blessed Press was partially due to the licking she'd once given it as an urchin. Considering the life she'd led since that day, maybe its anti-dullness properties had worked.

"Hello?" she called out as she stepped into St. Smeaton's cavernous interior.

"Hello, my child. Come forward." The words were spoken in a kind voice that came from somewhere by the pulpit.

Alex found a priest with a tufted halo of blond hair kneeling before a wooden diorama which had been temporarily placed on the flagstones. When intact, it would feature the Vengeful Queen threatening King Francis II with a bollock dagger, demanding that he give fair share—meaning all of—the English Channel's omnicite weed crops. However, some of the wooden figurines had come loose and there was a bag of light brown Femur's Animal Glue granules at the priest's side as he mixed a handful of them with some hot water.

Alex cleared her throat. "Father, I'm wondering if you could help me. I'm looking for an urchin named Grub who sleeps here sometimes. She's gone missing."

He responded with a distant smile. "Oh? Well, that happens. Could you hold Our Vengeful Lady, please?" He handed Alex the figurine and then picked up a paintbrush. The movement caused his cassock to hike up, revealing black hose. Alex wondered if he was one of Sadie Simms's customers, and if so, what colour of underwear he was wearing. Something told her that pink was an option.

She realised the priest was looking at her expectantly. She held out the figurine.

"Up a bit. Yes. I'm afraid my left hand shakes too much to get her steady. It's working the press—it wears on the nerves."

"Like this?"

"Yes." He poked his tongue out in concentration, giving the base of the figurine a precise dab of glue before taking it back and placing it firmly in the diorama. "That should do it. The children come in at night, you see, and sometimes they play with things they shouldn't." He stood up, giving Alex a warm smile. "Which child were you referring to again?"

"Grub." Alex watched him for a reaction.

He frowned. "The name isn't familiar to me. But we have many children coming and going. Can you share the reason you're looking for her?"

Alex fabricated an explanation quickly, in an effort to avoid mentioning the Lepers. "I hired her to deliver a message, but it didn't get to its destination. I'd feel responsible if anything has happened to her. If she comes back, I'd appreciate it if you could direct her to my office above The Armoury in Drury Lane. There'll be a reward for finding her, and a cut for the Church," she added.

The priest's expression transformed to a faint smile. "The Armoury—that takes me back. Is Gregor still running it?"

"He is. You know him?"

"I did once. When I was much younger, before the Vengeful Lady visited me in my sleep and threatened me to take up her cause."

"You can't resist a threatening when it comes," Alex said solemnly.

"Quite. Quite. The things I used to get up to. I trod the boards once." The priest wore a far-off expression. "The way Gregor used to snarl at us if we soliloquised... It takes me back. I'll never forget the taste of a pint of gin after a long day on the stage. I always liked to play the pretty girls."

"I'm sure you were beautiful."

The priest touched his balding pate. "I was, I truly was."

"About the girl..." Alex prompted him again.

"The girl? Oh yes. There are so many children." He fluttered his fingers in the air. "They come and go, and they change frequently. I hear you were once an urchin yourself, so you'd know. The Dread Pirate Purple Reign, aren't you? I recognise you from the scar, and the flying helmet."

"I am."

His face again took on a dreamy aspect. "I did enjoy hearing about your adventures on the Cry. The time you took that OverBrussels merchantman by swinging from the rigging with five cutlasses clutched between your strong thighs. Amazing."

Alex smoothed her hand over her helmet, preening. "It was nothing. Pirating is excellent for the thigh muscles."

"And the time you single-handedly took on the OverLondon fleet by firing yourself out of that cogcannon while singing that Norwegian song that was *so* popular a few years ago. What was it? Oh, that's right, 'Hug My Whale Til the Blowhole Blows.' I've always liked that one, especially if done properly in falsetto."

Alex gave the comment its due. "I'll admit, I've had my moments. But now I'm a privateer for the city." *At least until I get my ship back*, she added to herself.

The priest sighed. "I see. I see. Repentance is a fine thing. If you'd like to gain forgiveness, I'm doing a special rate on confessions today. Three sins for the price of one." He looked hopefully at her.

"I'll consider it. On the subject of the missing child, has anything odd happened lately at the church? Anything out of the ordinary?"

The priest shook his head. "Nothing that I can think of, other than last Thursday, when Father Bartholomew was visiting me. I was sure I'd taken my anti-spasm medication before I used the Blessed Press, but I came over all funny and he had to accompany me home." He made the sign of the pound. "May we all experience such ecstasy as to explode under the rapture of the Vengeful Word. I don't wonder if I didn't catch a small amount of his rapture before the actual event. If so, I was truly blessed."

"I see." Alex didn't, but she had to say something.

"As for your missing girl—maybe you could ask Crier Frank. He should be looking after Sweet Pete's cart right now, while Pete has his morning break. I fear it's the only time the children get a chance to have a good meal all day. Or maybe you could ask one of the Editors."

"You read my mind, Father. Thank you," Alex said, lying through her teeth. Why hadn't she thought of asking the Editors? Or the crier, for that matter? Oh, that was right—until recently she'd been a pirate, and pirates didn't tend to ask questions beyond "Where's the loot?"

"One last question," she said.

"Yes?"

"What's your preferred colour?"

"I'm partial to pink. It's our Vengeful Lady's colour, you know."

Alex grinned. "I appreciate the information."

"You're welcome, my child. The fee for this conversation will be tuppence." The priest smiled angelically.

Alex went through a performance of patting her pockets. "I don't have the money on me, but I'll send my cabin boy with it before the day is over."

"I close the doors at ten."

"She'll be here before then."

"Otherwise I charge twenty percent interest each day. Our Vengeful Lady was most exacting on the matter."

Alex glanced down at the little wooden figurine of the snarling queen in the diorama. "Yes, she was a lesson to us all. I'll be seeing you, Father."

"Bless you, my child, and bring me your cash."

Alex smiled politely and braced herself for a conversation with the crier, who could be heard nearby, bellowing out an unexpected bulletin.

Hear ye! Hear ye! This is an exclusive emergency bulletin. Father O'Malley of St. Weston's Cathedral has been discovered exploded by a Mrs Mildred Pondergrundle. She was quoted saying, 'There were bits everywhere!' A screwdriver was found at the scene, but it didn't explode when picked up. Stand by as events develop. Stop. Ye've heard! Ye've heard! Feeling like the world doesn't care? Need a flour to cheer you up? Buy Brovis wheat flour today! Less than ten percent sawdust guaranteed!

Alex turned at the sound of something breaking only to see Father Inigo standing in the aisle with the diorama smashed at his feet.

"Father," she called out. "Are you alright?"

He looked at her with wide eyes. "My Vengeful Queen! Father O'Malley. It's too awful—too rapturous and wonderful, I mean," he corrected himself. "I must find my bucket and shovel—I mean my mourning cassock—before Mother Superior bans relics and it's too late." He scurried from the church, not looking back.

Alex debated following him to St. Weston's, but decided against it. Exploding priests weren't her problem any more, and if Father Inigo's reaction *was* any indication, there'd be too many members of the clergy milling about.

Still, she was a pirate, and it would be remiss not to have a look around while the church was empty. She sauntered to the brass door guarding the Blessed Press and then muttered a curse when she found it locked. She'd never been able to afford admission as a child and it would've been nice to look at it.

Instead, she searched the pews and was about to check behind the pulpit when she spotted the broken diorama and the tiny mad queen who'd become dislodged once again. On a pirate-driven impulse, Alex placed the figurine in her pocket, then searched the rest of the church only to find nothing of interest. She left.

She found Crier Frank minding Sweet Pete's cart, as Father Inigo had said.

He was a tall, sallow man with mousy hair visible under his weathered green cap. The medals pinned to his similarly threadbare green uniform indicated that he was an industry veteran. Alex spotted a Medal for Window-Breaking Volume, a Medal for Stunning Passers-By and a Medal for Cracking Building Foundations.

"Crier Frank?" she asked.

"Yes!"

Alex winced at the man's volume, but it didn't seem to affect any of the urchins slipping past him to put their hands in the ice cream tubs. "Can I ask you a couple of questions?"

"What do you want? Get away boy, get away!" He waved at a small boy who'd ducked under his arm. Without the threat of Sweet Pete's scoop, the children were a feral, sugar-fuelled mob.

"It's about an urchin named Grub. She was last seen around here but she's gone missing."

"Why would I know where an urchin is? Filthy little devils. I said *get out of it*!" The man waved his arms again as a phalanx of children charged at him.

"Oi!" Sweet Pete came running down the street, scoop arm raised in the air, his expression furious. "Get away from there, you little demons!"

Seeing that their window of opportunity had disappeared, the children scattered.

"They're animals!" Crier Frank bellowed as Sweet Pete reached the cart, clobbering children around the head with clangs and bongs.

"Incredible!" Sweet Pete's chest heaved. "Every day, this happens. Every day. Can't a man have five minutes to go to the conveniences in peace? Thanks, Frank. Same time tomorrow?"

Crier Frank scowled at the children who'd retreated beyond scoop range. "You need to get me a spare scoop if you want me to do this any more, Pete! They're getting worse!"

Alex rubbed her ringing ear, now understanding why there were sometimes notices tacked up by the doors of tenements stating *No Criers*. Having someone like Crier Frank in the building would ensure a permanent lack of peace and quiet.

"Alright. Alright." Sweet Pete handed the crier a coin. "There's your payment."

"About that urchin," Alex said to Crier Frank. "Can you let me know if you hear anything? My name is Alex Reign, Captain Alex—"

"I know who you are! I've said your name enough!" Crier Frank bellowed indignantly and walked away. "That's the problem with you pirate layabouts who've never done a decent day's work—you expect to steal a man's time without a by-your-leave!"

"Fat lot of help you were," Alex muttered.

"What d'you expect?" Sweet Pete said. "You didn't offer him any money, did you? With the measly amount those blighters get paid? You got to offer 'em money before you can get a word out of 'em. Although there's no point with Frank. He's useless. He can't even watch my cart for five minutes without half of my produce going missing."

With that, he walked away, the wheels of his cart squeaking, his scoop flailing at random urchins.

Alex made a rude gesture at Sweet Pete's back, and the onlooking urchins tittered.

Taking one last look at St. Smeaton's, Alex decided it was time to get back to The Armoury. If she was lucky, Miss Sadie Simms and her four pounds would have returned.

CHAPTER 19

A ROGUE ARTIFICER HIRES A PIRATE, WHO HIRES A ROGUE ARTIFICER

As Elias alighted from a Black Hack at Drury Lane he accidentally jostled an actor in a harlequin costume who was prancing down the street, inflicting flyers on anyone stupid enough to make eye contact.

The actor spun around with an eager expression, the bells on his hat jingling as he thrust a playbill at Elias's face.

"Want to see the latest and greatest play in the world, bruvver? It's the new one from William Wobblespeare. It's got lions. It's got tigers. It's got sharks. It's got everyfink!"

Elias was momentarily thrown. "Sharks? Does it really have sharks?"

"Yeah, and they eat people and everyfink. It's gruesome, bruvver, gruesome! You've gotta see it!"

"Actual sharks?"

"Well, one shark, but it's a convincing one!"

"Yes, but is it a real one?"

"Maybe not *real* per se, but Torvald here has a good costume and the teeth are convincing, aren't they, Torvald?" He waved to another actor who was smoking a cigarette in the lee of a playhouse.

"Yah, convincing."

"I'm not interested," Elias said.

"There's an airship too! It sinks wiv everyone on it because it hits this thing, right. This big icy floatstone rock and—"

"I've heard enough. Please get out of my way."

"There's also this like, man who rules a woodland in far-off Verona! He's named Marzipan, King of the Monkeys!"

"There aren't monkeys in Verona." Elias looked around and spotted the sign for the Reign Agency above another sign featuring a snarling badger gnawing on a mime's leg.

"Look, mate, everything's in bleedin' Verona. It's what it's *for*. Anyway, there's this other one, Springtime for Genghis. Mountains of skulls! You'll laugh your head off!" The actor saw that he was wasting his time, blew Elias a raspberry and then capered off towards a group of Ottoman tourists.

Elias was just about to push the door of The Armoury open when a woman approached from the other direction.

He took in her flying helmet and facial scar. "Excuse me. Are you the Dread Pirate Purple Reign?"

The woman scowled fiercely at him. "That's *Privateer* Purple Reign to you. Say anything about my height and I won't be responsible for my behaviour. I'm in a hurry and I don't have the time to maim someone politely."

Elias fought confusion. "Height? Why would I do that? No, I need to talk to you. I'd like to hire you. It's about the priest. The new one that exploded, and the other one. I need you to find who did it."

"Well, that's another matter entirely." Her scowl transformed into a grin and Elias caught the flash of a gold incisor. She opened the door to the pub, gesturing for him to enter. "You can call me Captain Reign. After you."

Elias stepped inside and then stopped abruptly as a fug of gin, ale, sawdust and unwashed bodies assaulted his nostrils. He immediately concluded that his habit of avoiding pubs hadn't necessarily disadvantaged him socially, or nasally.

Captain Reign closed the door behind him, her expression thoughtful as she studied his face. "Where do I know you from?" She tapped a finger on her bottom lip, then her eyes widened. "St. George's! The woman with the floral dress and the full handbag. You carried her out of the church."

"My mother," Elias said. "I thought it would be wise to rescue her before she was injured in the fray."

"I don't think I've ever seen a woman who wanted to be rescued less."

"I'm afraid you're correct."

"No matter—here's to all vengeful women who worship vengeful queens!" Captain Reign clapped him on the shoulder. "Let's get down to business. Follow me." She led him through a haze of cigar and pipe smoke, winding through a throng of actors in various levels of debauchery and decrepitude, only to be confronted by a massive snarling badger man holding a fistful of empty gin flagons. His shirt was open to his navel, revealing a torso that resembled an overenthusiastic washboard.

"Tell the ferret that she needs to return what she took this morning, or I'll use her bones to pick my teeth." His voice sounded like an earthquake rumbling through gravel.

Captain Reign rubbed her forehead, wincing. "What did she take this time?"

"You want the list?"

"I'll send her down."

The big man glowered at Elias. "Make sure you guard your pockets. There are ferrets about."

"I'll keep that in mind." Elias cleared his throat. "Did I hear you correctly just then? Do you really eat people?"

That earned him a long stare. "I've been known to have a varied and nutritious diet."

"I see."

The badger man jabbed a finger at Captain Reign. "I want my pocket watch back in one minute. And tell her if she takes my buttons one more time, she's gonna be used as a privy brush."

Elias watched him stalk away. "Does he really eat people?"

The captain led him up some stairs. "I've never seen him spit out bones."

"That's not really putting my mind at ease." Elias cursed Vikram. He was in enough trouble as it was, and now people-eating badgers were somehow in the mix.

The walls either side of the stairs were lined with posters for a stomp ballet school. The women depicted looked more like Valkyries bent on carnage than the delicate dancers Elias had seen a few weeks ago when his mother had dragged him to the opera. It had been a useful expedition. He'd come up with an idea for a new corkscrew design while watching the dancers pirouette.

He hurried to catch up as the captain opened a door. She started speaking the minute she stepped into the room beyond. "Flora, where's Sid?"

"Out and away." The voice was singsong and dreamy. For some reason it left Elias thinking of daisies.

"Where?"

"To take Miss Sadie Simms back home."

Elias stepped through the doorway and immediately spotted a young woman lounging in a hammock with one leg hanging casually over the side. She was pretty in an odd way, with fair hair sticking out from under a floppy hat, her eyes shining black amid the dark brown mask on her otherwise fawn-coloured face. Obviously *homo furo*.

"She was here?" Captain Reign took off her cape with a flourish and hung it up.

"Yes. And there."

"There being?"

The young woman held her hand up in front of her left eye, her fingers forming an O, which she looked through. "Somewhere nearby. When she heard the Cry she came over and hired us again. Sid gave her gin and I had a cup of tea with extra sugar, because I borrowed some from Sweet Pete's cart this morning. It was very nice. Very sweet, which isn't what Pete is. Definitely not sweet." She moved her leg idly, sending the hammock into a gentle swing.

Captain Reign pinched the bridge of her nose. "Flora! Reverse from the sugar. Leave the sugar alone. This is not about sugar. What did Miss Simms want?"

"She said she'd pay us five pounds."

"Five pounds? Now you're talking." Captain Reign's posture relaxed. "Not bad."

Elias grimaced. Five pounds? That was beyond his budget. In fact, that was the entirety of his remaining savings. He was about to bring up the matter, when Flora continued speaking.

"And then Sid turned red and said he'd take her home and she said she'd be delighted, and then he turned even more red and his chest puffed up like that time he ate those clams, and she made a noise like this—" Flora made a bubbly giggling noise. "And then she said yes and then they left."

"With luck he won't terrify the money away," Captain Reign said. "I'll deal with that later. More immediately, did you take Gregor's watch?"

"Was it shiny with a chain hanging down, like it might fall out of his pocket at any minute? Because if it did, I might have *rescued* it."

"I see. Amazingly thoughtful of you."

"I know." Flora shrugged. "That's just how I am. Thoughtful and always thinking."

"Be that as it may, if you don't go down and let him know of this heroic, *thoughtful* deed within the next thirty seconds, you're going to be without a head to think with. And give the man back his buttons."

Flora jumped from the hammock, her long body swaying from side to side as she tucked her shirt into red breeches. "I've finished looking at them anyway."

"And while you're there, order us some gin. This gentleman and I need to have a business conversation."

"Aye aye, Cap'n." Flora saluted before smiling dreamily. "Hello. I'm Flora. You look like someone I've seen before."

"He was at St. George's, carrying his mother out of the church," the captain said.

"Oh yes! She bashed you with her handbag. I saw. I was in the church, sneaking." Flora's smile widened. "Do you like shiny things?"

"Do you mean metallic things?" Elias asked.

"Sometimes."

"If they're useful."

"They're *always* useful."

"I can see how that would be an opinion."

"I like you." Flora gave him a pat on the arm as she left.

Elias stared after her in bemusement.

"Okay, Mister—" The captain walked to a desk in the middle of the room, taking a seat behind it. "What should I call you?"

"Elias. Elias Dooley."

She frowned. "I've heard that name before."

"On the Cry. An urchin quoted me after Father Bartholomew exploded."

"Ah, I begin to see your predicament." She flashed him that gold-toothed grin again. "Take a seat." She gestured to a shabby velvet armchair.

"Thank you." He sat down.

"Now, tell me your story."

"It started when I accompanied my mother to church last Sunday."

She waved a hand. "Continue."

"I was working on an experiment when Father Bartholomew exploded." He paused as Flora reappeared holding three tankards. There were badgers on the side of them. "Thank you," he said when she handed him one. "I was also at St. Weston's when Father O'Malley blew up. I was showing him some things I found at the site of Father Bartholomew's explosion. Unfortunately, he exploded too, leaving me as the only witness."

Captain Reign looked at him beneath beetled brows. "And you're worried Mother Superior is going to give you the kitten treatment for blowing up clergy?"

"I wouldn't word it like that exactly, but yes."

She steepled her fingers in front of her mouth. "You say you found some objects of interest when the first priest died?"

"Like a cogcannon?" Flora asked.

"No." Elias twisted to catch her hopeful expression. "It was a fragment of paper with printed words on it."

"With a small cogcannon hidden under it?"

"Flora!" Captain Reign's voice was sharp. "There was no cannon. Leave the cannon. No more mention of cannons." She turned back to Elias. "Do you have this piece of paper on you?"

"Unfortunately, it was lost when Father O'Malley exploded. Or at least, I think it was. With all the blood seeping into the cracks in the flagstones I doubt it would've survived, but it bears checking. There was also a fragment of red satin, which I should still have." He patted his pockets, before remembering that he was wearing Vikram's awful knitted yellow cardigan. It smelled strongly of mothballs. "I had it in my coat, which is back at my shop drying."

"Where's your shop?" Flora asked.

"Ingenious Mechanisms? It's on Utopia Street, not far from St. Weston's, actually."

"Near Hamish Leek's shop?"

"If you mean the pawn shop, yes. About five minutes away."

"I like that shop."

"Flora, quiet! Mister Dooley, the fabric comes from a pair of knickers. As far as we know, they're not explosive."

"Knickers," Elias repeated slowly.

"Why don't you try some of that drink you're holding?" Captain Reign raised her tankard in a toast.

Elias studied the tankard in his hand. He took a sip and coughed. "This is very strong."

"It's that kind of day." She chugged her pint in a way that told Elias that she had a lot of trinkets on her body.

Elias took another sip. Phillips made a rude gesture but Elias didn't die, so it was probably safe. Besides, Father O'Malley's trinket was probably helping to counter the effects.

The captain wiped her mouth with the back of her hand, smacking her lips together. "Ahh, Recalcitrant Badger, OverLondon's finest gin. Okay, Mister Dooley, tell me the rest of your story."

Elias continued, becoming more relaxed by the minute, the words pouring from him as he recounted the whole sorry tale.

"And I also dropped a screwdriver," he concluded.

"The one mentioned on the Cry?"

"Yes."

"I'm sure we can take care of that," Captain Reign said enigmatically.

"I also seem to have acquired another trinket. I believe it's Father O'Malley's, which means it left the priest's body and attached itself to me before he exploded."

"That's odd."

"It is. That means it somehow sensed the explosion was about to happen. I found Father Bartholomew's trinket after his explosion as well. It was injured but its mouth parts weren't."

"If it'd been attached to him, its mouth parts should've been damaged, yes?"

"Yes. I'm not sure what to make of it," Elias said. "The scrap of paper I was showing Father O'Malley is also a puzzler. I'm certain that it was printed by the Blessed Press, but it isn't from the Book of Vengeance."

Captain Reign leant forward. "The Blessed Press?"

"I believe so. The type indicated as much."

"Hmm."

"There's also this. I found it at St. Weston's." Elias took the ring out of his pocket. "It's a signet ring. The stones look valuable."

Flora made a squeaking sound. "It's the same one!"

Captain Reign wagged a finger. "What have I told you about talking while I'm having a meeting?"

"You've told me that talking is inadvisable."

"So be advised to kindly shut up."

Elias twisted around to look at Flora, who was sitting up in her hammock. "There's another ring?"

Flora nodded. "At St. George's. I found it. It was on a finger that I had to give back. But I kept the ring."

"Flora! What have we discussed about handing over the booty before getting payment?"

"You said to never do it."

"And?"

"I'll be quiet now."

Elias turned back to Captain Reign, who'd just slapped her forehead. "If they both had a signet ring, it has to be connected. It's also strange they were wearing the rings during New Lent."

She raised her head. "Yes, I'm sure it is, but coming to that conclusion is my job. Which is precisely why I'm going to ask you to give me the ring for safekeeping." She walked over to Elias, holding out a black-gloved hand, giving him an expectant look until he dropped the ring into her palm. Her fingers snapped shut around it with lightning speed and then she strode back to her chair.

"Now, Mister Dooley, it's imperative we discover the connection between these odd little elements."

Elias recalled something that'd been pricking at him since the beginning of the conversation. "You mentioned the satin fabric I found was underwear."

"The red fabric came from a seamstress known to us. She makes knickers for priests."

"I see." Elias raised his mug to take another sip of gin, only to realise that he'd somehow drunk it all. "I've never heard about fabric being explosive, but as an artificer, I don't believe in discounting anything. It's important to go through all the possibilities systematically."

"Aha! That's exactly how I approach everything." Captain Reign tapped her bottom lip with a finger. "I have, of course, already devised an ingenious plan, but for the sake of covering every possible angle, why don't you tell me what these possibilities are as *you* see them?"

"Yes, of course. That's a logical thing to do." Elias set his tankard aside and counted off on his fingers. "Firstly, from what you've told me, we know Father Bartholomew was wearing satin underwear. It would be important to verify whether Father O'Malley was too."

"Go on."

"Secondly, we know they were both wearing signet rings with the letter 'S' on them. Thirdly, there's the paper fragment with print on it that I found at St. George's, which needs investigation because it made Father O'Malley uncomfortable when I showed it to him."

"Maybe it was in his underwear. That would be uncomfortable."

"Flora!"

"Sorry!"

Captain Reign turned back to Elias. "Your conclusions align *perfectly* with mine, which is why I'm curious about *how* you'd proceed, knowing what we both—of course—already *comprehend* about the situation."

Elias muffled a burp with the back of his hand, ignoring the way Phillips tried to smack his nose. "Logically, the first step would be to check if the seamstress sold Father O'Malley knickers too. I'd also endeavour to learn the names of the other priests who frequent her business, in the event that the underwear is the explosive element."

The captain rested her chin on her palms and grinned. "It's obvious that great minds think alike. Do go on."

"I'd also consult with an alchemical expert to learn if it's possible for fabric to self-ignite."

Captain Reign slapped the desk. "Alchemical expert! That's *exactly* what I was thinking. But who would be the best expert to talk to? Being an artificer of *phenomenal* skill, I'm completely sure you may potentially be our man!"

Elias blinked. "I never apprenticed at an alchemical workshop. But I know someone who has."

"*Excellent.* And just where would we find this person, who is *most definitely* the same person I'm thinking of?"

"Since it's the day of Mistress Fenderpossum's monthly demonstration, he'll be at the Artificer's Guild Hall, but—"

"The Artificer's Guild Hall!" Captain Reign exclaimed. "Exactly the place I intend to visit after our conversation!"

"Really?"

"Yes! And if I were to talk to an alchemical expert, what to your mind would be the next step in our investigation?"

"Oh, if the underwear is explosive, then I'd turn my enquiries to the seamstress and where she got the fabric."

"And if it's not the underwear?"

"Then I'd see if there was a link with the rings. I'd go through the list of priests who wore the underwear and question them individually, showing them the rings to see if there's a reaction."

"Obviously. *Obviously*. It's clear to me that your brain is full to bursting with ingenuity, Mister Dooley!"

Elias had rarely been praised to this extent and was beginning to feel light-headed, or maybe it was the gin. The Artificer's Guild didn't encourage apprentices to think or express ideas—quite the opposite, in fact. He kept talking, his mind given free rein on the topic. "Finally, I'd verify that the paper fragment I found at the site of Father Bartholomew's explosion came from the Blessed Press. I'm not sure of the connection, but there may be one. It's all about exploring all possible links between the exploding priests and the things that may have caused them to explode."

Captain Reign beamed at him. "Possible links! That's *precisely* what I was thinking. When we have eliminated all which is impossible and inconvenient—including witnesses and adversaries—then whatever remains, however improbable, must be..." She let her words trail off expectantly.

"The truth?"

"No, Mister Dooley. What remains is the booty. Or, in this case, the culprit!" She looked over Elias's shoulder. "Flora, are you paying attention? I have a list of things I need you to do."

"I'm listening."

"Find Miss Simms and ask for a list of all the priests who've purchased her special underwear. Sid will no doubt be somewhere nearby, so take him with you to St. Smeaton's. With luck, Father Inigo will still be away shovelling up—" She paused, looking at Elias. "What was the priest's name again?"

"Father O'Malley," Elias said.

"Yes. Father O'Malley. Either way, I want you to pick the lock on the room containing the Blessed Press and search it for anything unusual."

"Like?" Flora asked.

Captain Reign tapped her mouth with her forefinger. "Good question. I certainly have the answer, but since our guest is hiring us, why don't we consult him first?"

Elias blinked. "Oh? Yes. Thank you. I'd search for anything printed that doesn't appear to come from the Book of Vengeance. The words on the paper fragment I found were 'moist', 'insert', 'luscious' and 'plump'. It may also be an idea to retrieve a sample of the paper used for the press so I can determine if it's similar to the fragment I found."

"*So* helpful! You heard him, Flora. Look for anything that resembles the writing on the walls of the Hyde Park conveniences. While you're at it, tell Sid that he needs to find a rookery urchin named Grub, last seen near St. Smeaton's. Tell him this is an embarkation day situation and that he's not to come back until he's located her." Captain Reign looked at Elias. "It's entirely relevant to this investigation, I assure you."

"Alright." Elias cleared his throat. "I know what to look for and I know St. Smeaton's. My mother used to deliver bookbinding cloth to Bloomsbury when I was a boy and we visited frequently. Maybe I should go too."

A disbelieving silence filled the room as Captain Reign and Flora gave him the kind of once-over usually reserved for a soldier presenting for a military inspection with their underpants on their head.

"Do you know how to sneak?" Captain Reign asked.

"I'm not sure. I think I could if you explained the main principles."

"In a yellow woollen coat?"

Elias looked down at Vikram's hideous cardigan. "This belongs to someone else."

"It makes him look a bit like walking sick," Flora mused. "No one would believe walking sick would want to sneak into a church."

"Be that as it may, he's too memorable in that coat. His little thingummy doesn't even like it." Alex pointed to Phillips, who was trying to push back the sleeve of the hideous cardigan with the air of a disgusted teenager carrying a pair of their sibling's used underpants.

"You might be right." The only thing that would make Vikram's cardigan publicly acceptable was a splash of gin and a match.

"Is that all, Captain?" Flora asked.

"No. Once you're finished at St. Smeaton's, go to St. Weston's in the artificer district. Sneak in and retrieve the screwdriver our esteemed client left there, and if you can, winkle out the paper that fell through the cracks." Captain Reign looked at Elias. "Could you please tell Flora exactly where the paper fell?"

Elias described the location, as Flora stared dreamily up at the ceiling. "Did you get that?" he asked finally.

"Yes. It fell in the crack at the edge of the stone for Tabitha Noop," she repeated in her sing-song tone.

"Oh, you did hear me."

"I'm always listening."

Captain Reign clapped her hands together. "You most definitely are! While you're visiting the churches, I want you to also search the rectories for anything of interest, anything hidden. You're permitted to take anything shiny as long as it won't be missed. Speaking of shiny things, I also need you to give Father Inigo tuppence on my behalf. Leave it in the collection box with this note wrapped around it." The captain scribbled something on a scrap of paper and held it out.

Flora collected it. "Aye aye, Captain!"

"Did you just give her permission to rob two rectories?" Elias asked, darting a look at Flora.

Captain Reign gave him a wide-eyed, innocent look. "Of course not! I told her to search for clues that will exonerate you, Mister Dooley. Isn't that what you're hiring us for?"

"Yes, but—"

"Which brings us to my fee." All of a sudden, the gold incisor was flashing once again as Captain Reign leapt to her feet and started pacing. "Mister Dooley. You say you've just started a new business on Utopia Street."

"Yes. I haven't got any clients yet, but I'm hoping I will soon," Elias said earnestly. "To be honest, I have a limited budget for this investigation."

She sucked her teeth. "I see... I see. You understand that I have considerable costs when it comes to an investigation like this. There are badger overheads..."

Elias blinked. "Badger overheads?"

"If you didn't notice, my establishment is literally over a badger's head and Gregor likes the rent paid on time. There's also the allowance for hack fares, priest donations, and ferret bathing."

"Ferret bathing?"

"I like baths," Flora said.

"Flora's shampoo doesn't come cheap and she does insist on strict personal hygiene, as we all do. Or do you disapprove of ferret bathing?" The captain stared at him.

Elias looked at Flora, who was grinning. "I'm sure they like bathing as much as the next man, but—"

"Speaking of the next man, there's then my bo'sun, who you'll soon meet. He also needs soap. On a volumetric basis, much more."

"Yes, but I don't—"

"Then there's pirate tax, because I'm a pirate—or I should say *privateer* tax. Standard practice for anyone in my profession. Of course, we also have to accommodate emotional wear and tear. We are dealing with extremely traumatic subject matter, you understand."

"I'm aware of that, but—"

"*But*—" She held up a finger to silence him. "I also have to consider the fact that you're a man of science."

He latched onto that. "Yes. Or more to the point, I'm an artificer versed in scientific method."

She waved a hand. "Yes, yes. An excellent one. We've established that you think in a similar way to myself. For you see, Mister Dooley, artificers are much like pirates."

Elias blinked. "We are?"

"I thought artificers make stuff and we take stuff?" Flora said.

"Yes Flora, we are indeed stuff-based professions."

Flora grinned. "Booty stuff."

"Yes! Thank you, Flora. You can go now."

"Okay!" Flora skipped from the room.

Alex continued, "Booty is a subset of stuff, don't you agree, Mister Dooley?"

"Ah... I guess?" Elias wasn't quite sure where all this was going.

"It's stuff for coin! We are siblings in the mercantile. Which brings me to my point." She placed her hands on her hips. "Mister Dooley, I have a proposition for you."

"Yes?"

"I'd like to hire you to help with this investigation. I can only pay you two pounds, but I assure you it will be money well-earned."

Elias resisted the urge to tap the trinkets on his chest to make sure they were working properly. He couldn't be *that* drunk. "You're going to pay *me* two pounds?"

"Yes. Of course, we'll have to take into account my fee for this investigation, which is four pounds."

"Four pounds," Elias repeated, swallowing loudly.

Captain Reign nodded. "I do expect payment up front, given the danger involved in this situation. We're looking for someone with the ability to explode priests, after all."

"But I don't see—"

"I'll take the money off you now, if you don't mind. You *do* have four pounds, don't you?" Her brows beetled. "After all, we've already commenced this investigation and I'd hate to think I've just sent an innocent young ferret into peril for nothing. I took you for a man of honour!"

"Yes. Of course." Elias retrieved his coin pouch, taking out four pounds and watching all but one pound of his savings clink into Captain Reign's pockets. It was an extortionate fee, but as he saw it, he didn't have a choice. Money would be useless to him if Mother Superior decided that he was murdering her priests.

"Good man! I look forward to doing business with you!" She heartily slapped him on the shoulder. "I will of course withhold payment for your services until the job is done, as is standard business practice."

"But—"

"Not now, Mister Dooley. We have work to do. You're not paying me to pay you to waste my time, so let's get on with it and we'll have this problem solved by teatime!"

CHAPTER 20

AN IMPORTANT LETTER

*H*EAR YE! HEAR YE! *There is a fracas at St. Weston's Cathedral. Witnesses report many priests arriving on the scene with buckets and shovels. Stop. There has been an accident at Canary Wharf involving an overtly aggressive Icelandic hover pony. The Neptune Guards are investigating for an infraction of the OverLondon No-Fly Zone. Stop. Ye've heard! Ye've heard! Is it a lorikeet? Is it a giant piece of industrial machinery? No. It's Lilly BigSponge's famous* Play of the Damned. *See what the fuss is about at the Frunt Theatre Drury Lane. Bring your own umbrella!*

The cry filtered through an open window as Count Mendacium tapped the fingers of his prosthetic hand on his desk. He stared blindly at a pile of invoices from his tailor, haberdasher, wigmaker, bootmaker and tobacconist. Maintaining an image as ostentatious as his was expensive, but something was telling him that he'd just been handed the key to solving all future financial difficulties.

Yet another priest had exploded, at a time and date that should have been impossible. Something had gone wrong once again, but he was no longer alarmed. The key thing was that it was going wrong *consistently*. Consistency meant room for planning. Planning meant that he could engineer the situation to his advantage.

When he'd heard of Father O'Malley's explosion, he'd gone over every step of his methodology yet again, concluding that there had been no obvious error, which meant that an unforeseen aberration had happened twice.

This left him with the conclusion that two priests had exploded in spectacular fashion, leaving no evidence that could be linked back to him. Two priests out of five, which meant there'd be another three meeting the Vengeful Queen at any time, on any day. With luck, they too would do it publicly, with a splash. It didn't matter *how* the anomalously timed and amplified explosions occurred, the key thing was to take advantage of the situation *before* the rest happened.

It was dawning on him that acting now could gain him a small fortune, more than enough to leave this city and establish himself in OverParis living the life to which he'd become accustomed.

Yes, he could see it now.

For any plan to work, he'd need to dispose of the two idiots who'd planted the substance for him, eliminating any ties to himself. It wouldn't be hard to ensure that they'd soon be as lifeless as the urchin girl buried in their cellar.

He leant back in his chair. He had knowledge, and that gave him power. Three more priests were due to go splat within the next week, and he'd soon be the only man alive that knew why.

After giving the matter further thought, he selected a sheet of parchment, picked up a quill and got to work writing a letter.

CHAPTER 21

SID HAS AN EPIPHANY

MIDDAY CROWDS THRONGED THE streets between Theatreland and Bloomsbury as Sid and Flora walked to St. Smeaton's Cathedral. The city was travelling through a patch of clear blue sky for the first time in days. True to form, Sid was sweating, while Flora had a spring in her step and her hands in her pockets.

Sid mopped at his brow with a handkerchief. "I don't like it, Flora. I don't like it at all. What you're describing is ominous. Why does the captain need this list of priests?" He raised the floral-scented sheet of parchment in his other hand as if it was a precious artifact. "Miss Simms is an upstanding, respectable woman. She served me tea in a china cup with roses on it. On a doily. Only a respectable lady would do that."

"I don't think the captain thinks she's not respectable," Flora said.

"But it's not right. Miss Simms is a repeat customer and she had to find ink and a quill, and parchment and alluring perfume to write this. That's putting a good lady to unnecessary trouble." Sid's tone was self-righteous. "What do we know about this new cove other than the self-admitted 'fact' that he's seen two priests blow up? How do we know he's not accusing Miss Simms of blowing them up to divert attention from himself? In fact, I think that's *exactly* what he's doing!"

Flora frowned. "I don't think he accused her of anything. He just suggested we ask Miss Simms for a list of her priest customers so we know who might blow up next. Or at least, that's what I think he meant." Flora could see from Sid's expression that he wasn't listening. When Sid had his mind fixed on something, it was best to ignore him and focus on much more important things, like shiny things.

They'd walked for a few minutes in silence when Sid gripped Flora's arm.

"Flora! I have it! I have deduced what this cove is doing. It's like that book by Raymond Chandelier set in the ominous streets of Llandudno, with the seagulls and the lady in the red dress! *The Large Nappe*. This bloke's a femmy fartalley!"

"A femmy fartalley?" Flora frowned.

"Of course!" Sid said, radiating self-importance. "Femmy fartalleys always turn up begging for help when the hero is in the direst moment of need. Then they use their sexual whales and their charm to lure him to his doom. And the captain is susceptible! She's always been susceptible to romantic lures."

"Sexual whales?" Flora couldn't imagine anyone wearing Elias's yellow cardigan luring anyone to do anything other than perhaps buying him another cardigan out of pity. However, she'd always liked whales. From airship height, they looked cuddly. "Are you sure you read that right?" Flora knew that it was a side-effect of the books in OverLondon being copied by hand that spelling errors often happened.

"Yes! Of course I did. I know a common sense idea when I see it and sexual whales make sense Flora! The captain was ripe for the picking after that miracle had been announced at St. George's. Inconsolable, she was, and then this Elias turns up? She's practically a femmy fartalley magnet!" Sid stopped in his tracks and gripped Flora's arm. "Flora, this cove did it. I know it. It's all going to go pear-shaped. I can feel it in my waters."

Flora studied him thoughtfully. "Are you sure that's not because you're standing in a puddle of dog piddle?"

Sid let go of her arm and hastily stepped backwards. "No! No, I'm telling you, it's always the femmy fartalley that does the crime. Did the captain ask if he did it? She should have. Because I have no doubt he did. No doubt at all. He *definitely* did it!"

Flora frowned. "But aren't femmy fartalleys supposed to be women?"

The Academic Council of OverLondon had long ago given up trying to police what its citizens did, and was all for letting people do as much as they wanted, whenever they wanted, with whoever they wanted, provided those people could be taxed. However, Flora knew Sid tended to think in a rather old-fashioned way, which was strange, since he'd spent decades working for a captain who fancied anyone who looked good in a tight pair of breeches regardless of gender, race or species.

When entering foreign seaports, the captain always filled out the question on the immigration documents about gender or sex with the word 'pirate'. Since her writing was nearly illegible, no one ever questioned it, and probably assumed she'd meant to write 'private'. Meanwhile, Sid always wrote a long paragraph about how he had neither sex nor gender because they were both indecent. Flora liked drawing pictures of flowers for her answers.

Sid gave her a pitying look. "Flora, I don't think you understand the depth of this man's nefarious scheme. On the stage, femmy fartalleys are always played by men dressed as women, and this cove is a man, playing a femmy fartalley, dressed as a man! He's an evil genius, Flora. Evil!"

Flora knew better to argue. Instead, she changed the topic. "Why *don't* women play women in the theatre, Sid? It's been centuries since the Vengeful Queen burned down all the theatre houses after Princess Elizabeth got that bad review for her performance. You'd think they'd have got over it by now and would let women back. The captain said they only made that rule so the princess wouldn't try to act again, ever."

"They no doubt worked out it was better after they stopped women acting. Everyone knows that women don't have the right artistic temperament. Women are respectable. They're like Miss Simms. Miss Simms would *never* be a femmy fartalley. She doesn't have it in her. It's the *respectability*."

"What about women who dress like me and the captain? You always say that the captain's got a right temperament, especially when a ship we're chasing gets away. Could *we* be femmy fartalleys if we dressed as women?"

Sid looked momentarily nonplussed. "Well... I don't think it works like that. You don't have the right equipment, for one thing."

"Clockbows? Because the captain's got one of those. And I've got my dagger." Flora placed her hand on the hilt of the stubby dagger tucked into her belt.

"No! no, I mean—this isn't about the stage. This is about femmy fartalleys, and this cove's got the right *equipment* to lure the captain to her doom. Whales. He's got great big sexual whales." Sid mopped at his brow again. "You mark my words, Flora. It was him alright."

"I like him," Flora said as they took advantage of a gap in traffic to cross Marlowe Street, which separated Theatreland from Bloomsbury.

"That's because you're not *worldly*. You're not old enough to know about these things. Live a few more decades and you'll be as good at judging people as me," Sid said. "I guarantee you that we'll find something at one of these churches that points to him doing it. Mark my words."

They could now see the spire of St. Smeaton's, and they quickened their pace.

Sid carefully folded Miss Simms's list and slipped it into his waistcoat pocket. "Do you know who wants us to find this Grub?"

"I'm not sure. Could be anyone. If the captain wants you to find her, she must be worth some decent coin."

"Alright. It shouldn't take long. I've never failed to find someone before dawn."

"Okay, Sid."

"Wait until I've made a distraction and then slip into the church." Sid looked around and spotted a librarian strutting down the street dressed in the traditional leather armour and spiky boots worn by all members of the Order of the Knights Libris.

The Order of the Knights Libris was an ancient and secretive society feared throughout the globe for its members' ability to decapitate a man at twenty paces with a library card and was renowned for their terrifying battle cry, "Shhhh." They were however, universally welcome in OverLondon because they loaned free books and increased literacy levels, sometimes at sword point.

This librarian's book box was strapped to her chest, ready for her to aggressively administer literature to the unsuspecting. Her dreaded overdue stamp was currently sheathed, as was her inkpad, but the threat was always there. Bloomsbury's citizens scuttled out of her way either for fear of being forcibly loaned a book or, worse, being found overdue.

Sid, however, headed directly for her.

"Cor blimey! Here's just the person I wanted to see, and I've forgotten it!"

The librarian spun around, her hand automatically grasping the hilt of her overdue stamp. "Can I help you, sirrah?"

Sid slapped his forehead. "You could have if I'd remembered my bleedin' book! Overdue, I think I am."

"Overdue, eh?" Her eyes narrowed behind her pince-nez and she opened her book box, pulling out a notebook with the Knight's Libris motto *Legit aut mori* printed on it, which Flora knew meant 'Read or Die'. "Name?"

"Sidney."

"Sidney *what?*"

"Knickers."

Flora winced. Sid had never been good at making things up on the spot and tended to stick with the last thing he'd been thinking about. The last thing, in this case, was Sadie Simms.

"Well, Sidney *Knickers*. We shall see if you are indeed *overdue*."

Sid rubbed his palms over his waistcoat. "Good. Good. Because I'd hate to think I was. It happened once and I couldn't live with myself. I mean, with that big overdue stamp on my forehead and with all those broken bones—*justifiable* broken bones, don't get me wrong—" He held up his hands. "But I wouldn't want that to happen again."

"SILENCE!"

"Yeah. Right. I'll be silent. But I'd really hate it if I was *overdue*," Sid said, louder this time, just in case anyone in the street hadn't realised that free theatre was occurring.

People nearby slowed their step. An overdue stamping was always good value, as long as it happened to someone else.

Flora waited until she was sure no one was paying attention to St. Smeaton's, then quickly slipped inside. She scanned the interior and relaxed when she saw it was empty.

The brass door to the Blessed Press shone alluringly, but she resisted it for now, slinking along the walls, checking each pew.

She crouched to inspect the smashed diorama, but moved on when she saw it was merely wood. She then picked the lock on the collection box only to find it empty. Just for fun, she relocked the box, dropped in the captain's note and a tuppence—then repicked the lock and took the coin triumphantly.

The sounds of Sid being threatened by the librarian filtered through the doors as Flora skipped across the church to unpick the door to the Blessed Press and slip inside.

The gold thread of the printing cloth immediately caught her eye, but she resisted its lure, opening the large cupboard next to it and snaffling a clean piece of parchment. Then she checked under the cupboard and found two pieces of balled up paper. Tucking them into her pockets, she finally inspected the press, making a soft "ohhh" noise as she got a good look at the print cloth.

She admired it for a while, then moved on to inspect the trays of disappointingly dull lead type before making her exit, dropping the tuppence back into collection box on her way out. She wouldn't want the captain to get in trouble.

There was no sign of Sid as she darted down the alley beside the church. It was a moment's work to pick the rectory lock and another moment to learn that Father Inigo possessed a disappointing lack of shiny things.

Leaving the rectory as she'd found it, she tucked her hands into her pockets and whistling cheerfully, started for St. Weston's in the artificer district.

CHAPTER 22

ROGUE ARTIFICERS AND WEAPONISED STATUARY

A LEX WAS IN AN *excellent* mood. She was in possession of four shiny pounds, care of her new employee whose massive brain would no doubt lead to yet *more* pounds. Yes, he appeared to be backwards in the social skills department, and his cardigan required a mercy killing, but neither of these was insurmountable.

"Where exactly are we going? I missed you telling the driver," Elias asked while their hack was held up by a gang of belligerent mimes. They'd erected an imaginary roadblock and refused to raise it until commuters paid them tuppence toll.

"Artificer district. That's where you said your alchemical expert was."

"I said that they'd be at the Artificer's Guild Hall right now, since it's the day of Mistress Fenderpossum's monthly demonstration, but I didn't intend for you—for us—to go there. I'm not so sure it's smart for me to go to the Guild Hall given my current situation."

"Why? You're an artificer. It's the Artificer's Guild Hall. What's the problem?"

"I'm afraid I'm not, technically, an artificer any more. I've..." Elias paused. "As I said, my business is now in Whitechapel."

Alex grinned at him. "Do you mean to tell me that you've gone rogue? You're a rogue artificer?" She hooted with laughter. "What did you do to have them kick you out? Kill someone? Maim someone? Embezzle?" She leant towards him conspiratorially. "If it's the latter, I may have to increase my fee."

"No, no. It's not like that. All I did was inform my former employer that I wanted to experiment with getting a trinket to power a prosthetic limb without being attached to a human."

Alex glanced at the trinket on the back of Elias's hand. It waved at her. Inasmuch as she had learnt to relate to the creatures, it seemed quite amiable.

"And your experiment wasn't successful, so they fired you?"

Elias shook his head vehemently. "No, he fired me because I wanted to do the experiment in the first place. You have to understand that artificers don't innovate, they don't *invent*. They actively discourage it. It was one of the big reasons behind the interparish war between Shadwell and Whitechapel. The Clockmaker was doing new things with clockwork and prosthetics, and the artificers were trying to stop him. As the guild sees it, the job of an artificer is to maintain the status quo and to train others to do the same. Their motto is '*Si fractum non sit, noli id reficere*'. That means if it isn't broken, don't fix it. As far as the guild—and much of the Academic Council—is concerned, the city has reached mechanical perfection and any further technological innovation would cause an imbalance which would only lead to another war."

Alex considered this. "You mean technical innovation like that time someone worked out how to fire a palladium column over a record distance and ended the OverParisian war?"

"Yes! Although the column wasn't meant to be used as a weapon. The whole thing was a misunderstanding. An enthusiastic apprentice was merely attempting to dispose of some masonry that his employer had told him to deal with."

"So he fired it into the Palace of Versailles and accidentally ended the Over-Parisian siege of OverLondon?"

"He made some calculation errors. It was meant to be harmlessly catapulted into an empty part of the English Channel, using a decommissioned ballistic device that had only been *slightly* modified."

"Hmm, I've always found it curious that the Academic Council never credited the person who launched that column."

Elias shifted uncomfortably, causing the hack to rock on its springs. "I'm sure they have their reasons."

"Hmm. Before you went rogue, were you by any chance employed by a workshop that had an excess of statuary lying about? Any... decommissioned ballistic devices?"

He cleared his throat. "I've had many interesting apprenticeships in the artificer district. One of them did craft stone carving mechanisms, but that's beside the point. The point is that—"

"You've gone rogue," Alex finished for him. "The question is, do the artificers know that yet?"

"Not yet. I still have my apprentice badge."

"Then there won't be a problem raiding the place to visit your alchemical expert friend."

"Your choice of words is worrying, and it's not going to be as easy as that. You see, these people are like me—they have *enquiring minds.*" The pained way Elias spoke the words implied it was an affliction. "But unlike me, they're still apprenticed at the guild. You must promise me that whatever you see or learn, you won't tell anyone."

"You can rely on me, Mister Dooley." Alex schooled her face into a serious expression. It all seemed so silly to her. If someone wanted to do something, why not let them do it? If they did something worthwhile, the guild could always steal the idea and then make money off it. That's what a pirate would do. Sometimes the non-pirates of the world thought in such a *limited* fashion.

They fell silent as they drove through streets packed with midday traffic, urchins, vendors and the odd loose chicken. While Elias fidgeted at her side, Alex spent the time imagining what she'd do once she got her ship back.

"Artificer's Guild," the hack driver announced in a monotone, a while later. "You owe me an extra tuppence because of the mimes. Traumatic, they were. If you'd said we were going to pass mimes, I wouldn't have taken the fare."

"You were the one who drove us past them!" Alex said.

"Aye. But if I hadn't picked you up, I wouldn't have gone that way. Seems to me that you owe me a compensatory fee."

Alex rolled her eyes. "And they call me a pirate. Pay the man, Mister Dooley." She jumped down from the carriage and strode to a pair of massive iron gates guarded by two Hammer Men.

Despite its prominence in the city, this was the first time she'd had any reason to visit the Artificer's Guild Hall. The Purple Reign's various mechanisms had been the design of the notorious Norse Boatmen, and any weapons or prosthetics she or her crew had needed had been picked up on the black market, mainly in places like the infamous shipyards of Kampong Ayer in the Sultanate of Brunei, or Singapore's treacherous floating docks. In those faraway locations, innovation rather than tradition had been the key, and she was curious to see what the Guild Hall looked like on the inside. It was, after all, one of the most famous buildings in the city.

While OverLondon was stuffed to The Edge with remarkable architecture like the Tower of OverLondon, Westminster Palace and Big Basil the Faulty Clock, the two most unique attractions for the discerning tourist were the Artificer's Guild Hall in Shadwell and the Tower of Screams in Whitechapel. While the Guild Hall was not so much one building as a sprawling Tudor-era complex with numerous high towers, workshops and astral observatories, the Tower of Screams was a decrepit granite tower whose topmost sections were almost always wreathed in cloud.

For the residents of Shadwell and Whitechapel, being proximate to these two great structures was like living near neighbours who had been arguing over a privet hedge for fifty years. There was always the worry that just one leaf growing in the wrong direction would send the whole thing pear-shaped, with pitchforks thrown in for free. The other OverLondon parishes approved of this, figuring that a cold war kept the idiots busy and away from their own metaphorical hedges. Plus, it was good for tourism.

Where the Artificer's Guild Hall was frequented by tourists keen to witness such remarkable features as the Arborrery, the Upside-Down Fountains and to peer through the great telescopes in the public observatory, no one wishing to return from their holiday entered the Tower of Screams.

Looking over her shoulder, Alex could see the Tower of Screams now, looming over Whitechapel, the stones green with moss and lichen, the narrow windows overlooking the city with the air of a malevolent creature monitoring its future victims for weakness. It was said that The Clockmaker's Room of Lost Souls was at the very top, which was why the screams could be so easily heard when he was working on his latest cogwork nightmare.

Alex could well be the one screaming if she didn't find the urchin, but she'd been in far worse situations before. It was all a matter of perspective, and her perspective was piratical. She turned her attention back to Elias who was shifting his weight from one foot to another like an urchin about to pick their first pocket.

"Do you have your badge, Mister Dooley?"

"Badge? Oh. Yes." He fumbled in his utility belt and withdrew a brass disc with a hammer on it. "This will get me in, but you'll either have to pay the tour fee or—"

"Be your guest," Alex said. "You're allowed to take guests in, aren't you?"

He blinked. "I've never done that before. I think it's a possibility, but I'll have to register you."

"Lead the way."

"That means that we'll have to go into the Hall of Patents."

"By all means."

"But it's the Hall of Patents! I've only ever been there once, on the first day of my first apprenticeship."

"There's a second time for everything, if you're lucky." Alex clapped him on the shoulder and he stumbled, arms flailing, to the amusement of the Hammer Men guards who'd been taking an interest.

Elias showed one of them his badge. "This is my guest. I'm going to sign her in."

One of the Hammer Men withdrew an official-looking notebook from his leather apron.

"Name?"

"Elias Dooley."

"Position in the guild?"

"Apprentice."

"Not in that getup you're not," the guard chortled. "Why's your uniform all black like that? That's no apprentice green."

"There, ah... there was an accident," Elias said lamely.

"I'll say. Seems to me that it's still happening." The guard looked the horrible cardigan up and down with a smirk. "Where'd you get that, then? Cat sick it up?"

"His mum knitted it," Alex said cheerfully. "I'm sure he could ask her to knit you one too if you'd like."

"That would be a cruel and unusual punishment." The guard looked sideways at his fellow Hammer Man as he tore off a sheet of paper and opened the gate. "Take this to the admissions desk in the Hall of Patents."

Alex followed Elias into the famous courtyard, coming to a halt when she first caught sight of the Arborrery. She'd seen the postcards and woodcuts in books, but seeing it in person was to experience its true grandeur.

Towering over the courtyard, the tree was a clockwork marvel, constructed of brass and copper that had tarnished to green to give its far-reaching branches the appearance of being alive. As winter still hadn't given way to spring, the branches were bare, the leaves presumably tucked away somewhere. Here and there, clockwork squirrels scampered along them, their jerky stop-motion movements making them look alive, with the exception of the broken one banging its neighbour on the head with a brass acorn, the headless one with an *Out of Service* sign and the one scampering upside down in reverse. Although, Alex had to concede these were still metaphorically lifelike to a certain sort of thinker.

"Is this your first time seeing it?" Elias asked.

"Yes. I thought you said the guild didn't like innovation."

He looked pained. "It's just a basic sculpture of an oak tree that changes with the seasons by means of simple clockwork elements, powered by a steam pump. A cogloom in a factory is far more technologically advanced."

"But is it as beautiful?"

"Some would say so. Come on. We might as well get this out of the way."

"You really do seem to have a negative outlook. Where's your sense of adventure, Mister Dooley?"

"What part of being a rogue artificer isn't adventurous?"

Alex paused at that. Maybe it was a matter of levels. While her idea of adventure was swinging from the rigging of the Purple Reign hundreds of feet up in the air, while firing her clockbow at someone trying to blow her to bits with a cogcannon, perhaps Mister Dooley saw the simple act of walking into a building as being just as daring. The lad obviously needed to get out more.

The door leading to the hall was two storeys high and operated by means of a complex mechanical apparatus that swung it open soundlessly.

"Impressive," Alex said.

"Yes, it is. The mechanism takes five artificers to maintain it every day," Elias said.

"Wouldn't it be easier to not have the mechanisms and just have one person opening and closing the door?"

Elias looked at her in horror. "You can't say that!"

"Why not?"

"Because the last person who said that loud enough for people to hear was sent home via catapult to demonstrate that sometimes the most efficient way of doing something, isn't the most ideal."

"I see." Alex shrugged. "Well, each to their own and I've always heard artificers were touchy about their instruments."

"It's a matter of scientific principle. You probably wouldn't understand. Anyway, wait here," Elias said, leaving Alex standing just inside the building's entrance.

Looking around, she was immediately struck by the massive, vaulted ceiling and the walls covered in a multitude of patents and designs, with large, easy-to-read signs above them stating the date they'd been approved. From what she could see, there were none from this century. She examined a storey-high diagram of OverLondon's plumbing and stabilization systems and was surprised by how many tunnels ran through the place. She'd heard the rumours, but seeing it was another thing.

High on the far wall was a spectacular clock with the movements of the sun and the moon mapped out on its face in brass, copper and silver.

The room was bustling with clerks wearing blue flat caps and aprons. A tour group wove between them, led by a man holding a bright yellow parasol above his head. Over the din of voices Alex could hear a continual thumping sound, like an aggressive heartbeat. Scanning the gaps in the crowd, she spotted a sprawling desk and a large wingback chair that was occupied by a man who looked like he had a twenty-a-day lemon habit. The noise of a large hammer repeatedly banging onto an anvil was coming from a huge machine at his side.

As Alex watched, various artificers approached and gave the man rolls of paper, presumably blueprints. The man examined the papers, sneered, and then placed them on the anvil for the hammer to stamp them.

"Who's he?" she asked Elias when he finally returned.

Elias shuddered. "Master Spittiful. The Head of Patents."

"What's the big loud thing next to him?"

"His automated rejectionator."

They watched as a hulking artificer was handed back his documents with the word *REJECTED* punched through the parchment. He turned and scurried from the hall, visibly in tears.

"And what's he doing?"

"Rejecting patents," Elias said with a sigh. "There's a rumour he's got an 'approved' stamp locked away somewhere, but no one's ever seen it." He handed Alex a slip of paper. "Take this. Keep it safe. I have to return it when we leave."

Alex tucked it into a pocket. "What now?"

"You follow me and don't make eye contact with anyone. The key is not to draw attention to ourselves."

"With you wearing that cardigan?" Alex snorted.

Elias frowned. "It's a funny thing, but while I was signing you in, Mistress Fearsum walked right past me without recognising me."

"Maybe she was preoccupied."

"No, you don't understand. She always notices me, usually to tell me I'm doing something wrong. She was the one who I did the apprenticeship at the ah, marble carving workshop with."

"I see. Then you'd certainly be memorable."

"Yes!" Elias plucked at the cardigan. "It's like some strange kind of reverse camouflage. Maybe that's why Vikram likes these awful things. They're so hideous that no one wants to admit that anyone would wear them voluntarily. It bears further investigation." He caught Alex's expression. "Later. Come on. Mistress Fenderpossum's demonstration will begin in fifteen minutes."

"We're going to see it?"

"In a manner of speaking."

Alex gestured to the door. "Lead the way. And if I may make a suggestion, Mister Dooley, you need to work on your strut. A strut implies you have *purpose*. No one questions someone who's strutting. It's elementary pirating. Get a swing to your arms, set your shoulders back and *strut*."

"Like this?"

Alex supressed a wince as Elias did an excellent impersonation of a man with a hedgehog down his pants. It was, however, effective, as people were noticeably trying to keep their distance.

"It'll do."

"Good. Follow me."

Elias led the way out of the building, then along a narrow passageway between the Guild House and the wall that surrounded the building, which opened onto another courtyard surrounded by a cluster of workshops and forges.

They veered to the left, down a series of much narrower passageways that took them past kitchens, stables and a massive, pungent compost heap. Behind this was a squat stone tower. From its crumbling appearance, Alex assumed it had been abandoned.

"Could you please stand back?" Elias pointed at the foothills of the compost heap. "Further. A bit further. Alright. Don't move."

He walked to the single door of the tower and applied the knocker in a complex series of raps and pauses before scuttling backwards.

Seconds later, a great pile of muck dropped from the sky in the precise spot where he'd been standing moments before.

"What in the Vengeful Lady's buttocks just happened?" Alex exclaimed.

Elias waved a hand. "It's nothing. Just a deterrent. A simple jettison lever concealed on the roof. It's safe now. Follow me and don't step on every third stair."

"Why? What will happen?"

He frowned. "I'm not sure. Percy's never told me, but I don't think it'd be pleasant. Please close the door behind you." He entered and started climbing the steps circling the interior of the tower.

Alex followed, scanning every third step for booby traps. She couldn't see any, but that only meant that if they were there, they were well hidden. Maybe she needed to talk to Elias's friend about designing something for the Purple Reign once she got it back. Preferably some kind of maiming device positioned at tax collector head-height.

She was so busy counting stairs that she bumped into Elias's back when he stopped before a door at the top.

He gestured for her to stand back as he knocked in a complex rhythm before ducking to a crouch.

Seconds later, a hatch opened and a boxing glove on a spring shot out at head height.

Elias straightened and knocked again.

The door was pulled open by a young woman wearing a green apprentice artificer's flat cap, a green apron and a pair of woolly pink socks. She was holding a steaming cup of hot chocolate and took a sip as she looked Elias up and down, pausing on the cardigan.

"Elias? I almost didn't recognise you. Come in. Percy's setting up the telescope. Who's your friend?"

Alex bowed with a flourish. "Captain Alex Reign. You may know me as the Dread Pirate Purple Reign." She was met with a blank look. Obviously yet another person who needed to get out more.

Elias cleared his throat. "Hello, Neha. We're here to ask Percy some questions. It's about chemicals with explosive properties."

Neha moved aside so they could enter a cramped, circular room also occupied by a bear of a man with a bush of ginger hair and the most horizontal beard Alex had ever seen. He was standing amongst a confusion of mechanical and technical detritus—cogs, lenses, levers, buttons and pasted-up diagrams—and was currently peering through a telescope that pointed out of the room's single narrow window.

"Hello, Percy," Elias said.

"Elias." Percy didn't look up from adjusting the telescope. "You've come the wrong month. As you well know, explosive chemicals were last month. She's doing projectiles today. Cherubs. It's already evident she's going to maim at least one of those blighters down there. She doesn't know it, but some idiot's only gone and given her a Spinning Buonarroti. The damned things ricochet. I heard one of them took out half a squadron the last time the OverPisans tried to attack OverFlorence."

"I thought Spinning Buonarrotis were a just a myth." Elias hurried over to the window and looked out. "This is not good. She's using the closed firing range!"

"What's going on?" Alex asked.

"Every month, Mistress Fenderpossum invites representatives from the Academic Council, parish heads, beadle bosses and the odd tour group to the Guild Hall and demonstrates a different foreign device or mechanism," Neha said. "I'm sure you've heard about the demonstrations on the Cry."

"I have," Alex said. "But I never gave them any thought." She looked at Elias. "I thought you said the Artificer's Guild was against change?"

"It is. The purpose of the demonstration is to show that foreign technology is inferior and that further innovation is unnecessary."

"But aren't OverFlorentine spinning cherubs one of the most lethal projectiles on the market?" Alex asked. While she'd been lucky to never have one aimed at the Purple Reign, she'd heard a lot about the damage they inflicted, mainly from OverFlorentines crowing about their military superiority.

"Yes! The evidence is insurmountable!" Percy boomed, straightening from his position at the telescope. "My prediction is that Mistress Fenderpossum will conduct this demonstration in a way that makes the cherubs seem too unpredictable for the city to adopt. Hence doing the demonstration in the confined firing range with the over-powered mangonel. Plus, you'll note that she's put herself and all the bigwigs in a bunker and has only left the tour groups standing outside. What do you think, Neha? Thirty or forty dented noggins?"

Neha joined them at the window, making a *tsk*ing sound. "Maybe more."

Alex was fascinated. "And what are you doing here? Spectating carnage? It seems poor form not to give them enough warning to at least duck."

"We observe the demonstrations impartially, record our findings and then work out how to *improve*." Neha thrust a hand into the air, index finger pointing to the ceiling. "Innovate!"

"Innovate!" Percy made the same gesture, as did Elias.

"I see," Alex said. "And have you come up with anything interesting?"

Percy scowled. "Not yet. But we intend to. For example, I'm currently looking into last month's experiment. If I can work out a way to mix both substances properly, the explosion would be truly *magnificent*." He waved at the numerous beakers and alembics on the shelves that lined the room. Many had the word *Dangerous* painted on them in red.

"The one with acid and omnicite?" Elias shook his head. "Percy, I've told you multiple times that there's no feasible way to improve on the demonstration, because for once Mistress Fenderpossum's right. Acid and omnicite do not mix, they *repel* each other. The best result you'll get is a localised ignition and a large amount of unmixed acid and omnicite sprayed all over the place, damaging property and wasting money. I suspect Mistress Fenderpossum only undertook last month's demonstration to disprove the rumour that the OverAlexandrians have developed an omnicite-based ballistic device."

Alex stared at Elias. "Are you telling me that if you mix acid and omnicite together, they explode?"

"There's *technically* an ignition," Elias said. "But it has all the force of a balloon popping. When both substances meet, they cause a small, localised exothermic reaction at the point of contact. What you're left with is a lot of acid being sprayed around. It's highly inefficient and extremely messy."

"Understatement," Percy said. "Oh, the energy density is high enough for a magnificent explosion, but the two substances repel each other too quickly to mix. Impossible to combine them, but that doesn't mean it's not *inconceivable* that there's a method we don't know about, but I wouldn't put money on it." He guffawed as he turned back to peer through the telescope, picking up a pencil and holding it poised over a sheet of lined parchment. "Here we go. She's about to launch it."

They all gathered around the window as Percy counted, "One, two, three!"

"Ohhh—ewww—aggghhhh—uggghhh," they all said collectively.

Moments later, a series of apprentices ran into the courtyard equipped with bandages and stretchers.

"Messier than I expected." Percy scrawled a series of notes. "I don't think this group will be recommending the tour to their friends any time soon, but the silly blighters signed the waiver." He looked up and, for the first time, Alex noticed the shine in his eyes. A fanatic. "I think I can definitely improve on the spin to make it even *better*. It's the hair. The OverFlorentines are obsessed with curls, but I think that if we gave the cherubs some kind of pompadour there'd be more blunt-force trauma. It'd be a truly formidable weapon!"

"Going back to the *fascinating* discussion from before," Alex said. "If omnicite and acid are useless, is there anything else that'd cause a large explosion like the one that killed the two priests recently?"

"Why are you asking?" Neha asked, sipping her hot chocolate.

Alex shrugged. "Curiosity. It's not something that happens every day."

Percy frowned. "I've already given the matter some thought, and the only effective method I can think of is an old solution."

"Yes?" Alex leant forward. Here it was.

"Black powder."

Elias and Neha immediately burst into laughter.

"What?" Alex demanded. "What's so silly about black powder?"

"Everything!" Elias wiped tears from his eyes. "Trinkets are allergic to it. If there was a significant amount of black powder anywhere in OverLondon, we'd know about it from all the people scratching like monkeys! Remember that time Patrick smuggled a grain of black powder he'd found in his grandfather's house into the forge?" They fell into laughter again. "It was the most hideously uncomfortable day of my life! No. It can't be black powder. Percy is making a joke. Humour. He used it to break the tension after the discomfort of the demonstration."

"I know what humour is," Alex said through gritted teeth. "But I don't see why this is a laughing matter. Didn't the trinkets leave the priest's bodies before the explosion?"

Elias hesitated, his smile disappearing. "Yes, they did, but they didn't cause anyone to itch. So it definitely wasn't that." He turned to Percy. "What we're looking for is something that could be impregnated into fabric."

"What kind of fabric? How much?"

"A fine satin, enough to make a pair of large knickers."

Percy frowned. "Is there an ignition source or some kind of steam device? Any evidence of a hose from a compressor pump?"

"None of the above."

"That's a knotty one. Have you considered a cogcannon? Projectiles can move very quickly, as you just saw."

"I don't think it's a feasible option given the location." Elias turned to Neha. "Has your grandfather speculated about the priest explosions? Anything that could happen in the human body to cause them to explode?" Addressing Alex, he added, "Neha's grandfather is Master Malik."

"The prosthetics artificer who developed quadrupedal movement?" Alex asked. Everyone had heard of Master Malik. He'd been an OverLondon institution for centuries.

"The same."

Neha shook her head. "He was talking about it over dinner only last night, and said there's absolutely nothing he knows of that could do it—save black powder, but again, it's completely unfeasible. This will sound terribly odd, but

I overheard him talking to Father about the potential of the explosion genuinely being some form of miracle or divine retribution."

Alex guffawed, expecting to be joined by the others, but she was met with thoughtful frowns.

"Given Ockham's Shaving Hypothesis, the most obvious answer may well be the right one," Percy said. "Not that I'm religious. But since there's no other way..." He stroked his beard. "If that was the case, imagine the possibilities. It'd have to be some form of invisible substance, probably floating in the air. If it *does* exist, would it mean we could trigger divine intervention? How would we do it? Could we create an armament, say, by piling a bunch of followers of the Church of Vengeful Acquisition into a goat cart and getting them to profane a lot? They'd have to be willing volunteers."

"I see where you're going," Neha said thoughtfully. "It'd be like some kind of holy grenade. Again, they'd have to *willingly* volunteer to go into enemy territory and profane—"

"You're not being scientific, and you're also assuming it was the Vengeful Queen that did it instead of one of the hundreds—maybe thousands—of other gods represented in this city," Elias said. "And even if it was divine intervention from the Vengeful Queen—which it *wasn't*—you're assuming it's because of profanity. It's widely accepted that Father Bartholomew exploded because of his devotion."

"True..." Percy said. "But you have to wonder, if it *was* religious devotion, how much of it would cause that big an explosion?"

"Hmm," Neha said. "The question is, how would you test if someone is truly experiencing devotion to a religious deity? And how would you measure the intensity level? This bears consideration."

It was obvious to Alex that they weren't going to get any more useful information out of this lot. Just as Percy opened his mouth to reply, she raised her voice to say, "Thank you. You've been very... interesting," and bowed.

Alex walked out the door to the backdrop of Neha and Percy starting a debate about the most repeatable experiment to measure religious fervour.

CHAPTER 23

SID POTTS FINDS HIS MAN

SID POTTS WAS EXPERIENCING a wobble in his waters. He'd never had a problem finding someone in the past, no matter what crack or crevice they'd winkled themselves into, but right now he was flummoxed, stumped and beswiggered.

He'd traipsed around Bloomsbury for hours and, as far as he could tell, the entire population of urchins in the parish had gone missing. This was not normal. Urchins were to OverLondon what fleas were to an old dog snoozing before a fireplace. They were a part of the comfortableness of the city. As Sid saw it, they were vital. Since no one questioned them crossing parish boundaries, they ran errands, sold news to the Cry, and everyone knew that various parish beadles hired them as spies. So, it seemed to him that the coves around here should be worried. After all, the only dog without fleas was a dead dog.

Sid had put this to a couple of Editors patrolling Chaucer Street, but they'd just threatened to write up an infraction for using unnecessary and alarmist adjectives.

The criers in this part of town hadn't been useful either, with Crier Frank from near St. Smeaton's proving to be a miserable bastard.

Finally, Sid had found Sweet Pete and questioned him. Pete had told him the urchins had cleared off not long after talking to the captain. Since Sid couldn't think of anything the captain could have said that would scare off a pack of urchins, he discounted that explanation. For all he knew, this was some kind of scheme Sweet Pete had cooked up to save his ice cream supply. In fact—Sid squinted his eyes at the thought—there could be something to that.

Since the criers and the Editors had proven useless, Sid trawled the local bars, but didn't have much luck questioning the locals. While they drank like fish in Bloomsbury, they were a boring lot.

Whoever heard of a pub where everyone talked about books? Books weren't for talking about. They were for *reading* with concentration, pointing a finger at every word on every line so they couldn't escape.

The Cracked Spine in Pinchpenny Alley had been promising due to its lack of reading types. Sid had just started to get friendly with a couple of odd-job men named Roddy and Keef when a Sugar Gang Lieutenant dropped by. Put off by the newcomer's posturing, Roddy and Keef had cleared off before Sid could ask more than their opinion about the weather.

This task had been proving a lot harder than finding the Purple Reign's crew members, and Sid didn't like it. It didn't sit right that one of his most dependable abilities was now failing him. Sid Potts always found his man.

Eventually, he'd ended up checking around the cheap curry and chicken houses on Bookbinder Street. But in the entire time it took him to eat a large plate of chips with Number One Chicken Curry on top, all he'd seen was a beggar attempting to sell a second-hand cup of tea, before drinking it himself.

Would you credit it? Sid thought as he ambled into Woolsey Lane, stopping briefly to browse at a penny dreadful stand and experiencing a moment of ego-bolstering pride when he realised that he'd read all the books the writer was furiously copying out with a white-knuckled hand.

Here he was, walking in a parish renowned for making all the books in OverLondon, and none of the smart blighters roaming these streets had spotted the missing urchins. It was only Sid's unique intellect that allowed him to see it.

He sampled the idea as he watched two engravers hurrying by, noting that *neither* of them looked up to see that someone more gifted in the observational department was watching their every movement.

The captain had always said that Sid's ability to put two numbers together and end up with a different result every time never ceased to astound her. Come to think of it, even that librarian had recognised that Sid had a unique way of seeing the world. After working out he wasn't overdue, she'd loaned him a book called *Thinkinge Fore Cretines*. That was one smart woman, but even *she* hadn't noticed the lack of urchins.

He pulled out his pipe, lit up and puffed, thinking the situation through. It was like the penny dreadfuls he'd read, the ones where Hercules Pirouette turned up at a village and noticed that the vicar had been murdered. Pirouette always found out who did it, because he had special observational skills from having travelled the world, just like Sid. And Sid wasn't even a foreigner to OverLondon, so he had a head start.

The crimes in the books were usually done by the butler, a jilted spinster or a femmy fartalley—

Sid choked on an inhalation of smoke.

That was it—the new cove who'd hired the captain! He'd not only blown up those priests, but he'd also kidnapped all of Bloomsbury's urchins!

But how could Sid prove it? Femmy fartalleys were tricky. The captain was already under the spell of the man's whales. That'd mean Sid would have to move tactfully. He'd have to write down all the clues, and then he'd need a library or parlour with enough chairs so that everyone could sit around and listen to him explain the cove's evil plan.

Mandatory, that stuff was, mandatory. But how was he going to find all the clues and protect the captain at the same time? Sid had no doubt she was in danger. The femmy fartalley always tried to lead the hero to his doom so she could laugh wickedly and toss her hair coquettishly. The captain was blind to all these goings on, but Sid could see it all. He saw *everything*!

He tapped out his pipe, straightened his waistcoat, set his jaw and looked ahead with purpose, which was why he failed to see the hammer being raised behind him and lowered onto his bowler hat with enough force to make a *kang* sound.

As the last mouthful of smoke puffed from his lungs, Sid Potts slumped to the cobblestones and didn't observe much more at all.

CHAPTER 24

BIG IVAN MAKES CAPTAIN REIGN AN
OFFER SHE CAN'T REFUSE

WHILE ELIAS RETURNED HER visitor slip, Alex leant against the trunk of the Arborrery and contemplated what she'd learnt from the rogue artificers.

She was convinced they were wrong about there not being an explosive substance. Their skulls were no doubt so full of brains that there wasn't any room for interesting ideas.

With pirates, nothing was impossible. Improbable, yes, but never impossible.

If Alex discounted cogcannons, she'd just been given three ways to make an explosion. These were black powder, acid combining with omnicite, and someone being blasted with a great quantity of steam. Sure, one was highly toxic to trinkets and caused people to itch horrendously, another was incapable of creating an explosion big enough, and the other required a hose to carry the steam, but if those methods existed, so could something else—she just hadn't figured out what it was yet. But she would, because she was a pirate, and pirates thought in a bendy fashion. It was all a matter of perspective.

"Are my eyes deceiving me? Am I looking at *the* Dread Pirate Purple Reign?" As the question boomed around the courtyard, a passing artificer looked over Alex's shoulder with an expression of horror before scuttling away.

Alex reached into her doublet, withdrew a cigar and lit it before turning around. It never paid to appear too eager to respond to someone yelling one's name. Particularly if it was in an OverKrakow accent. A couple of years ago, she'd had a little altercation with the OverKrakow fleet, and they had a reputation for holding a grudge.

A short, wide, wall of a man was advancing on her with the kind of arrogant strut that would bring a tear to any pirate's eye. He was flanked by two towering figures in red-and-white sequined suits.

Alex catalogued the squat man's black sequined suit, his stocky limbs, rotund torso, beady black eyes and the great whiskered brown jowls that unmistakably marked him as *homo phodopus*. It all added up to her being in the presence of one of the scariest bastards in the city.

"Big Ivan?" She blew a puff of smoke from the side of her mouth.

"Who else would it be? Of course it is." OverLondon's most notorious hamster gangster came to a stop in front of her. He grinned, showing off a wicked pair of yellow buck teeth.

There were stories about what Big Ivan was capable of doing with those teeth, and none of them were pleasant. Rumour had it that back in OverKrakow there were grown men who whimpered whenever they saw a chisel.

Luckily, Alex knew Big Ivan's type like most people knew their own mothers. The trick was to never show fear and to make a speedy exit before their mood changed.

"What the hell are you doing here?" Big Ivan boomed. "Seeing the demonstration? I didn't see you, but then again, I was too busy watching that cherub. Amazing thing, amazing. I said to the boys that it was amazing. Didn't I, boys?" he asked the two mountains flanking him.

There was a chorus of, "Yes, boss."

"I'm here for the same reason you are," Alex said.

He chortled, his jowls wobbling. "It was spectacular! Aggie Fenderpossum thinks those cherubs aren't useful to us, but I think they are. What I wouldn't give to have a couple of those guarding my sugar shipments! Especially from pirates like yourself!" Ivan's eyes reflected Alex's face back at her, clearly conveying the message that he was aware of every single time the Purple Reign had captured one of his ships. His expression said he couldn't prove anything, but he'd remembered.

Alex played along, her shudder not entirely involuntary. "Perish the thought."

Big Ivan's face cracked and he let out a great bark of laughter. "Funny! Didn't I tell you that she would be funny, boys?" He looked at the men either side of him, his smile vanishing when they didn't answer immediately.

"Yes, boss."

The smile resumed. "It's an honour to be in your presence, Reign. That job you pulled with the Academic Council? Mastery! And taking out that OverDublin merchantman last year by dropping that bedstead! I said to myself, if I ever run into the woman, I'm buying her a drink." He slapped Alex on the shoulder, and it was only her experience of standing on ship decks in high winds that ensured she kept her balance. "And there's no better time than now. Get into my rig." He indicated a red-and-white-striped carriage that resembled a boiled sweet on wheels. The six black goats harnessed to it were Transylvanian Fangoras, which were much larger than the OverLondon Grey Slump. All had red plumes attached to their bridles.

Alex took another puff of her cigar, doing a mental calculation of how much more complicated her life would get if she said no.

She gave Big Ivan her most roguish smile. "It'd be my pleasure. Give me a minute to tell my associate that I don't need him for the rest of the afternoon, and then I'm all yours."

CHAPTER 25

AN IMPORTANT VISITOR

"UGH, IT'S RETURNED. HAVE you fixed your problem, or are you still a candidate for Mother Superior's most wanted?" Vikram demanded the minute Elias returned to his shop.

Elias exorcised the hideous cardigan, placing it back on its hook. "I hired the pirate."

"And?"

"And she's investigating the matter." He strode to the privy and inspected his coat, which was drying nicely.

"And?"

"And I'm helping her do it," Elias said, although he wasn't sure what he was supposed to do next. He'd been waiting in line to hand back the visitor slip when Captain Reign had come to tell him that she'd call on him later. Before he could ask any questions, she'd sauntered off, puffing cigar smoke into the air.

"That's not reassuring."

"My job isn't to reassure you."

"It bloody well is, because if I have to, I'll be the first to pay a visit to Mother Superior and—" Vikram stopped abruptly as the bell on the shop door rang, indicating the arrival of a customer. "If you're here for a nasty little book, walk to the left. If you're here for some stupid mechanical reason, lurch to the right."

Elias hurried from the privy to greet the newcomer, then experienced a spark of genuine pleasure when he recognised the neat man in the doorway. "Mister Gripes! What are you doing here?"

"Mister Dooley." The Cry's Master of Information took off his bowler hat and performed a short bow before removing his coat and draping it over his arm. His worn but well-maintained dark-green doublet and hose, neat pencil moustache and small wire spectacles only reinforced Elias's opinion that this was the kind of man of business that he wanted to emulate. Mister Gripes conveyed that he was someone important without being ostentatious. He was calm, he was analytical and he was respected.

Mister Gripes looked around Elias's side of the shop, taking in the neat desk, the trinket aquariums and the tool racks with an approving smile. "I can see you're settling in, and in such a short amount of time too. What has it been? A matter of days. You astound me, Mister Dooley."

"Thank you, sir," Elias said with pride.

Mister Gripes turned his attention to the other side of the shop, where the wall of questionable books hid Vikram from view. "And such an interesting business to share premises with."

Vikram snorted.

"It's only temporary," Elias said swiftly.

Vikram blew a raspberry.

"I'm afraid my colleague is indisposed," Elias said. "How can I help you?"

Mister Gripes offered a rueful smile. "This is somewhat embarrassing, but I'm wondering if you can help me with my hand? I stopped by Hovepipe's Workshop after seeing the flying cherub demonstration, but I'm afraid he was unavailable. Cherub foot to the nethers after foolishly attempting to aid some tourists in the line of fire."

"You saw it?" Elias asked.

"Oh yes. I attend all of Mistress Fenderpossum's demonstrations. It's my job to keep abreast of developments. I've devoted my life to keeping the citizens of this city informed about everything that concerns them. I'm always on duty and the clock never stops. My poor secretary has a devil of a time keeping track of me," Mister Gripes said solemnly. His mouth ticked up at the corner. "Although I could happily have missed this demonstration. All I learned today was that Mistress Fenderpossum shouldn't trust her apprentices to source cherubs. I think she's set a new record for injuries."

"That's what I heard, sir," Elias said, not wanting to admit that he'd seen it. "How can I be of assistance?"

For a moment, Mister Gripes looked nonplussed, but then he recovered. "As I was saying, I dropped into Hovepipe's, but they couldn't help me. Then I recalled you saying that you can repair prosthetics when you placed your advertisement the other day. What do you think about helping me with mine?" He slid off a dark green glove to reveal a prosthetic hand that had to be over a hundred and fifty years old. It was made of age-darkened oak, and the fingers were ink-stained. The little finger had cracked at some stage and had been repaired with pine. "Think you can assist me with this old thing?"

His first client! Elias worked to maintain a calm expression. "What seems to be the problem with it?"

Mister Gripes looked at the hand ruefully. "It's the index finger. I don't know if the trinkets are getting old, but it's sticking when I try and hold a quill."

"Please, show me." Elias handed him a pencil, and noticed immediately that the index finger wasn't bending at the knuckle. "Ah. I think I know the problem. It's the second spear cog in the knuckle. The teeth must've worn down. It simply needs replacing."

Mister Gripes responded with a pleased smile. "That's *excellent* news! How long will it take to fix it?"

"Only a matter of minutes, once you take it off," Elias said confidently. "Would you like a cup of tea while I'm working?"

"No need for refreshment. Can you do the repair without me removing it?" Mister Gripes asked.

Elias realised he'd made a layman's mistake. A hand this old wouldn't have a prosthetic attachment that would allow for the hand to be removed and interchanged. Instead, it would be hooked straight into the trinkets attached to the stub of Mister Gripes's wrist.

"Of course. If you'll take a seat here—" Elias rushed to his desk and pulled out a chair, then retrieved a crate for himself. "Please put your hand on my desk." Swiftly, he found his magnifying eyepiece and located his smallest screwdriver.

"If you don't mind me asking, how did you lose your hand?" he asked as he began painstakingly unscrewing the knuckle attachment so that he could access the damaged cog.

Mister Gripes shrugged. "Much the same way as anyone who has lived as long as I have. While trinkets like these little chaps in your aquariums are excellent at keeping our plumbing working, they don't replace damaged limbs. In my case, it was a simple carriage accident." He looked at Elias questioningly. "I'm surprised you're unscathed. Don't artificers frequently lose limbs?"

"Brains," Vikram muttered.

"They do," Elias said. "Usually hands, as a matter of fact, but I've been lucky."

"And you're young. How old are you exactly, if you don't mind me asking?"

"Seventeen."

"Seventeen." Mister Gripes whistled. "Oh to be so young again. And to have achieved so much in such a short time."

A book dropped on the floor on Vikram's side of the shop.

Elias beamed with pride. "Thank you sir."

"I hope you'll have continued good fortune." Mister Gripes tapped on the aquarium containing the late Father Bartholomew's trinket. "What happened to this poor chap? I've never seen one with its carapace damaged like that."

"It belonged to Father Bartholomew from St. George's," Elias said.

Mister Gripes's eyes widened behind his spectacles. "Oh? I remember now, we quoted you. I'm terribly sorry for bringing up the memory."

"It's alright. I don't mind talking about it." Elias searched in a small box of cogs for a replacement, ignoring Vikram's mutter.

"Such an awful business. Awful—but also wondrous, seeing a miracle up close like that," Mister Gripes said swiftly.

"It was confusing." Elias leant over the hand once again, slotting in the new cog with a pair of jeweller's tweezers.

"Confusing? I guess it would've been. However, even a man as versed in mechanisms as yourself would have to admit that it was a truly *remarkable* occasion."

Elias glanced up, recognising a similar tone to the one his mother used when talking about the incident. All criers were members of the Church of Vengeful Acquisition because their leader, Loud John, had made it mandatory, but it seemed Mister Gripes was an actual believer.

"It was a unique experience," Elias said honestly.

"I said to the people in my office, there's no other explanation. It *has* to be a miracle. The Vengeful Lady is showing herself." Mister Gripes ran the index finger of his unscathed hand over his moustache. "If you don't mind, could you tell me a little about it? The miracle, I mean."

Elias continued with his work. "I'm not sure what to tell you. One minute I was sitting next to my mother, and the next minute there was a splatting sound and the odd smell of burnt... person and incense, and then there was a lot of unnecessary hysteria."

"Incense, you say?" Mister Gripes cocked his head to the side. "Such a strange thing to remember."

"It is. But it was terribly pungent and—" Elias paused. The incense! Why hadn't he considered that the explosion could have been caused by that? The altar boys had been walking directly in front of the priests, swinging their thuribles. And they had been large thuribles...

What if the thuribles had been full of something that caused a vapour detonation? It would have to be a substance unknown in OverLondon, which would explode under the right conditions. Was that possible? And if it was possible, why had the trinkets left both priests' bodies before the explosions?

Elias distinctly remembered one of the thuribles having a dent in it. That could hint at the incense being behind Father Bartholomew's explosion, but what about Father O'Malley's? Had there been incense burning at St. Weston's? Elias had a vague memory of the smell in the air, but he couldn't be sure.

"And?" Mister Gripes was looking at him expectantly. "You drifted off there."

Elias recovered himself. Now wasn't the time. "Nothing. I merely became distracted screwing in your cog. I believe that's fixed the hand." He leant back and surveyed his work. "These old ones were made to last. Some of the best Hovepipe ever made."

The comment earned him a satisfied smile. "That's what I say. Why replace something merely because it looks old? Good workmanship is good workmanship." Mister Gripes formed a fist and the finger moved smoothly. "Ah, this is excellent work. How much do I owe you?"

"No charge, but I would appreciate it if you could tell anyone you know about me."

"No, no, I insist. A man of business must always charge for his services." Then Mister Gripes paused. "I'll make you a deal. Why don't we run your advertisement on the Cry for an additional week? Would that be sufficient payment?"

"That would be wonderful, sir."

Moments later, Elias stood at the door, watching Mister Gripes cross the road, the worry of the morning evaporating. His first client! An important client that he could tell his mother about!

There was another snort from behind him.

He turned to find Vikram standing before the stove, warming his fingers while giving Elias a disdainful look. "Idiot."

"Why? What do you mean?"

"You have a bigwig from the Cry come in and you fix his hand for *free*? You should've charged him extra for spraying religious dogma around this sacred secular space!"

"He might bring further business, or repeat business," Elias said defensively.

"Mark my words, you give it away for free, they'll expect it for free forever. I know that type. Give them an inch and they'll demand a banana, then a fruit basket and before you know it, you've got a cumquat deficit. You'll get nothing from him."

Elias looked through the window, following Mister Gripes's progress along Utopia Street, admiring the confident way he navigated the traffic. One day he would be a respected man too, able to walk the streets with such self-assurance.

"We'll see about that."

CHAPTER 26

THE MORTALITYE POOLE

E VERY PARISH IN OVERLONDON has a pub. There are multiple pubs in
every parish, of course, but usually only one *pub*. It doesn't have to be the
oldest pub, or even the most notorious, but it's the pub that acts like a magnet,
attracting anyone who's anyone.

If you spend enough time in Theatreland, you will gravitate towards The
Armoury. If you're in the Docklands, you will gravitate towards the Affectionate
Squid. If you're in Westminster, you'd end up in the Henry the Late.

This venerable establishment is located in a small alleyway, not far from
Westminster Abbey, and is marked by a sign featuring Henry VIII's severed
head, which manages to look simultaneously surprised and disgruntled about
its fate.

Inside, you'll find a large, open space with proper chairs and tables. The sawdust on the floor is replaced every day, and the ale and gin on tap is never watered
down. The barman, Mister Loom, is a former accountant who's worked out
that drunk men are a much better source of money than sober. He's a neat
man rumoured to be the by-product of an abacus breeding with a human. He's
also an excellent listener. The reason for this is related to the large blackboard
above the shelves of bottles. There are names written there, along with odds,
but we'll learn about those in a moment, because Captain Reign and Big Ivan
have entered the premises.

W HEN ALEX WALKED INTO the Henry the Late in Big Ivan's wake she knew immediately this wasn't her kind of pub. It was far too orderly and had obviously been designed to emulate a watering hole for the common man, while—importantly—being pretentious enough to dissuade that same man from tarrying too long.

Rather than following Big Ivan and his henchmen across the room, she paused in the doorway and blew a smoke ring as she catalogued the exits. Any pirate with a career as long and varied as hers knew better than to simply walk into an unfamiliar place.

The pub was sparsely populated, but that could be explained by it being New Lent and by the proximity of the pub to the headquarters of the Church of Vengeful Acquisition. Half of the patrons were dressed in forest-green crier uniforms, complete with the medals that denoted their status. Alex had always found it interesting that the Cry had long ago worked out that awarding medals was as effective in managing its employees as paying them. She'd always thought the whole thing was downright piratical, and not in a good way. The Cry didn't follow the Pirate's Code, which mandated that crew was king. A pirate without a loyal crew was a pirate without a ship.

The Cry's medal system was one that Alex's former first mate, Mister Lemons, had always said he liked.

The rest of the pub's occupants consisted of a table of MPs (Masters of Pugilism), from the Academic Council, exhibiting all the cuts and bruises of a recent debate, a couple more Sugar Gang lieutenants and a man with a long, cavernous face and bushy, silver eyebrows who was wearing a dark green bowler hat, doublet and hose. He was sitting alone at a long, scarred table.

Big Ivan made a beeline for the man in the bowler hat, his stubby arms flung out. "My dear friend John, I have a present for you!"

The man looked up, his expression dour. "What now, Ivan? And before you start, I don't want to hear about the demonstration. I got acid all over my coat last time and I told you I'm never going to attend another one again. I'm only here at my usual time because a man has to eat." His voice sounded like someone had taken sandpaper to his vocal cords.

"I've brought none other than the Dread Pirate Purple Reign!" Ivan chortled with a level of glee that told Alex there was more afoot than him wanting to buy her a drink.

"Oh?" The man looked Alex up and down, his lip curled. "That's nice, Ivan. Very nice. And breathing too, I see."

"Never say I'm not a good friend." Ivan turned to Alex, who by this time had strutted across the room. "What'll you have, Reign?"

"Gin." She puffed a stream of cigar smoke out the corner of her mouth. "Whatever sort is going."

"Gin it is!" Ivan looked sharply at a nearby lieutenant. "Get the woman a gin. I'll have a carrot botanical and John will have a glass of water because he's a miserable bastard and New Lent isn't over yet."

"Yes, boss. Whatever you say, boss," The Sugar Gang heavy tripped over her own feet hurrying to get to the bar.

"You're paying for that water. I didn't ask for it, so I'm not paying for it," the man muttered, before turning to Alex. "I won't say it's a pleasure to meet you. The fact that you're still breathing cost me twenty pounds, I'll have you know."

"I don't follow you." Alex straddled a chair. It was obvious she wasn't going to get out of whatever was going on here, so she may as well be comfortable.

"The mortalitye poole, woman! I had twenty pounds on the Academic Council hanging you, and what did they do? Gave you a bloody letter of marque!"

"That they did! You should have seen him, Reign. He was inconsolable!" Ivan boomed as one of his men placed two chairs together for him to sit on. It wasn't that he was fat so much as tremendously wide. Like all hamsters, the width increased the more comfortable he got. "I said I owed you a drink, and here it is," he announced as his lieutenant brought over a tray of drinks before hastily retreating to lurk at the bar.

"And you are?" Alex asked the man in the bowler hat.

"Loud John, Herald of the Criers. As if you didn't already know." Loud John's tone reminded Alex of the croak of a disgruntled vulture circling a disappointing carcass.

That explained the voice. Alex had never met the Cry's boss before, but everyone knew of his legend. Loud John had once been the loudest crier the city had ever known. It was said that in his prime, his Cry had stunned the trinkets off bodies, concussed goats and caused buildings to crumble. That had all changed during the early days of the OverParisian War. Loud John had taken on the role of hub crier in Westminster, but the updates had been so frequent that his vocal cords had been irreparably damaged.

When she'd first heard about it, Alex had felt sorry for him, but then the rumour started circulating about his rise to the top having been aided by undercover string-pulling by powerful city leaders—namely Cardinal Chudleigh—which was confirmed by Loud John's decree that every crier in the city had to donate forty percent of their yearly earnings to the Church for New Lent or be fired. Nowadays, people rarely spoke of the man without calling him a miserable git. Having now met him in person, Alex was inclined to agree.

"What's this mortalitye poole, then?" she asked casually.

Big Ivan turned to Alex, his chairs creaking ominously, his eyes shining with glee. "You never heard of it, Reign?"

"Enlighten me."

"As with the many fine traditions of your country, it goes back to the time Queen Anne put Henry VIII in the Tower. This place was called the Sniffling Stoat back then, and the barman started a bet on how she'd do him in."

"Beheading, drowning or screaming him to death," Loud John muttered.

"Bets were placed, and after it was all over, with old Henry's head on a spike, the barman realised he'd made a tidy profit and the mortalitye poole was started. Although nowadays the bets are on *who* is going to kill someone, not *how*, because it makes it more interesting. My good friend, Mister Loom here, manages the odds." Ivan gestured grandly to the barman who was idly cleaning a glass, giving the impression that he was both uninterested in the conversation and yet listening intently at the same time.

"But with respect to your trial, Mister Loom decided to resurrect the original terms, and we placed bets on how the Academic Council would kill you," Loud John muttered.

"Wonderful," Alex said dryly. "And the odds were?"

"Not important! All you need to know is that John bet on you hanging and he lost a pretty penny," Ivan chortled.

Alex studied the board. "If this mortalitye poole is over, why's my name still there?"

"New poole!" Big Ivan slapped the table, causing their drinks to slosh over the sides. "Mister Loom set it up the minute he heard about this private ear business of yours. You're a safe bet to be done in by someone soon. The Academic Council named you a privateer for the whole city, but that doesn't mean anyone likes it. Take it from me. My gang crosses parish boundaries and it pays to have protection, doesn't it, boys?" Big Ivan looked over his shoulder at the various Sugar Gang members in the premises.

They chorused, "Yes, boss."

Alex noticed that Loud John's odds of killing her were one to two, followed by The Clockmaker at three to two, followed by the words *Blacke Hak Driver* and the odds three to one. Judging by the smudged chalk, the latter odds had been recently changed, which *could* have something to do with all the times she'd threatened hack drivers with her clockbow lately.

She looked at Loud John. "You've got top odds on killing me?"

"Of course!" Big Ivan said. "It makes sense, given how much of a scene he made when you failed to die. Personally, I'm happy you're alive. The look on John's face when you got that pardon? Priceless."

"You're a prince, Ivan," Loud John said.

"Among men!" Big Ivan chugged his carrot botanical, which Alex suspected was simply straight gin with a carrot for garnish.

"I don't know whether or not to be offended or complimented," she said.

"Complimented. All eyes are on you!"

Alex looked at the board again. "Alright, alright. Is it just me? No, I see you've got Cardinal Chudleigh up there."

"There's a poole on Chudders every New Lent, although he doesn't like it," Ivan said. "The man takes forty percent of his congregation's money every year. One of these years someone'll make him disappear. Although not John." He winked at Alex. "Wouldn't buy you a drink if you were dying of thirst, but he gives the Church a pretty purse every year. Anyone would think he's worried about the afterlife." He chuckled at Loud John's snort of disgust.

Alex continued reading the names on the board. There were a few she didn't recognize, and then the word *Priests*.

"You're betting on who killed the priests?" she asked.

"Of course."

Alex looked at the names written beneath. "Mother Superior, three to one, Cardinal Chudleigh, five to two." She looked at Big Ivan. "Wouldn't they be the last people you'd suspect?"

"It makes perfect sense!"

"To you. I believe the leaders of our Vengeful Lady's congregation are above reproach," Loud John said.

Big Ivan ignored him. "Think of all the times the Church of Vengeful Acquisition has been mentioned in the Cry. With all the other competing religions in this city, it's good for business. It would make sense," he said. "And then there's internal Church politics. It's Chudleigh's chance to nominate replacements who side with him—word on the street is that Bartholomew and O'Malley were Mother Superior's men. Then there's the wealth a new saint will bring to the relic market. Since Cardinal O'Connery announced the miracle, Mother Superior's been hoarding relics like gold bars." He snorted. "They're even more valuable than gold bars, so why stop at just one priest? Chudleigh has the same motivation. Makes sense they're on the board."

Alex filed away this information and kept reading. "The Hare Krishnas, sixteen to one. Big Ivan, four to one." She raised an eyebrow.

Big Ivan waved a hand. "I had what you may call a mild altercation with the Church a while ago, over their refusal to classify my ice cream as fish during New Lent. Profits drop dramatically at this time of the year. No reason for it. Ice cream is cold and slimy, fish is cold and slimy. Same thing, as far as I'm concerned, but with better flavour."

"I see." Alex didn't, but arguing with Big Ivan didn't seem wise. "'No more bets on divine retribution from the Vengeful Queen'," she read, then looked at Big Ivan and Loud John. "Why?"

"Mister Loom thinks it's too likely that she did it, and it's bad business for him," Ivan said. "So does my friend John. How much did you try to put on it? Ten pounds to be paid when the second priest gets declared a miracle?"

"Of course it was the Vengeful Queen," Loud John said. "I told you, Ivan, the Vengeful Queen works in mysterious ways, and exploding priests is the very definition of mysterious. It was a glorious ascension to Vengeful Heaven, and may we all be so lucky."

"Mister Jim of the Mysterious Pies, eight to one," Alex read.

"Bad curry fish pie. That's my bet," Ivan said. "I've got inside intel."

"Oh?" Alex asked.

"Father O'Malley was heard complaining about one of Jim's pies by one of my people a year ago."

"And you think it took a year for him to explode?"

"Ever eaten one of Jim's pies, Reign? They sneak up on you. It probably followed him home and waited for its chance to strike."

"How could a curry fish pie explode someone?" Alex asked.

"How can a mad queen who's been dead for centuries?" Big Ivan countered.

"You won't be so smug when you're burning in the fires of eternal damnation and I'm living in my luxury penthouse in Vengeful Heaven." Loud John glowered at Big Ivan before turning to Alex. "You haven't offended anyone else lately, have you, Reign? I could do with recouping my funds and due to an annoying technicality, I can't bet on myself for releasing you from the mortal coil."

"Everyone and no one." Alex tapped her cigar into an ashtray shaped like Henry VIII's severed head. She looked at Big Ivan. "I've always wanted to know, what *do* you do when you give people the carrot?"

Big Ivan's razor-sharp teeth glowed yellow in the lamplight. "We put them in an ice barge with a carrot and an ice cream churn, and send them up to where the air is freezing."

"And?" Alex asked.

He looked at her innocently. "How else do you think we get our ice cream?"

"And the carrot?" she asked.

Big Ivan's shiny black eyes blinked innocently. "Why, to stir the ice cream."

"Sounds a bit inefficient. Doesn't it get all bendy?"

"That high up? Nothing stays bendy for long." He chuckled in a way that wasn't entirely pleasant.

"Ah." Alex formed a mental picture and shuddered. She quaffed the last of her gin. "Thanks for the drink. It's been a delight to meet you gentlemen, but I really must go. I have ears to be private with." She stood and bowed.

"Someone's hired you? Who?" Big Ivan asked.

"Client confidentiality is my middle name," Alex announced.

"I see." Loud John croaked sourly. "I'll be watching your career with interest, Former Dread Pirate Purple Client Confidentiality Reign."

After glancing at the mortalitye poole one last time, Alex left.

CHAPTER 27

FLORA MAKES A SMUG DISCOVERY

A s a rule, Flora enjoyed sneaking, but lurking in St. Weston's was proving to be a fruitless exercise.

She'd made the mistake of stopping by Hamish Leek's shop beforehand and had lost track of time admiring his window display. By the time she'd finally arrived at the church there were far too many priests inside, trying to shovel bits of the late Father O'Malley into buckets. Where there weren't priests, there were Bad Habits hitting priests.

Flora had been excited to see the Bad Habits at first. She'd hoped to meet Sister Barry again, but the nun was nowhere in sight, which was a pity.

The only people in the church who weren't trying to get a relic, or stopping someone else from getting one, were the three priests huddled together near the confessional booth where Flora was now hiding.

One of the three—a thin man with a torturously worry-lined face—was sobbing into a handkerchief. A tall, stooped priest with a pinched face was scowling and telling him not to be foolish. The third of the trio was a much younger, sweaty priest who had the kind of face Flora associated with the boys who used to throw rocks at her and call her names. For some reason, he kept demanding they search for something, but the stooped priest continually hushed him.

Since their conversation wasn't about shiny things, she darted out a hand and picked the sobbing priest's pocket out of boredom, finding a pocket watch and a cloth pouch.

Feeling sorry for the man, she immediately returned the watch, but kept the pouch. She'd give it back later. Maybe she'd use it as an excuse to find Sister Barry. She could always say she'd found it in the street.

Right now, she had to decide what to do. She'd found Elias's screwdriver, which had been dumped amongst a pile of things that she'd overheard a priest declare were *definitely* not relics, but the piece of paper Elias had dropped was proving trickier. She couldn't see a way to pry it out from between the flagstones without being spotted.

Flora decided that her best option was to come back later. The captain would understand. After all, one of her favourite lectures was about strategic retreat, which was usually delivered while the Purple Reign was retreating at high speed, often while on fire.

Peering out of the confessional box, Flora picked up a wooden bead someone had dropped on the floor. Waiting until the right moment, she threw it at a passing Bad Habit. It hit the nun on the ear and she rounded on the three priests, brandishing her cane.

The men scurried away and Flora used the opportunity to slink from the booth and out of the church.

The design of St. Weston's was similar to St. Smeaton's, so it wasn't hard to find the rectory. Unfortunately, the doorway was blocked by a crying woman in an apron who was being comforted by another woman in an artificer's uniform.

Sticking her hands in her pockets, Flora sauntered by, to the rear part of the rectory. There, she found an open window leading to the rectory's kitchen. It was the work of seconds to winkle herself through, and once inside she jumped to her feet immediately.

In the tradition of all thieves everywhere, she immediately checked the icebox, but was disappointed when she only found a depressed-looking fish and a large jar labelled *Haemoroyde Ungente*. Flora wasn't sure what a haemoroyde was, but she figured it was probably some kind of cow, because the substance in the jar smelled like butter.

Making sure the women outside were still occupied, she hurriedly searched the other rooms, ending her investigation in a room furnished with a single desk, a chair with a wonky leg and a wardrobe containing a single priest's cassock.

She studied the room with her hands on her hips. There *had* to be something more. Even Father Inigo had pink satin underwear hidden under his mattress. But here, there was nothing. There had to be—

Yes!

Her eyes lit on an irregularity on the desk's surface.

She smoothed her hands over the wood, searching for a button or lever, and found one in the guise of a nail that hadn't been properly hammered in.

She pressed it, and heard a click, then a rectangular section popped up, revealing a concealed compartment. Reaching inside, she pulled out a roughly bound pamphlet and a cloth bag which contained brown sugar, if the writing on the side was correct.

She snaffled both on the principle that hidden meant important, and had just closed the secret compartment when she heard a man telling the housekeeper that he required some unguent for his haemorrhoids.

Footsteps sounded, getting closer.

Knowing she had only seconds to escape, Flora searched for a way out. The window was bolted and if she opened the wardrobe, the door would squeak. Her only option was to hide behind the door.

A mere heartbeat after she'd flattened herself against the wall, the door was pushed open with enough force to smash the wood into her nose. Eyes watering, she held her breath, recognising the click of the secret compartment opening, followed by a scrabbling sound.

"Where in the Vengeful Lady's moustache did he put it?" a man's voice muttered. "He said he always kept it here."

Daring to peek around the door, Flora recognised the sweaty young priest from the church. He glared at the empty compartment with his hands on his hips before spinning around and looking at the wardrobe.

"Aha!" His frown changed to a crafty grin. He darted over and wrenched the wardrobe door open.

Knowing that he'd see her if he looked sideways, Flora tried to make herself as small as possible.

The man uttered a curse when all he found inside was the priest's cassock. Pulling it out and throwing it to the ground, he glared at the wardrobe. "Where could it *be*?" Flora heard hollow sounds as he knocked on the interior, searching for another secret compartment.

He stepped back and looked up. "On top!" He collected the chair from behind the desk and stood on it, stretching to run his hand over the top of the wardrobe.

Flora could hear breathless huffing noises and could see dark sweat stains under his arms. Her nose twitched with the smell of the strong cologne that he'd used to cover up his body odour, but which only served to make it worse.

Unable to reach far enough, he jumped up with a grunt, causing the chair to skitter backwards. He was left hanging, with his hands gripping the top of the wardrobe, his feet flailing for purchase.

With his cheek now mashed against the wardrobe, he was looking directly at Flora in her hiding spot.

"Who are *you*?" he demanded.

"No one," Flora squeaked. This close, his red face looked like every one of the boys who'd beaten her up when she'd been small. She knew she should run—she was fast, and he didn't look fit enough to catch her—but her feet wouldn't move. She started to shake. The hair all over her body stood on end.

Primitive instincts taking over, she tried to squeeze herself further behind the door. If she could just make herself invisible, she'd be alright.

The priest's legs flailed at the air until his foot finally found the chair again. "You're bloody well some*one*. What are you doing here? Have *you* got it? You're a ferret, aren't you? A ferret *thief*. Give me back my pamphlet, you *dirty* ferret thief," he snarled with a malevolence that Flora recognised all too well.

She willed herself to run, but all she could do is look into his eyes and feel small. This was going to be bad. It was going to be very bad.

"I'm not dirty." The words left Flora's mouth just as the priest let go of the wardrobe to step down from the chair.

He didn't count on the wobbly leg. As the chair pitched sideways and he started to fall, the spell holding Flora immobile broke. She burst into action.

Just before she could get past the priest, he hit the floor.

Flora caught the look of surprise on his face before hearing a great wet glugging sound.

Then there was priest splattered all over the room.

CHAPTER 28

A DIVINE VISITATION

A LEX HAD JUST RETURNED to The Reign Agency when the Cry echoed down Drury Lane. Cocking her ear for any news useful to her current cause, she took the tiny figurine of the Vengeful Queen that she'd snaffled from St. Smeaton's out of her pocket and set it on her desk. It promptly fell over due to the lint-covered glob of dried glue stuck to its base.

Hear ye! Hear ye! The investigation into the priest explosion at St. Weston's Cathedral is ongoing. Stop. The Icelandic hover pony that caused the fracas at the docklands and stunned six passing seagulls earlier today has been claimed by Lady Widdershins Napkin. Its name is Fluffy Napkin Snookie Blanket IX. Stop. Ye've heard! Ye've heard! Do you have a small mechanical difficulty? Do your parts not work as well as they should? Visit Ingenious Mechanisms in Whitechapel, next to the Happy Times Bookshop. All parts welcome, small and large!

Alex considered the wording of Elias's advertisement as she took a seat behind her desk and put her feet up. The lad was certainly unique.

She picked up the rumpled pile of wanted posters she'd peeled off the walls of the Hyde Park conveniences and rifled through them. Even at a glance she could see that Flora had collected the cream of the crop during her earlier foray.

As she lowered her goggles and studied the poster on top of the pile, the stairs creaked with heavy footsteps.

"You know Sid, I'm beginning to wonder at our wisdom in thinking we could find someone called—" She turned the poster sideways, then back again. "Sam Mother Fearing Jacksun. Who calls themselves Mother Fearing? And while I'm at it, who holds up an airship with a bag of live cobras? Ridiculous! Anyway, what took you so long?"

She lowered the poster and saw the nun.

She was big—hulking would be a much better term—with a chin of healthy black stubble and a brow that would make a gorilla envious.

Alex added all this up, along with the red wimple, and came to a conclusion.

"Sister Barry, I presume?" She swiftly removed her goggles and stood up.

The nun responded with a smile that showed a lot of gaps where teeth should be. "Dat's right. Where's da cabin boy from da church? I liked her. She smiled at me." Sister Barry scanned the room with the air of someone expecting Flora to jump out of the stove, or from behind Sid's shelf of penny dreadfuls.

"Flora? She's doing a little job for me. Can I help you?"

"Yeah."

Alex waited, until it was obvious that no more information was forthcoming. "*How* can I help you?"

The nun's brow was a tilled field of furrows for a painful five seconds before it smoothed. "Mother Superior wants to see you, an' you can't tell no one."

"Mother Superior?" Alex's pirate senses tingled at the prospect of a high-stakes encounter. A visit from the head arse kicker of the Church of Vengeful Acquisition was never a good thing.

"Yeah."

"When?"

"Now. An' you can't tell no one or you'll get der kitten treatment."

"Yes, I think you've made that clear." Alex considered the situation, debated whether she could make a quick escape, and decided that, like Sid, she preferred her insides firmly inside her body. Besides, it had been hours since she'd had some excitement in her life. She set her shoulders back. "Alright, take me to her."

"No."

"Why?"

"'Cos she's here."

"She's here?" Alex looked around. "Where?"

"Here, Captain Reign." The words were a sultry purr. A slim figure draped in a hooded black cloak sauntered through the doorway.

Mother Superior placed a hand on Sister Barry's hefty shoulder. Alex noted the inch-long, blood-red fingernails. "You can go now, Sister. Wait at the bottom of the stairs and make sure no one interrupts our little... tête-à-tête."

"Okay." The nun lumbered away. Alex and Mother Superior stayed right where they were until the sound of footsteps on the stairs receded.

Alex bowed with a flourish. "Mother Superior, it's a pleasure to be in your presence. To what do I owe the honour of this visit?"

The other woman lowered the hood of her cloak, revealing a face that was all cheekbones, tawny brown skin and green eyes sharp enough to cut you open and steal your heart without leaving a scar. Her hair was covered in a turban that matched her crimson nails. "It seems I need your help, Captain Reign. I'm *desperate*."

Alex grinned in a way she knew flashed her gold tooth. She'd heard rumours about this woman, but being the focus of so much charisma was like being melted by a sexy blowtorch.

"As I'm sure you've heard, I never abandon a damsel in distress. Why don't I take your cloak? Then you can take a seat and tell me what the problem is."

"How gallant. Could you hold Pippin?" Mother Superior retrieved a ball of fur from a pocket and handed it to Alex. It blinked and meowed before sinking its teeth into Alex's thumb. Its jaw strength would make a mousetrap proud.

The kitten was by far the ugliest creature Alex had ever seen. It had patchy ginger fur, the underbite of a miniature bulldog, stubby ears and a single boggle eye that was five sizes too big for its face. The space where the other eye had once been was covered in a small black eyepatch, much like the one worn by Slasher Harry's Daphne.

"Cute cat." Alex subtly tried to save herself from losing her thumb as Mother Superior took the cloak off, revealing a shimmering red dress. It wasn't a pair of breeches, but in this case, Alex's libido was willing to make an exception.

Mother Superior held out the cloak with a knowing smile. "Can I have my kitty back?"

"Of course." Alex handed Pippin back. He resisted for a moment, obviously wanting to take her thumb with him, then detached, dropping into Mother Superior's hand with a watery purr. Mother Superior cradled him in the crook of her arm before slinking over to the tattered velvet armchair. She took a seat, crossing her legs and revealing that the dress had a slit that went right up to her hip.

Alex enjoyed the view before hanging up the cloak and returning to lean against her desk. "I wasn't expecting you. If I knew you were coming, I'd have arranged for a more suitable welcome."

Mother Superior shrugged. "No one expects the Bad Habits, Captain Reign. It's one of the two things we're famous for." Mother Superior stroked the kitten and looked around. "Interesting. You're now calling yourself a private ear?"

"Yes. I like to think a good pirate is an alive pirate because they've got keen hearing and keep secrets *very* private." Alex resisted the urge to wink. It was one thing to fancy a lethal beautiful creature, it was another to commit suicide by being too familiar.

Mother Superior nodded. "I trust that whatever your ears hear in the next few minutes will be kept *very* private. Because I warn you that if you tell anyone of my visit..." Pippin made a high-pitched growling noise.

"I get a pat?" Alex asked.

"After a fashion. Let's call it excessively heavy patting, with prejudice."

Alex raised an eyebrow. "Prejudice?"

Mother Superior waved a hand languidly. "Sister Prejudice joined our order recently. From what I'm told, she's working through some very deep and... disturbing anger issues."

"I see." Alex shrugged. "In that case, I can assure you that whatever you tell me will be kept highly confidential."

"*Wonderful*," Mother Superior purred. "Captain Reign, I'm here to hire you."

Alex frowned, caught off guard. "Hire me?"

"Yes. I need you to solve a little problem for me. It's about two unfortunate priests."

"The ones that exploded?"

"Exactly. I knew you would understand immediately."

"I thought that they were both miracles—I mean—I thought that they were blessed by the Vengeful Queen."

Mother Superior shrugged. "Of course they were, after a fashion. After all, *everything* is the work of our most vengeful of queens. But what I need to know is *who* she's working through, if you get my meaning."

"I do get your meaning, most clearly. She's the most mysterious of vengeful deities," Alex said smoothly, then paused deliberately. "Is there a reason you need me to find who did it—ah, the vessel of the Vengeful Queen's miraculous works?" she corrected herself quickly.

Mother Superior reached into her cleavage and withdrew a piece of folded parchment. "Take this."

Alex took the paper. Although she wasn't wearing her goggles, she could see clearly enough to understand the contents. "Is this a blackmail letter?"

"Yes." Sharpness crept into Mother Superior's tone. "As you'll see, they're demanding this year's New Lent takings or they'll explode Father Chudleigh in five days, at the Festival of the Queen's Ascension. They've said that they'll explode more priests if the Bad Habits try to trace them."

Alex whistled, turning the note over to study the back, finding it blank. "This was all?"

"Yes, Captain Reign. That was all."

"When did it arrive?"

"Two hours ago. It was delivered by an urchin, who we detained, but he couldn't tell us anything other than that he'd been given it by a man with a foreign accent."

Alex looked into those green, green eyes. "And where did that urchin pick the letter up?"

"Westminster, the alleyway behind the Henry the Late."

Alex thought back to the mortalitye poole, and the names that had been on it. OverLondon was full of foreigners. It was famous for it. Big Ivan was one of them. But how would he have done it, and why?

"The urchin couldn't tell you any more?"

Mother Superior's lips formed a displeased moue. "Unfortunately, no. My people have searched the area and have asked questions. Discrete questions, of course."

"Of course." Everyone in OverLondon knew that when it came to the Bad Habits, 'discrete' meant that they gagged you before they caned you.

"But then Sister Barry mentioned that she'd met your cabin boy at St. George's after Father Bartholomew's glorious ascension to the afterlife. And I wondered to myself, why is a pirate like you taking an interest?" An eyebrow arched questioningly.

"We were in the area seeing an old friend of mine," Alex said, feeling like she was engaged in one of the better types of air battle with a worthy opponent. "An old sky dog named Slasher Harry. He's now a flower seller who works in the area."

"Harry?" Mother Superior repeated with a faint smile. "How is the old rogue? And Daphne? I don't enjoy dogs as a rule, but I have a special soft spot for her. Something about the temperament." She scratched Pippin under the chin. The kitten dribbled with happiness.

"You know Harry?" Alex asked, genuinely surprised.

Mother Superior laughed. If Alex had to describe the sound, she'd lean towards words like 'velvety', 'syrupy' or 'the noise you hear just before you die happily'. "*Everyone* knows Harry. Let's just say we're *old* acquaintances. But that's not important. What *is* important is that I'd like you to find whoever sent that note. Can you do that, Captain Reign? The payment will be fifty pounds on delivery of the individual. Alive, preferably."

Alex spent a few seconds trying to unswallow her tongue. Fifty pounds was a fortune. Fifty pounds would be enough to pay off her tax debt with change left over. Fifty pounds would see her back in the skies, never to be caught again.

"I'll have to consider it. We are *exceptionally* busy," she said.

"Too busy for me?"

Alex paused long enough to feel the tension build deliciously, then smiled slowly. "I'll make the exception. But I have a question."

"Ask away, Captain."

"What if I don't catch them?"

Mother Superior looked knowingly at Alex as Pippin swiped at the air in her direction.

"I see. And if I refuse?"

Pippin snarled.

"In that case, I would be honoured to take this assignment," Alex said. "Do you mind if I keep this letter? I have a colleague who may be able to help me uncover its secrets."

Mother Superior shook her head. "I don't think it's intelligent to leave any evidence of our association, do you? I'd be *most* upset if anyone were to suggest that my Bad Habits couldn't resolve an issue for me. As far as the denizens of The Armoury are concerned, I'm currently threatening you for some unrelated matter, so please look suitably penitent when you next venture downstairs." She stood up and held out her hand until Alex handed back the blackmail letter. "I expect a conclusion to this matter by tomorrow evening, or Sister Barry will be paying you another visit."

Alex collected Mother Superior's cloak, draping it around her shoulders. "May I say that's a unique hair shirt you're wearing, milady." She knew the words were impertinent, but given the way the Church of Vengeful Acquisition policed its followers during New Lent, the pirate in her couldn't resist a barb.

It earned her a sharp look. "Captain, please don't misunderstand me. During New Lent, I abstain. But in my own special way." Mother Superior ran an index finger down the buttons of Alex's doublet. "Tread carefully, Captain Reign. Offending me can be a *very* bad habit."

"Yes... yes, I can see that." The two women looked into each other's eyes for a long, charged moment before Alex grinned. "Thank you for blessing me with your presence, milady."

"I assure you, the pleasure was all mine." Mother Superior headed for the stairs in a metronomically hypnotic walk. She looked at Alex over her shoulder. "Don't disappoint me, Captain Reign."

"I promise you I—" Alex realised that the woman was already descending the stairs. "—won't." Laughing to herself, high on the adrenaline of a near-death experience, she threw herself into the armchair, inhaling the scent of swirling perfume. It smelt like money with a lashing of danger, much like piracy. And like piracy, getting it wrong could be a terminal affair.

The thought sobered her, until she realised that she now knew that the person who'd blown up the priests was a man who frequented Westminster alleyways, which meant that *someone* had done it. Divine intervention? Like hell.

Galvanized into action, she leapt to her feet and plucked the figurine of the Vengeful Queen from her desk. Shoving it into her pocket as a talisman, she followed in Mother Superior's wake.

CHAPTER 29

UNKNOWN UNKNOWNS

S ID POTTS WAS NO stranger to being hit on the head and tied up. While crewing on the Purple Reign, he'd been banged on the bonce so frequently that he'd had a Bavarian hatsmith reinforce his bowler with a lightweight mesh dome. That dome was the reason his hat had a dent in it, rather than his skull. It was no doubt also why he woke up with all his thinking parts working, ready to deduce the whys and whatnots of his current situation.

Sid had many thinking parts, and the captain had once said he was a "thinly distributed intelligence". He'd liked that. There were his waters, which wobbled if anything was out of sorts, his guts, which communicated situations clearly to him, his neck hair, which stood on end if needed, and a gammy leg, which pained him if he had to think while walking long distances. In fact, he had so many thinking parts he barely had to use his brain at all.

He tried to move his hands and deduced that he was definitely tied to a chair. He was also blindfolded, but it was easy to surmise that he was being kept in a dingy cellar, or the back room of a disreputable establishment. It certainly smelled disreputable. Or at least, it smelled of goat. *Ominous* goat.

He knew *exactly* how this was going to play out.

Sid Potts read books. Sid Potts saw plays. Sid Potts knew that the hero always got hit on the head and tied up so that the villain could question him about what he knew. And this was where Sid had the advantage. He had an ace up his sleeve that would thwart the villain and lead to his capture: Sid didn't know anything.

He contemplated this fact smugly before wondering what his next step ought to be.

In some of Sid's books, the hero would use his contortionist skills to loosen his ropes, while feigning that he was still tied up. He'd then wait for the opportune moment, leap at the villain, knock him down and bring him to justice. The only problem was that in those books, the hero had already worked out what the villain had done. Sid didn't know what this cove had done beyond kidnap him.

He figured that meant he was in the other sort of book, where the villain questioned the hero and made dastardly threats, which outraged the hero so much that he found a way to escape, swearing he'd get vengeance. In those books, the hero didn't yet know who the villain was and had to work it out, which always led him to the femmy fartalley. Since Sid knew who that was, he had a head start!

Yeah, Sid concluded that all he had to do was wait and get ready to be outraged.

He settled as comfortably as he could in the chair and began mentally cataloguing every book he'd read where the hero got outraged and escaped. There'd been the one where hero gulped in great lungfuls of air, expanding his manly chest until his ropes snapped. And the one where the hero used bendy skills learned in a far-off ashram to untie his ropes using his toes. Then there'd been the ones where the hero found a convenient sharp thing nearby and sliced his ropes free in a flash. Sid figured that would be the most likely option for him. He'd just have to move this chair until he reached something sharp.

He made an experimental bouncing motion and started to sweat. This was harder than he'd expected.

He was saved from having to try it again when he heard a door creak open, followed by footsteps. This was obviously the villain coming to question him. He tried to think of what heroes said at times like these.

"Who goes there?" Sid demanded. "Show yourself! I know what your game is!" He jutted his jaw out in a manly fashion so the villain would know he was belligerent and brave in the face of all kinds of torture. The only problem was that being brave in the face of torture was normally the captain's job. Usually it was Sid's job to keep the Purple Reign in the air while suggesting to the captain that maybe it'd be a good idea to run away and take up farming on a nice Greek island—after all, the captain liked tomatoes, melons, peaches and even eggplants. Although, Sid wasn't sure what kind of bird laid those.

"My game?" a low voice asked. The accent was foreign and posh. This was *definitely* the villain. "I should ask you the same." Sid heard a match being struck and then smelled clove cigarette smoke that did little to override the stink of goat. "Who are you?"

"Me? I can't remember," Sid said. "Someone hit me on the head. Boggled my memory, it did."

"Did it? I'm sure it will come back with the correct persuasion."

"I'm not going to tell you anything!" Sid announced.

"I assure you that you are. Starting with why you have a list of priests in your pocket, along with a questionable library book about thinking for idiots, which I can only assume is some kind of unfortunate joke. Why do you have the list? Tell me?"

The mention of the library book threw Sid for a moment, and then it dawned on him that his current predicament was because of the list of priests he'd gotten from Miss Sadie Simms. Aha! This was the moment when he, the hero, realised that he'd been kidnapped because of the femmy fartalley. That cove Elias had asked the captain to find out who'd exploded the priests, and now here Sid was.

"What list?" he asked.

"The one with the two priests who've exploded written at the top. Why have you got it?"

"I don't know what you're talking about."

"Alright..." There was the sound of the man inhaling on his cigarette, and then Sid coughed as smoke was blown into his face. "We'll get that information out of you in a moment. Why were you asking after the urchin?"

"What urchin?"

"You know which urchin. What do you want with her?"

"I don't know what you're talking about. I don't know anything."

"Ah, but I know that's a lie. You know something. Or you wouldn't have been asking questions."

Sid puffed up. This was where he played his ace and enraged the villain into making a mistake. "Ah, but what you don't understand is that there are things I don't know that I don't know. Things I know I don't know. Things I know I know that I don't know, and things I don't know I don't know... that I don't know. It's an ouroboros of not knowing—" He paused to let the word sink in. "But the *important* thing is that I don't know anything that you're talking about. Especially anything about the urchin that the captain told me to find."

"Captain? What captain? Who is the captain you're talking about?"

"That's something you don't know that I know you don't know."

"I have no idea what you are talking about."

"That's because I don't know what I'm talking about. Which is why *you* don't know." Sid was getting good at this. He was outsmarting the villain. He was making him angry. That's what was supposed to happen, so that the villain slipped up and told him who he was. Then Sid would get free and tell the captain. Afterwards, the Academic Council would give him some kind of medal, and he'd show it to Miss Sadie Simms and her bosom would heave in rapturous desire. Sid didn't really know what heaving meant when it came to bosoms, but he suspected it had something to do with high winds and desiring one's hatches to be battened down. This made a lot of sense, the reasoning being that since all ships were female, it followed that all females were ships. This nicely explained all the extra rigging.

Admittedly, Sid's stomach stuck out further than his chest nowadays, which would draw attention away from the medal, so he hoped it would be a big one.

"I know you're going to be *very* sorry if you don't tell me who your captain is!" the villain said.

"Pirates never give away other pirates. It's the Pirate Code, and I'll never break it," Sid said smugly. "I'm no Mister Lemons. I won't tell you anything and you can't make me."

"Pirate? Ah, I think I begin to see. You wouldn't be talking about Captain Reign, would you? Wasn't she turned in by her first mate? Wasn't his name Mister Lemons?"

Sid flailed for a moment and then remembered the thing the actors in The Armoury always talked about. Improvisation, it was called. "Yes! But not the one you're thinking about. I work for *another* pirate named Captain Reign, who was double-crossed by an entirely unrelated Mister Lemons." There, that should do it.

There was a long pause. "I see. And why does this pirate who is definitely not the Dread Pirate Purple Reign want to know about the urchin girl?"

"I don't know. They didn't tell me," Sid said. "I warn you, you will never get away with this." He said this because it's what the hero always told the villain. In the books it always made the villain angry, so that he did something stupid.

"I think you'll find that I already have."

"No you haven't."

"Quite. I won't say it's been good to meet you." There were more footsteps, the sound of a door opening, and then Sid heard the villain tell someone to keep him blindfolded and tied up until he sent word.

The door closed and Sid was left alone, feeling faintly worried that the whole thing hadn't gone exactly how it should have, which was all the more reason for him to find a sharp thing to cut his ropes with.

Bracing himself, he rocked from side to side, jiggling the chair across the room. It worked quite well and he managed to move at least a foot before one of the legs hit a patch of uneven floor. Sid's momentum overbalanced the chair.

His head was the first thing to hit the floor, and this time he wasn't wearing his hat.

CHAPTER 30

A BLOODY APPARITION

E LIAS SAT AT HIS desk, studying the words he'd just written on a sheet of the butcher's paper he used for drawing his designs. The word *incense* was underlined at the top. Underneath, he'd written a series of questions: *Cane it explode? How woulde the explosione detonate onlye the priests and nothinge else? Is there a forme ofe black powder toe which the trinkets have noe allergye?*

He glanced at the measurements he'd written in his notebook after Father Bartholomew's explosion. They pointed to the explosion originating either on the priest or right next to him. As neither he, Neha or Percy could conceive of a way the priests could have had the explosive substance on them, it *had* to have been next to them, which meant the most likely culprit was incense.

The stuff had already been alight, which took care of the ignition source. Maybe the explosive element had been coated in something that had to burn away before detonation.

Father Bartholomew had been in proximity to incense-laden thuribles when he'd exploded. Father O'Malley hadn't been holding a thurible, but he *had* been standing next to his pulpit. Elias couldn't recall the smell of incense at St. Weston's, but maybe there'd been some burning on a brazier nearby.

He set his quill down with a scowl.

An explosive agent that could be concealed in incense, which possessed the force to completely destroy a human body? Something like that would change the face of global warfare. The consequences would be horrific. In this, Elias agreed with the Artificer's Guild. Some innovations should be prevented. But *what was it?*

Phillips waved at him and Elias felt a jolt of memory. Yes! He picked up the quill and wrote *The trinkets knew aboute it and left thee bodeys before the impacte.*

If the trinkets knew about it, then it was something in the air, something in the priest's physiology itself, *or* someone had devised a way to treat black powder so that it repelled the trinkets but prevented them from making their hosts itch. But how? And what?

"I got your screwdriver." The words were spoken in a small, watery whisper by Elias's side.

He looked up and yelped.

A gore-covered apparition was standing before him, holding a screwdriver.

With his heart pounding, it took Elias a moment to catalogue a pointy face dripping in blood and two tear-filled black eyes. There was a floppy hat with a chicken feather that had obviously once been white but was now mostly red with a glob of something best left unidentified sticking to it.

"What in the Vengeful Lady's spleen is happening over there?" Vikram bobbed up from behind his wall of books. "What is it?" he screeched. "How'd it get in? Get it away! Get it away!"

"Don't call me an it! I'm Flora! I'm a *person*, not an *it*," the bloody figure wailed before bursting into great wracking sobs that created crimson runnels down her cheeks.

"Flora? What happened?" Elias stood up and scrabbled in his pockets for a handkerchief, then held it out. "Here."

"I was sneaking in the rectory and a priest saw me and called me a bad name. Then he exploded and I'm all—I'm all m-m-manky!" Flora wailed, taking the handkerchief and burying her face in it. "He splatted all over me and covered my best hat and coat. And it smelled so *bad*, which was bad, because he already smelled bad. And I had to hide, so I snuck here because I remembered your shop was here." The words ended up in a hiccoughing sob. "And I forgot to get a relic! Unless I'm a relic because I've got bits all over me. But if I am, how can I sell *me* to get a new coat and breeches? And I've got priest in my shoo-oo-oes." She burst into fresh tears, gripping Elias's handkerchief tighter to her face.

"Another priest?" Vikram exploded from behind his books, running towards Flora, waving his arms. "Out! Out! I will not be a known associate twice over! Get her out of here!"

Flora squeaked and shied closer to Elias.

"Calm *down*, Vikram." Elias stepped in front of Flora. "Use your brain. What if the Lepers saw her leaving like this? Besides, if another priest has exploded, there may be clues to how it happened." He turned to Flora. "Where did it happen? Was there any incense present? Is that what the bad smell was?"

Flora opened her mouth to answer just as the shop door burst open to reveal Captain Reign. She strode towards Elias with a triumphant expression.

"Mister Dooley! Time to earn your keep. I have new information that's pertinent to your problem and my getting paid—Flora! What in the Vengeful Lady's third nipple happened to you?"

"Captain!" Flora ran towards Captain Reign and Elias suddenly found himself looking at the tip of a clockbow bolt.

"What have you done to my cabin boy?" The captain's tone and expression suddenly matched every blood-curdling description of the Dread Pirate Purple Reign Elias had heard.

"It's nothing to do with me!" Vikram shrieked. "She just came in here. It's his fault. Whatever it was. *Don't shoot me.*" He yelped and huddled on the floor when the captain focussed the clockbow on him.

"Shut up." The captain's words were calm and deliberate. "Flora. You're going to stop crying, then you're going to tell me which one I'm going to shoot first."

Flora sniffed. "Neither of them, Captain. It wasn't them. It was a priest, in the rectory. He exploded."

The captain looked at her sharply. "Another priest?"

Flora nodded.

"Exploded?"

"Yes. And I came here after to hide. Because I was manky."

"These two didn't have anything to do with you looking like you've been basted in strawberry jam?"

"No."

The clockbow was lowered and holstered.

Elias exhaled in relief, while Vikram crawled behind his desk. Within seconds, books began thumping on top of each other as he reinforced his dam.

"What sort of priest?" the captain asked.

"A sweaty one in a grey robe. I didn't like him," Flora said.

"Alright. Tell me what happened and then we'll see about getting you scrubbed. I'm sure Mister Dooley has a bathroom you can use."

Elias didn't think this was a wise moment to say that due to Vikram's hygiene standards, Flora would possibly come out of the bathroom in a worse state than when she'd entered.

Flora sniffed. "I was in the rectory. The priest came in looking for the things that were hidden, but he couldn't find them because I'd already taken them. I was hidden too. I hid behind the door, but he saw me and called me a bad name, and then he fell and exploded." She swiped at her nose, looking at Elias. "There wasn't incense. There was just a secret place in the desk holding a bag of sugar and these papers." Flora pulled a pamphlet from the back of her breeches. Other than the bloody fingerprints she'd just left on it, it was unscathed, telling Elias that she'd been facing the priest when the explosion happened.

Elias considered this. No incense, but now there was a pamphlet and some sugar that, for some reason, had been hidden. An idea began to form in his mind but was interrupted when the captain read the cover of the pamphlet aloud.

"Sister Lascivious's Forbidden Fancies. It's in print, Mister Dooley. Blessed Press, by the looks of the 'e's."

Vikram yelped. "What?" Books toppled to the floor as he skittered around his desk again to look over the captain's shoulder as she thumbed through the pages. "This is a real copy! In print! There's the moist vanilla sponge with the extra creamy centre, the dripping custard, the wobbly puddings, the spotless dick! It's all here. The book exists!" Vikram looked at them all with wild eyes. "I thought it was just a myth. There weren't supposed to be any more copies after the Vengeful Queen had the presses burnt! Do you know what this means? It means that there's an original out there somewhere! And this— Do you know how much this is worth? Did you say this was printed on the Blessed Press? Because if it is, do you know how many perverts would kill each other to have it? The Church of Vengeful Acquisition's most sinful cookbook, printed on the Blessed Press itself!" He made a gurgling noise that Elias realised was an attempt at laughter. "How much do you want for this, girl?" he asked Flora. "I'll pay you now."

"You can't have it because I don't like you." Flora scowled at him. "I got it for the captain. It's so we can find out who blew up the priests."

"Elias!" Vikram gave him a pleading look, and Elias realised that for the first time he had the upper hand. "Convince her to sell it to me. I won't report you to Mother Superior, I swear. I'll even let you take back your bathroom slot at Mrs Nevins's. Whatever you want."

"Did you just threaten to report him to Mother Superior?" Captain Reign looked at Elias. "Is this the owner of the horrendous cardigan?"

"Yes," Elias said. "His name is Vikram."

"He has the same personality as his cardigan."

"Yes." Elias experienced a brief moment of satisfaction over Vikram's scowl. "Vikram, you can't have the pamphlet because if it was concealed in a hidden compartment it definitely bears investigation, and so does the sugar, although that may be unrelated." He looked at Flora. "Do you have the sugar?"

She produced a cloth bag. "Here."

"Thank you." Elias placed it carefully on his desk, experiencing a spark of hope as his thoughts continued on their earlier track. A cookbook and sugar hidden in an exploded priest's desk. Another priest looking for the cookbook, maybe the sugar too, and then exploding also. There *had* to be a connection.

Vikram wasn't about to let the topic go. "What about afterwards? After you've found whatever you need to find? Will you give me the book then?"

Elias looked at Flora.

"You called me an it," Flora said, glaring at Vikram.

"That was just surprise, dear, ah, dear... lady." Vikram was trying to form what was possibly his first ever smile. His cheeks quivered with the unaccustomed effort, his lips stretched as nerves kicked muscle groups into unfamiliar contortions, exposing a pair of large buck teeth.

"I'm not a lady, I'm a pirate."

"You could start ingratiating yourself by offering her your cardigan, so she has something to wear after she washes off," Captain Reign said coolly.

"My cardigan? The one this cretin infested? You expect me to—" Vikram caught himself in time, the strange face contortion happening again. His eyebrows were undulating in the effort to keep the expression fixed. "Of course! Whatever the young lady wants, the young lady gets."

"The one that looks like sick that you were wearing before?" Flora asked Elias, having obviously spotted it on the hook on Vikram's side of the shop.

"I'm afraid so," Elias replied. "But it'll be better than what you're currently wearing."

She looked down at herself and then at the cardigan.

"Marginally better," Elias corrected himself. "The privy is through that door. On the sink you'll find an object pretending to be soap. Afterwards, we'll discuss what happened." He looked at the pamphlet in his hands, then at the sugar, then at Captain Reign. "I think we may have a way forward in this investigation."

"Yes, Mister Dooley, and not only that, we have a new development."

"What is that?"

"Let's just say that Mother Superior has given me her blessing—" Captain Reign looked at Vikram. "What's going on with your face?"

"He's trying to smile," Elias said. "Vikram, you can stop now. What you're doing with your mouth is best kept to dark alleys."

Vikram's face immediately reverted to his usual scowl. "What's this about Mother Superior?"

The captain looked around. "Are there any more chairs in the vicinity? This may take some time."

CHAPTER 31

"S" STANDS FOR SOMETHING

A LEX HAD JUST FINISHED telling Elias and a hovering Vikram about
Mother Superior's visit when an unexpected Cry bulletin sounded down
Utopia Street.

*Hear ye! hear ye! This is an exclusive emergency bulletin. Stop. Another priest
has been discovered exploded at the late Father O'Malley's rectory in Shadwell.
Father O'Malley's housekeeper, Mrs Smith, was quoted saying that she found
Novice Lice splatted all around the study. The investigation is ongoing. Stop. Ye've
heard! Ye've heard! Do you cower at the coo? Use Perisham's Pigeon Deterrent
today. Curse the coo and free yourself from pigeon persecution with Perisham's!*

Elias grimaced. "That's problematic. I was hoping there'd be some way we
could investigate the scene, but now there'll be too many priests and Bad Habits
present. Wait—" He frowned. "Are we currently employed by the Church of
Vengeful Acquisition?"

"I believe we are officially unofficially working for the Church of Vengeful
Acquisition," Alex said.

"That sounds complicated."

"Not to a privateer, Mister Dooley! Being unofficially official is practically our *oeuvre*." Alex paused to see if anyone had noticed her use of French.
No—ignorant, the lot of them. "In fact, I should charge more for the unofficial
aspect, since it's not been officially stated that we're unofficial." She realised she
may have got too ahead of herself, and cleared her throat. "Anyway, they'll have
shovelled up anything interesting by now."

"I'm afraid you're right," Elias said.

Alex glanced up at an aquarium holding a trinket with an injured carapace and another with leg splints. "It's also put a stopper on us finding out if this Novice Lice had a ring or another one of these on him." She tapped at the pamphlet, aware of Vikram hovering like a fly at a picnic. "At least we now know that we are *definitely* dealing with someone who thinks like a pirate."

"How do you mean?" Elias asked.

"Blackmail, Mister Dooley. It's the most straightforward sneak attack there is! Although I always preferred to give them more of a running start. He blew up two priests before asking them to hand over the booty. It's unsporting and I don't like it."

"Are we being lectured about ethics by a pirate?" Vikram exclaimed.

Alex turned to him. "Am I being censured by a man who sells books about large bananas?"

"She's got you there, Vikram," Elias said.

"She doesn't have anything." Vikram sniffed. "Except for Mother Superior breathing down her neck."

"That *is* a point," Elias turned pensive again. "Is Mother Superior going to hold you accountable for this new explosion?"

Alex caught herself before she revealed that she hadn't considered that. "Come now, Mister Dooley! Do you think she'd hold me responsible for something that happened while I was in her company?"

"Yes."

"Of course she wouldn't!" Alex persevered, keeping her tone hearty. "And you heard on the Cry yourself that the man was a mere novice, and a repugnant one at that, by the sounds of it. Who ever heard of anyone going out of their way because of a novice priest exploding?"

"I would just like to make it clear that I have *nothing* to do with any of this!" Vikram announced as he started pacing the red line down the middle of the shop. "I do one good deed and see where it gets me?"

"If you want this cookbook once we're done, you have *everything* to do with this." Alex spent a moment wondering if it was against rookery law to keelhaul someone under a goat cart for being bloody annoying. As far as she knew, The Clockmaker hadn't included anything like that in his Rules.

"The question is, what do we make of this?" Elias hefted the sugar bag and looked at the cookbook. "I'm beginning to get an idea of what may be happening but—"

"Captain, I've found another ring!"

They turned as Flora burst out of the privy, covered to the calf in the horrible yellow cardigan.

"Another one? In the privy?" Alex asked sharply as Flora skidded to a stop in front of her, holding the ring up in the air with a wide grin, proving that gold rings could be an effective, if expensive, distraction from a traumatic experience.

"In the pouch that I took, that I was going to give back," Flora said.

"Give back to who?"

"The crying priest who was talking to the one that blew up, and the other one that was really tall and all hunched over." Flora did an impersonation of what a vulture would look like if it was wearing a horrible cardigan. It didn't look all that different from Vikram.

"And these priests were where?" Alex asked.

"In the church! I was stuck in the confessional booth and it was boring, so I thought I'd see what the crying priest had in his pockets. And he had this ring!"

Alex turned to Elias, who had a thoughtful expression. Vikram paused in his pacing.

Alex tapped her chin. "Two rings from the blown-up priests."

"Found upon the floor," Flora said.

"And one ring from the crying priest."

"Maybe there are more!" Flora said. "In Father O'Malley's rectory, where the splatted priest lies!" Her smile dimmed and she bit her lip. "Although I don't want to go and check. He scared me and he smelled bad."

"No, I don't think we'll put you through that again. We'll work with what we have." Alex retrieved the other two rings from her pocket—the one she'd found and the one she'd collected from Elias. "An S. What do you think this stands for?"

"Sugar?" Flora pointed to the bag on Elias's desk. "That starts with S and I found it somewhere secret."

"Secret! That's *precisely* what it stands for!" Alex exclaimed. "Mister Dooley, a man with your humungous intellect should've seen it already."

"Why would three people wear rings that say they're secret? Why couldn't the S stand for shiny?" Flora asked.

"Because that would be silly," Alex said decisively. "No, it's obvious to me that these priests are all members of a secret society!" She waited for the admiration that was her due, then gave up when all she got was confusion.

"Why would priests have a secret society?" Elias asked.

Vikram threw his arms in the air. "Vengeful Lady, forgive this humble idiot for his lack of a brain. Of course priests would have a secret society! Do you know how many secret societies order books from my shop? Too many to count, that's how many. You name me a group of people in this city and I'll show you a publication they've ordered. The Knights Libris order *Page Tearer Monthly*, the Neptune Guards like *Figure Head*, and the Banking Guild inexplicably loves a book called *Gardening On a Budget with Absolutely No Money*. Perverts, the lot of them! It's no surprise that Church of Vengeful Acquisition priests are running a secret society. In fact, come to think of it, it's mandatory."

Alex spared the stacks of books on the other side of the room a thoughtful glance, then made a mental note to keep Flora from looking too closely at the covers. "Flora."

"Hmmm?" Flora was studying the rings in Alex's hand with a dreamy expression.

"Would you recognize the other two priests if you saw them?"

Flora frowned. "I think so. Especially the one that looked like this." She hunched over again. "And the crying priest had a lot of lines on his face. Not many people have as many as he had."

"I see." Alex lit up a cigar and puffed on it. "Did Sid get that list of priests from Miss Sadie Simms?"

"He did. It had the names of the priests who'd exploded at the top of it."

Alex looked at Elias. "Ah. This confirms that there may be more. We may have a way of finding two more priests who could soon explode. The question is *how* they'll explode."

"Wait. Wait. Exploding priests aren't important," Vikram interjected. "What's important is that if we're dealing with a secret society, we are dealing with secret things, and *that* book is a secret thing." He pointed with a shaking finger at the illicit cookbook. "Which means..." He paused, his eyes shining. "Promise me that you'll give me all the copies you find once you're done. Please? I'll help in any way I can. Just promise me—"

"You think there are going to be more than this one?" Elias asked.

"There are multiple rings, ergo there are multiple books!" Vikram yelled. "You found that one and bits of the other one, which was blown up."

"I haven't verified it yet."

"You don't need to. How many copies of the Book of Vengeance have the word 'moist' in them? None, that's how many. There are three rings. That means there are at least three books."

Elias looked at the pamphlet and the half-empty bag of sugar. "You may be right." His forehead wrinkled. "Captain Reign, I think we may be dealing with some form of illicit cooking group. Why else hide the sugar?"

"New Lent?" Flora asked. "Sister Barry said she couldn't share one of Mister Jim's mysterious pies with me because it was New Lent. You can't eat pastry on New Lent. Or ice cream. Or anything nice. It's all fish or nothing."

"Sister Barry?" Elias asked.

"The nun."

"Who I met this afternoon, by the way. He—she—*they* asked after you," Alex said to Flora.

"Really?" Flora beamed. "Did she tell you that she was a boy even though nuns are girls?"

"No, I think that would've taken more of a mental run-up than she had time for," Alex said. Flora had always championed the oddest of characters. Slasher Harry's dog Daphne was a fine example. No matter how often Alex explained that Daphne was a peg-legged killing machine, Flora insisted that she was just a little under-patted and would be fine once she received enough love. It had to be a ferret thing.

Alex turned to Elias. "What do you think, Mister Dooley?"

Elias nodded slowly. "You may be onto something. Your meeting with Mother Superior established that someone is deliberately attempting to kill the priests." He hefted the bag of sugar. "This is a half-formed idea—"

"What idea have you ever had that wasn't?" Vikram sniped.

"Why does he keep opening his mouth and letting words out?" Flora asked.

Elias ignored both of them. "What if this *isn't* sugar and is just something in a bag with 'sugar' written on the side? What if it's a substance that explodes if it's eaten? I've been thinking about it, and while I still believe there's no way that acid and omnicite can cause a large enough explosion, the stomach *does* have acid in it..."

"You believe it's some form of powdered omnicite?" Alex punched the air. "Aha! I *knew* you were wrong about that. There's always a way, Mister Dooley, always a way! The priests baked it into their wicked dumplings, ate them and then painted the walls!" She looked around to see if anyone was admiring her powers of deduction, but Flora was examining a random piece of paper in her hand and Elias was peering into the bag, giving it a sniff.

"It smells like brown sugar," he said. "It's high-quality too, which would hide the presence of ground omnicite or some other substance we don't know about yet, but there'd be no way of knowing without experimentation."

"My Vengeful Lady! It's like walking behind a goat with the slumps." Vikram snatched the bag from Elias's hands. "Who wouldn't want to taste high-grade brown? The stuff is worth more than gold! It's simple. Taste it and see what it is, don't just talk about it."

He dipped his finger inside and brought it out covered in granules. He was raising it to his mouth when Elias said, "Vikram, while I admire your willingness to die in order to prove my hypothesis, I'd advise against it."

Vikram glowered at him. "If you were any more histrionic, they'd hire you at the Sphere in Drury Lane!"

Alex stubbed out her cigar on a cracked porcelain plate that held a couple of spare cogs and a screwdriver. "I think what Mister Dooley is saying is there's a good chance you'll be coating the walls if you eat that sugar."

"Captain, don't warn him. I'd like to see him go splat," Flora whispered.

"I know." Alex patted Flora on the shoulder. "But sometimes we have to put up with idiots, even big ones."

"You're all *very* dramatic." Vikram wiped his finger on his trousers and sniffed at the bag. "It smells like brown sugar—extraordinarily expensive sugar—but since you insist, I won't taste it." He looked at Elias. "Well? What are you going to do about it?"

"Would your friends be able to help, Mister Dooley?" Alex asked.

"I believe so," Elias said slowly. "Percy keeps a quantity of acid for his experiments. It shouldn't be too difficult to test whether or not this sugar is responsible for the explosions."

"What are we waiting for? Let's go and see if this stuff can blow up a priest."

"Captain." Flora tugged at Alex's sleeve. Her hair was beginning to dry now and was standing up around her head like a dandelion.

"Hmm?"

"You haven't asked me about the other things that I found."

"What did you find?" Alex asked.

"These. I found them at St. Smeaton's." Flora held out a folded piece of blank parchment and two other pieces of screwed-up paper.

Alex examined each of them in turn. Not wanting to come to any conclusions that would diminish her previous victory, she turned to Elias. "What do you think?"

Elias studied them. "Is this the parchment used on the press?"

"Yes."

"I'll compare it to the pamphlet in a moment."

He flattened out the other pieces of paper. "From the spur on the 'e', both seem to have also been printed on the Blessed Press."

"Don't leave me in suspense! What do they say? Is it something as good as the cookbook?" Vikram hovered over Elias's shoulder.

"One is a transcript of the Cry, as if someone set the words in type." Elias read it out loud before setting the paper aside. "If I remember correctly, it's from last Thursday night. I know that because I heard it before I went to bed."

"Ah." Alex held up a finger. "That's the night that Father Inigo told me he didn't take his medication and Father Bartholomew had to take him home. What if Father Bartholomew then came back with the other priests and used the press?"

"That fits." Elias carefully studied the other piece of paper. "This appears to be a shopping list. Red herrings and some mackerel."

"Who bloody cares about some red bloody herrings?" Vikram yelled. "The important thing is to work out if that stuff you almost killed me with by making me eat it is blowing up priests. Then you can clear your name, find the other cookbooks and give them to me so I can sell them to the highest bidder. Am I the only sensible one here?"

They all looked at him.

"Mister Dooley?" Alex asked.

"Yes?" Elias asked.

"If we find out that sugar is explosive..."

"Yes?"

"Can you please make sure that your friend here eats a good helping of it?"

"It would be my pleasure."

Vikram threw up his hands. "Ungrateful! You're so ungrateful! If it weren't for me pointing out how valuable that pamphlet was, you never would've worked out that it was related to your silly investigation." He pointed at Flora. "And she's wearing my cardigan. That's my best one, you know."

Alex looked at Flora. "It's hers now."

"I don't want it," Flora said.

"Then collect your other clothes and go back to The Armoury."

Flora shuddered. "They're manky."

"I know, but they'll be good enough until you get home. I'll see you later this evening. And give the rings back. I know you snaffled them a few seconds ago." Alex held out her hand and Flora dropped the rings into her palm.

"But Captain, I want to see him blow up." Flora pointed at Vikram.

"Flora, sometimes we don't get what we want. But I promise I'll make up an extra gruesome bedtime story about an obnoxious bookseller who eats from a bag of poisoned sugar and explodes into chunky bits."

CHAPTER 32

THE ACID TEST

E LIAS HAD ONCE HEARD that the Apache Nation had a form of amusement where tourists paid to sit on the back of floatbison which were then persuaded to stampede. Apparently, the thrill of the ride was enhanced by the knowledge that one could die at any second. Elias was getting an inkling of how that must feel as he sat in a hack next to Captain Reign, trying to think of anything but the bag of potentially high-powered explosive tucked into his coat pocket.

Dark had settled over the city, and omnicite lamps lit streets congested with private carriages, cabs, delivery merchants, food carts and stray animals. Up ahead, Elias could see a flock of OverLondon's infamous flightless numpty pigeons, whose slow waddle had the ability to hold up traffic for hours.

There had long been petitions to eradicate OverLondon's numpties, or *numptea domestica*, but no one had volunteered to do the job, mainly because the birds were extremely hostile and responded to any perceived aggression by releasing their bowels with ballistic force and accuracy. Their street name was 'gutter cannon.'

Captain Reign reached into her doublet and withdrew a cigar, offering it to Elias, who shook his head. She shrugged and produced a small cigar cutter to remove the end before striking a match on the side of the hack to light up. As if reading Elias's mind, she exhaled a puff of smoke and then said, "Relax, Mister Dooley. If it was going to explode, it would've done so when Flora had it."

"I hope you're right," Elias said, but was greatly relieved when they finally arrived at the Rogue Artificers' tower.

Captain Reign opted to stay outside while Elias ran upstairs and ducked the boxing glove before bursting through the door.

Both Percy and Neha were standing at a table set up with a complex array of equipment. Beakers bubbled and retorts wafted pungent smoke.

"Elias!" Neha beamed at him. She was wearing goggles, as was Percy. "We're just about to begin an experiment to see if it's possible to turn tea into coffee with alchemy."

"Can you delay it?" Elias asked.

"What? Why?" Percy looked up. In deference to safety precautions, his horizontal beard was restrained in a conical leather cup. In the past it had occurred to Elias that it looked like a codpiece for the chin, but he'd never tell his friend.

Elias reached into his pocket and withdrew the bag of sugar. "Because I may have a way to prove Mistress Fenderpossum wrong about acid and omnicite."

Thirty minutes later, Elias, Percy and Neha stepped back after setting up the experiment, which involved a beaker containing an acid solution that had been nestled into the compost heap in front of the tower. Meanwhile, Percy was brandishing an outstretched broom handle with another beaker attached to one end. It contained a thick white mixture.

The three rogue artificers stood huddled around the candle Neha was holding and consulted *Sister Lascivious's Forbidden Fancies* for the tenth time in as many minutes.

"I think we should be okay with our 'luvely jubbly pancake batter' using half a cup of the adulterated sugar," Neha said thoughtfully. "You're right Elias, if they baked it into the food, it's vital to replicate the ingredients they baked it with as closely as possible. Although the love dumpling recipe does call for one cup of the sugar and the biscuits that resemble nun's... biscuits call for one and a half, which *does* seem excessive." She looked up. "Do you have any idea which recipe they may have used?"

"No, but I think the pancake batter is our best bet so that we have enough sugar for further analysis if the experiment is a success." Elias fitted his goggles over his eyes.

"Then we're in agreement that the experiment is to proceed." Percy turned to Captain Reign, the candlelight reflecting from his goggles. "All civilians must step back from the experimentation area, behind the blast shield."

"Aye aye, sir." Captain Reign saluted at Percy and went to stand behind the table they'd set on its side, twenty feet away.

Percy snorted in approval. "Right. Let's get started. The omnicite sugar, flour, egg and milk mixture should ignite within seconds of making contact with the acid."

"That's why I'll be the one pouring it in," Elias said. "It's my experiment, my responsibility."

"Spoken like a true pirate," Captain Reign said.

"Your reasoning is sound. Good luck, Artificer Elias."

Neha patted Elias on the shoulder. "Good luck, Artificer Elias."

Elias took a moment to readjust the numerous leather aprons they'd 'borrowed' from the blacksmith's workshop and to fit a pot onto his head—it was the best protective wear they'd been able to come up with at short notice. Then he took the stick from Percy, careful to keep the beaker stable so that none of its contents poured out. "Thank you, Artificer Percy and Artificer Neha. Innovate!"

"Innovate!"

"Innovate!"

Elias waited until Percy and Neha had retreated behind the blast shield, then carefully approached the beaker of acid. Sweat broke out on his body as he positioned the beaker full of batter over the top of it. Then, with a swift movement, he poured one into the other, dropped the broom handle and ran as fast as he could, diving over the upturned table to where the others had made space for him.

He landed on his face with a thump, the pot coming free of his head and clanking as it skittered away. A few moments of silence followed. Then more silence.

He righted himself. Four goggled heads popped up from behind the table.

"Nothing's happening," Percy said.

"No," Neha agreed, her voice tinged with disappointment.

"No. But this might *not* be omnicite," Elias said. "If we allow the time it would've taken for Father Bartholomew to eat something made with it and then to walk to the church, or for Father O'Malley to do the same, then have a conversation, I'd calculate that we should wait at least ten or twenty minutes."

"I'm in no rush, Mister Dooley." The end of Captain Reign's cigar glowed in the dark.

They waited as Neha's candle sputtered and the cacophony of the city drifted over the walls of the Artificer's Guild.

Finally, after what Elias calculated to be at least thirty minutes, he exhaled a puff of air. "What do you think?" he asked Percy and Neha.

Percy hummed thoughtfully. "I think we can safely say it's not omnicite. And it's probably not something else in the sugar either, otherwise it would've gone off by now. Or at least it'd be doing *something*."

"I think you're right." Elias felt disheartened. He'd been so hopeful.

"Have you considered that it could merely be unadulterated sugar and that it was hidden because the priests weren't meant to have any at this time of year?" Neha asked.

Elias's shoulders slumped. "I'm beginning to consider that as a possibility."

Captain Reign clapped him on the back. "Take heart, Mister Dooley. We can't capture every ship with promising booty."

"Thank you, Captain."

"I'll see you in the morning. My bo'sun will be back with the list of priests' names and we'll locate the surviving two Flora saw. Why don't you give me the remaining sugar? At the very least, it'll be evidence to Mother Superior that her priests were up to mischief."

"Yes. Yes," Elias said distractedly, handing over the bag.

"Shall we leave the beaker here, just in case?" Neha asked. "I don't think we'll have to worry about anyone finding it. I've put the word out that a flock of flightless numpties have been roosting on this side of the heap." She spoke the words with a painful kindness that told Elias she was saving face for him.

"I think that's wise," Percy said with the same excruciating care. "Just in case."

"Yes. Just in case," Elias looked at the two of them, the heat of embarrassment rising to his cheeks. "Thank you for your assistance."

"No need to thank us. All in the name of scientific inquiry," Percy said with forced cheerfulness. He stuck his index finger in the air. "Innovate!"

"Innovate!"

"Innovate." If Elias's voice didn't contain the usual enthusiasm, no one questioned it, and before long he was handing back the captain's visitor slip at the Hall of Patents and making his way back to Mrs Nevins's boarding house.

He was vaguely aware of Phillips patting his hand comfortingly as he walked along the artificer district's busy streets, heading for the depths of Whitechapel.

CHAPTER 33

DREAD THE PIRATE

A LEX DECIDED TO WALK home to Drury Lane. Lost in thought, she purchased a cone of roasted chestnuts from a vendor who looked like he'd washed his hands at least once in the past year, then continued to consider the day's events as she navigated the streets.

Despite Elias's disappointment, Alex wasn't discouraged. If the sugar hadn't blown up the priests, then something else had. A pirate didn't need to know the make and model of the cogcannons being pointed at her ship to know they'd make a bloody big hole. The key information was *who* was firing the cogcannons, and where they were going to aim next.

Munching on a chestnut, she decided that they were definitely in a good position. Sid had a list of priests. Flora would identify the ones she'd seen at the church and Elias would come up with the right questions to ask them.

Alex congratulated herself on bringing the lad on board. Now that Lemons had turned out to be a double-crossing demon reptile from the fiery pits of hell, Alex needed additional brains to complement her crew.

She was contemplating offering Elias a permanent position once she got her ship back when someone tugged on the back of her cape.

She spun around with her hand on the hilt of her clockbow, but didn't see anyone.

"Down here, bruv," said a jaded voice at waist height.

Alex adjusted her gaze and saw an urchin she'd last encountered while he'd been wiping his nose on a kitten. The kitten was nowhere in sight, but given the state of the boy's nose, its services were desperately needed.

Alex raised an eyebrow. "Yes?"

The kid sniffed, which didn't help the nasal situation. "Clockmaker says he's watchin' you an' that. Like, he's watchin' to see if you find Grub."

"That's all?" Alex asked.

The boy shrugged.

"Are you meant to take him a message from me?"

"Nah. He just wan'ed me to threaten you and he wan'ed me to tell you that you had to give me those ches'nuts." The boy eyed the cone in Alex's hand.

"Ah." Alex sighed. "He's not only a dark master of torture and torment, but concerned about the feeding of urchins. I see."

"Yeah."

"If I must. Please tell him that I have my best man on the job and I'll have a result soon." Alex handed the chestnuts over. "Now bugger off."

The boy snatched the cone, holding it to his chest, then looked at her speculatively. "You're not gonna be gettin' any other stuff t'night, are you? Like some fish an' chips, an' some chicken, an' some ice cream, because The Clockmaker said you had to give me those too."

"Did he mention anything about dinging you around the ear for pushing your luck?" Alex asked.

"No, but I fink I've got some other stuff to do now." The urchin sauntered away, stuffing chestnuts into his mouth and spitting out the shells. As Alex watched him go, he picked the pocket of a passing woman with a deftness that trumped even Flora's abilities.

Alex continued on her journey.

The Clockmaker was having her watched. That didn't surprise her. And if there was one watcher, there'd be others. But no matter. Sid would come through by dawn. He'd find Grub even if he had to visit every pie vendor and pub in the city.

Alex entered Drury Lane at nine, as the early shows finished and punters poured into Theatreland's already cramped streets. All around her, touts flogged tickets to late-night plays, dandies paraded their fripperies and milkmaids handed out flyers for their respective 'dairies' in the butter district. Alex stepped to one side to let a mob of drunken Macaronis from OverRome pass.

They looked like bloated wasps with their towering wigs, cinched waists and trousers so tight that she expected to hear sad little crunching noises whenever they took a step. She overheard one of them speaking about William Wobblespeare's latest at the Sphere. Apparently, the play included a set of twins who looked like another set of twins, who got lost at sea and ended up in Verona.

Due to the high proportion of William Wobblespeare's plays set in Verona, rumours had long been circulating through Theatreland that he'd been paid off by the Verona Tourist Board. Alex knew from Gregor that this was entirely untrue. Apparently, Wobblespeare was getting generous under-the-table donations by the Association for the Awareness of Twins Lost at Sea.

A fanfare sounded at the far end of the street and was met by a chorus of groans. A royal was travelling, which meant that the streets would soon be even more congested than usual. Royals were always accompanied by a procession that included trumpeters, mimes, jesters, and their personal dribble moppers.

Alex was debating whether or not to watch the procession so she could share the details with Flora, when someone wrapped a length of rope around her neck and dragged her into an alleyway.

Reflexes honed by years of experience kicked in. She immediately went limp, dragging her feet on the cobbles in the hope of gaining purchase, but the ground was too slippery.

Overhead, she saw a washing line strung with a pair of Sid's underwear. She was in the alleyway next to The Armoury. Her turf. No one got the drop on her on her own bloody turf!

Some monumental idiot was about to get their buttocks handed to them on two separate plates. To attack her by her favourite pub? Her *home*? It wasn't just idiotic, it was unforgivably impolite. Fury arced through her veins.

She caught sight of another cove in the darkness. He was a large, brutish shape wearing a hat, with his face covered by a rag.

So, she'd have to teach two idiots some manners.

She gripped the rope at her throat, using it as leverage, and lashed out at the hat-wearing man with her boot, connecting with his kneecap.

He howled.

"No need for that now, miss," a voice said in her ear. "Come quiet and we won't hurt you. His Lordship just wants to talk to you."

Alex's feet finally found purchase and she rammed the cove holding her against a wall. He grunted in pain as she slammed him into the wall again with enough force for him to loosen his hold. It took a second to twist free to face him and another second to draw her arm back and smash her fist into his nose.

Bone crunched and he slumped to the ground at her feet, spluttering.

"Agh! She broke by nobe! By nobe!" he howled.

Alex ignored him, rounding on the other assailant, who by this time had straightened and was limping towards her, his hat shadowing his face.

"What idiot with a suicide wish tries to mug a pirate near her own damn pub?" she demanded, reaching for the hilt of her clockbow only for her fingers to close around air.

"One that's pointing your own clockbow at you." He limped into a patch of dim light, her clockbow held in a shaking hand. "Now miss, we don't wanna hurt you any more'n we have to. Although we will. 'Cos it's you or us, an' I'd rather it not be us." He looked at the cove on the ground behind Alex. "Pick up that rope, Keef. Stop moanin'."

"She broke by nobe!"

"I'll break more than that before the night is over." Alex shielded her face with her left arm and charged the man brandishing her clockbow, taking him off guard.

He yelped, there was a click, and the bow fired.

With a *ka-thunk*, the bolt lodged deep into Alex's arm, but she kept charging, low tackling the man and flipping him over her shoulder.

The clockbow flew from his hand and skittered along the alleyway, the impact triggering the emergency tension release which made a *vreeeee* noise as pre-tensed springs and flywheels spun away their stored energy. It would be useless until it was rewound.

She turned to find both men piled together in a groaning tangle of arms and legs.

Advancing on her quarry, Alex looked around for another weapon. There was a pile of junk to her right with a broken bar stool sticking out of it. She wrenched off two of the legs, brandishing one in each hand. They weren't belaying pins, but they'd be good enough for a bo'sun's handshake.

"Which one of you curs is going to try it first?" she asked.

"You go, Roddy. You're godda hab to use da habber. Knock her oud," the one called Keef said as they staggered to their feet.

"Yeah. Alright. I don't want to. But I will if I have to." The man named Roddy rushed at Alex. There was the flash of metal as he raised a blacksmith's hammer in the air.

Alex blocked it with the first chair leg, only for the wood to shatter. She threw the stub in Roddy's face, taking advantage of his distraction to smash him on the cheek with the second chair leg.

He stumbled backwards, only for Keef to push past him. Blood was streaming down Keef's face from his mangled nose. He was brandishing a butcher's knife, waving it erratically.

"It doesn't hab to be like dis, miss. *Pleade* comb quietly an' we'll go easy on you. Pleade," he said. "We *really* don't wan' to hurt you. We don't like the idea ob hurtib woben."

"If you know anything about me, you'll know that I *never* come quietly." Alex spun on her heel, drew back her left hand and punched the stone wall above the steel bars covering The Armoury's basement window.

"Ere! What are you doin'?" Roddy asked incredulously.

Alex punched the wall again, this time feeling the mortar crack. "While I appreciate your gallantry, if you're going to—" *punch* "—fight with a pirate, gentlemen—" *punch* "—you had *better* be ready for it." *Punch*. She grabbed at one of the window bars and wrenched it free from the fractured stonework.

"What's she doib', Roddy?" Keef shrieked. "She can't do dat!"

"No, she can't! You can't be doin' that!" Both men backed away, the whites of their eyes showing in the dim light.

232

2ionOVERLONDON

"On the contrary, gentlemen. I can and I am. Need I remind you that you're messing with the *Dread* Pirate Purple Reign." Alex stalked towards them, scraping the bar along the stone wall, sending sparks flying into the darkness.

Keef dropped the knife as he gripped Roddy's arm. "Bloody 'ell. I fink we better run, Roddy."

Alex charged.

They legged it for the other end of the alley.

Alex would have reached them if it weren't for two trapdoors being thrust upwards directly in her path. Gregor launched himself through them, into the alley with a roar. "Keep the bloody noise down!"

Alex's momentum made it impossible for her to stop and she plummeted head first into The Armoury's basement, landing on a pile of something soft.

A trapdoor hinge squeaked.

"Who's down there?" Gregor snarled.

"Me!" Alex yelled up at him. "Don't let them get away, and get my bloody clockbow."

"Right." There was the sound of heavy footfalls overhead.

Alex righted herself. She'd fallen into a basket, which, until moments before, had only contained various items of unwashed clothing. The furniture in the room included a single bed and a small stove. She'd fallen into Gregor's bedroom or, as he'd refer to it, his sett.

She was dusting herself off when Gregor returned, dropping into the basement and pulling the doors shut.

"They got away. Too many people." He focused on the metal bar still in Alex's hand. "Is that from my window?"

"Might be." Alex dropped it amongst the clothing at her feet.

"That's going on your tab." He looked at her arm. "Want me to pull that out?"

Alex looked at the bolt sticking out of her forearm. "*Damn.* Yes. I only had the bloody thing tuned last month."

"Brace yourself." Gregor took hold of Alex's shoulder and pulled on the bolt. There was a scraping metallic noise before it came loose.

"Thanks." Alex pulled off her glove, revealing the polished metal beneath. She flexed her fingers and growled when her fist didn't close properly. "The bastards damaged the internals!"

"Good thing you know an artificer." Gregor handed over her clockbow and the bolt he'd retrieved.

Alex examined the bolt. The tip was too bent for her to use it again—yet another reason to be annoyed. "Flora told you about Mister Dooley?"

"Aye. And about this mess you've gotten yourself into with the priests."

"And she's stolen your buttons again, I see." Alex looked pointedly at his chest.

"Gave 'em to her to look at just for tonight. She looked peaky when she came in earlier."

Alex grinned at him. Gregor grunted.

"Sid back yet?" she asked.

"Do I look like your servant?"

"Apprenticeships are always available."

"Don't push it, Reign. And he isn't, but if he wakes me up when he comes in, I'll bite his head off and sell his guts to Mister Jim for pie filling. Bloody pirates and actors. I sometimes wonder how you all stay alive."

CHAPTER 34

FATHER POLK ENCOUNTERS A PIOUS DILEMMA

F ATHER POLK HURRIED THROUGH Maye Fayre, his worried distraction causing him to stumble.

It was past midnight, but OverLondon never slept and the streets were congested with the city's wealthy, flittering from ball to ball in lacquered carriages and sedan chairs like so many exotic birds in cages.

Father Polk had always felt uncomfortable in this part of town. His congregation at St. Noris's—formerly St Paul's, until the Vengeful Queen burned it down—were a restrained lot, quietly focused on moving cash around in the high-stakes equivalent of the cup and ball magic trick. The most he had to do was threaten the accountants in his congregation with a visit from the Bad Habits if they didn't pay their forty percent, and he found even that stressful.

Until a few months ago, Father Polk had lived a largely untroubled life. But then Father O'Malley had talked him into joining the Saccharine Society and everything had gone wrong.

Father O'Malley, Father Bartholomew and Novice Lice had exploded, which left himself and Father Bollard, who Father Polk didn't like very much.

A thrill of panic shot down his spine as he spotted the over-ostentatious façade of St. Brereton's and the giant statue of Pope Gregory XIII being kicked in the buttocks by the Vengeful Queen.

The cathedral's great doors were open and he stepped inside, scanning the gilt and marble interior before breathing thanks to the Vengeful Queen when he saw Father Bollard's stooped figure. The other priest was standing before a giant fresco depicting the famous Battle of the Borders, with Mary, Queen of Scots leading her army while riding her hovering hairy coo, against the Vengeful

Queen, who was standing on the shoulders of a Yorkshire peasant, thus demonstrating her famously direct approach to metaphor.

"Father!" Father Polk cried out.

Father Bollard spun around and the candelabra in his hand dripped wax onto the flagstones at his feet. "Father Polk. It's you." He exhaled. "I thought—I don't know what I thought. What are you doing here?"

"My ring. It's gone!"

Father Bollard reared up to his full height. "What do you mean, it's gone?"

Father Polk twisted his hands in his cassock, feeling like a novice who'd just forgotten the Currency Litany at New Mass. "My ring! I had it in my pocket when I entered St. Weston's, but I can't find it anywhere now!" He glanced at Father Bollard's finger, seeing the glitter of gold and rubies. "How can you be wearing yours so openly after what happened today?"

Father Bollard shrugged defensively. "It's late. No one's going to see, and it felt like the right thing to do in memory of our departed brothers. And Novice Lice. He was a terrible, smelly boy and a worse novice, but it's still unfortunate."

"Terribly, terribly unfortunate." Father Polk wrung his hands. "What do you think happened?"

"It's obvious, isn't it? The Vengeful Queen visited him with her blessing where no one could see it," Father Bollard sniffed loudly. "Stupid boy. We both told him that searching O'Malley's rectory was a foolish thing to do, but did he listen?"

"What are we going to do?" Father Polk asked.

Father Bollard stared at him. "Pray to our Vengeful Queen."

"But it won't be enough! Our Vengeful Queen is punishing us." His stomach lurched as he blurted out the words he'd come here to say. "What we've done is wrong, and I can no longer be a part of it. We must destroy the pamphlets! I already have. I threw mine into the OverThames. I can only hope that the Vengeful Queen is appeased."

Father Bollard reeled back in shock. "You threw it out?"

"Yes! I just cannot risk Our Lady's wrath any more. I'm pleading with you to do the same. Your ring, too. You must destroy it, somewhere hot, somewhere it will melt. Oh, if only we had a volcano on English soil! The Vengeful Queen would see it as a sacrifice to the city and forgive us."

"You're being foolish." Father Bollard shook his head. "It's been made official. The explosions are a blessing, not a curse. To say otherwise is sacrilege. And I'm not giving you my ring. It's mine, and far too precious to throw away."

Father Polk stared at him. "Doesn't the thought of blowing up scare you?"

"I'd be foolish to say it didn't give me pause, but I've decided that our society has been blessed, Father Polk, not censured." Father Bollard's voice boomed around the church's cavernous interior. "This is a sign. The more I think about it, the more I believe that it is our *duty* to recruit new members and to expand."

"But Father—"

"As the senior member of our society, I feel it is also my duty to rebuke you, Father Polk! You have thrown away the sacred book. You are suggesting I throw away my sacred ring even as you admit you've lost yours! Your behaviour is *blasphemous*!"

Father Polk looked into Father Bollard's eyes and saw the light of fanaticism, stirred up into a noxious vindication. He backed away. "You are wrong Father. Wrong!"

Father Bollard slashed a hand through the air, his ring catching the light. "It is you who is wrong!"

"No! We never should have started the society. We never should have angered the Vengeful Queen."

"We celebrate the Vengeful Queen. *Celebrate*!" Father Bollard advanced towards Father Polk, the candlelight casting shadows beneath his eyes.

"No! I no longer want to be a part of this. I no longer wish to be a member of the society!" Father Polk's cassock tangled about his legs and he fell on his backside to scuttle along the floor like a fleeing crab until he reached a pew, grasping it to regain his footing.

"You will leave the society when I tell you that you can!" Spittle flew from Father Bollard's lips. "I will not hear any more of it. You *will* come to our next meeting on Monday night and you *will* be ready to face the penalty for your disloyalty. May our Blessed Lady strike you down if you don't arrive on time."

"You don't mean that!"

"I mean exactly that. Afterwards, you will aid me in recruiting more priests to our order. The Vengeful Lady wills it!"

Seeing the determination on Father Bollard's face, Father Polk's shoulders slumped. He'd never been a strong man and he'd joined the Church of Vengeful Acquisition precisely because it had so many rules. He didn't have the capacity to make a stand on his own.

"Alright. I will be there on Monday and will receive my punishment. But my ring..."

Father Bollard waved a hand dismissively. "If anyone finds it, they'll merely assume that someone has dropped an expensive ring, which they'll no doubt take for themselves and be eternally cursed by our Vengeful Queen. Now go, before you embarrass yourself more than you already have. You are making too much of an issue out of this."

"Am I?" Father Polk ran from the church with the dreadful premonition that this was the last time he would see Father Bollard. He just didn't know which of them was going to explode first.

CHAPTER 35

A BRAZEN BET

A LEX PAUSED IN FRONT of the Henry the Late to light a fresh cigar. She worked up a good puff for the sake of appearances before entering the pub with a swagger designed to command attention.

The place was packed with criers, Sugar Gang members and Bad Habits. The latter would no doubt claim they were drinking water in accordance with New Lenten dictates, but Alex was certain that anyone checking their tankards would see crystal-clear liquid rather than the tannin-brown substance that passed for water in this city.

Big Ivan held court at a distant table, surrounded by a group of his lieutenants. Alex had heard a rumour that the hamster man was nocturnal.

During the journey from Drury Lane, she'd played through how this visit would go.

Gregor had given her the idea with his parting words in The Armoury. When he'd said he wondered how she stayed alive, it had immediately reminded her of the mortalitye poole, which had sent her thoughts in an interesting direction. There were a lot of people with a vested financial interest in seeing her dead right now, which meant she had to devise a way to make it more appealing for them to keep her alive, at least for the next few days.

The crowd parted as she approached the bar and looked up at the board behind Mister Loom, studying the list of possible bets written beneath her name. None of the odds had changed. Right.

She blew three smoke rings languidly, then said, "Mister Loom, I require your assistance."

There was a satisfying lull of sound, with the exception of two criers discussing her lack of 'height' at full volume.

"Aye?" Mister Loom looked up from pouring gin into a tankard that had *Warter* written on its side, confirming Alex's earlier suspicion. People were painfully predictable.

"I would like to place a bet."

His eyebrows rose. "Oh? Who on?"

"I'd like to place a wager that whoever kills me will be killed *by me*."

Mister Loom set the tankard down, giving her his full attention. "Come again?" Behind Alex, a low murmur grew in volume.

"It's simple." She took her time inhaling another lungful of cigar smoke, then blew a stream from the corner of her mouth. "I, the Dread Pirate Purple Reign, wish to create a new mortalitye poole for whoever kills me."

Mister Loom frowned and nodded. "Okay, that's odd, but I'm with you so far."

"And I want to bet on *myself* as being the one that kills my murderer."

"Now you've lost me again," Mister Loom said.

"What's this, then?" The words boomed. "You want to bet that you'll kill your own murderer?"

Alex turned to see that the crowd had parted, leaving her looking directly at Big Ivan.

"That's exactly what I want to do. And I want to bet fifty pounds," Alex announced, enjoying the collective gasp from the pub's patrons. It was an absurd amount of money, but that was the point. She turned back to Mister Loom. "Will you take the bet?"

Mister Loom looked thoughtful. "Who would it be for, again?"

"It's obvious, Loom!" Big Ivan said. "Start a new poole under the words 'whoever murders Captain Reign'. Makes sense to me. Don't see why it wouldn't make sense to you."

"Yes, yes, I see that, but how are you going to kill someone if you're dead?" Mister Loom asked Alex.

"It's simple," Alex said. "If Big Ivan asks one of his lieutenants to kill me, who's murdered me?" She looked around the room slowly. "You'd say it was Big Ivan, wouldn't you, because he gave the order and his people obey his every command. They're loyal in the Sugar Gang."

There were a series of murmurs amongst the Sugar Gang members, most of them insisting that they were indeed loyal, while shooting sideways looks at Big Ivan.

"She's right there!" Big Ivan said. "People don't say that Sweet Suzy here gives people the carrot." He slapped a hulking lieutenant on the shoulder. "They say I do."

"Precisely," Alex said. "Using the same logic, it stands to reason that if I order one of my crew to kill my murderer, I'm the one responsible for their death."

Mister Loom shook his head. "Now you're getting into lawyer territory. I'm not sure I can agree to this."

"There is a precedent," a small man sitting at the end of the bar said. He was dressed in the peacock robes of a lawyer, and a towering wig was slumped beside his tankard of gin. "Five years ago, when Lonny Threeshanks died, you ruled on the poole that The Clockmaker had done it, even though it was a Leper who killed him."

"He's got you there, Loom!" Big Ivan said.

There were a series of titters and murmurs.

"What do you say?" Alex asked. "Will you take my bet?"

Mister Loom remained silent even as the bar's inhabitants clamoured for him to agree. This was good gossip, and everyone wanted to say they'd been present at such a historic occasion.

"I'll have to work out the odds," Mister Loom said finally. "I've heard rumours about your crew, Reign. Especially the fat one with the bowler hat. He's been seen with books. Can't trust a reading man."

Alex hoped no one ever learnt how long Sid took in the privy while reading those books. "The most well-read and deadly crew a pirate has ever known," she said grandly.

"What were those odds?" Big Ivan yelled.

"Give me a moment." Mister Loom consulted an abacus, his fingers moving hastily as the beads clacked. Then he scribbled for a while on a grubby notepad. Finally, he put down his pencil. "Odds would be three to one."

Big Ivan slapped the table before him. "Too good to miss! Put me down for ten pounds on Reign."

"I'll put five shillings against her!" Alex recognised the voice immediately as Crier Frank's.

"I'll put fifty pence on her!" This came from a Sugar Gang pusherman.

Alex allowed herself a smile of satisfaction as the betting went on, with Mister Loom climbing up on a stepladder and writing up a poole for *Thee Murderer Off Captaine Reign*. Within ten minutes he'd had to adjust the odds twice to make betting against her more attractive.

When the betting died down, Mister Loom climbed down the ladder and scowled at Alex. "Hold it. In all the excitement I forgot there's no way you could have fifty pounds on you. The last I heard, your ship was impounded precisely because you were skint."

"Mister Loom, everyone knows pirates don't walk around carrying great bags of money. We instead keep it safe, buried in treasure chests where it belongs," Alex said with a wink. "I assure you I will have the money for you within the three-day limit defined by the Gentleman Joe Rule."

"Come again?" Mister Loom said, just as the lawyer at the other end of the bar chuckled.

"Well played madame." The lawyer turned to Mister Loom. "The Gentleman Joe Rule, Mister Loom. Named after the late Earl of Spline who died whilst undertaking a five-hundred-pound wager that he could eat fifty cogcannon balls fired at close range. It bankrupted his entire family for five generations to come and prompted the Academic Council to create a new law." He looked at Alex with an amused smile. "Which Captain Reign has just alluded to. It stipulates that payment for any unconventional wager made on English soil, which is deemed foolhardy, dangerous, or downright stupendous will be delayed for three days. During this time either the family of the punter, or the punter themselves can withdraw the wager as long as they pay the bookmaker the penalty fee for any inconvenience they have experienced. However, until the three days are over, or the bet is cancelled, the wager stands."

"But I've just taken all these bets! If the wager is cancelled I'll have to pay the money back."

"Yes." The lawyer shrugged. "And Captain Reign would have to pay the penalty fee to reimburse you for your trouble."

"I didn't agree to this!"

"Ah." Alex took a long draw on her cigar. "But you did, when you calculated the odds for a bet that was by its very definition foolhardy, dangerous, and downright stupendous. Piratical, in fact." She grinned. "What's your penalty fee, Loom?"

Mister Loom glared at her before pulling out his abacus again and doing some quick-fingered calculations. "Two pounds, Reign."

"Make it three. I'd hate for my reputation as one of the most generous pirates on the globe to be tarnished. It won't be necessary though," Alex said as the murmurs—or in the criers' case, bellows—about where she may have buried fifty pounds rippled through the room.

Yes, she was going to soon be owing Mister Loom three pounds after she cancelled the bet, but she had no intention of wasting Mother Superior's reward.

For her plan to work, she'd had to wager an amount mind-boggling enough to be credible. OverLondon ran on gossip, and no one wanted logical thought to get in the way. Knowing her fellow citizens as she did, Alex could guarantee that the bar's inhabitants would spend the next twenty-four hours sharing the story of the night's events, increasing the amount with each retelling until they'd be insisting that she'd placed enough gold on Mister Loom's bar to purchase an entire fleet of airships. No one wanted to tell a story about a pirate who bet fifty pounds and couldn't pay. To the average OverLondoner, that would be inconceivable. The bigger the lie, the more everyone wanted to believe it.

Mister Loom glowered at her. "Alright. But if you cancel this ridiculous thing and don't pay up, you realise you're not just going to have to deal with me, you're going to have to deal with him too." He nodded at Big Ivan who was engaged in an enthusiastic conversation with a group of his henchmen.

"You doubt my word as a pirate? Mister Loom I'm deeply offended." Alex tutted.

Mister Loom grunted before turning away from her to serve a Bad Habit who was ordering 'purified' water.

"Congratulations," the lawyer at the end of the bar leaned towards her and murmured as he raised his tankard to her. "You've just made killing you *very* unattractive. At least for the next few days."

"That was my plan," Alex replied, keeping her own voice low enough so no one else would hear.

"How did you know about the Gentleman Joe rule?"

"Family secret." Alex tapped her nose. "Thanks for your assistance."

She then turned and bowed to Big Ivan, grinning at his booming laughter. Until he'd put that ten pounds down, she hadn't been able to count him out as being behind her attempted kidnapping. You never knew with Big Ivan.

"Can I get a quote so I can sell it to the Cry?" a crier in a threadbare uniform asked her.

She looked him up and down, feeling charitable when she took into account his gaunt cheeks, worn boots and lack of medals. "Of course, my good man. Tell them that anyone who murders Captain Alex Reign, proprietor of the Reign Agency—no job too expensive—will die within a day by her hand."

The crier took out a stubby pencil and a scrap of paper, muttering as he wrote. "Reign... expensive... hand. Yeah, got it."

"Wait." Alex grabbed onto his coat before he left and placed two coins in his hand. "Tell them I'll pay them a shilling if it runs tomorrow. The other one's for you. More people will hear it and the Cry'll be able to charge more for the advertisement they run with it. Eight in the morning should do it."

"Alright. I'll make sure of it. I've gotta hurry though, before anyone else gets in before me." The man hurried away.

Her work done, Alex spent a few more minutes playing up to the crowd before she headed back to The Armoury. Dawn wasn't far away and Sid would soon be back with news of the urchin. Before that happened, she needed sleep.

CHAPTER 36

SWEET PETE GIVES HIMSELF A TREAT

T HE DAWN CRY ECHOED over the city as Sweet Pete rolled out of bed.
Yawning hugely, he caught an advertisement for holiday packages to
the Welsh Republic, then shook his head at the ridiculousness of people in this
city. He never understood the desire to go abroad, especially to strange foreign
places. There were more than enough strange types infesting this city to keep a
body occupied. Strange types, pestilential urchins and Sugar Gang lieutenants
wanting to know why Pete hadn't sold as much product this week as the last.
This, when they knew that last week's sale had been a special exception! In all
his years walking the streets of Theatreland and Bloomsbury, Pete had never sold
four pounds of high-grade brown like he had to those priests. It was unheard of.

He scratched his belly through his nightshirt and walked bow-legged to the
stove in the corner of the room. He scooped a spoonful of omnicite shavings
onto the embers within, waiting until the flame glowed red, then checked the
kettle on the hob and measured a fresh scoop of tea leaves into the brown tannic
sludge already lining the pot.

In the time it took for the kettle to boil, he got dressed.

Crouching by his bed, he pulled away a piece of skirting board, revealing a
hidden compartment. He reached into it and pulled out a small snuff tin and
two bags. One bag was labelled *Bilder's Chalke* the other *Femur's Animal Glue
Granyools*. He placed them on a rickety table, upon which was already a set of
measuring scales and the two bags of sugar he'd picked up from the depot the
previous night.

After fastening his scoop to the trinket attachment on his stub, he got to
work.

He cursed as he weighed the bag of brown sugar from the depot. "Ten bleedin' ounces. It was supposed to be twelve. Miserable bastards." Muttering to himself, he mixed in enough glue granules until the bag weighed twelve ounces. He debated increasing the mix of glue granules and skimming some off for himself, then decided against it. Any more and it'd clump when the damp got into it. His customers expected brown to be a much higher standard than white, and the last thing he needed was some bleedin' lieutenant breathing down his neck again.

Setting the brown sugar aside, he moved on to the white.

Over the years, Pete had trained his customers to expect a mix of two parts chalk to five parts sugar. So much so that when he'd once upped the sugar percentage, his clients had complained the taste was off.

By the time he'd returned the glue granules and the chalk to their hiding place, the kettle had come to a simmer.

He bent backwards to ease the kink in his spine, and scowled.

Who the hell did Big Ivan think he was? Who was he, asking him, Pete, who moved more product than anyone else in this city, to *increase* sales? To who? The people in this country ate more sugar than anyone else on the globe. Half of 'em used it as tooth powder. Sugar was practically the English national dish. Was Big Ivan out pushing a cart in all weather, fending off urchins and freezing his chilblains off? Not bloody likely.

No, it was suckers like Pete doing all the work, and for what? These dingy lodgings and a landlady who stole anything that wasn't nailed down.

He collected his mug from the floor next to his bed and poured himself a cup of tea, giving the kettle a shake to loosen the leaves stuck in the spout.

At his age, he should be entitled to some *respect*. The criers got medals for their service, but did esteemed members of the Sugar Gang? If Big Ivan started handing out medals, Pete wouldn't be able to walk for the weight of 'em. He was due a reward. He'd done his time. He sold his quotas, day in day out.

He raised the mug of tea to his mouth, then paused as his eyes alighted on the snuff tin on the table. That tin contained the one precious ounce of uncut brown that Pete had skimmed off the top of the priest's order before cutting it with glue granules. He'd been saving it for his birthday, but why not? Why *not*? After the week he'd had, he bloody well deserved it.

Setting the mug down, he opened the tin and raised the contents to his nose, inhaling with a faint smile. Then he upended the tin into his mug, swiping the spare granules of sugar, chalk and glue from the table before considering his day.

First, he'd drop by the depot to pick up his ice cream tubs. Then he'd swing by the Nile Publishing House to drop off the brown delivery. If the weather was good, he'd make enough ice cream sales to sell out by two, which would mean another trip back to the depot...

He took an experimental sip of the tea. It was deliciously sweet, made all the sweeter because Pete knew that there were coves in this city who'd shop their grannies to taste this much brown at once. Fools with a problem, they were. Pete knew how to manage his tastes. He only ever sampled his own supply on special occasions.

Smacking his lips and bracing himself for the big hit, he gulped a mouthful of scalding liquid, embracing the sugary kick and the burn like a true connoisseur.

The liquid flowed to his stomach in a great rush, but rather than warming his belly, something else happened—something sharp and excruciatingly painful.

Later, Sweet Pete's landlady would swear she hadn't heard the screams or the noises caused by a grown man thrashing in agony, smashing a window and toppling a chair and table in the process. But by the time anyone started asking questions, Sweet Pete, sugar pusherman of Drury Lane and Bloomsbury, was dead.

CHAPTER 37

THE CAPTAIN'S ARM

T HE SUN WAS STILL to rise when Elias walked along Utopia Street towards Ingenious Mechanisms with a porridge pail in his hand.

He'd slept fitfully before getting up early to walk to Father O'Malley's rectory to ask the Bad Habits on guard if they'd found an injured trinket on the premises. An unfortunate creature missing a wing case had been dropped into his hand by a nun who'd said she'd been about to flush it down the privy. It was now resting safely in Elias's pocket, and he would construct a lightweight foil replacement for its carapace later.

As he walked, he went over his failed experiment of the previous night and decided that he needed to revisit the idea of incense being the culprit. He'd go to St. George's and return to St. Weston's later and gain samples of the incense they used in order to conduct some experiments. It was just a matter of elimination and deduction. Last night's setback was the kind of thing that happened when one undertook proper scientific research.

His step faltered when he saw Captain Reign leaning against the door of his shop with her arms crossed.

"Mister Dooley." Elias noticed that she didn't appear any more rested than he felt. She glanced at the pail in his hand. "Planning to feed an army?"

"It's porridge. Porridge *puttanesca*, actually. I think it's an Italian word meaning friendly, but I've yet to look it up." Elias unlocked the door of his shop. "How can I help you?"

"How good are you at fixing prosthetics?"

"I consider myself competent."

"Good. You can fix my arm. And then we have two priests to find. Flora will bring us the list from Sid when he returns, which will no doubt be within the hour." She followed him into his shop, waiting as he lit the lamps and gently lowered the new trinket into an aquarium. It swam to the bottom and hid behind a knot of omnicite weed.

"Where'd you discover that one?" the captain asked.

"Father O'Malley's. I stopped by the rectory before coming here. Can I take your coat?" Elias asked.

Captain Reign shrugged out of her cape and handed it to him.

"Would you like a cup of tea?"

"Yes, thank you. I've had a long night, heavy on swashbuckling and poor in booty, if you get my meaning."

"I don't, really."

"Never mind—we'll make a pirate of you yet." Captain Reign peeled the black glove from her left hand, setting it on Elias's desk. She then unbuttoned her doublet and shirt, draping them on the back of Elias's chair.

Kettle in hand, Elias did a double take, staring open-mouthed. He swallowed past the lump in his throat. "Is that—"

The captain looked up at him. "Take it all in, Mister Dooley."

"I've never seen anything so *spectacular*." Elias stumbled towards her. The smoothness! The appearance of suppleness!

He came to a halt and just stared. "Beautiful."

"Of course it is. Countless have fallen at my feet in awe."

"Can I touch?" Elias asked, his mouth dry.

"Be my guest." The captain raised her arm and the light once again flickered over the most impressive prosthetic Elias had ever seen. The sculpted muscles rippled as if they were real flesh, the metal plating moving as if it were the smoothest skin imaginable.

He vaguely noticed the captain's intact arm, which was tattooed with numerous complex images that would have been interesting if her prosthetic wasn't so captivating. The leather straps belted over her sleeveless undershirt presumably provided an anchor point for the device's immense strength without damaging the trinkets connecting it to her body. The prosthetic's attach-ment to her shoulder was seamless, skin merging with metal in perfect symbio-sis.

Elias ran a finger over the bicep and shook his head in wonder. "This is re-markable." Looking closer, he realised that the 'skin' wasn't completely smooth. On the upper arm were a series of small words engraved into the metal, with names in the Latin alphabet and other strange characters he'd never seen before. He studied them. "Amaka Ibe! Snori Larsen! Helga Schmid! Yahuar Capac! Did they all work on this?"

The captain shrugged. "Among others. Over the years it's turned into some-thing of a competition over whoever can make the most advanced addition."

"Who are these? I can't read the writing." Elias ran his fingers over some of the foreign characters.

The captain glanced down. "That one you're now touching is Noor Khan, the one below it is Zuou Biyu and, if my memory serves me correctly, the one next to that is Hiroyuki Kenichi of the Iron Artificers."

"Zuou Biyu," Elias breathed. "I thought she was only a myth. A librarian once loaned me her book, *Martial Devices Fore Intimat Interpersonal Engagement*. I've read it at least thirty times."

"She's the one responsible for the metal skin you're currently touching."

"Unbelievable. Can I see inside?"

"You'll have to, in order to fix it." The captain touched a small indent on her wrist. The outer skin lifted with a series of clicks, revealing one of the most complex mechanisms Elias had ever seen.

Each cog, each screw, each rod had been hand-tooled. They were all stamped with the insignia of the workshops they'd come from and were made from a heady combination of metal alloys. An arm like this would not only be incred-ibly strong, but it would be as flexible—if not more so—than the real thing, especially when reinforced with the leather harness.

Elias patted his pockets until he found his handkerchief, then mopped his brow with it. "And how... how can I help you?"

"If you look closely you'll see there's a bloody great hole in my forearm," the captain said wryly.

Elias focussed on the area in question. "Oh! How did that happen?"

"A clockbow bolt. Mine, actually. Shot at me last night." She shook her head when Elias looked at her sharply. "There are far too many details for me to go into, and we have far too much to do today. As you'll see, my fingers aren't working properly." She closed her hand into a fist and Elias saw the delay in the finger movement.

"Can you do that again, this time slower?" He snatched up his eyepiece, studying rods and gears. "And again? Yes. I see it. The bolt has warped this rod here."

"Can you replace it?"

"Honestly?" Elias looked up. "I'm not sure. I've never worked with something so bespoke. The sizing of the parts may not be standard."

"I don't need the technicalities—just tell me if you can do it. It's been a long night, Mister Dooley, and I would be *incredibly* grateful." The captain gave him a tight smile.

"Yes. Okay. Yes." Elias selected a pair of measuring callipers and held them up to the damaged part. "It looks like this is a five-inch timing rod. A number three Clayton's, with a Fenton bevel. I may have one of those. It's not brand new, but I think it'll fit. There's not much I can do about the outer layer, though," he said sadly.

"Function over beauty is the important thing." The captain's smile was genuine this time. "But before you start, why don't you make us that cup of tea? And make it strong."

By the time Elias had brought two mugs of tea back to his desk, Captain Reign was slumped in his chair with her chin on her chest as low snores filled the room.

Carefully, Elias removed the cigar from between the fingers of her non-prosthetic hand and stubbed it out. He then pulled up a crate, took a seat and got to work.

He painstakingly unscrewed the gears and cogs to get to the damaged part, setting everything aside on a square of watchmaker's black velvet. All the while, he marvelled at the turn his life had taken in only a few days. If he'd stayed with the Artificer's Guild he'd have never worked on something this specialised. It was a masterclass in prosthetic artistry, and he could already see how he could make significant improvements to the prosthetics of future clients with little extra expense.

The shop door opened, letting in a gust of frigid air as well as Vikram, who was draped in multiple layers of noxious woollens. He came to a stop when he saw Elias and Alex.

"Oh, you're here. Did you solve your little problem? Can I have the cookbook now? Why is she undressed? This is a distinguished disreputable establishment, I'll have you know."

Elias fitted the new rod into the captain's arm carefully. "To answer your questions in order, not yet, no, and I think it's obvious, don't you?"

There was a pause as Vikram made sense of the answers. "Why not? What happened with your little experiment?"

"It didn't work." Elias screwed in the rod. "Which means we have to conduct further enquiries."

"With the priests, you mean? If they tell you who did it, can I have the books then?"

"What's your last name?" Captain Reign opened her eyes lazily. She reached for the cigar Elias had stubbed out earlier, and placed it in her mouth before selecting a match from the box on his desk, striking it against the surface and lighting up.

"My last name? Belvoir," Vikram said.

"Pronounced 'beaver' in old English," Elias said, eliciting a glare from Vikram.

"Mister Belvoir?" The captain took a draw on her cigar.

"Yes? What? What do you want?"

"Kindly shut up. It's too early in the morning for me to feel this annoyed."

Vikram sputtered, obviously wanting to make some kind of sarcastic reply while also knowing that doing so would mean kissing his cookbooks goodbye.

"How long to go?" Captain Reign asked Elias.

"Another few minutes should do it. And then I'll get you to test it," Elias said. "May I ask how many trinkets you're using for the attachment?"

"Twenty, last count," the captain replied. "Necessary to be able to do all that swinging from the rigging. Even then, I need this so they don't get wrenched off." She patted the harness that criss-crossed her chest.

"Impressive," Elias said. "And how did you lose the arm?"

"That, Mister Dooley is a long and ancient story." She blew out a puff of smoke. For a moment, the scar on her cheek looked starker and her eyes more piercing than normal.

"Yes, yes we're all unique and special butterflies with tragic backstories," Vikram muttered to himself, having retreated behind his dam of books.

He was saved from the captain's reply when the shop door opened again.

The young lad, Michael, walked in chin first, exhibiting all the bravado of a mouse squaring up to a hungry cat.

"Good morning, Michael. Your porridge is here, as promised." Elias nodded to the pail he'd left by the captain's chair.

"Hello, mister. Thanks." The boy sidled over. "What are you doing?"

"I'm repairing Captain Reign's arm," Elias said. "If you take a look, you'll see that I've replaced this part, which was damaged last night."

Michael peered closer. "How'd it get damaged?"

"Someone shot me," the captain said with a serious expression that was belied by a twitch at the corner of her mouth. "So I had to scare the life out of them."

Michael's eyes rounded. "Cor, you mean you scared them to death?"

"I would've, if they hadn't run off with their tails between their legs."

"Like Novice Lice exploding yesterday? I heard Mister Khmalo at the Foundling House say that the priests exploded because they worshipped the wrong god. Do you think that's right? Because if it is, I *definitely* need to convince my parents to move heavens before the Vengeful Heaven property market crashes."

Elias was still deciding how to respond to such an ecclesiastical twister when Vikram's head popped up above his book crenulations. "You mean you know the name of the priest that exploded yesterday?"

Michael shrugged. "Yeah. Everyone does. It was on the Cry. But I knew him anyway because he was at Father O'Malley's all the time. Every Monday. Him and the other one that blew up, and the other two. Sometimes Thursday and Fridays as well."

"The other two." The captain repeated, looking awake now. "Do you know their names?"

"Not exactly," Michael said. "But I know what churches they come from 'cos I had to drive 'em both home on Saturday night when Gravid Bickle at the stable was sick and couldn't do it. It was late and we weren't really breaking the rules. One gave me a whole penny, but the other one just told me to say my prayers. I told him that I did every night, but he told me to say them more."

Elias, the captain and Vikram all looked at each other.

"Did any of them carry papers? A book, like this?" Vikram scrambled on his desk until he found a roughly sewn together pamphlet about the benefits of massaging grapefruit, and brandished it in the air. "Did you see anyone holding *anything* like this, anything at all?"

Michael wiped the too-big sleeve of his smock under his nose. "Yeah. At least the one from St. Brereton's did. He was talkin' about how he was lookin' forward to some wobbly cake or somethin'."

"Aha!" Vikram exclaimed. "There *is* another cookbook! And where there's another one, there'll be another two!"

Captain Reign ignored him. "Which churches did you take them to?" she asked Michael.

"St. Noris's in the banking district and St. Brereton's in Maye Fayre." Michael looked at Elias's hand, where Phillips had been surprisingly well-behaved for the past hour, perhaps as awed by the captain's arm as Elias. "Have you made my thing yet? Cos I really need one, cos I have all kinds of jobs that I need it for. It could hold bits of straw for the goats to chew and it could wave at people when

I don't want to. It's important to be polite, even when you don't want to be. Mister Khmalo told me that."

"That's excellent advice, but it won't be finished for a month." Elias braced himself for an argument. Instead, the boy merely hefted the porridge pail.

"Alright. I've got to get to work now. Tulip the goat's been off her food and I promised I'd sing at her until she feels better."

"Good lad," Captain Reign said.

"Will there still be more porridge tomorrow?" The boy's tone was painfully hopeful.

"I assure you, there will be porridge tomorrow," Elias said.

"Okay. Uhm. You're not looking for any real estate in Vengeful Heaven, are you?" Michael asked the captain.

"No, but if I hear of anyone who is, I'll be sure to let you know," she said solemnly.

"Alright. Good. I'm going now." Lugging the pail, he staggered through the doorway and down the street.

Captain Reign looked thoughtfully in Michael's wake, puffing on her cigar while Elias replaced the final cog in her arm.

"Well?" Vikram demanded, breaking the silence.

"Yes?" Elias asked.

"He just told you where to find the other cookbooks! What are you waiting for? Go get them!"

Elias leant back and studied the arm. "That should do it. Can you clench your fist for me and then raise each of your fingers in turn?"

The captain did, moving each of her fingers to make a rude gesture at Vikram, who snorted. She grinned. "Good as new, Mister Dooley. *Excellent* work."

Elias's cheeks became warm. "It was my pleasure."

"No, I assure you, it was entirely mine." She closed the arm's outer casing. "Normally I'd charge someone to look at it, being such an *exclusive* item, but since you've done such excellent work, I'm feeling generous. Why don't you sign it instead? To show you've joined the ranks of your fellow skilled artisans."

Elias blinked in disbelief. "You'd really let me sign it?"

"Just here will do." She pointed to a spot two inches above the hole made by the clockbow bolt. "Do you have an engraving tool?"

"I do!" Elias scrambled on his desk until he found it. "This is such an honour."

The captain smiled benevolently. "I know, but you deserve it."

She held her arm steady as Elias carefully engraved the words *Elias Adaze Dooley* in his neatest hand.

Captain Reign stubbed out her cigar, stood up and pulled on her shirt, buttoning it up swiftly. "Right, Mister Dooley, we have priests to question. I'll take the one in Maye Fayre, you take the one in the banking district. We'll rendezvous at the Reign Agency at two." She shrugged on her doublet. "And with that, I'll leave you." She turned to Vikram. "If Flora comes with a list of priest names for me, tell her that I don't need it any more and direct her home."

"What am I? Your servant?"

"You're someone who wants to be in my good graces if you want that cookbook." With those words, she swirled her cape around her shoulders and left.

Elias watched her go, marvelling at what had just happened. He'd worked on the same arm as Helga Schmid, Amaka Ibe and Zuou Biyu!

A book hit him in the chest. He turned to find Vikram glowering at him.

"What?"

"You worked for over an hour and the only payment you got was signing an arm! You'll be shutting down within the week."

Elias stuck his nose in the air. "This is something you wouldn't understand, and anyway, I have important business to take care of in the banking district."

"Go on, then. And when you find the next cookbook, be sure to give it to me. I'll even let you sign it, if that kind of thing tickles your fancy so much."

Vikram ducked behind his literary battlements as Elias threw the book back across the room at him.

Outside, the Cry echoed down Utopia Street.

Hear ye! Hear ye! It's been officially announced that a compost heap exploding at the Artificer's Guild Hall at five thirty this morning was responsible for the

large amount of fertile doings covering the surrounding area. Mistress Fenderpos-
sum was quoted as saying that it was the result of a virulent numpty build-up in the
vicinity. Stop. The Dread Pirate Purple Reign has placed a fifty-pound bet at the
Henry the Late that she will kill her own murderer, if murdered. Bets in Captain
Reign's favour have reached one hundred pounds. She was quoted as saying,
'Anyone who murders Captain Alex Reign, proprietor of the Reign Agency—no
job too expensive—will die within a day by my hand.' Mister Loom has stopped
further bets until more people bet against her. Stop. Ye've heard! Ye've heard! Do
you have too much money? Why not invest in Ephemeral Shares? Meaninglessness
made profitable! Buy Ephemeral today!

Captain Reign burst through the shop door again, her expression gleeful.
"The heap exploded. Your experiment worked!"

"It worked," Elias said faintly. "But there was a delay. A ten-and-a-half-hour
delay." The implication of this dawned on him. "We need to go and see the other
priests!"

"Immediately," the captain said. "And when we see them, we need to find out
who gave them the sugar and stop them from eating any more of the stuff!"

CHAPTER 38

COUNT MENDACIUM HEARS SOME UNFORTUNATE NEWS

C OUNT MENDACIUM WAS WALKING through Westminster on his way to a meeting when he heard the Cry. His step faltered and his composure began to slip, but he managed to recover it in time. Turning away from his destination, he headed instead for the Henry the Late. Despite the early hour, it was open, but then again, no OverLondon pub would ever admit to being closed.

Taking a table in a dark corner, he glared at the mortalitye poole. There it was, the poole Captain Reign had set up last night. Even now, a cretin from the Sugar Gang was trying to place a bet in her favour only to be rejected.

Vengeful Lady only knew who Reign had commissioned to assassinate her murderer. He'd once heard a rumour that she'd started life as a Whitechapel urchin, which could even mean The Clockmaker had an interest in the matter. A Clockmaker affiliation would certainly explain why she'd had her man sniffing around looking for the urchin girl.

Thanks to Roddy and Keef failing to capture her last night, Reign would no doubt be sniffing around for them too. If the Count wasn't careful, that would lead her directly to him, which would be untenable.

He ordered a mug of stomach-corroding coffee and drank it while considering this new development.

His original plan had been for his men to abduct Reign and take her to their dingy stable in Whitechapel. Once she'd been tied up next to her idiot employee, the Count would have set the next wheel in motion.

However, the damn pirate was still loose in the city. This meant he was now forced to decide if she still posed a risk to him. After all, if her man and his lackeys couldn't tell her anything, would she ever link him to the priests' deaths?

Maybe not.

At least, not in any way that could be unravelled before Mother Superior paid up. After that, the Count would be on his way to OverParis. It was only a matter of days until he was free of this disgusting city and the imbeciles that infested it.

He reached into his coat and pulled out the letter he'd penned earlier. It had been pleasantly diverting to carry someone else's death sentence around, but now was the time to act.

The envelope was sealed with crimson wax, but he didn't need to open it to recall what it said. It contained only two sentences.

Clockmaker, the urchin you seek is buried in a basement in the building that was once Beazel's Whitechapel Livery Company. The three men you'll find there were responsible for her death.

It was to the point, which was exactly what the Lepers would be. Rookery justice was fast and the Lepers rarely asked complex questions if they found a man standing next to a corpse holding a bloody knife, or—in this case—three men in some stables with a murdered urchin buried in the cellar.

Until this moment, the Count had never experienced the thrill that came with holding the power of life and death. In fact, until a few days ago, he'd only thought about power in the context of wealth and respect.

Suddenly, he wished he could be there when those two fools and the pirate idiot realised they were about to die so he could see the expressions on their faces.

No, he'd have to delay his gratification until another day, another time. If his plan worked, there'd be ample opportunity to later witness someone's life being extinguished by his order, but for now, he'd have to settle for one of his spies relaying the events to him.

He finished his coffee, then pulled the hood of his cloak over his face and left the pub. Looking around to make sure he wasn't being followed, he veered off into a dank alley, wincing at the muck squishing beneath his shoes. He continued until he reached a pile of empty gin barrels stacked on their side.

Covering the lower half of his face with his handkerchief, he knocked on a barrel with his walking stick, waiting for the sound of movement within.

He cleared his throat, modulated his tone of voice, and adjusted his accent to be unrecognizable. "I have a message to deliver to The Clockmaker. Any urchin willing to make five pence had better crawl out of there now."

A grubby face appeared at the end of the barrel, looking at him suspiciously. "Five pence? What you done, mister?"

"What I've done is offer you five pence to take The Clockmaker a message," he replied coolly.

There was the sound of scrambling and the urchin crawled out. She was weedy, even for her kind. She wore a tattered purple knit cap that was too big for her and she was wrapped in a disgusting threadbare blanket.

"That all?" she asked.

"Yes. And if you keep quiet about this conversation for the next seven days, I'll return and pay you another five pence." He'd be in OverParis by then, but she wasn't to know that.

She gave him a world-weary look. "I weren't born last night. If you want me to keep quiet, you gotta pay me ten pence now and the other five in seven days."

"Fine. How long will it take you to get there?"

"Hour if I run fast. More if I get held up."

"Make it an hour. Here, take this and here's your ten pence. I'll know if you open my missive or don't deliver it." He handed her the letter and the money.

"Yeah. Whatever."

He watched as she scurried off, then went about his day.

In a matter of hours, the only connections between him, the exploding priests and the missing urchin would be eliminated. He could now spend his remaining free time in this dreadful city conducting his experiments. It was imperative that he learn how the reaction between the acid and the omnicite had not only been delayed, but amplified so dramatically. If he could learn the key to the aberration, he'd be the most powerful man in the world! An explosive device that was ingestible, with a delayed effect? He'd be able to assassinate anyone. And if a measly cup of sugar could explode a man, what would a barrel do? He'd be able to blow cities out of the sky! OverLondon would be the first to go.

The OverParisians would reward him handsomely. If they knew what was good for them.

CHAPTER 39

AN ALARMING MEETING WITH
FATHER POLK

A S ELIAS'S HACK NAVIGATED through congested streets, the clothing of the pedestrians changed from flat caps and aprons to the traditional black bowler hats of bankers.

Spurred on by Elias's promise of a bonus for speed, the driver almost slammed into an Auditor, a banking district Beadle, who was crossing the street. Shaking a fist covered in the traditional abacus knuckle dusters, she yelled for the hack to slow down, but the driver ignored her, racing on until he reached his destination.

Elias paid the driver and sprinted up the steps of St. Noris's Cathedral, pushing through the half-closed doors and looking about wildly.

"Father?" His voice echoed around the cavernous marble interior. "Is there a priest here?"

A stern-looking woman lighting a candle before a statue of the Vengeful Queen glared at him. "Young man, the Vengeful Lady doesn't approve of hasty marriage. May you atone for your sins."

"This isn't about a wedding," Elias said impatiently. "What's the name of the priest here?"

"Father Polk. But I don't see why you need to bother him this early in the morning, I hope he gives you a lecture about manners." With another censorious look, she bustled away.

Elias cupped his hands around his mouth. "Father Polk!" The sound echoed off of the reliquaries, the vaulted gilt ceilings and the cathedral's famous tryptic, which featured the Vengeful Queen opening the First Bank of OverLondon, the

Vengeful Queen bathing in her wealth and the Vengeful Queen hunched over her hoard, demanding more wealth while wearing her flaming hen finery.

"What? What's the matter, my son?" A priest hurried from a side door, his footfalls echoing. "What's the problem?"

Elias focused on the priest's lined and harried face, his simple black robes and his shock of white hair. "Have you eaten any of the sugar?" he demanded.

Father Polk tripped, grabbing a pew to steady himself. "Sugar, my son? I have no idea—"

"You don't have *time* for this!" Elias said impatiently. "I just need to know. Have you eaten any of the sugar? Have you made any of the recipes?"

The priest blanched. "How do you know about the recipes?" he whispered.

"It's not important. Have you?"

Father Polk shook his head. "No, but—"

"Where is it? The sugar? It has something in it that detonates when you eat it."

"I threw it into the river last night." Father Polk clutched his wealth beads. "Are you saying the sugar is poisoned?"

"It's an explosive," Elias said. "I believe it detonates ten-and-a-half hours after it's eaten."

"Vengeful Lady forgive us all. This is horrific. And I almost ate one of the scones! It's too much to bear." The priest slumped onto a pew, cupping his head in his hands. "Father O'Malley, Father Bartholomew, Novice Lice!"

"Who else has the sugar?" Elias asked. "I need to know, Father. They're in great danger."

"Father Bollard is the only other member of our group." Father Polk's words were muffled by his hands. "I saw him last night. He said he wanted new members to join, because of the miracles—" He shot to his feet. "I have to warn him!"

Elias put a hand on the priest's shoulder. "Someone's already doing that, Father. What I need from you is the name of the person who sold you the sugar. Where did you get it from?"

Father Polk's face turned a sickly grey. "Sweet Pete from Bloomsbury. Father Bartholomew arranged it. It was meant to be a batch of finest brown. It was terribly expensive, but Father Bartholomew assured us that the taste would be worth it. I just couldn't bring myself to make a recipe and eat it. It's New Lent!"

"Thank you for the information, Father. Please don't tell anyone of this conversation," Elias said before running from the church.

Sweet Pete. He had a name. All he had to do was find the man.

CHAPTER 40

CAPTAIN REIGN TAKES THE CAKE

A LEX PUSHED THROUGH THE crowd lining the marble steps of St. Brereton's, OverLondon's most picturesque cathedral, dodging a heavily
bandaged tourist who'd no doubt attended Mistress Fenderpossum's recent
cherub demonstration.

There were portrait painters everywhere. Alex noticed that a few of them had
caricatures of her on their stands, and one of them had even managed to give her
more 'height' than both her wanted poster artist and Blowhardi combined.

She pushed on one of the huge wooden doors only to find it locked.

"Doesn't open until one," a portrait artist said without pausing the sketch
he was doing of a young woman wearing a huge hat and a black lace face veil.
So far, he'd only managed to draw a massive pair of buck teeth, conforming to
the universal truth that any portrait artist stationed in front of any picturesque
landmark will in fact be a frustrated dentist, drawing anyone brave enough to
pay for a portrait as a massive set of chompers with a face wrapped around them.
"Father Bollard doesn't like early punters."

"Oh." Alex put her hands on her hips, examining the church's Gothic façade.
"Where's the rectory?"

"Over there." He tilted his head to the left side of the building. "It won't do
you any good. He doesn't like visitors either. He'll set the Vengeful Lady against
you, he will. Rumour has it that he fired his housekeeper last night for telling
him he needed to sweeten up. Kicked her out without a reference, onto the street
and all. Last I saw she was headed for Westminster to put in a complaint with
Cardinal Chudleigh."

"Charming. I think I'll risk it." Alex made her way to the rectory and knocked on the door. When no one answered, she peered through the windows. She couldn't see anything, but that didn't stop the hairs on the back of her neck rising.

Using her prosthetic arm, she knocked again, only this time a lot harder. Wood splintered, the lock gave way and the door swung open.

Alex didn't need to walk more than two steps into the hall before she saw the pool of congealed blood on the floor.

She sighed. "Too late."

She walked back outside and looked around. The alleyway was clear. She re-entered the house, closing the door firmly before bracing herself to look into the room leaking all the blood.

It had once been a bedroom. Now it was what the curator of an art gallery would call an 'Installation of Deconstructed Priest'.

Other than a bed that had once contained the late Father Bollard, the room consisted of a floor-to-ceiling shrine to the Vengeful Queen. Or, more to the point, the Vengeful Queen and the late Father Bollard. Studying the various amateur portraits of the Vengeful Queen embracing, whipping—and, in one instance, standing on the head of a gaunt-looking priest—Alex had a feeling that the late Father Bollard would have been a frequent customer of Vikram's shop if he'd known about it.

What remained of Father Bollard was mixed with paper confetti. On closer inspection, she saw that it was printed parchment. Leaning over the bed, Alex spotted the word 'scone' on one fragment and uttered a curse.

He'd been reading the cookbook in bed, maybe even as he exploded. There was no sign of a ring.

She debated collecting a relic or two, but realised that she didn't have a bucket or a bag to put them in. Besides, there was something about the scene that didn't sit right with her.

Her eyes alighted on a painting of the late Father Bollard being flown through the air in the clutches of the Vengeful Queen in her flaming chicken form. The picture was now coated in priest.

Alex left the room. She searched the rest of the rectory, checking for anything that looked out of place, only to be disappointed.

The kitchen was her final port of call. As she walked through the doorway, movement caught her eye and she stopped to pick up a limping trinket. Recalling Elias's hospital aquarium, she placed it gently in her pocket and resumed her search.

The sink was full of dishes that showed clear signs of baking. Examining spoons, mixing bowls and an empty sugar bag, Alex started to form a picture of what had happened. The priest had fired his housekeeper and had then taken advantage of her absence to finally make a recipe from the cookbook.

Her suspicions were confirmed when she opened the ice box and discovered a large slice of cake sitting on a silver tray. It was covered in cherries and creamy white icing. The cake itself was strawberry pink.

It was the prettiest lethal thing Alex had ever seen.

With great care, she picked up the tray with the cake on it, then left the rectory. Maybe Elias would be able to learn something by analysing it. At the very least, she'd just saved some other unfortunate from exploding by giving in to sweet temptation.

On her way back to The Armoury she ran into one of Maye Fayre's Butlers and informed them that Father Bollard required their immediate attention.

CHAPTER 41

THE LANDLADY WHO DOESN'T KNOW NUFFIN'

E LIAS WAS AWARE OF the eyes of Sweet Pete's landlady, Mrs Shaft, boring into his back as he knocked on the door of a third-floor flat of a tenement building situated in a dingy alley on the edge of Theatreland.

He was still breathing heavily after running all over Soho trying to learn Sweet Pete's address. He'd finally got it from an urchin who'd been wan with sugar withdrawals due to the ice cream pusherman not having turned up to work. Elias had immediately experienced an awful premonition of why that may have been.

"I told you, 'e's not in there. No good reason for 'im to be in at this hour," Mrs Shaft said in a high-pitched, irritated voice. She was a haggard woman with a tight bun and hollow cheeks that she sucked in with disapproval.

Elias tried knocking again. "Can you let me in? I fear something terrible has happened."

"Can't do that, lovey. Not wivout his permission."

"I'm worried that he may not be in a state to give permission at this moment."

Mrs Shaft's lips pursed. "But fink of what people would say if I just started letting people into other people's places. It's not right, is it?"

"I'll give you sixpence," Elias said desperately. "Please."

She sucked in her cheeks again. "That might work. It *might* work but see, sixpence ain't an awful lot in today's economy, lovey, is it?"

"A shilling. It's all I have to spare."

"Alright, but you have to pay up first."

Elias scrambled in his pockets and handed over a coin.

Snatching it up, she produced a ring of keys and walked past him. Before slipping a key into the lock, she turned and said, "Don't tell him I got a key, alright, lovey? He changed the locks last month and don't know our Garry told our Les to make a copy."

"Fine. Fine. Hurry."

The door swung open, revealing a room that was empty except for Sweet Pete lying in the middle of it wearing his red-and-white-sequined Sugar Gang uniform.

"Will you look at that. 'E's dead," Mrs Shaft said in a flat voice.

Elias took a step forward. "Sweet Pete?" He knew even as he said the words that Sweet Pete wasn't going to answer, not lying on the floor like that. A cold breeze whisked through broken windowpanes, ruffling the dead man's sparse hair.

Elias scanned the room, noticing the unfaded squares of wallpaper where pictures had once hung. The room smelled strongly of tea, sugar and old socks, overlaid with the deceased odour of Sweet Pete.

"Why isn't there any furniture?" he asked.

Mrs Shaft tried her best to look baffled. "Lord knows, lovey. It's 'ow it was when I found it."

"You already found him like this earlier?"

Mrs Shaft's face was blank. "Figure of speech, lovey. I'm *findin'* him now, ain't I?"

Elias approached the body and crouched down to turn it over, feeling for a pulse, just to be sure.

He then took out his notebook and a pencil, making a sketch of Sweet Pete before scanning the floor, which had been recently swept. There were streaks of what looked like spilt tea and some kind of chalky substance on the boards, along with small pieces of china and broken window glass.

He examined Sweet Pete's prosthetic scoop. There was a dent in it.

Whatever had happened, Sweet Pete hadn't died without a struggle and he was certain Mrs Shaft was lying about everything, even potentially her name.

"What time did you hear the windows breaking?" he asked.

Mrs Shaft half-heartedly placed a hand to her mouth. "Oh my lord," she said, deadpan. "Would you look at that. The windows are broken. Didn't hear a fing. Anyway, why'd you want to know?"

"I'm a concerned citizen."

"Yeah? Of this parish? Pull the uvver one."

"Have you called the Sugar Gang?"

"Yeah. I imagine they'll be along shortly. But I didn't call 'em because I knew 'e was dead. Just because I had this, like, hunch. You know Big Ivan don't like people keepin' news from 'im."

"That's something, at least." Elias unbuttoned Sweet Pete's shirt carefully.

"Ere, what're you doin'? You can't do that!"

"It's okay. I'm an artificer and possibly a privateer."

A lost-looking trinket fell onto the floor. Elias placed it in his pocket. Studying Sweet Pete's prosthetic, he pulled on it gently and both the scoop and the attachment sleevette came away immediately, revealing another two alarmed trinkets. Elias stowed these with the other one, ignoring Phillips's high-pitched coos and waving arm.

"You're not stealin' 'em, are you? Because that's illegal. I'll be forced to tell the Sugar Gang when they come, I will. It's not right." Mrs Shaft sidled over, her eyes focused eagle-sharp on Sweet Pete's body, obviously cataloguing anything she may have missed earlier.

"My shop is Ingenious Mechanisms in Whitechapel, and you can collect them once they're rehabilitated. I will, however, require proof of ownership." Elias continued undoing Sweet Pete's buttons, revealing a massive dark bruise on the man's stomach.

Elias's own stomach clenched as his suspicion became a reality. Something had broken or erupted inside Sweet Pete's body—something that had caused dreadful damage. Given what Elias had recently learnt from Father Polk, his thoughts immediately went to omnicite. This was the exact reaction he'd expect to see if someone had ingested the substance. But if Sweet Pete had been the one to put omnicite in his sugar, he wouldn't be stupid enough to eat it.

But what if... what if the sugar had already been adulterated with the omnicite ahead of time? And what if Sweet Pete had added a mystery ingredient that caused the explosion to not only be delayed, but that allowed the omnicite and stomach acid to mix together fully before reacting? What if Sweet Pete *hadn't* added that ingredient to the sugar he consumed? He'd want to have it straight and uncut, wouldn't he?

It was a tenuous theory, but at the same time, every OverLondoner expected their food to be 'spiced up' in some way, whether it was sawdust in baking flour or water in milk. The problem was that every single food vendor in the city used different 'ingredients' and kept their special 'recipes' to themselves so that no one else could copy the unique flavour of their specific product.

What could Sweet Pete have added to extend his brown sugar that could have delayed the omnicite's reaction? Elias looked at the white residue on the floor. His first guess was that Pete had used chalk for his white sugar, but what would he have used for the brown?

"Did you find any sugar in the room when you cleaned it out?" Elias asked. "Any sweet food? Cakes, ice cream? And was there anything else? Anything that could be mixed with brown sugar to bulk it out?"

"He's Sweet Pete! Of course there was sugar—but I wouldn't know about that, because it's mysteriously disappeared," Mrs Shaft said quickly. "And I wouldn't know about any uvver stuff because I weren't 'ere, but I can say that if I '*ad* been 'ere before now, I didn't see anyfink but the sugar, some tea leaves an' some dried up old bread."

Elias closed Sweet Pete's eyes, rebuttoned his shirt and stood up. Giving Mrs Shaft his full attention, he said in an urgent tone, "This is important. The sugar that was in this room could hurt people. You have to make sure no one eats it."

Mrs Shaft sucked her teeth and looked shiftily over his shoulder. "That's all good an' well, lovey, but since I 'ave no idea what 'appened to it, I can't 'elp you."

"But if someone were to take the sugar from here, who would they be?" Elias asked. "Can you give me a name?"

"I didn't 'ear or see anyfink so I can't 'elp you there an' all."

Elias looked into the woman's eyes and pictured multiple people around this city—children, women, even some of the city's few elderly—drinking tea laced with brown sugar they'd bought cheap on the black market, and ending up like the dead man on the floor.

"It's gone, isn't it? You've already sold it, haven't you?" he asked.

Mrs Shafts voice took on a menacing edge. "I 'ave no idea what you're talkin' about, an' if you don't leave soon I'm goin' to be forced to call for the Ushers an' tell 'em that you stole all Sweet Pete's stuff."

Realising that he'd have to find some other way to inform people, Elias rushed to the door.

"'Ere, where you goin'?" Mrs Shaft demanded.

Elias looked over his shoulder. "If you won't tell people, I will. Goodbye, Mrs Shaft."

CHAPTER 42

THE LEPERS COME CALLING

"Roddy's goin' out for a pie. Do you want one, Sid?"

Sid woke with a start, looking around before remembering the blindfold covering his eyes. "What? Who goes there?"

"Me, Sid."

"Keef?" Sid asked, frowning. There was something odd about Keef's voice, as if his nose was blocked.

There was just enough light coming through the blindfold to tell him it was day. Sid must've passed out after his fourth escape attempt. Even though Roddy and Keef had assured him that their boss was going to let him go soon, he'd still figured that he had to make the effort. The captain valued Sid's dependability, and his reputation was being damaged every minute he remained tied to this chair.

He'd woken up from his first escape attempt with Roddy and Keef righting his chair, moving it to a place where they could keep an eye on him, telling him he'd do himself an injury if he kept wobbling about. Sid had gone through his repertoire of heroic threats, but after they'd explained that they didn't like the situation any more than he did, he'd agreed to a cup of tea. Roddy had held it up for him to sip, intermittently dunking a biscuit for Sid to suck, which had been nice of him. It had been a Lady Kipling's Fancy. Sid hadn't had a Lady Kipling's since he'd been a lad.

It wasn't long afterwards that Sid realised there was a kid hanging around as well. Further questioning revealed that she was the very urchin he'd been looking for. He'd asked some decisive questions and Roddy and Keef had admitted that the villain had nabbed Grub and had ordered them to kill her, but they hadn't.

Now she spent most of her time asking Roddy and Keef if she'd definitely have her own bed and her own pillow when they moved to the farm that they kept talking about.

"Yeah, Sid. It's me," Keef said. "We're finkin' we're hungry and Grub wants an anchovy and egg pie—" Sid heard a girlish whisper. "Wiv pickles, yeah, I won't let Roddy forget the pickles, poppet. An' I'm havin' a liver an' onions. What do you want, Sid?"

Sid's stomach chose that moment to growl loudly. "I could do with you untying me, Keef," he said. "I'm gettin' leg cramp."

"Can't do that, Sid," Keef said in a regretful tone. "His Lordship said we had to keep you tied up until he said. And blindfolded. In case you recognise us. It's like that evil mastermind fing you told us about. You can't just have the henchmen take the mask off the good'un so he can recognise the evil mastermind. The good'un's gotta work it out on his own."

"I could work it out by you telling me who he is," Sid said, thinking it wouldn't hurt to try this line of reasoning for the fifth time.

"I'd like to help you there, but like we told you, if we did that, he'd grass on us to Big Ivan and that'd drop us right in it." There was a faint noise before Keef said in a syrupy voice, "What, poppet? You fink we should untie him? But if we do that an' he gets away, the bad man will find out an' we'll get in trouble and won't get to live on our farm."

"That's right," said Roddy. "We can't do anyfink that messes wiv our farm plan."

There was another quiet whisper before Roddy spoke again. "Well, yeah, we could scrag him, but that's not very nice, is it? I fink the uvver night proved we wasn't too good wiv kidnappin' people, let alone scraggin' 'em. The pirate woman almost had our guts tied in a knot."

"The captain?" Sid asked. "You tried to scrag the captain?!" His chest expanded as anger filled his belly, exactly the way it did in the books whenever the hero was outraged. That was the secret. He just hadn't been outraged enough before, but now he was. He was full to his earholes with fury. No one hurt his captain!

"Not *exactly*—more kidnap her so His Lordship could question her. Sid, you better be careful there. You're turnin' red, an' we don't want you gettin' all worked up and wigglin' your chair and fallin' over again. How many times is it now?"

Sid inhaled great gulps of air. He was going to burst free of these ropes and he was going to save the day and—

A great crashing sound filled the room.

Sid heard shouts, footsteps and the dreaded scrape of knives on stone. His insides clenched painfully. He knew that noise.

He heard a sing-song voice that sounded like it'd been gargled through a dead fish. "Come out, come out, urchin-killing scum. We've got a little game we want to play with you."

He couldn't see them, but their stench was rank enough that there had to be more than one. Awful laughter echoed in his ears.

"Hide, poppet!" Keef shouted.

"What do you want?" Roddy asked, panic in his voice.

"Your guts!" The word was a satisfied hiss that sounded all the more terrifying for Sid not being able to see the mouth that produced it. "The guts of all three of you for breakin' the Rules and killin' one of The Clockmaker's urchins. We're gonna enjoy this. It's been *weeks*!"

"No!" The word was a girlish shriek. "Don't kill them. I'm alive!"

"Who are you?" the voice demanded.

"Grub! I'm alive. They saved me. Another man kidnapped me and they saved me." Grub was clearly young, but her voice had an edge of command that reminded Sid of the captain.

"What do you mean they saved you?" The voice was sceptical.

"They did save me! They stopped the bad man from killing me. And the tied-up man is the one who found me. He works for a pirate and he was looking for me."

"Bad man? Who's this *bad man*?"

"The one who kidnapped me."

"Do *you* know who this bad man is?"

This was followed by an audible gulp from either Roddy or Keef.

"'E's some kind of posh nob," Keef wheezed. "Don't know anyfink else. We just came along at the right time an' saved her, like she said."

"Can't we just kill 'em and tell The Clockmaker they'd kidnapped her?" The words were hissed in a blood-chilling whisper by another Leper. "We could do her too. He thinks she's dead already. I ain't killed anyone for months, Beryl."

"Yeah, but if we do that, it's breakin' the Rules, innit? The Rules say we can't kill rookery coves."

"Yeah, but it wouldn't be killin'. We'd be followin' Clockmaker's orders."

"But I'm alive, so you wouldn't be followin' orders," Grub said. "And he'll find out. He always knows. They saved me an' they gave me a pillow and they're gonna adopt me an' we're gonna live on a farm wiv ducks."

Sid, who'd been following this conversation by turning his blindfolded head like a hooded pigeon, stopped abruptly as he felt a blade pierce through his clothing and press against the soft skin of his belly. The stench of the Leper's breath washed over his face.

"What about this one?" said a voice in his ear. "We could gut 'im now an' say they did it, an' then do them."

"We could."

In the moment of silence that followed, Sid tried not to widdle his pants. Through the quivering tip of the knife he could sense the urge to deliberately make the blade slip, to rip and tear.

"We can't," the other Leper said finally. "She's right. He'd find out."

"But if no one's dead here, why'd The Clockmaker get a message?"

When no one replied, sheer panic drove Sid to find his voice. "It's a villain plan, isn't it?" he croaked. "Frame the heroes and then get away while they're being punished for a crime they didn't commit. There's millions of books about it. And plays."

"Yeah. Like in the books an' plays," Keef said. "Sid knows fings like that. He's told us all about it."

"Why's he tied up like this if you're not the villains?" the Leper holding the knife to Sid's stomach demanded.

"Ahhh," Keef and Roddy said together.

"It was a game," Grub said hastily. "We were playing 'tie a man up so he can't move'. It's very fun. You should try it."

"I've never heard of this *game*."

"Yeah you have. You just kills 'em once you tie em up," the other Leper cackled. "Come on. No one to kill here. You're bleedin' lucky we're feelin' generous."

"Yeah. You are."

The blade was removed from Sid's belly and he heard footsteps clunking and the scrape of blades on flagstones as the Lepers left.

Still Sid didn't move, unsure if he was safe yet.

Roddy exhaled. "I fink someone just tried to kill us, Keef."

"Yeah, Roddy. I fink it was His Lordship."

"We can't stay here. He'll send someone else." This was Grub speaking. "Or they'll change their minds and come back."

"Yeah," Roddy said.

"Yeah," Keef said. "You know that money stashed in your pillowcase? Fink that's enough for you, me and Grub to get to your cousin's farm near Slough? He should still 'ave that little cottage empty. You know, the one he talked about the last time he was 'ere?"

"Should be enough. But what if His Lordship tells Big Ivan about us and that cart? He told us he'd do that if we told anyone about him or left the city."

"He just tried to have us killed, didn't he? Whether it's Big Ivan or the Lepers, we're still dead. An' I'd rather be somewhere picturesque like Slough when that happens."

"You've got a good point there."

"Can someone untie me?" Sid asked. "If the villain tried to have you killed, it means you're not on his side any more, doesn't it? So you can tell me what his name is and where he lives, so my captain can sort him out. That way you won't have to worry about him ever again."

There was a whispered conversation before Roddy replied, "Yeah. Alright. His name is Count Mendacium, or somefink like that, an' we always meet him at that posh club in Maye Fayre owned by the Krabb brothers. That's all we can give you 'cos that's all we know. Stay still now."

Sid yelped as his ties were cut and blood rushed back to his hands and legs. Squinting in the sunlight, the first things he registered were two hulking shapes and a much smaller one standing between them with her hands on her hips. The next thing he registered was just how much he needed the privy after having been tied up for almost an entire day.

CHAPTER 43

ELIAS SEEKS PROFESSIONAL HELP

E LIAS FOUGHT HIS WAY through the usual throng of urchins, criers, citizens and loiterers in front of the Cry's offices in Westminster, navigating through a labyrinth of corridors towards the intake desk. The ancient building was a catacomb converted from sixteenth-century tenements and the mustiness filling it was centuries old. The smell got stronger when he reached his destination, only to find a snaking queue. At the front, an urchin was trying to sell information about Mister Jim's Mysterious Pies being full of toads' ears, while behind him a woman announced that she wanted the Cry to decry the belligerence of the city's goats.

Elias didn't have time for this. An OverLondon queue could go for hours. It was a mark of civic pride. Swerving around the people, Elias veered down a corridor from which he'd seen Mister Gripes emerge days before.

He got lucky at the third door when he spotted the Cry's Master of Information sitting at a desk piled high with papers.

He knocked on the door. "Mister Gripes?"

Mister Gripes looked up sharply, a frown of concentration transforming to a welcoming smile. "Mister Dooley! To what do I owe this pleasure? Come in, come in."

"I need your help." Elias took off his cap and twisted it in his hands. "I have some alarming information that I need to share with the public immediately."

"Alarming information?" Mister Gripes leant forward. "Don't dilly dally, my boy—what is it?"

Elias gulped in a deep breath before the words poured out of him. "It's Sweet Pete, sir. I've found him dead, and I suspect he was poisoned by something put

ELIAS SEEKS PROFESSIONAL HELP

in his sugar. The only problem is that I have reason to believe that his sugar stock was stolen, meaning that people could be at risk at this very minute if it's sold on!"

Mister Gripes reeled back in his chair. "Sweet Pete. The ice cream pusherman? Poisoned? This *is* alarming news! Horrible news."

Elias's shoulders slumped in relief. Mister Gripes believed him. "Can you arrange for a warning to be spread on the Cry? Something that will let people know not to eat the sugar?"

"Of course! It's our duty." Mister Gripes reached for a sheet of parchment and picked up his quill. "You must give me all the details."

Elias explained how he'd found Sweet Pete and that the room had been empty. "There's more, but I don't want anyone to know it yet, not until I'm sure."

"Yes?" Mister Gripes looked up sharply.

"I believe Sweet Pete was somehow involved in the priest explosions. Although he may not have known it. I'm almost positive that the sugar he ate had omnicite in it. It reacted with his stomach acid."

"Omnicite." Mister Gripes blinked. "Like the demonstration Mistress Fenderpossum gave last month?" He grimaced. "That's an awful way to die, but Mister Dooley, the priests didn't die like you've explained Sweet Pete did. They exploded."

Elias nodded. "I understand that, sir, but I've been giving it some thought and I believe he added something to the sugar, probably to bulk it out as usual. Whatever that thing was, it delayed and amplified the effect of the omnicite. Since he didn't know about the omnicite in the sugar, he wouldn't have thought anything of it." Elias paused. "This is all theoretical, but the important thing is that people are informed not to eat *any* sugar they haven't brought from a Sugar Gang pusherman, and even then, I'd be worried." He sent silent thanks to the Vengeful Queen that his mother purchased her sugar in bulk and was still working through a bag she'd bought months ago.

Mister Gripes's hand scrawled across the page. "This is an alarming claim, Mister Dooley. Very alarming indeed." He looked at the steaming mug of tea on his desk and pushed it away as if expecting it to explode. "Do you have any evidence to back up your words? Big Ivan is a formidable foe and he's friends with Loud John. There would be repercussions if I put this on the Cry only for it to be a hoax."

"I have some of the sugar remaining from one of the priests who exploded. Not much."

"On you?" Mister Gripes looked at Elias sharply.

"No, no—it's at Captain Reign's office in Drury Lane."

"Above The Armoury. Yes, we've been running some advertisements for her. May I ask why?"

Elias paused. "Ah, she needed my help to fix something, and I gave her the sugar for safekeeping because I didn't think my shop was secure enough." The words had enough truth in them that they didn't quite feel like a lie.

Mister Gripes put down his quill. "Would you be willing to conduct an experiment like the one Mistress Fenderpossum did, to demonstrate your claims?"

"Yes."

"Then I will take you at your word. Have no fear, Mister Dooley. Once I gain Loud John's blessing, we should have an emergency bulletin going out about the poisoned sugar within the hour."

He rang a bell on his desk and a clerk came in.

"Yes, Mister Gripes?"

"Is Loud John in the building?"

"Yes, Mister Gripes."

"Tell him I'd like to talk to him. You may go now."

The clerk bustled off and Elias went limp with relief. "Thank you, sir."

"Of course, but I can share the news about Sweet Pete's unfortunate death straight away, as I'm sure at this point it's public knowledge."

"The landlady said that the Sugar Gang had been told." Elias was feeling lightheaded now.

Mister Gripes stood up and hurried around his desk and took Elias by the elbow to steady him. "You appear to have sustained quite a shock. Can I arrange some tea, maybe a biscuit to calm your nerves?"

"No, no, I'm fine. I need to tell Captain Reign what's happened," Elias said.

Mister Gripes nodded. "That's sensible. If you learn anything new, please don't hesitate to contact me. My door is always open and remember I am in your debt. My hand has been working better than ever." He held up his wooden prosthetic and smiled as he moved the fingers. "Your workmanship is excellent."

"Thank you. By the way, sir, how do you ask your barber to shave your moustache?" Elias asked, surprising himself with the question, but wanting to know all the same.

Mister Gripes looked nonplussed for a moment, then flushed with pleasure. "I'm glad you asked. It's a style of my devising. Mister Peters has named it after me. Here, let me give you his address." He scribbled it on a scrap of parchment and handed it to Elias, who took it gratefully.

"Thank you. I'll take my leave now." With a bow, Elias left the building.

He was so intent on hailing a passing hack to take him to Drury Lane that he didn't notice the two men muscling through the crowd behind him.

However, he did notice when someone grabbed his arms, stuffed a bag over his head and bundled him into a cart.

CHAPTER 44

PRIVY CAKE

A LEX RETURNED TO THE Armoury in a foul mood, which wasn't helped by Gregor accosting her the minute she walked through the door. She inspected his shirt. "She hasn't taken your buttons, so what has she taken now?"

"Nothing."

She arched an eyebrow. "Then how can I help you, other than paying for a new window bar once I get paid for my first job?"

Gregor scratched his jaw. "I've been thinking about that poole you started last night at the Henry the Late. I was wondering how it is that you can't pay me a shilling, but you can put down a bet for fifty pounds. Then I remembered that we were blessed with a visit from Mother Superior yesterday. If she was here to punish you for something, you don't look very inconvenienced. And why are you holding cake?"

Alex considered the platter with its slice of lethal patisserie. "It's to celebrate Mother Superior allowing me to live another day. If you don't mind, I'm far too busy for this conversation. Got to make window bar money." She ducked under his arm and headed for the stairs.

Gregor's hand on her shoulder stopped her. "If you bring the Bad Habits down on my establishment, I'll not only bite your head off, I'll use your spine as a back scratcher."

"I assure you that absolutely *nothing* is going to happen to your fine establishment and the cultured types who infest it." Alex nodded to a drunken actor drooling on a nearby table. "Is that all?"

"For now." Gregor stalked off.

Moments later, Flora greeted Alex at the top of the stairs. "Sid's not back!" she said. "He always comes back before dawn, but he hasn't!"

Alex gripped Flora by the shoulder with her free hand. "Can you be sure he hasn't come back and then left again?"

"I've been here all morning and I would've noticed." Flora twisted her fingers in her hair. "Do you want me to go and look for him? I was going to, but then I wanted to be here when he got back, just in case something bad happened and he needs me to cheer him up. I always cheer him up."

"Good girl." Alex walked to her desk and set the cake down.

"Is that cake for Sid? Because he doesn't like cake, remember? He likes pies and curry and sometimes fish and chips. Maybe I could get him a pie!"

"It's only for him if he wants to be splattered all over the place." Alex said, studying the room for somewhere to store the cake out of sight.

"I don't think he'd like that. Although he ate one of Mister Jim's oyster and pickle pies once and said it worried his insides."

"Flora, remember what I told you that day we were in OverFlorence and you walked into the cathedral and saw all the gold?"

"Close my eyes, and remember to breathe?"

"Do that now." Alex ordered, trying to ignore the way Flora immediately started inhaling dramatically and whistling through her teeth on the exhalation.

"Calming down?" Alex asked after a few seconds.

"Yes, Captain."

"Good. Now let's sort out where to put this slice of cake and then we'll find Sid. I don't want it anywhere someone might see it and eat it."

"You could put it in the privy. No one likes privy cake."

"An astute and brilliant observation." Alex stowed the cake on top of the wardrobe in the privy, dusting off her hands. "That should do it. Now, let's sort Sid out." She walked back into her office and poured herself a cup of tea from the kettle simmering on the stove, taking a sip and feeling it doing her good. "You left him at Bloomsbury, which is where we'll start. I'll take the pubs and the criers, you question the Editors and any urchins you find. If they're not helpful, we'll spread out—"

"Captain! Captain!" Sid burst into the room. His face was red with exertion, his expression frantic. "I know who the villain is, Captain!"

"Sid! I was so worried!" Flora rushed over to him. "Did you get hurt? Are you sad? What happened? Do you want a pie? I can get you a pie. Or do you want to see my shiny things? They'll make you feel better. I have them here." She started rummaging through her pockets.

"Flora!" Alex yelled. "Breathe."

"Okay!"

"Sid, take a seat before you fall down, and tell me what happened. And why's your hat dented?" Alex directed her bo'sun to the armchair and pushed him into it as Flora's whistling huffs filled the room.

Sid slumped like a lumpy sack of potatoes, looking up at Alex with wild eyes. "Got hit on the noggin, Captain. I found the urchin, but she went to Slough with Roddy and Keef after the Lepers came to kill us."

"You found the urchin?" Alex asked, relief a very real thing. "Did the Lepers know that you were associated with me?"

"Yes, but that's not the important bit. Roddy and Keef told me who exploded the priests. It's all a part of his nefarious plan! The villain got Roddy to add some stuff to the sugar in Sweet Pete's cart while he was making his regular trip to the conveniences, and he sent Roddy and Keef to attack you, but you messed 'em up good."

"I did at that," Alex said. "Continue. How do you know this Roddy and Keef?"

"They hit me over the head and took me to their place on the villain's orders. He's got something over them about a stolen cart. Anyway, the villain tried to kill all of us by telling the Lepers that we'd killed the urchin. But Roddy and Keef hadn't killed her and she was alive and—" Sid drew in a gulp of air just as his face was beginning to turn purple. "And I'm right tired, Captain. I haven't slept since yesterday unless you count the times my noggin took a hit."

Alex grabbed him by the shoulders. "Sidney Potts, you're not sleeping until you tell me the name and the address of this villain who blew up the priests. Tell me now!"

Sid gulped. "Yes, Captain. His name is Count Mendacium, and Roddy and Keef always meet him at Krabb's Private Members' Club in Maye Fayre. He's definitely a villain, like in the books. He's got a foreign accent and everything! I didn't see him but I heard him."

Alex looked over his shoulder. "Did you hear those details, Flora?"

"His name is Count Mendacium and we can find him at Krabb's Private Members' Club," Flora repeated in a sing-song voice.

"Excellent. Let's go." Alex checked the tensioner on her clockbow was at maximum before re-holstering it.

Sid struggled to get out of the chair. "I'll come too, Captain! I should be there. I'll recognise him the minute I hear him. He interrogated me and I know a villain when I see one."

"We need our best man at the office, Sid. Stay here and get some rest. You'll need it to identify him once we catch him."

"But Captain!" Sid staggered to his feet, only to fall back into a slump.

"That's an order, airman!" Alex said. "Come on, Flora—if we move quick enough, we'll have him before he knows what's happening."

Stopping just long enough to grab her cape and twirl it dramatically around her shoulders, she rushed down the stairs.

Now *this* was pirating. She'd spotted her quarry and all that remained was to chase him down! She may be doing it in a Black Hack instead of the Purple Reign, but a chase was a chase.

CHAPTER 45

AN UNHAPPY HAMSTER

E LIAS BLINKED AS THE bag was lifted from his head. He was queasy after being rattled around in a goat cart before being manhandled into a large, echoing building that smelled like the finest brown sugar. His captors had then half-dragged, half-carried him into a quieter—presumably smaller—room and had searched his pockets before shoving him onto the hard chair he was now seated on.

His first impression was of red and white striped wallpaper, carpet and curtains. He was sitting in front of a black lacquered desk with a huge red wingback chair behind it, which was facing away from him.

He took in the two men flanking him. They were wearing red and white sequined suits and fedoras. Sugar Gang.

The sick feeling intensified.

"Excuse me. There's been a mistake," he said.

The man to his left cuffed him on the back of the head. "No talkin' until the boss says you can."

The other Sugar Gang lieutenant cleared his throat. "We've brought 'im, boss. The one who scragged Sweet Pete an' stole all his stuff."

"What? No!" Elias exclaimed. "I didn't do anything to Sweet Pete. He was dead when I found him! Does it look like I'm carrying any of Sweet Pete's belongings?"

"What are those trinkets in your pockets, then?" asked the man who'd cuffed him.

"I rescued them because they were in shock. They would've died if I hadn't taken them. You're free to take them if you can rehabilitate them."

The man screwed up his face. "Yeah. Never liked touchin' 'em myself. What about the other stuff? Where have you put it? The brown an' the white Pete was due to deliver today, an' all his stuff?"

"Nowhere. I left Sweet Pete's and went straight to the Cry's offices," Elias said.

"Who took his stuff, then?"

"His landlady!" Elias's voice echoed around the room. "She took everything, including his sugar, which is why I went to the Cry. I had to warn everyone. Someone may have poisoned Sweet Pete's sugar with omnicite, and it could kill people! You have to believe me. This is extremely important." He looked to each side at the Sugar Men, but both of them were looking directly ahead. Following their gaze, Elias saw a plume of smoke rising above the chair behind the desk.

"Are you telling me that my sugar is poison?" The voice spoke in a rumbling OverKrakow accent. "Are *you* saying that the Sugar Gang distributes a substandard product?" The question was followed by a strange squeaking noise, like a winch being wound. The chair turned a fraction before it juddered to a halt.

"Bernie, this chair ain't gonna turn itself," the voice said. "See to it."

"Right, boss." The henchman who'd questioned Elias walked to the chair and began working a crank that squeaked rhythmically.

With glacially slow stop-motion jerks, the chair rotated to reveal the widest man Elias had ever seen. He was wearing the deadpan expression of someone who knew that something ridiculous was happening but that no one would ever dare say anything.

Elias gulped as he took in the great hairy jowls, the small black eyes and the black sequined suit. Big Ivan.

A bald, chubby pink hamster was held in the crook of the big man's arm. It was eating a carrot while wearing an expression that suggested that the vegetable was its mental equal.

Big Ivan glared at Elias as he stubbed out his cigar. "Answer me, lad. I haven't got all day."

"I'm not saying *your* sugar is poisoned, sir," Elias spoke in a rush. "I'm telling you that someone poisoned some of the sugar Sweet Pete was selling. The priests who exploded bought it and it killed them."

Big Ivan's brow lowered as he pulled another cigar out of his pocket, biting off the end with a click of two yellow buck teeth before he lit it up. His cheek pouches inflated, then he exhaled a great cloud of smoke in Elias's direction. The lieutenant at Elias's side stifled a cough.

"Are you telling *me*—" The words were a deadly monotone, the OverKrakow accent getting thicker with each word. "—that *my* product is blowing up *priests*? Are you actually going around this fair city saying that I poison people? That *my* pushermen poison people? Is that what you're telling me?"

Elias swallowed around the lump of dread in his throat. "No sir! I'm telling you that Sweet Pete's brown sugar was poisoned and I believe it killed him and the priests he sold it to. That's the news I was trying to spread—that people shouldn't eat any brown sugar they've bought on the black market."

There was a rumble from the lieutenant who had cuffed Elias earlier. "I fink he did it. I fink he's talkin' too much. People who did it always talk too much."

"Do I pay you for your opinions, Tony?" Big Ivan asked.

"No, boss."

"Then shut up before I shut you up."

"Yes, boss."

Big Ivan paused with his cigar halfway to his lips. "On second thoughts, don't shut up. I want you to go to Loud John and put a stop to this lad's foolish message before it goes out. Tell him that if he doesn't, I'm gonna start telling people how he really lost his voice. Got it? Johnny boy should know better than to put false rumours about me out on the Cry."

"Yes, boss. Going now, boss."

"Now, back to *you*." Big Ivan's wicked teeth flashed as he glared at Elias. "How many other people have you told about this little theory of yours?"

"Just Mister Gripes so far," Elias said. "And Captain Reign knows the sugar is explosive. She was there when I conducted the experiment. But we didn't know it had come from Sweet Pete then."

The big man seemed to swell, his body getting wider even as his huge head receded into his shoulders. "Reign's in on this?"

"She's investigating who blew up the priests. Yes."

"Is she telling people that *my* sugar blows up priests?"

"No, sir!" Elias said hastily. "Not yet. I mean, we aren't sure who poisoned the sugar yet. Once we know that, we have plans to notify the relevant people."

"Like me?" For a moment the only sound in the room was the crunch of the bald hamster gnawing on the carrot.

Elias nodded. "Like you and, and Mother Sup—the other people relevant to our investigation."

Big Ivan cupped his free hand to his ear. "Was that Mother Superior you almost said, lad? You're going to tell *her* that my sugar killed her priests?"

"No, sir! Not that your sugar is killing the priests. As I said, it's something someone else has *added* to your sugar that's doing it."

"No, no, *no*, lad." Big Ivan slammed his hand down on his desk. The hamster squeaked, spitting out a mouthful of carrot. Big Ivan stroked its back to calm it. "Look what you did. You upset Mister Snagglesworth. D'you know what happens when people put Mister Snagglesworth off his food?"

"I don't know, sir."

"It's the same thing I do to people who go around telling the Dread bloody Pirate Purple Reign that *my* sugar kills priests, so she can then tell Mother Superior. But you haven't actually told her about Sweet Pete yet, have you?"

"Not yet, sir."

Big Ivan grinned wickedly. "Then she's never going to find out. You see, lad, I worked out long ago something Mother Superior hasn't learnt yet. There's no need to give the stick, when you've got a nice big carrot." He turned to the henchman at his side. "Anyone getting the carrot today, Bernie?"

"Yeah, boss. Leonard the Nose. Remember?"

"In that case, put the lad in storage and he can go up tomorrow. Make sure you give him an extra-large carrot. I don't want him going hungry." Big Ivan's jowls shook with a chortle that quickly transformed into another scowl. "Now get out of my sight before Mister Snagglesworth gets really upset. And Bernie, come back when you're done with him. I've got a message for you to take to Captain Reign."

"Yes, boss."

Bernie yanked the bag back over Elias's head and he was once again dragged somewhere, this time to be left alone. This place echoed, smelled like sawdust and was very, very cold.

As Elias huddled into himself, shivering, he heard the faint echo of the Cry outside.

Hear ye! Hear ye! Ice cream pusherman Sweet Pete has been found dead by his landlady...

CHAPTER 46

ALEX AND FLORA CHECK THE LEDGER

*H*EAR YE! *H*EAR YE! *Ice cream pusherman Sweet Pete has been found dead by his landlady who said she had no idea how he lived with nothing in his house. Stop. Mistress Flan of Stepney Feather Imports has warned that there is a white feather shortage for this year's Festival of the Queen's Ascension. She's quoted as saying, 'If you want to look like a giant hen to honour our lady, you're going to be disappointed, deary.' Stop. Ye've heard! Ye've heard! Are you in need of a good buttering? Feel like the cream has gone sour in your marriage? Why not consult your local dairy today? First second free, smile guaranteed!*

"Did you hear that, Captain? Sweet Pete's dead!" Flora exclaimed as she sprinted away from Krabb's Private Members' Club to the yells of a lot of angry people giving chase.

"That's sad news, but we've got more pressing things on our mind right now." Alex ducked into an alleyway and yanked Flora in behind her, before swiftly grabbing empty soap boxes and gin barrels, piling them up in a barricade. The rich of OverLondon weren't known for their intellectual prowess and she doubted they'd think to look behind or under anything.

Flora hugged a book that was almost as big as her torso to her chest. "Gregor said Pete was really old. Maybe his trinkets got sick from being close to all that sugar."

Alex hefted a final gin barrel on top of the pile she'd created before dusting off her hands. "Or they got sick of sucking on something so bitter." She caught Flora's censorious look. "Maybe he was old," she corrected herself.

"That's what it must have been. Do you think we're going to get in trouble for stealing the club ledger?" Flora bit her lip. "How will the rich people know where they live if they can't get someone to look it up for them? You know they're not that smart."

"We didn't have time to argue with the doorman, and we didn't *steal* the ledger, we've *relocated* it to this alleyway so that we can look for an address."

Flora didn't look any less anxious. "Do you think the doorman is okay? You hit him really hard."

"I merely gave him an extra friendly bo'sun's handshake. Anyone who calls a pirate his 'good woman' deserves everything they get. Now put the book down here." Alex set a wooden crate in front of her just as someone nearby bellowed for the 'miscreant' to be caught.

"What's a miscreant?" Flora asked, making an *oomph* noise as she set the book down.

"It's an unmarried lady from Crete." Alex licked her finger and flicked through the heavy vellum pages. "Now let's find this bastard Mendacium. Lord Hammingway... no."

"Really?! I've got a Top Toff's collector card for him. He has a Berkshire lifting pig named Emsworth."

"Astounding." Alex ran her finger down the page. "Viscount Protuberance..."

"He's allergic to rubbing himself in marmalade."

"Fascinating. Flora, your adoration of the aristocracy will never cease to amaze me. The Honourable Mister Quantitate—no, don't tell me, it'll be something to do with not being able to add anything up."

"He likes swimming in custard."

"Custard?"

Flora nodded enthusiastically. "But he can only swim with two inches or less in his bathtub, because his doctor is worried he'll drown."

"Princess Elvira Bottomley. Do I even want to know?"

"I like her. She has a pointy face like me, but I don't mash peas into my ears like she does. It's a princess thing."

"Riveting." Alex kept going down the page. "Ah! Count Mendacium. Here." She tore the page out. As she shoved it into her doublet, she heard someone yell that the thieves could be hiding in the alleyway behind all the barrels. "It seems that they've made a mistake and hired someone with brains. Leave the book and come with me." She grabbed Flora's hand.

Flora looked at the ledger longingly. "But Captain, there might've been some valuable ones listed in there! We haven't even gotten to the Earl of Soap. He paints rocks with purple glitter paint and throws them at people, yelling, 'Paff! Poff!' He's my favourite."

"We'll borrow it again another time." Alex dragged Flora to the end of the alleyway just as someone burst through the makeshift barricade. Luckily, finding the ledger was enough to stop the pursuit and they were able to reach safety two streets away, where Alex skidded to a halt and pulled out the sheet of vellum and read it. "Fifteen Harlequin Street. We've got him!"

"Isn't that the street where you used to visit that lady whenever we were in port?" Flora asked. "The one with all the height and the tight breeches who always called you 'darlink'?" She did a passable impersonation of a theatrical Russian accent while fluttering her stubby eyelashes.

Alex looked at her sharply. "How do you know about Natashia?"

"You talk in your sleep."

"I talk in my sleep? What do I say?"

"It's not so much words as noises—"

"Alright! We'll discuss this later. Come on, and no more mention of Natashia or noises."

Deciding that a Black Hack would take too long to hail, Alex led Flora past Tudor mansions, along rows of stately Princess Elizabethan town houses and across parks with more topiary than was healthy. Finally, they reached Harlequin Street, the last street before Maye Fayre turned into Westminster. It was lined with Tudor-era row houses that were respectable enough to maintain a certain social standing, but cheap enough that country aristocrats could hire them for the social season each year. For the knowledgeable, this was also *the* place to maintain the special person in one's life without too many questions being asked. In Harlequin Street, so many people came and went that even the most dedicated curtain twitchers had given up.

It was the perfect street for a criminal mastermind to hide in plain sight.

"This is the street!" Flora said. "Your lady Natashia lived at number twenty-nine, didn't she? And she had a little kitty that you liked, because you always talked about it in your sleep. You said it was a very good kitty."

"Flora!"

"Sorry! What number are we looking for?"

"Fifteen." They trotted along the street, Alex counting off house numbers under her breath. "Twenty-one... seventeen. Fifteen!" She stopped so abruptly that Flora bumped into her back.

Alex put her hand on the hilt of her clockbow. "Do you have your dagger ready?"

"Yes—are we sneaking or raiding?"

"Sneaking first. Then raiding." Alex's blood warmed. *This* was pirating. Loping up the stairs to a newly painted blue door, she knocked and waited for an answer. When she didn't get one, she nodded to Flora, who produced her lockpicking kit from one of her many pockets.

Alex then lit up a cigar, smoking nonchalantly, as Flora crouched behind her to work on the lock, which yielded within seconds. They stepped inside, closing the door behind them.

Her nose twitching from the unmistakable smell of Axiom wig powder, which was rumoured to repel moths, rodents and possibly entire continents, Alex motioned for Flora to stay still as she listened for movement.

When she didn't hear anything, she nodded at the stairs. "I'll take the top floor, you take the bottom."

It didn't take more than a minute to confirm that most of the rooms were empty, not just of people, but of any furniture or personal touches.

Alex frowned as she looked around a room that would normally function as a bedroom, but didn't contain anything other than an empty grate where a fire should be. She walked to the next room, which contained a lone desk and some empty bookshelves. No matter how much she searched the desk's surface and underside for a hidden compartment, she found nothing.

"Captain?" Flora called out.

"There's nothing here, Flora."

"There is here." There was a reverence to Flora's words that was only ever prompted by the presence of things that sparkled.

Alex rushed downstairs and found Flora in a room at the rear of the building. While the rest of the house was empty, this room was overflowing.

A floor-to-ceiling gilt mirror on the back wall amplified the magnificence of the luxurious clothing spilling from four massive wardrobes, their open doors showing every kind of satin and silk. Breeches, doublets, waistcoats, stockings, shirts, cravats, ruffs, codpieces and collars, all in a myriad of colours. Racks of shoes with buckles caught the faint light seeping through the open doorway, glinting alluringly.

Upon a table were five wig stands, four of which held towering white wigs, the other bare. The rest of the table was covered in a mishmash of tins, pots and brushes. Alex spotted white lead ceruse, a cake of red vermillion and a jewelled cigarette case.

"We're dealing with a dandy." She shook her head in bemusement. "One who doesn't sleep and who likes to admire himself."

Flora dragged her eyes away from a tray of pocket watches. "You didn't find a bed?"

"No. Did you?"

"No, only this. The kitchen doesn't even have an icebox." Flora picked up a shoe. "This buckle is so *shiny!*"

"This house is so *strange*." Alex walked back through the house, reinspecting each room before returning. "What we have here is a ghost ship."

Flora looked at her sharply. "You think Count Mendacium is a ghost? I haven't got his collector's card and all the best aristocrats have one. If he was a ghost, he might not have a card."

"Interesting perspective, but what I meant is that I think he doesn't live here," Alex said, "Or if he does, he likes sleeping on the floor and only eats at his club."

"Don't private members' clubs have bedrooms for hire?" Flora asked. "I read on Baroness Marchpenny's collector's card that she sleeps at her club because the baron burned down their house while doing embroidery."

"That could be it." Alex stroked her chin. "But something doesn't feel right." As she said the words, she heard a click as the front door opened, followed by the sound of someone muttering.

Both Alex and Flora peered around the door into the hall to see a hunched woman wearing a dowdy brown dress. She was carrying a mop and bucket and wore spectacles with the thickest lenses Alex had ever seen.

Alex evaluated the situation quickly. There was no way they could escape without detection. She decided to brazen it out.

"Hello!" she said heartily, stepping into the hall. "You must be the housekeeper. Count Mendacium said you'd be stopping by."

The woman shrieked, dropping the mop, her hand pressed to her heart. "Vengeful Lady's corsets! You scared me! Who are you?"

Alex bowed. "Alex Reign, privateer, at your service."

"Wot?" The woman held a hand to her ear. "I'm not good at hearing, dearie."

Alex raised her voice. "I'm looking for your employer. He told us to meet him here!"

"'E's not here! 'E rushed out earlier." The woman peered at Alex with eyes magnified to the size of plums. "Who are you? A debt collector?"

"No, I'm a privateer," Alex yelled.

"Wot?"

"A privateer!"

"Wot?"

"A pirate!"

"Oh. You should've said so in the first place."

Alex cupped her hands around her mouth. "Where is he?"

The woman picked up the mop, setting it against the wall. "I don't know! Somewhere in Drury Lane. 'E lit out of here in an 'urry not long ago, 'E almost bowled me over, 'e did. I was just droppin' by to see if 'e needed seein' to today, and the language 'e used when I asked 'im where 'e was going in such an 'urry!

It's not acceptable. I'm respectable, I am. Not someone that 'as to put up with words like that!"

"Drury Lane? Where in Drury Lane?" Alex was aware of Flora beginning to fidget next to her.

The woman set the bucket down. "Some pub. Odd for 'im. 'E's a quiet type and I rarely see 'im. Before seein' you here, I've never seen 'im with a visitor. But it's nice 'e has lady friends. You'll teach 'im to be nicer." The woman peered at Alex. "You *are* a lady friend, aren't you, dearie?"

"Not at all," Alex said. "I'm a business associate."

"She's a kitty inspector," Flora chimed in.

Alex slapped her forehead.

"Wot? 'E doesn't have a cat. No pets allowed."

Alex recovered. "Ah, well, that's the *very* business I'm here to discuss with him!"

"Business? Right then. When you see 'im, tell 'im that 'e can't go about bein' rude to me like 'e was earlier. 'E yelled at me for not setting 'is good wig out the other day. Rude, that was. I'm not a mind reader, dearie, I said." She dunked the mop in the bucket as she spoke. "And do you know what 'e said?"

"What?" Alex asked.

"'E told me to go to 'ell! Can you believe that? Not a peep out of 'im for three years and then 'e says that. Well, I says, I don't have to put up with people who speak like that. I don't get paid for that kind of language. The other ladies and gentlemen who live on this street never use that language with me when I take care of 'em."

"Do you remember what the pub was called?" Alex asked.

"Wot?"

"What was the pub called?"

"Something starting with A. The Amulet, no. The Armadillo. The Army—no."

"The Armoury?" Alex asked.

"Yes! That's it. The Armoury."

"Captain! Sid's there!" Flora tugged at Alex's cape. "We have to warn him!"

"Yes." Alex bowed at the woman. "Thanks, you've been very helpful."

"Tell 'im to mind his language next time 'e talks to me," the woman yelled at Alex and Flora's backs as they rushed by her and into the street.

CHAPTER 47

COUNT MENDACIUM MAKES HIS MOVE

OUNT MENDACIUM WALKED UP the stairs to the Reign Agency from The Armoury, ignoring the catcalls and whistles from the ignorant cretins who were amused by his fine clothing. Actors were the worst kind of human, second only to every other scoundrel in this benighted city. He couldn't wait to see the last of them.

If the damn Lepers had done their job he wouldn't be in this situation, but the urchin he'd had watching Roddy and Keef's stables had confirmed that Roddy, Keef and the urchin girl—who very definitely *wasn't* dead—hadn't been killed. Neither had Captain Reign's idiot.

That meant that Roddy and Keef may have told Captain Reign's man about the Count, which meant that he could tell the captain and ruin everything. So, as always, it was up to the Count to do everything himself.

He reached the top of the stairs and froze when he saw the captain's prize idiot slumped in an armchair, snoring.

He did a quick mental calculation as to whether or not this would be an issue, then remembered that the idiot hadn't seen him at the stables—he'd merely heard his voice, which could be disguised.

He stepped into the room and cleared his throat. "Pardon moi, monsewer," he said in possibly the worst French accent that had ever been attempted. "But I am lookeeng for a preevate eeyoor to feeend sooomewone."

"Find someone?" The idiot jerked awake, staring at the Count as if he'd never seen another person before. "A client! You're a client. Of course, sir!" He staggered to his feet and gestured to the chair he'd just vacated with vigorous sweeping motions. "The captain will be back soon, sir. Take a seat, sir, and we'll soon get you sorted, and we'll wait for Captain Reign. She's just off solving a *very* important crime, but she'll be back soon, I'm sure. Don't you go anywhere!"

"Mersee." Giving the imbecile a simpering smile, the Count crossed the room and took a seat.

"Can I get you some refreshment, sir? Tea, coffee? Gin? Gregor does a very good gin."

Count Mendacium steepled his fingers and smiled. "A brandy, seel vous plate, and oui, whay note soome geen too? Lots and lots of geen in great beeg tankaaards." He held his hands apart to indicate the size, noting the way the imbecile's gaze was drawn to the filigree and pearls on his prosthetic. "We, ah, *French* are particulaaar aboot the quantitay of our bevarrrages."

CHAPTER 48

ELIAS IS LEFT IN THE COLD

E LIAS'S BODY SHOOK FROM the cold.

It hadn't taken him long to realise that the hessian-covered crate he was leaning against wasn't wood, but a giant block of ice. The floor and the air were freezing. There was a sweet smell in the air that was no doubt the ice cream that the ice was keeping cold. The realisation was anything but comforting.

Even more alarming were the muffled industrial sounds he could hear in the distance. He had no doubt that he was in a Sugar Gang warehouse at Canary Wharf. Worse, he was getting sleepy and he knew that wasn't a good sign. Once, he and Thomas Cheapside had gone skating on the OverThames Reservoir in the winter, but he'd forgotten to wear a vest. The chill had been like this. At first he hadn't realised how cold he was, then his hands and his feet had gone numb, then he'd become extremely tired.

What he wouldn't give for one of Vikram's disgusting cardigans and a pair of woollen gloves right now.

He experienced a sharp pain on the back of his hand, then jerked as it happened again. "Phillips?" he croaked. A tiny spark of hope flickered. "Can you untie me?" He tried to move his hand so the trinket would know what he meant.

There was a prickle on the back of Elias's hand as Phillips disconnected, his little feet walking up to Elias's wrist until the ropes there stopped him. Phillips made a high-pitched noise and Elias realised that the trinket must be irritated that something was encroaching onto his territory.

Moments later, Phillips walked back to his preferred spot and attached again. A few seconds later there was another tug on Elias's ropes.

"That's it!" Elias injected as much enthusiasm into his voice as he could muster. "Untie me and you can have my hand back. No more horrible rope and we can both be warm." He jerked against his bonds, trying to encourage the little trinket along. "Come on!"

Phillips continued plucking at the rope with his tiny prosthetic arm, then stopped, detaching to yet again to trot up to Elias's wrist.

Elias slumped in disappointment. It'd been a good idea, but as eccentric as the creature was, it was too much to expect.

He'd fallen into a shivering almost-sleep when he was pinched again, harder this time. Phillips must have settled back on his hand.

There was another tug on the ropes, faint but insistent. Then another. Then another, as if Phillips was plucking the rope apart, one strand at a time. Elias didn't know how long it went on for, but before he knew it he was trying to help Phillips along, struggling against his ties and wrenching his wrists as far apart as he could. Then Phillips made a cooing sound and Elias worked himself free.

Elias pulled the bag off his head with numb hands, fished his flat cap out of it and shoved the hat back on his head. Then he stroked Phillips's carapace as the little arm waved. "Good work boy!" he exclaimed.

Phillips pinched him hard enough to draw blood.

"Ouch! Yes. Okay. Annoying creature." Elias used the penknife from his utility belt to cut his ankle ties, then staggered stiffly to his feet.

Something clattered to the floor and he felt about, only to encounter a large frozen carrot. He threw it across the room, where it shattered against a wall.

There was a sliver of light limning a door. Hurrying to it, Elias tried the handle, finding it unlocked. Opening it a fraction, he peered out.

He was definitely in a warehouse at Canary Wharf. In the foreground were great wooden crates painted in the Sugar Gang's red and white stripes, and in the distance he could see an open gate leading to a busy dock where great airships were being offloaded. There was a near-deafening cacophony of cranes, traffic and dock workers speaking every language on the globe at high volume.

Evaluating his situation, Elias debated the pros and cons of sneaking or sprinting away, and opted to make a run for it.

It was the right choice.

Within seconds, he'd merged into the throng of people, winding and weaving around goat carts, dock workers and a small flock of sheep.

With his arms pumping at his sides, his heart pounding and Phillips making a high-pitched *weeeeee* noise, Elias sprinted back towards Soho.

CHAPTER 49

A VILLAINOUS CONFRONTATION

A LEX IGNORED GREGOR'S SHOUT for her to mind his customers as she pushed through the crowd in The Armoury, Flora at her heels. Without missing a beat, she raced up the stairs, bursting into her office with her hand on her clockbow, only to find Sid hovering near a man with a painted face and a towering white wig.

She took aim as Mendacium leapt to his feet, grabbed Sid and held a dagger to his throat.

"What? No, this is the captain!" Sid yelled. "Captain, this is a new client. A fancy gentleman! Although he's a bit worked up right now."

"Shut up, idiot." The blade pressed against the fleshy skin of Sid's neck as the Count withdrew a single shot clockbow from his coat with his free hand, aiming it at Alex and Flora. "No one move and we will discuss this like civilised people."

Flora squeaked. Alex maintained her aim on Mendacium's forehead. At the very least she'd be able to shoot the bastard's wig off, scaring him enough to let Sid go. The only problem was that if he staggered backwards, he'd slice Sid's jugular clean through.

"I'm giving you only one more second," the Count said coolly, shifting the focus of his clockbow to Flora. "Or I'll shoot her and kill him. Do you want that, Reign?"

"Why's your voice changed?" Sid asked. Then his face reddened. "Captain! I know that voice! It's the villain! The one who tried to have the Lepers kill me, Roddy and Keef."

"I gathered that." Alex lowered her weapon slowly. "What now, Count?"

"Now we go about our business with civility." The Count sniffed, then waved his clockbow at Flora. "You. Ferret," he said with a sneer that made Alex's teeth itch. "Take the belt off the captain's breeches and tie her to that table leg. Now."

Flora looked at Alex and she nodded. They'd been in this situation numerous times in the past. The trick was to wait for an opportunity.

"I knew you were the villain," Sid said. "I was just pretending that I didn't to keep you here so the captain could come and I could give the speech in the library where I explained how you did it, like the heroes do. Although this isn't a library."

"Silence!" the Count commanded. He jerked the clockbow at Flora. "Hurry up. Hurry up! Have you done it?"

Flora stood back. "Yes."

"Damn you." Alex made a show of unsuccessfully struggling against the leather securing her to the leg of the table near the stove.

"Now take her clockbow and bring it over here," he told Flora.

Flora met Alex's eyes. Alex winked at her.

"Okay." Flora reached for the bow, and then pretended to sneeze, her hand fumbling on its hilt, flicking the tension release.

Vreeeeeeee.

The whir of it unwinding filled the room. It would be useless now, unless the Count got Flora to rewind it, and Alex had the impression that he didn't have the time to spare.

"Idiot!" the Count screeched, his composure slipping. It was almost impossible to tell what he looked like under all that white face paint, but Alex could see a red flush on the man's neck above his lace ruff.

"Sorry," Flora squeaked, hurrying over and throwing the clockbow onto Alex's desk.

"Now take this fool's belt and tie him up too. Tie him to that chair behind the desk." The Count stepped back from Sid, removing the knife but still aiming his bow at Flora. "And don't get any ideas, Captain Reign, or the ferret will die."

"Are you okay, Sid?" Flora asked as she and Sid walked around the desk with the Count's weapon aimed at them.

"Hurry!" the Count ordered. "Take your belt off, give it to the girl and sit on the damn chair."

Sid undid his belt. His breeches immediately fell to the floor, revealing brown woolly underwear that, if implemented as a contraceptive, could lessen the city's birth rate overnight.

"He's the villain, Flora!" Sid hissed.

"I thought villains were meant to wear black and laugh like this." Flora did her best villain laugh.

"Some of them. But this one's *undercover* as a peacock. It's like the *reverse* femmy fartalley."

"Vengeful Queen save me from idiots! Hurry up, girl, before I shoot you just to save myself from your ridiculous prattle." The Count held the clockbow directly at the back of Flora's head as Sid sat on the chair and Flora tied him up.

"What are you hoping to gain?" Alex asked the Count calmly. "Gregor would've seen you come up here. You'll be caught. We've told people your name and your connection to the sugar. Mother Superior knows," she bluffed. "Do you think she's going to give you all that money now? She knows where you live, she knows how you did it. You'll be dead by the end of the day."

The Count laughed derisively. "You're a simpleton, Reign. You think I care about Mother Superior and this pathetic city when I now possess a weapon I can sell to anyone I want, for whatever price I want?"

"The sugar?" Alex shrugged. "Omnicite and acid is old news. Mistress Fenderpossum proved that last month."

"Yes, but she didn't know how to delay the explosion or make it bigger!" the Count retorted.

"And you do?" Alex raised a brow. "Because that makes me wonder why you're here instead of in the skies, travelling to the first place that'll buy your secret. Why *are* you still here, Count Mendacium?"

The Count glared impatiently at her, his tone dry. "Excellent question, Reign. I'm a man in a hurry and this is taking far too long. It's all a matter of tying up loose ends." His hand visibly twitched on the trigger of his clockbow. "Have you done it, girl?" he asked Flora.

"Yes."

"Show me."

"I can't because it's behind him and he's tied to the chair."

The Count backed up until he could see behind Sid. "Yes. Good. Now I want you to go over to those books there, on that shelf. Put them on the armchair."

"Sid's books? What are you going to do with them?" Flora asked.

"Do it!"

"It's okay, Flora. I've read them all and this is exactly how it's meant to go," Sid said. "The villain's going to make a mistake soon and then we're going to catch him—"

"Shut up!" the Count commanded. "Do it, girl!"

"Okay." Flora moved at a snail's pace, but it wasn't long before the chair's seat contained a neat stack of penny dreadfuls.

The Count nodded at a tray of gin tankards on Alex's desk. "Now pour them on the books."

"But they're Sid's!"

"Do it, Flora." Alex looked into the Count's eyes. His voice was calm but there was something there that told her he was edging out onto the thin ice of sanity. If he was pushed any further, he may fire the bow. Even if he was a bad shot, his chances of hitting Flora were too high.

"Okay." Flora's eyes welled with tears as she poured the gin onto the books and backed away with a whispered apology to Sid.

"Good. Good." Keeping his aim on Flora, the Count sheathed the knife at his waist. He then reached for the box of matches on Alex's desk, selected a match and struck it against the surface. A flame flared to life. "I won't say it's been a pleasure to meet you, Captain Reign. But I'm glad to see you go up in flames." With a jerky movement, he threw the match at the chair and the books ignited with a *whoosh*.

A great lick of flame curled into the air, catching Alex's attention for a second. It was a second too many. When she looked back, the Count's finger was moving on the trigger of his bow.

"*Flora!*" Alex bellowed just as the bolt *thunk*ed into Flora's chest, throwing her backwards.

The armchair was now a ball of flame, acrid smoke filling the room as the Count dashed for the stairs.

With a roar, Alex jerked her prosthetic arm outwards, snapping the belt binding her hands and causing it to ricochet off a wall. She launched herself at the Count, slamming into his back just as he reached the doorway at the top of the stairs leading to The Armoury below.

He squealed as she grappled him, stumbling sideways, his head slamming against the wall and knocking his wig askew so that it covered one eye.

He swatted at her, gouging at her eyes, but Alex was faster. In a quicksilver movement, she grasped the sleevette of his prosthetic in an unbreakable grip, yanking him towards her.

She saw the panic in his eyes before she staggered backwards as the trinkets holding the Count's hand in place gave up their grip.

With a shriek, the Count fell down the stairs, sliding headfirst.

Great billows of black smoke followed in Alex's wake as she raced after the Count, yelling for Gregor to catch him. But even as the words left her mouth, the Count was picking himself up and scrambling for the door.

"Captain!"

It was Sid's bellow that stopped her in her tracks. Alex caught sight of Gregor as he vaulted over the bar to give chase, only to be tripped up by a drunk actor.

"Captain! It's getting worse, Captain!"

Alex looked back up the stairs. There was no decision to make.

She sprinted back into her office to find Sid straining at his bonds. Either he wasn't twisting his hands the way that Alex had drilled into her crew, or in his panic he'd accidentally tightened his belt.

Meanwhile, Flora was lying on her back on the floor, showing no signs of life.

After another look at both of her crew members, then at the raging fire that was now licking up the walls, Alex grabbed her cape and rushed at the chair, beating at the flames.

The paint on the ceiling had caught fire by the time Gregor burst into the room with a fire bucket full of water, which he hurled at the chair.

There was a hissing sizzle, but it wasn't enough.

As Alex continued to beat at the flames, Gregor repeatedly filled the bucket in the privy, hurling its contents at the ceiling and the wall until all that was left was the rank smell of ash, scorched paint and sodden paper.

"What did I tell you about messing with my establishment?" he yelled, the usually white stripes on his face red with anger.

"Now is not the time." Alex raced to Flora's side. "Flora's been shot. Help me."

Gregor strode over, every hair on his body bristling.

The bolt had entered Flora's chest right above her heart. Alex touched Flora's neck. There was a pulse, but it was a faint one.

"There's no blood, so there might still be hope. We have to get her clothes off to see what the damage is. You hold her up. I'll unbutton her."

Gregor had just reached for Flora's shoulders when a breathy sound escaped her lips.

"I like buttons. They're shiny." The words were so faint that they were almost inaudible.

"Flora, you've been shot. Stay still," Alex commanded. "Gregor and I are going to help you."

"I don't think I've been shot." Flora's eyes popped open, before she coughed and grimaced in pain. "It doesn't feel like it. It feels more like that time when you told me not to climb up the rigging and I did and I fell down onto the deck and couldn't breathe."

"It might feel like that, but there's a bolt sticking out of you. No, Flora, stay still."

Gregor reached for Flora's hands to restrain her, but she twisted out of his grip and jumped to her feet, swaying.

"I'm fine, I think," she said, then looked down. "Except for that." She grabbed the shaft of the bolt, just as Alex and Gregor yelled for her not to, and pulled it out.

Expecting a spurt of blood to spray across the room, Alex lurched towards her, but it wasn't necessary because Flora had pulled something from her breast pocket that looked suspiciously like a pocket watch.

"Oh no." Flora looked at Gregor, her eyes round with guilt. "I was going to give it back. I promise. I was just looking at it."

"Is that my watch?" Gregor asked, finally finding his voice.

"I think it *was* your watch." Alex put her hand against the wall to support herself as her body slumped in relief.

Gregor stared at Flora for a long, silent moment before his nostrils flared in a snort. "You owe me a new watch, Reign. A new bar for my window, a new paint job and my rent on time or I'll—"

"Bite my head off." Alex patted him on the arm. "I understand the sentiment."

Giving her a lethal glare, he stomped back downstairs.

"Well, that went worse than it could have," Alex said. "Sid, you'll never cease to amaze me. One minute you're saving the day and finding out who the villain is and the next minute you're serving him gin."

She turned when she didn't get an answer. Sid Potts had somehow managed to tip his chair sideways and was snoring on the floor.

CHAPTER 50

SID EXPLAINS EVERYTHING IN AN
IMAGINARY LIBRARY

"**S**ID, WAKE UP." ALEX untied Sid and shook his shoulders gently. "He's out cold."

"I tied the belt so he could twist out of it," Flora said. "I don't know why he didn't."

"He must have been so tired he wasn't thinking." Alex shook Sid again, harder this time. Every impulse was telling her to hunt down the bastard who'd just threatened her crew and scuppered her office, but she couldn't yet. Her crew came first. "*Sid!*"

Sid groaned.

Flora knelt at Sid's side, shouting in his ear. "Wake up!"

Sid's eyes popped open, and he struggled to a seated position, giving the overturned chair a confused look before his wits returned and he looked at Alex with panic in his eyes.

"The villain! He shot Flora! I tried to burst out of my bonds, Captain, but my belt was too tight. Where is the little mite? Is she alive?"

"I'm here." Flora patted him on the shoulder. "I'm not dead."

"But you could've been!" Sid surged to his feet and gave Flora a relieved hug before stepping back and grabbing the desk to support himself. "It's the femmy fartalley, Captain. He's behind all this. He lured you with his whales and look where it got us!" He gestured wildly to the armchair with the soggy scorched books and the blackened wall and roof. "Almost burned to a cinder, and I know who was responsible!"

"Count Mendacium? The fop who just had us tied up, shot Flora and tried to burn down the building?" Alex asked wryly.

"No! It was the femmy fartalley!" Sid's voice shook with conviction.

Alex shook her head. "I have no idea what you're talking about. How hard did you hit your head?"

"My head has never worked better! I'm telling you it's him, that cove who came to hire us."

"He means Elias." Flora righted the chair Sid had been tied to. "He's not bad. He's nice."

Sid shook his head vehemently. "No, he's not. He's evil through and through. He's obviously working with the Count. It's like I explained, Flora. The captain is under the spell of his sexual whales!"

"I've got no idea what these whales are," Alex said, "but I'm going to beat you with them if you don't shut up about them soon. We have a villain to catch."

Footfalls sounded on the stairs and Elias burst into the room, looking just as wild as Sid.

"Captain! Something awful has happened." He skidded to a halt, staring at the blackened walls and the chair. "Vengeful Queen's fiery eyeballs! What happened?"

"Aha!" Sid charged at Elias like a bull who'd spotted a promising china shop. "Own up to it! It was *you*." He shoved a finger under Elias's nose. "Where are your whales? Show them! Show them right now!"

"Sid, what the *hell* are you talking about?" Alex yelled.

"I don't have any whales," Elias stepped back to prevent Sid's finger going up his nostril.

"Yes you do!" Sid poked him in the chest before spinning around to face Alex and Flora. "I'll explain it all. Just give me a chance." He looked frantically around the room. "We don't have enough chairs, though, and this isn't a library, and we've got to have a carpet for him to kneel on to beg forgiveness."

"Forgiveness for what?" Alex asked.

"The crime!" Sid exclaimed. His face scrunched up in thought. "I think I've got a solution. Can you all pretend that this is a library where all the chairs and books got burnt by the villain? It'll work if we do that."

"Will that get this out of your system quicker?" Alex asked. "Because we've got a genuine villain to catch."

"Yes! And I've caught him! This man—" Sid pointed a shaking finger at Elias. "Is really a man dressed as a woman, dressed as a man!"

Elias looked down at his clothes. "I'm not."

"And he hired you, Captain, so that he could lure you into a false sense of security using his whales—"

"Whales again. What's going on with the whales? Where did you catch this whale idea?" Alex asked.

"I hope he didn't catch any," Flora said. "I don't think they'd be happy out of water."

"It's in the books!" Sid pointed to the dismal steaming pile on the burnt armchair. "I've read them. Some more than once! You'd believe me if I smoked a pipe and wore a funny hat and had a silly moustache. I might not be foreign, but I can tell a villain when I see one."

"I think I'm beginning to understand." Alex covered her face with her hands, counting silently until she no longer wanted to introduce Sid's head to the nearest wall.

Sid slumped with relief. "I knew you'd see that I was talking sense."

"I can see that you're talking something. A lot of something. Now, what I need you to do, to prevent this man's—woman's—*Elias's*, sexual whales from influencing me any more, is get me some gin. I'm going to drink some sense into me."

"You believe me?" Sid asked, his expression a map of relief and gratitude.

"I believe that you can get me some gin. Five pints should do it. And please ask Gregor to pour it into those little glasses the panto dames like. Helps with the clarity. If I'm going to understand a man who dresses as a woman pretending to be a man, who's in league with an office-burning Count, I've got to drink the same drinks they do, right?" Alex said.

"Of course, Captain! Anything so that you see sense and we can apprehend this blaggard!" Sid pointed at Elias again. "Just you wait. I'm on to you, and the captain will be too, the minute I get back."

With that, Sid hurried downstairs.

Alex cleared her throat. "Now, Mister Dooley, please tell me what's happened."

"What's a sexual whale?" Elias asked.

"Some things are best left a mystery," Alex said.

"Yes. Ah." Elias shook his head, and then the panicked expression he'd worn when he'd arrived returned. "Sweet Pete's been killed by adulterated sugar! Big Ivan tried to give me the carrot and I escaped. I think I know what happened. I don't know who did it, but I know how they did it, almost."

"The carrot? To one of *my* crew? Why?" Alex demanded, all of Sid's daft accusations forgotten. "Tell me everything. Start at the beginning. Quickly, if you please. Gregor might turn out to be a quick pour."

She listened as Elias relayed everything that had happened, then she recounted how the Count had tried to kill them by burning down the building. When she got to the bit about Flora being shot, Elias asked to see the pocket watch to understand how it had been constructed to withstand a clockbow bolt, but Alex held him off. "Later—the important thing is that we apprehend Mendacium. We know where he lives. Even if he tries to hide, someone will catch him. Peacocks like him are easy to catch, take it from me. I've run down many a peacock's ship in my time. They're always so full of self-importance that they never think anyone can outwit them."

There was the heavy *thunk* of footsteps on the stairs. Far too heavy to be Sid. Alex spun around as two hulking figures entered the room.

One wore the red and black uniform of the Bad Habits and the other was wearing the red-and-white-striped suit of a Sugar Gang lieutenant. With their blank expressions, width and girth, they looked like two boiled sweets that had been left in someone's pocket long enough to collect fuzz.

"Sister Barry!" Flora rushed to the nun, dancing from one foot to the other. "Are you here to get a pie with me? Because now isn't a good time, because we have to catch a villain."

The nun looked down at Flora with a benevolent smile. "Hello cabin boy. I can't get a pie now because I'm on da clock. Wanna go after New Lent?"

"Yes! We can get one with anchovies and cheese and apples and—"

"Flora!" Alex shouted. "Later." She bowed to the two henchmen. "To what do I owe the pleasure of your company?"

They both stared at her with identical blank expressions. Briefly, Alex wondered why there wasn't an employment agency representing this kind of tall, wide and not-so-bright employee, but then she realised that in OverLondon, there was a good chance there was. "Why are you here?" she clarified.

"Ladies first," Sister Barry said to the Sugar Gang heavy. "Dat's me."

"You're a lady?" the Sugar Gang lieutenant asked.

"I'm a nun."

"Nuns are officially known as ladies." Flora gave Sister Barry an admiring smile.

"In da ecclesiastical sense," Sister Barry said. "Yeah."

"Like I'm a cabin boy in the piratical sense."

"Yeah."

"Someone start talking!" Alex commanded.

Sister Barry brightened. "Oh yeah. Mother Superior wants to know if you've solved her little problem."

"An' Big Ivan wants to have strong words wiv you about some lies concernin' his sugar bein' bad," the Sugar Gang heavy announced.

"I see." Alex scratched her jaw. "Well, Sister Barry, I have excellent news for Mother Superior. I have the name of her miracle man and she can find him at this address." She grabbed a pencil from her desk and scrawled Count Mendacium's details on a paper bag that had formerly contained a pie. "Also, please tell her that my man here will be conducting a demonstration about divine miracles tomorrow morning at eight, at the compost heap near the Hyde Park conveniences." She looked up and caught Sister Barry's panicked expression. "I'll write that down too, shall I?"

"Yeah. Dat would be good."

"And as for Big Ivan," Alex said to the Sugar Gang heavy, "tell him that a man named Count Mendacium of fifteen Harlequin Street, Maye Fayre is responsible for poisoning his sugar and killing Sweet Pete. Also, tell him that I'll prove my claims at the compost heap near the Hyde Park conveniences at eight tomorrow morning."

"Can you write that down too like you did for the nun?" the Sugar Gang heavy asked.

"Yes, yes." Alex found another grease-stained paper bag, thinking that she really should get Sid and Flora to vary their diets. All these pies couldn't be good for them.

"It's only because he's got one of your boys an' is going to give 'em the carrot tomorrow mornin' at nine if he doesn't get answers." He turned to Elias, who looked like he was going to throw up. "You look a lot like the boy that we've got waitin' for the carrot. Are you his bruvver?"

Alex loudly cleared her throat to cover up Elias's stuttered reply. "Pure coincidence! Standard uniform for all privateering artificer apprentices. It's a guild thing." She looked at the man's face. His mouth was moving, albeit slower than Sister Barry's had been.

"Want me to write that down too?"

"Yeah."

Alex wrote the information down and ended the note promising that no more would be said to the Cry on the condition that Elias's life was no longer threatened.

After rereading both notes, she folded them carefully and handed them over. "There you go. I won't say it was a pleasure to see either of you, but please send my regards to your respective employers."

"Yeah. What you said. I'm goin' now." The Sugar Gang heavy departed, leaving Sister Barry behind.

"Will you be coming tomorrow, Sister Barry?" Flora asked. She'd been beaming at the nun for the past few minutes and Alex was becoming concerned about whether or not getting hit by the clockbow bolt had rattled her brain. "I can show you all the wanted posters at the Hyde Park conveniences. There's all kinds of things on them!"

"Dunno. But I will try."

"Yay!"

"I have to go now," Sister Barry said, then frowned at the smouldering armchair. "Don't let the librarians know you've been barbequin' books or they'll come down on you like an avalanche of almanacs."

"Barbequing books? Thank you for that genius deduction," Alex said.

"Yeah. I'm smarter dan I look. I cultivate resting fick face for professional reasons. It's expected, like," Sister Barry said solemnly. "Although there are some *really* fick nuns. Sister Scrofula is a bit lost in der brain department. She once tried to cane a chair because it looked at her funny."

"Fascinating." Alex bowed to the nun. "Please give Mother Superior my regards."

"I will do dis thing."

"Excellent."

"I am going now."

"Even better. Flora, why don't you show Sister Barry out."

"Okay!"

Alex waited until the nun and Flora had left, then turned to Elias, who was closely examining something in his hands.

"What have you got there, Mister Dooley? The Count's hand? Oh yes, I pulled it off him. Took me by surprise." Alex inspected the prosthetic, whistling as she saw the filigree and the pearls. "I haven't seen that kind of frippery since I visited an artificer in Bohemia. Must be where he's from."

Elias nodded, running his fingers over the attachment sleevette. "Can I take this to study it? I might learn something."

"Do whatever you like as long as you bring it back afterwards. It'll sell for good money and I've got a badger downstairs who's got a running tally on how much I owe him." Alex collected her clockbow, inspected it for damage and began to wind the tensioner. "I need you to set up that experiment with the sugar and the acid again so it goes off at eight tomorrow. I picked the Hyde Park compost heap because no one'll be around at that hour, and it should be spectacular enough to eliminate all doubt in our findings. And to prove your innocence, for that matter."

"To Big Ivan?" Elias asked, tucking the prosthetic into his coat pocket.

"I was thinking of my bo'sun," Alex said wryly.

"Is there a reason he's obsessed with whales? Because I've never seen a whale, other than in books."

"Pray you never find out. Anyway, let me get you that sugar." She walked to her desk and opened the drawer, only to find it empty. She looked around the room. "It *was* here."

She focused on the empty tankards on the desk, experiencing a terrible premonition just as Sid came up the stairs carrying a huge tray covered in tiny glasses full of gin.

"I've got the gin Captain!" He bustled over with a keen expression. "Gregor said that you were barmy and that it was going on your tab, but I said it was for vital deduction work!" He puffed up with pride. "Now drink up."

"Sid..." Alex asked. "When you got those pints of gin for Count Mendacium, did you leave him alone in our office?"

Sid looked lost. "Of course. I didn't know he was the villain then."

"Hmm." Alex put her hands on her hips. "And where was he standing when you came back up the stairs?"

"Behind your desk, Captain. He said he needed to stretch his legs. All that lording all day took it out of him."

"Ah." Alex closed her eyes, counted backwards from ten and then gave the room a manic grin. "No fear! We still have the cake!" She hurried into the privy only to see that the top of the wardrobe contained a bare tray. "Sid?"

"Yes, Captain?" Sid asked, hurrying to the privy door.

"Did you, or did you not—and this is important—feed Count Mendacium privy cake?"

Sid flushed. "I wanted to keep him here because I thought he was a customer, and it's not just a privy, is it? We store the potatoes in here, and the onions." He pointed to the hessian sacks in the wardrobe. "And we use it for our laundry." He waved at Flora's wet clothes strung across the room. "So it's not *exactly* a privy. More of a multipurpose storeroom."

"Storeroom." Alex repeated, pinching the bridge of her nose. "Sid, did you feed Count Mendacium storeroom cake?"

SID EXPLAINS EVERYTHING IN AN IMAGINARY LIBRARY319

"It was so pretty. I thought you'd put it on the wardrobe especially for visitors. And I assure you, Captain, he would never have known this was the privy. I told him it was the larder, which it is, after a fashion, when you think about it."

Alex pursed her lips. "I see." She left the privy to see that Flora had returned and was now showing Elias Gregor's damaged pocket watch. "Crew, it seems that we no longer need to hunt down Mendacium because he'll be exploding in—" She looked at Sid. "When did you feed him the cake?"

"Must have been an hour ago."

"In nine and a half hours. The trick will be listening to the Cry for news of a large and dramatic explosion." She recalled the Count's colourful clothing. "A large, dramatic, peacockish explosion."

"What about the demonstration for Mother Superior and Big Ivan?" Flora asked.

"It's simple. We'll wait to hear the news about the Count blowing up on the Cry, go to wherever he is and find the sugar amongst the bits."

"What if the sugar gets blown up too?" Elias asked.

"Good point." Alex gnawed on her lower lip. "No! I have a much better idea. We'll inform Mother Superior and Big Ivan that the demonstration has moved in time and location."

"To where?"

"To wherever Count Mendacium has exploded," Alex said emphatically. "With luck, we'll find enough sugar there to point the finger at him. Mother Superior said she'd pay us for the delivery of the cove who tried to blackmail the Church, preferably alive. She didn't say *definitely* alive. And if that's not enough evidence, Mother Superior has a note in his handwriting and I have his address written in his hand from the club ledger!" She pulled the sheet of parchment from her doublet. "It will just be a matter of showing they're by the same hand."

"That's the clue that solved the case of the missing Maltese poodle in *Thee Case Ofe The Missinge Maltese Poodle*!" Sid exclaimed, gesturing to the sodden and scorched penny dreadfuls.

"I have, on occasion, been known to read also," Alex said. Looking at the books had given her an idea. "Sid, it's just occurred to me that while your conclusions about Mister Dooley here are undoubtably unique, you're looking at this whale from the wrong end."

"What do you mean, Captain?"

"Mister Dooley—" Alex paused for dramatic effect "—is *not* a femmy fartalley, no matter how much he looks, acts and talks like one."

Sid nodded enthusiastically. "He does, Captain! I can see his whales working even now!"

"Quite. But it's all a case of mistaken identity," Alex said. "What we have here is, in fact, a damsel in distress who's been mistaken for a femmy fartalley! He came to us for help and fell victim to Big Ivan's carrot. That's damsel behaviour if ever I saw it. Would a femmy fartalley almost get the carrot? I don't think so." She caught Elias's shocked expression and shook her head while Sid was staring off into space, his face screwed up in concentration.

"A damsel in distress?" he asked finally. "But if it's not him, then it was all the Count, and that's not right because he didn't tell us why he did it. They always tell the hero why they did it."

"We may still catch him before he explodes. And Mister Dooley's damsel-in-distressery was hard to detect because…" Alex tried to come up with a reason but floundered.

Thankfully, Flora saved the situation. "Because of his *natural* sexual whales!" she said triumphantly.

"*Precisely.*" Alex left Sid to contemplate that and approached Elias, patting him on the shoulder. Then she remembered the trinket in her pocket from Father Bollard's rectory, and handed it to him.

"It's from the priest in Maye Fayre?" Elias asked, as the odd little trinket attached to the back of his hand made cooing noises and waved its tiny arm.

"Yes. Why don't you take this little fellow and go home? Get some sleep. I'll need you up and alert in around nine and a half hours, to explain to Mother Superior and Big Ivan why Mendacium is our man. Even if he explodes in private, someone's sure to discover him not long after." Alex rounded on Sid. "In the meantime, Sid, get some sleep—your noggin has obviously been dented. You did a good job learning Mendacium's name and address. And feeding him the cake, come to think of it. Flora and I will keep watch on the Count's club and his house. If we spot him sooner, we'll let you know." She started to collect her cape from the hook on the wall, only to pause, chagrined when she remembered that it was a sodden, charred heap on the armchair. Then she rallied. "I've got a villain to catch and a ship to get back. Let's make it reign!"

CHAPTER 51

A HANDY REALISATION

E LIAS LABORIOUSLY CLIMBED THE stairs to his room at Mrs Nevins's boarding house, closed the door and slumped against it. Then he took the trinkets he'd collected over the course of the day and placed them carefully in the small aquarium he kept next to his bed for any creatures that needed overnight monitoring. Seeing their sluggishness, he shaved some omnicite into the water and then gave some to Phillips and his longevity trinket. Phillips cooed his appreciation, only for the trinket on Elias's chest to coo back, which would have been disturbing if Elias wasn't so exhausted.

Divesting himself of his coat and cap, he collapsed on the bed and fell into a deep sleep.

Hear ye! Hear ye! A large number of Sugar Gang members and Bad Habits have entered into an altercation in Harlequin Street, Maye Fayre. A witness standing nearby named Flora was quoted as saying that it had started because of a miracle. Stop. Big Ivan of the Sugar Gang has announced that he is offering a five-pound reward for information on the whereabouts of a miscreant named Count Mendacium who lives at fifteen Harlequin Street, Maye Fayre. Stop. Ye've heard! Ye've heard! Do your feet hurt? Do you need to get somewhere at medium speed? Why not take a Black Hack? All the cynicism, all the time. Black Hacks, we've got an opinion for you.

Woken by the Cry, Elias sat upright. It was dark. Scrambling to light a lamp, he checked his watch, breathing a sigh of relief when he saw he still had approximately one and a half hours until the Count was due to explode.

He got up and washed his face, then paced as he considered the situation as it stood, trying to add up everything he knew. He now knew who'd blown up the priests, and he knew how, but there was something about why the Count had done it that bothered him. Why kidnap an urchin and why blow up those priests specifically? If the Count's only intention had been blackmail, wouldn't anyone have done? Why four—almost five—priests from a secret society? The question gnawed at him. It was as frustrating as attempting to assemble a jigsaw with a missing piece.

His eyes lit on his coat and he picked it up, removing the prosthetic hand the captain had pulled from the Count.

He sat on the bed, examining the flexibility of the finger joints and admiring the craftmanship. He'd seen all kinds of prosthetic hands, but other than Captain Reign's arm, he'd never seen one this beautiful or expensive. It was constructed from a mixture of metal alloys in a filigree pattern with inlaid pearls as decoration. Each strand of intertwined metal had been bevelled in a way that caught the light like a thousand diamonds. It was truly a masterpiece.

Turning it over, Elias looked for a maker's stamp. If he could identify the artificer who'd made it, maybe the information would be useful in some way. He couldn't find one externally and began searching the surface of the hand for a method of accessing its internal mechanisms. When he couldn't find anything, he flipped it upright to examine the wrist attachment sleevette.

After studying the hooks and levers there that were meant to connect with the wearer's trinkets, he retrieved a set of pliers and gently tugged on them.

CHAPTER 52

JUST DESSERTS

MINUTES LATER, ELIAS WAS huddled in the back of a Black Hack as it raced through Whitechapel's drenched streets, heading for Westminster. The hack's awning provided little defence against the rain and sleet and he tugged his cap down tighter, hiking his collar up to cover the back of his neck.

By the time the hack halted in a narrow street where the buildings bowed towards each other, he was soaked through. Shivering, he paid the driver, then looked up and down the street, experiencing a jolt when he saw a barber's pole through the curtain of rain that was turning the street into a shallow river. He ran towards it and burst through the door.

Once the barber finished berating Elias for alarming a man holding a razor to someone's throat, he gave him the information he wanted. Elias thanked the man, then consulted his pocket watch and braved the streets again. The sleet had now turned to hail that pummelled his head and shoulders as he sprinted through Westminster, searching barely visible street names until he found the one he was looking for. It was on the very edge of the parish where Westminster met Maye Fayre.

Perisher Street.

From Harlequin Street, the next street over, he could hear the sideshow of street vendor's calls and interparish taunting that always accompanied a large OverLondon mob. Elias had no doubt that Big Ivan's offer of a reward had half the city out on the streets, breaking the Parish Agreement and causing no end of trouble in the search for Count Mendacium. He just hoped that the captain and Flora were keeping out of the fray somewhere dry.

Wiping water from his eyes, Elias counted down the street numbers attached to the stone facades of modest townhouses.

He skidded to a halt in front of number twenty-five, breathing a sigh of relief as he saw light creeping around the curtains covering the front windows. Bracing himself, he knocked on the door.

The curtain twitched and moments later the door opened, revealing Mister Gripes wearing a floor-length dark green dressing robe. One hand was in a pocket, while the other held the door. He was shivering due to the invading cold.

"Mister Dooley! What are you doing? Don't answer that. It's frigid out here. Come in, come in and dry yourself. Come in to the warm. You're soaked through."

He ushered Elias down a narrow hallway and into a cosy room full of comfortable armchairs and lined with overflowing bookcases. A fire was crackling in the hearth and despite his urgency, Elias moved towards it. Steam radiated from his clothing.

"To what do I owe the pleasure of this unconventional visit? Here, drink this, it will warm you." Mister Gripes hurried to a small table that contained a decanter and glasses. He sloshed some spirit into a tumbler and carried it over to Elias who took it but didn't drink it.

"Thank you, sir," Elias said. "I have to speak to you about a personal matter."

"Of course. Of course. Let me take your coat so you can make yourself comfortable." Mister Gripes gestured to an armchair.

"No thank you, sir. I don't plan on being here long." Elias glanced at a grandfather clock on the other side of the room. The seconds were ticking away and time was running out.

"I see." Mister Gripes smoothed the index finger of his good hand over his pencil moustache, drawing attention to a small speck of white there. "How can I help you?"

"It's this, sir." Elias fumbled with his coat pocket and pulled out Count Mendacium's prosthetic hand. "I believe it's yours. You left it at the Reign Agency after you tried to kill the captain and her crew."

Mister Gripes blinked, his expression momentarily blank before he burst into hearty laughter. "Come now, Mister Dooley. You came here on a horrible night for this? What are you accusing me of? I'm a glorified clerk. The person that Mother Superior and Big Ivan are currently seeking lives in Maye Fayre and is a foreign aristocrat." He waved his hand to encompass his study. "Does this look like somewhere a member of the gentry would live?"

"No, it doesn't," Elias said. "But it doesn't need to, because Count Mendacium doesn't live here. He lives at fifteen Harlequin Street, which I'm almost positive backs directly onto this house. Once your barber told me your address, I was sure. You see, I used to make deliveries to this part of town for my mother, and I once delivered an order of fabric to number ten Harlequin Street. The man there complained about the sound of his neighbour in Perisher Street playing the violin all night. His walls were thin and the sound came right through. And then I remembered the captain telling me about number fifteen being empty except for the one room at the back of the house which had a great big mirror and a lot of clothes. I bet that mirror hides a doorway to this house, doesn't it?"

Mister Gripes responded with a condescending smile. "I can see your reasoning, but just because one house in this street adjoins another, it doesn't mean they all do. You're a bright young man, but I'm afraid your imagination has run away with you. Any other man would be offended, but I'm feeling generous. Why don't we put this down to a large intellect with too much time on its hands?"

Elias continued, "I have evidence. I'm not imagining things. The hand is definitely yours."

"I'm getting impatient now. How do you think a man of my meagre wages could afford something so grand?" Mister Gripes asked, his tone painstakingly reasonable.

"I'll admit that I was confused at first, until I realised that it's not a prosthetic. It's a glove." With the tips of his fingers, Elias gripped the hooks and loops at the prosthetic's wrist and pulled. The filigree sleevette slid off, revealing an aged oak hand with a little finger repaired with pine.

Mister Gripes snorted. "Ridiculous. There have to be hundreds of other old hands in this city. You told me you practiced on them yourself."

"If it's so ridiculous, why won't you show me the hand in the pocket of your robe?" Elias asked.

"You want to see my hand?" Mister Gripes asked. "Fine." He withdrew a new looking pine prosthetic from his pocket. It was clutching a Nelson's clockbow—small and only good at short-distances, but lethal all the same.

"I think we've talked enough, don't you?" he asked, raising an eyebrow.

"You don't need to shoot me," Elias said, his pounding heartbeat and Phillip's hiss belying his calm tone. He set the tumbler Mister Gripes had given him on the mantelpiece. "I have no intention of forcing you to give yourself up. I just want answers."

"Answers?"

"I want to know why you did it. I already know how. You got your men to put omnicite in the priests' order of sugar after the urchin girl told you what she'd overheard. It wouldn't have been too hard if they did it when Sweet Pete took one of his regular breaks, or while he was distracted. You would've known about the omnicite exploding in acid after seeing it demonstrated by Mistress Fenderpossum last month. I remember you told me you attended."

"Yes, yes. What of it?" Mister Gripes asked, his tone impatient now.

"That was quite smart, sir. But it didn't go to plan, did it? Something happened that caused the explosion to be much bigger than you expected. When the second priest exploded in the same way, you realised that whatever was going wrong was doing so consistently, so you sent the blackmail letter to Mother Superior. But I don't think blackmail was your first intent," Elias said earnestly. "Otherwise you would've sent the letter after blowing up Father Bartholomew. So what I'd like to know is why you kidnapped the urchin and why you targeted that specific group of priests. Their secret society can't have been a threat to you."

Mister Gripes stared at Elias for a long moment before his face contorted into a furious scowl. "You want to know *why*? They printed a copy of the Cry!" he snarled. "The urchin even overheard one of the priests saying that they could sell printed copies of the Cry in the street! Do you know what would've happened if the idea got back to Mother Superior or Cardinal Chudleigh? The divine bloody leaders of the church of never-ending vengeful acquisition would've jumped at the chance to make more money. They'd have been competition! It had to be stopped!"

"So the urchin *did* overhear the priests," Elias said. It had just been a theory until now. "She came to sell the information to you, didn't she?"

"Yes. Yes. They all come to me. Everyone in this disgusting city has a story to sell."

"And then you kidnapped her."

"I had no choice!" Mister Gripes exclaimed. "Do you know how many people are employed by the Cry? We would've lost advertisers. Hundreds of people would've become penniless. I was protecting their interests!"

"That doesn't explain your alternate identity as Count Mendacium." Elias watched the clockbow carefully. The tip of the bolt was wavering with Mister Gripes's every word. His trinkets would still be getting used to the new prosthetic.

"Doesn't it?" Mister Gripes scoffed. "I gave undying fealty to the Cry for decades. I lived and breathed the knowledge that I was the caretaker of every bit of official information that every citizen in this city heard. I was even next in line to take over, until Loud John became a bloody war hero. It wasn't long before rumours came out about him promising the Church that he'd give them forty percent of everyone's income if they pushed for him to get the job. Forty percent of my income disappeared overnight. *Forty percent.* And the idiot didn't even know the basics of accounting! It was but a small matter to take the money back. I deserved it. It was mine. I created the Count because he was the man I was born to be! My mother was Bohemian. If she'd only been someone elevated enough to marry my father, the title would have been mine instead of leaving me working day in day out for a city that never appreciated me."

Elias frowned. "It would cost much more than forty percent of a clerk's income to maintain a second house in Maye Fayre and a membership at Krabb's, not to mention the fine fabric and clothing Captain Reign described."

"Forty percent of my income... forty percent of the others employed by the Cry... what's the difference? It had already been stolen. All I did was steal some of it back."

"I understand, sir, but you kidnapped an urchin and ordered her killed, had four priests exploded, poisoned Sweet Pete, and you attempted to kill Captain Reign and her crew," Elias said. "I can't excuse that."

Mister Gripes guffawed. "You could if you were in my situation, I assure you. But you're young and stupid and don't realise how unfair life is. Unless you take, you don't get. And thanks to four exploding priests, I now have the means of getting whatever I want." Mister Gripes's eyes shone in the glow from the fireplace. "You're an artificer—you understand the significance of what I have discovered. An explosive with so much power that a small amount can blow a man to bits with a delayed effect? All I need to do is learn the additional substance Sweet Pete added to his sugar and the world will be mine! Just think, if you helped me, you too could be a part of that. You said you had theories about what Sweet Pete used to bulk his sugar out. If you shared them, you'd never have to worry about money again. A fortune halved is still a fortune. You wouldn't have to work in that dismal little shop. You could raise your family out of the squalor they no doubt exist in and truly *live*."

"No thank you," Elias said calmly. "My mother would take great offence about her lodgings being described as squalor. And your plan won't succeed."

Mister Gripes scowled. "What do you mean?"

"Because in order to work out what Sweet Pete used, I'd have to analyse the sugar, and I don't have it any more."

"I have the sugar! Dear boy, if that's all you require—"

"I won't help you because it's wrong," Elias said.

Mister Gripes raised the clockbow. "You *will* help me, or you'll die. Surely you must know I can't let you leave here alive."

Elias shook his head. "I'm afraid you're the one who is going to die, sir. Remember the cake you ate at The Armoury earlier?"

As he spoke, the Cry became audible, filtering into the house from the street.

Hear ye! Hear ye! Big Ivan has increased the reward for the capture of Count Mendacium, of fifteen Harlequin Street Maye Fayre, to six pounds. Stop.

Mister Gripes's eyes widened in horror as he processed the magnitude of Elias's words. "No!"

"I'm afraid so, sir. Any minute now. Do you have any last wishes? Any family members you'd like me to inform?"

OverBerlin has officially declared war on OverMunich due to a dispute over the correct shape and size of the Germanic potato. Stop. Ye've heard! Ye've heard!

Mister Gripes twisted around to check the clock and Elias could see him counting the hours. "No, it can't be."

"It can."

"To hell with you!" Gripes re-aimed his clockbow and tried to pull the trigger, but his fingers remained rigid. As he looked at them in surprise, both prosthetic and clockbow fell to the floor with twin *thunks*.

Do your parts not work as well as they should? Do you have trouble with your moving bits? Visit Ingenious mechanisms on Utopia Street today.

Elias rushed to scoop up the trinkets that were now scuttling across the carpet, then dived sideways into the hallway, scrambling out of sight just as a loud, too-familiar wet splat sounded around the house.

Then there was silence.

He lay motionless until his heartbeat returned to normal, then regained his composure. Using the wall to support himself, he got to his feet and placed the trinkets carefully in his pocket.

Then, without looking into the parlour, he located Mister Gripes's bedroom at the rear of the house. There was a large mirror attached to the wall. After a few seconds Elias found a hidden catch at the top of the frame and the mirror swung inwards to reveal another room in fifteen Harlequin Street, Maye Fayre.

Closing the secret door, Elias searched Mister Gripes's house—avoiding the library—until he found the kitchen.

The room looked like a chemical laboratory belonging to a particularly deranged alchemist. Ignoring the scattered omnicite pods, beakers full of acid, bags of various brown substances ranging from sawdust to brown flour and the acid burns on almost every surface, Elias located the bag of sugar that Mister Gripes had taken from the Reign Agency. There was still a small amount inside.

After tucking it into his coat pocket, he cleared the items Mister Gripes had been experimenting with from the kitchen counters, placing them in the parts of the house where one would expect to find them. If anyone asked him to speculate about Mister Gripes's methods, he was determined to say that while he knew omnicite had been involved, it would be impossible to speculate on any other ingredients. If it came to it, he knew Mistress Fenderpossum would back him up and that any experimentation would be shut down by the Artificer's Guild. For once, her dislike of innovation would work in his favour.

Finally, after checking the kitchen one last time, Elias let himself out the front door.

He found Captain Reign and Flora in Harlequin Street, huddled in the dubious shelter of a winter-bare oak tree, smoking a cigar and eating a pie respectively as they watched the chaos in front of Count Mendacium's house. By now, Maye Fayre's Butlers had turned up and were attempting to assert their authority over the brawling Sugar Gang members and Bad Habits.

It didn't take Elias long to explain what had happened and within minutes Flora had been dispatched with messages for Mother Superior, Big Ivan and Loud John. Meanwhile, Elias took Captain Reign to number twenty-five Perisher Street to show her what remained of Mister Vernon Gripes, Master of Information for the OverLondon Cry.

CHAPTER 53

A ROGUE ARTIFICER SAVES THE WORLD

D AWN WAS JUST PUSHING its fingers through OverLondon's fog-choked streets when Elias finally left Mister Gripes's house.

Mother Superior, Big Ivan and Loud John had come and gone, and Captain Reign and Flora had departed for The Armoury only minutes before, with the agreement that they'd see Elias later.

Elias's voice was almost as croaky as Loud John's after having explained his carefully tailored version of events multiple times. He was tired but he wasn't ready for bed yet. He needed to think.

It was a long walk back to Mrs Nevins's, but Elias didn't hail a hack. Instead, he wandered through the city's early-morning streets, through Westminster, along Drury Lane, through Covent Garden and to the banks of the Over-Thames Reservoir.

Hands in his pockets, lost in thought, he avoided the offers of the boatmen touting fares to Southwark and dodged out of the way of the odd scavenger at the water's edge searching for detritus to sell.

As he trudged along, water lapping against the shore in ripples caused by the city's never-ending flight through the sky, Elias considered the night's events.

Nothing felt right to him.

He replayed the bargaining that Big Ivan and Mother Superior had conducted with Loud John over how to keep the story quiet. Then he thought about the way Captain Reign had stood by, smoking her ever-present cigar. She'd appeared completely unsurprised by the scene, waiting until the fuss had died down before casually mentioning that in order to retain her silence, Loud John would have to pay some kind of penalty fee on a wager she'd made at the

Henry the Late. Loud John had erupted into a furious protest, but Big Ivan and Mother Superior had backed the captain. It seemed to Elias that their support was only because it contributed to their sense of justice over making Loud John pay for his employee's crimes.

At the time, Elias had fought the feeling that things shouldn't be like this.

Mister Gripes had killed people and had tried to have others killed, but no one in the city other than the people who'd been present in that house tonight would ever know. Elias had overheard Loud John ordering in a cleaning crew. He'd heard Loud John announce that Mister Gripes had, in fact, not died, but had suddenly taken a job in OverParis. He'd heard Big Ivan announce that he'd heard from reliable sources that the count he'd been seeking had left the city at the same time.

Meanwhile, the Church of Vengeful Acquisition would maintain that the priests' deaths were miracles. Elias had listened incredulously as Mother Superior had said she wouldn't even be surprised if they weren't still made saints.

As for Sweet Pete, no one cared. The urchins of Bloomsbury and Drury Lane might miss him until the next pusherman took his place, but as far as the people in that room were concerned, he'd been no one, only a man who'd worked every day for someone else before dying alone.

Elias thought about that.

He understood Mister Gripes's desire to be another person. He'd experienced that same urge himself—although he hadn't desired wealth or prestige. He only wanted to be able to innovate and invent without censure. However, he understood the desire for something *more*, since realising that the rules ordering his society didn't make sense and that others didn't appreciate or understand his view of the world. He understood all of that.

Elias could even—if he pretended that he didn't have the moral code that his mother had drilled into him from childhood—understand Mister Gripes's motivation to steal from the Cry's tithe to the Church of Vengeful Acquisition. From a certain perspective, it had merely been the theft of a theft, even if the only truly honourable thing would have been to return the funds to their rightful owners.

However, what Elias couldn't understand was Mister Gripes's desire to kill. That had been wrong. There'd been no need for it. Elias had an enquiring mind, but he'd never been curious about how it would feel to have the power of life or death over others. A power like that should be a burden, not something to be sought, savoured or exploited. He knew this deep in his soul.

He reached a curve in the OverThames Reservoir where the water was deeper, and he pulled the bag of sugar from his coat.

If he took it back to his workshop and analysed it, there was a good chance that he'd eventually be able to work out which additive Sweet Pete had used. Once he determined that, he'd have the power of life and death in his hands. He'd have the formula for the greatest weapon the globe had ever seen. He'd be a man of wealth and notoriety, the first artificer to truly invent something for decades, maybe centuries. He'd be able to buy his mother whatever house she wanted. She'd never have to work again. He'd be able to establish his own workshop in a better part of the city, with apprentices working on experiments to develop things that could improve the lives of people all over the globe.

Elias stood on the OverThames's muddy banks as the city travelled above English soil and the sun rose, and he considered this for a very long time.

Then he loosened the top of the bag, turned it upside down and poured its contents into the water. He turned the bag inside out, filled it with stones and dropped it in too.

Afterwards, he walked the rest of the way to Ingenious Mechanisms, stopping at Bumbridge's Tea Shop for a cup of tea and two buns. One was for him and the other was for Vikram, who was certainly not going to be happy when he learned that Mother Superior had confiscated the cookbook.

CHAPTER 54

THE GLARING ABSENCE OF GIN, COIN AND SHIP CONTINUES

A ND NOW IT'S THE day of the Festival of the Queen's Ascension, and The Armoury is packed with actors dressed as the Vengeful Queen in her fiery chicken form, ready to participate in the day's events.

Outside, the streets are swathed in bunting made from anything Soho's residents could find, and cheers can already be heard as people parade effigies of a decapitated Henry VIII that will be later thrown on ceremonial bonfires located on the banks of the OverThames.

Everywhere there is laughter and frivolity, with old disputes momentarily set aside for the one day of the year when every OverLondoner gets to take the day off work and celebrate their good luck in living in a time of such peace and prosperity.

Every OverLondoner, that is, except for the four people sitting in a corner of The Armoury, who are looking distinctly glum.

A LEX TOOK A SWIG from a tankard of gin and scowled at the other five empty tankards lined up on the table in front of her.

"We've been scuppered, crew," she said to Sid, Flora and Elias, who was perched on a stool opposite her. "Scuppered and our booty looted—there's no other way to put it, and we're still stuck in this blasted city."

"Cheer up, Captain—there's worse cities to be stuck in."

"No, Sid, there are no worse cities. Although I will admit that this is the best worst city on the planet, because it's mine and not some other blighter's."

"For better or worse, that's what I always say."

"Better and worse, Sid. Better *and* worse. There's no other way of looking at it."

"I guess it's true, Captain. It was such a shame about that mortalitye poole bet you placed being cancelled like that. You could have made a tidy profit if you'd won it!"

"What you're failing to grasp is that I would have had to die to win that bet."

"Yes Captain, but everyone knows the Dread Pirate Purple Reign wouldn't take being dead lying down. Not with all that booty to collect," Sid said, earnestly.

"Excellent point. I laugh in the face of death. Ha ha," Alex said glumly.

"And in the mirror. You laugh when you look in the mirror all the time," Flora said. "Especially when you're going to consult with a lady or gentleman about a quote for your services. You do a lot of laughing. And afterwards too."

"Your contribution, is, as always, valued Flora," Alex sighed. "But reminding me of happier times isn't cheering me up." She gulped another mouthful of gin. "I'm not saying we didn't do an outstanding bit of private-earing, crew. Especially you, Mister Dooley. You did some excellent work deducing that Mister Gripes was our man, but we've been routed. It's like an entire party of Mister Lemonses has descended from up on high to sink us in one fell swoop."

"Is it really that bad?" Elias asked. "After all, we learnt who was responsible for killing the priests and Sweet Pete. And we prevented it from happening to anyone else."

Alex waved a hand. "Yes. Yes, we did all that. And I have to say that Sid's touch with the privy cake was an unexpected stroke of genius, whether or not he intended it." She looked sideways at Sid, who nodded emphatically. There were another four empty tankards in front of him, and he didn't have nearly as many trinkets on his body to filter out the alcohol as Alex.

"Of course I knew, Captain!" he said. "Heroes always thwart the villain in the end. It was my heroic intuition hard at work."

"Pointing you towards the privy cake," Flora said.

"Aye! Pointing me at the privy cake, which *you*, Captain, craftily put in a place, knowing that I'd immediately *assume* it was the correct place for a villain's cake to be."

"I'm not sure that holds up logically," Elias said.

Sid's chest puffed out, his expression condescending. "You wouldn't be sure because you're in distress. Damsels in distress never know things. That's why they're distressed."

"We're all distressed, Sid—extremely distressed," Alex said. "Our booty has been looted and there's nothing we can do about it." She held up her hand at the look of alarm on Elias's face. "Never fear, Mister Dooley, I have the payment for your services. Never let it be said that I don't take care of my crew." She reached into a pocket and withdrew two shiny pound coins.

Elias took the money with obvious relief. "Thank you. Although I'm sorry about the cookbook, and the rings."

"Mother Superior didn't have to take the rings," Flora said with a long face.

Elias cleared his throat. "Logically, she did. Because if she didn't, we'd have evidence that her priests had been doing something untoward during New Lent, which completely contradicts the Church's story about their religious devotion. It makes sense."

Flora huffed a sigh. "At least the horrible beaver man isn't going to get his cookbooks now that Mother Superior told us she'd get her Bad Habits to find and destroy the others."

"There is that," Elias said.

"And just think, Captain," Sid said, "we've now got a fifty-pound credit note for a nice place in Vengeful Heaven. You never know when you might need it."

"You're not helping." Alex went back to glaring at the empty gin tankards. That had been the grating part. She'd shown Mother Superior Mister Gripes's exploded body, the rings and the cookbook Flora had found in Father O'Malley's rectory—all with the expectation of earning a reward, only for the woman to snatch the lot and give her a *credit note* that was only cashable in Vengeful

Heaven. A credit note! What self-respecting pirate wanted a credit note for a heaven she didn't even want to go to?

"And at least Big Ivan doesn't want to give the lad the carrot any more." Sid gave Elias the sort of smile one gives a simpleton who's worked out how to put his breeches on the correct way. "We'd just rescue you, all the same, but it means you don't have to worry about being frozen any time soon."

"That's something." Elias sipped his gin. Alex noticed the lad had taken to it, his posture not being quite as stiff as it had been the day she'd met him.

"See, it's not so bad, Captain," Flora, the eternal optimist, said. "I mean, Miss Sadie Simms didn't pay us in money because she'd lost so many customers with all the exploding priests, but she made you a new cape. And she made me some nice new red stockings because of priest splatting on the other ones. And she made the other things for Sid, with the extra fabric."

"Which will not be talked about in my company, as long as I live," Alex said quickly.

"Oh, I don't know, Captain." Sid shifted on the bench at her side. "I'm happy to talk about them all day, every day. They don't restrict my nethers at all. And I think red is a respectable colour. It warns everyone that they shouldn't be looking at what they're looking at. And might I say what they're looking at is—"

"Sid!"

"Well, Captain, it's a free city and a man can wear any underwear he wish-es—Why are you hitting your head on the table, Captain?"

"Oh, no reason. Just trying a new way to erase my memory."

A shadow fell over the table and Alex looked up to see Gregor glowering over Elias's shoulder.

"I expect that you're wanting the rent?" she said with a sigh.

"Plus the extra money for the window, the fire damage, my pocket watch and a bond to cover any future eventualities. I've decided you're a liability," Gregor growled.

"How much?"

"A pound."

"Are you sure you're not a pirate?" Alex asked sourly, dropping the last of her funds into his palm.

"I'm cautious and omnivorous," he said gruffly, before giving Sid a glare that changed to a slightly less surly glare when he took in Flora and Elias. To anyone who knew the man, it was a sign of the utmost approval. He then strode back to the bar, cuffing the head of an actor admiring Alex's 'height' on her wanted poster.

Alex smacked the table. "Well, that does it, crew. Other than being in possession of a new cape, which would never have been needed if we hadn't started our little enterprise, some stockings and some red silk *unmentionable* things—yes Sid, I mean it, no mentioning them *ever* again, I don't care *how* comfortable they are—we're in exactly the same situation that we were when we started."

"Not exactly," Elias said.

"What do you mean, Mister Dooley?"

"By directing this investigation, you've stopped someone from developing a weapon that could have been responsible for the annihilation of entire cities."

"Ah." Alex paused, her dour mood lifting a tiny amount. "Ah. I do see what you mean. As captain of the Reign Agency, it is I who should take responsibility for all victories and defeats that my crew experience." She straightened, her mood beginning to brighten as this new perspective took hold. "Yes, this was a victory—my victory for hiring you, Mister Dooley, and for directing Sid and Flora in their investigations. This was *our* victory as a crew."

"This was a city adventure. An OverLondon adventure!" Flora said.

"Yes," Alex said. "A brave and daring adventure." The idea was certainly growing on her. "And sometimes pirating adventures don't produce booty, but they do produce—"

"Friendship!" Flora finished with a toothy grin.

"Also, I wouldn't have met Miss Sadie Simms and she wouldn't have made me—"

"Sid! You've been warned." Alex cleared her throat. "I feel a speech coming on. A mighty captain's speech." She stood up and put her hands on her hips.

"Crew, I can see it now. This was merely a chase where our prize got away. We haven't lost the battle! There will be more booty."

"Shiny booty," Flora said.

"All we have to do is spy it and run it down," Alex said.

"I'm not sure—" Elias began, but Alex cut him off.

"Of course you're not, Mister Dooley! You're not a pirate, you're an artificer, but you're an artificer with a magnificent brain who is working *for* a pirate."

"I'm not sure I'm still working—"

Alex cut him off once again with a booming laugh. "Come now, Mister Dooley! Of course you are. Why wouldn't you? Think about it. You've managed to make more connections with important people in the past week than you would've in years of working in your shop. Tell me, would Big Ivan know your name if you hadn't met me?"

"Yes, I see your reasoning, I think, but he tried to give me the carrot."

"The carrot is a thing of the past!" Alex waved her hand in a grand, sweeping gesture. "It's all a matter of looking *forward*. Now that he knows who you are, there's always the chance for it to improve your business. The next time he needs an artificer who innovates, who is he going to call?"

"He might need you to work out a better way to give people the carrot," Flora said.

"Yes! Very helpful," Alex said. "He very well might. Just think about the other influential important people you'll meet if you continue to fly with us. What do you say, Mister Dooley—how do you feel about joining our crew as an honorary member? Picture yourself as a lone ship that flies under our colours whenever you're needed."

"Pirate colours!" Flora said.

"You're already dressed for it," Alex said, looking at Elias's coat and flat cap. "You're the only artificer who wears black. You've already got the pirate spirit, whether you know it or not. What do you say?"

Elias appeared torn. "I'm not sure how I feel about this."

"That's exactly what a damsel in distress would say," Sid said knowledgeably. "They don't know what's good for 'em. They always need help to save 'emselves."

"I'm not sure what I'm saving myself from," Elias said.

"Mundanity!" Alex announced.

Elias frowned in thought. "It would only be when you need me?"

"Of course!"

"And you'd pay me?"

"Definitely, taking into account all expenses incurred," Alex said grandly.

"I've never been a part of a crew before." Elias's expression transformed into a tentative smile.

"That's as good as a yes. Welcome to the crew of the Reign Agency, lad! May your booty always be plundersome!"

"Your shiny things shiny!" Flora said.

"And your nethers always free!"

"Sid!"

"Well, Captain, they *are* free. Even freer than if I wasn't wearing anything."

Alex waved a barmaid over. "Another gin for my good friend here, and for the rest of us."

"Gregor says you have to pay first," the barmaid said.

"Of course!" Alex reached into her pocket, searching for change, but she came up empty except for the tiny figure of the Vengeful Queen that she'd snaffled from St. Smeaton's Cathedral. She set it on the table and it promptly fell over.

"Pay the woman, Flora," Alex commanded.

"But they're my shiny—" Flora began, but at Alex's sharp look she said, "Okay." They both knew that Flora had visited the bar earlier and she'd returned looking pleased with herself, her pockets clinking.

As the barmaid went off to fill their order, Alex sat back down and picked up the figurine of the Vengeful Queen, studying the dab of glue covered in lint that was stuck to its base. The way she saw it, it was a lucky charm. After all, she'd found the urchin, and The Clockmaker was no longer a threat.

Sid glanced at it. "Is that the one you took from the church, Captain?"

"Borrowed. Yes." Alex pulled her dagger from her belt and carefully shaved the glue from the figurine. She placed it back on the table and this time it didn't fall over.

"It would be nice to know what Sweet Pete added to his sugar that blew those priests up like that, wouldn't it?" Sid said. "Just to know."

"Working out what it was through experimentation could take a lifetime," Elias said quickly.

"Quite." Alex swiped the glob of glue from the table. It fell amongst the sawdust on the floor. "Crew, we have much better ways of spending our time. We have wanted coves to catch!"

"And shiny things to find!"

"And distressed damsels to save," Sid said.

"Indeed! Before long we'll have the Purple Reign back and take to the sky! Or may the Vengeful Queen strike us down!" Alex said just as the barmaid arrived with their order.

Alex hoisted her tankard. "Drink up, crew! A toast. Let's make it reign!"

CHAPTER 55

A HAPPY ENDING

W E'LL LEAVE CAPTAIN REIGN and her crew as they depart The Armoury and stride through OverLondon's bunting-laden streets in search of their next adventure.

Instead, let's travel to the OverThames Reservoir, following its winding waters until we detour briefly to a stable in Shadwell, where we spy a small boy with soup-ladle ears, wearing a Black Hack smock. He's sharing a pail of *boeuf a la porridge* with an elderly goat and is cheerfully telling her about a trinket he will soon receive from an artificer in Whitechapel.

Leaving him, we continue along the reservoir until we reach Stepney and the textile district, where a three-legged pirate and his small dog are threatening some passing tourists from OverLisbon into buying a bunch of daffodils.

Finally, we reach the Wharf Gate.

As we exit OverLondon, we note that the piers extending from the city now have nets beneath them. One of the nets tinkles with the sound of a tambourine as a crowd helps a blissfully smiling lemming Hare Krishna in orange robes back up to safety.

OverLondon moves on through the clouds and we descend to England's verdant green countryside to travel a little to the west until we reach the small, nondescript village of Slough.

At the edge of the village, we see a small stone cottage situated in the middle of a newly ploughed field.

On the roof of the cottage we spy a burly man repairing the thatch. His name is Roddy and he's whistling that tune that was so popular in OverLondon some years ago, 'Hug My Whale Til the Blowhole Blows'.

There's a small garden behind the cottage, and there we find another heavily built man named Keef. He's wielding a hoe and is thinking about the vegetables he will grow throughout the summer. There will definitely be potatoes.

And finally, to the side of the cottage we spy a small girl named Poppet sitting amongst a clump of daffodils. There's a discarded dolly at her side, and on her lap she's holding a fat white duck that she's just named Grub.

As she tells the duck about the new pillow and bed she has in her very own room, she looks at her two new fathers, the one on the roof of the cottage and then the one in the garden, and she smiles.

ACKNOWLEDGMENTS

The authors and the various parishes, guilds and gangs of OverLondon wish to enthusiastically award the following individuals for their services to the city's creation:

The Parish of Maye Fayre would like to award Anja Dreyer a golden plaque for her services to building homes that are safe for even the dimmest of aristocrats to stand in for five minutes without inexplicably choking on a light bulb.

The Butter District would like to award Rhyll Vallis a luxurious whipping with extra cream for her invaluable early reading and encouragement, which reminded the authors that it's not the number of words you have, it's how you use them.

Mrs Nevins, proprietor of Mrs Nevins's Boarding House for Respectable Young Gentlemen, wishes to award Angela Murphy an endless supply of porridgewurst for keeping the authors sane, well-fed and feeling well cared-for during a rather pesky pandemic.

Miss Ignatia Crump's Agency for the Correction of Wanton Stupidity wishes to award Mersedeh Badrian a sash of Eternal Screaming Into the Void for her services to educating the un-educatable. (Namely, the authors.)

The Ushers of Theatreland wish to award Lesley Seldon with the rarely-given Pantomime Horse's Tail for her services to creative fancy dress.

Hamish Leek's Experience of a Lifetime would like to endow Vanessa Stubbs with a special Definitely-Gold-No-The-Tarnish-Is-Just-For-Effect-Dear Ring of Snooping, for her services to observation and writing things down.

The Editors of Bloomsbury would like to award Andrea Robinson their highest accolade, the Red Pencil of Smite, for services to eradicating extraneous prose.

The Happy Times Bookstore would like to award Dean Mayes a special edition of *How Big Is My Eggplant?* for his services to helping us doctor our prose.

Mistress Fenderpossum of the Guild of Artificers would like to award Alessio Turchi and Elena Bombardelli with a magnificent Spinning Buonarroti for their services to keeping the authors inspired, educated about Florentine art and laughing during a rather pesky pandemic.

The OverLondon Cry would like to award Caimh McDonnell with a Sash of Charismatic Bellowing for his services to producing words that attract people, rather than scaring them away.

Gregor, barkeep of The Armoury would like to award Elaine Ofori a pint of Recalcitrant Badger gin for her invaluable advice, which should be written on a wall in great big capital letters.

The Textile District would like to award Heide Goody with their special Pillowcase of Side Splitting for her services to humorously sewing words together. The authors would also like to send a personal thanks to Heide for stopping us from shooting ourselves in the footnote.

The Lepers of Whitechapel would like to gift some especially rusted Blades of Stabbiness to Kaaron Warren for her services to shock, awe and horror—and for the awesome cover quote!

The Ushers of Theatreland would like to award Brendan McDonald an Extra Splatty Throwing Tomato of Accuracy for his magnificent performance in the audiobook... And for not incoherently screaming at us when he realised that we required him to voice more than sixty (sixty!) separate characters. (He did a phenomenal job.)

If anyone has been left off of this honours list, they're encouraged to visit the Armoury in Drury Lane where Captain Alex Reign will gladly write them up an Award for Services to Swashbuckling on the back of a pie bag. Thanks to her crew's love of Mister Jim's Mysterious Pies, there are plenty of pie bags to go around.

ABOUT GEORGE PENNEY

Class: Barbarian-Researcher
Alignment: Chaotic Workaholic Omnivore
Ancestry: Pansexual Pirate

George Penney is a best-selling comedy fiction author who was once saved from being a bunny-slipper-wearing academic by an unexpected three book publishing deal. She's a driven workaholic who spends her spare time voraciously reading and researching for fun—when she's not actively trying to wind up her partner-in-crime and co-writer, Tony Johnson.

George has lived a determinedly eccentric life, spanning over fifty places around the globe and blames her life choices on watching the Indiana Jones movies at an impressionable age. While no rolling boulders were available, she's found her fair share of adventure, including being chased by a rock wielding mob, being nearly rammed off the road in a high-speed chase, and almost being poisoned by a spitting cobra. She once rescued a kitten from a troop of hungry monkeys.

She loves English, Scottish and Irish comedy, will fight to her death for a morning cup of tea, would cuddle an entire zoo if she could, adores staying up late debating philosophy, enjoys world cinema, absurd anime and new music every day. She considers both Ripley and the Alien Queen to be strong female role models.

She is utterly obsessed with sharks and would like to be eaten on her hundredth birthday by a low-flying great white.

ABOUT TONY JOHNSON

Class: Swashbuckler
Alignment: Thwarted Chaotic Stubborn
Ancestry: Diva Cat

Tony Johnson considers writing to be the third most fun thing you can do sitting down, and has co-written multiple best-selling comedic novels with his writing partner, George Penney.

In a past life he worked as an engineer, hammering a creative shaped brain into an analytic shaped career. During this time, he got to play with most kinds of radiation, chaotic simulation, the dark arts of metallurgy, neural networks, competitive bacteria and nearly exploded once or twice. He can't fix anything smaller than a house that doesn't operate at steel bursting pressures and tries to fit a normal distribution to everything. One day he would like to train an AI to replace CEOs.

Tony has lived all over the planet, from deserts to rain forests, and enjoys being a stranger in a strange land, as opposed to being a deeply weird suburbanite. He once sold everything he owned to start travelling the world because it seemed like a good idea at the time.

He loves astrophysics, particle physics, durians, techno-utopianism, excessive complexity and 99.9% of cats. One day he will mash together enough tabletop role-playing games for them to achieve sentience.